A PERSIAN
REQUIEM

S0-ABQ-672

A PERSIAN REQUIEM

A Novel by
Simin Daneshvar

Translated by
Roxane Zand

GEORGE BRAZILLER / New York

First published in the United States in 1992 by George Braziller, Inc.
Published in Great Britain in 1991 by Peter Halban Publishers Ltd.

Originally published in Iran under the title *Savushun*
Translation copyright © 1991 Roxane Zand
Map © András Bereznay

All rights reserved

For information write to the publisher:
George Braziller, Inc.
60 Madison Avenue
New York, NY 10010

Library of Congress Cataloging-in-Publication Data

Dāneshvar, Simīn, 1921–
  [Sāvushūn. English]
  A Persian requiem : a novel / by Simin Daneshvar : translated by
Roxane Zand.
    p. cm.
  Translation of: Sāvushūn.
  ISBN 0–8076–1273–1 : —ISBN 0–8076–1274–X (pbk.) :
  I. Title.
PK6561.D263S213   1992
891'.5533—dc20   91–40933

Printed in the United States of America
First U.S. Edition 1992

Acknowledgements

I would like to thank the following for their generous help and involvement with this translation, ever since it was first undertaken, and throughout the many years it collected dust or met with misadventure: Dr. John Gurney, Keyvan Mahjour, Mohsen Ashtiani, the late Dr. Hamid Enayat, Aamer Hussein, Iradj Bagherzade and Ali Gheissari.

A special thanks to Simin Daneshvar whose place in our hearts extends beyond that of artist and humanist to a particular kind of inspiration. My gratitude for her patience and loyal support.

Finally, my love and thanks to Hamid who has journeyed with me through this book, and to my sons, Vahid and Karim.

Roxane Zand

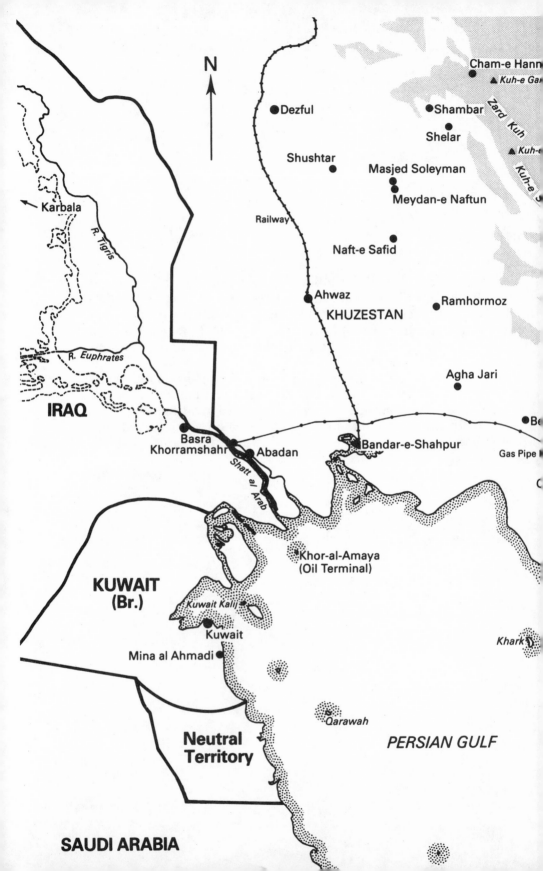

About the translator

Roxane Zand was born in Tehran, educated in Sussex and at Harvard University where she read Comparative Literature. She is currently completing a D.Phil. in Social History at Oxford University, and takes a strong interest in women's issues.

1

It was the wedding day of the Governor's daughter. The Shirazi bakers had got together to bake an impressive sangak loaf, the likes of which had never been seen before.

Groups of guests filed into the marriage room just to admire the bread. Zari Khanom and Yusef Khan also managed to see it close up. The minute Yusef set eyes on it, he blurted out loud: "Those fools! Licking the boots that kick them! And to waste so much at a time like this . . ."

The guests nearby who overheard Yusef first edged away and then left the room. Zari, suppressing her admiration, caught Yusef's hand and implored him, "For God's sake, Yusef, don't talk like that, not tonight."

Yusef laughed at his wife. He always tried to laugh her off. His full, well-defined lips parted to reveal teeth which had once sparkled, but were now yellow from pipe-smoking. Then he left, but Zari stayed behind to gaze at the bread. Bending over, she lifted the hand-printed calico tablecloth to reveal an improvised table made of two old doors. All around the table were trays of wild rue arranged in flowery patterns and pairs of lovers. And in the centre was the bread, baked the colour of burnished copper. A poppy-seed inscription read: "Presented by the Bakers' Guild to our honourable Governor" with "congratulations" written all around the edge.

"Where on earth did they find an oven big enough to bake it?" Zari wondered silently. "How much flour did it take? Yusef's right—what a time for all this! A time when a loaf like that would make supper for a whole family, when getting bread from the bakery is a major feat. Only recently there was a rumour in town that the Governor had threatened to throw a baker into his own oven as an example to others because everyone who had eaten his

1

bread had come down with stomach cramps and vomiting. They said the bread was black as ink from all the dirt and scraps mixed in it. But then, as Yusef says, how can you blame the bakers? All the town's provisions—from wheat to onions—have been bought up by the occupying army. And now ... how on earth do I cover up for what Yusef has just said?"

Suddenly a voice broke into her thoughts.

"Salaam."

She looked up and saw the English missionary doctor, Khanom Hakim, standing in front of her with Captain Singer. They shook hands with her. Both spoke only broken Persian.

"How are being the twins?" Khanom Hakim asked, adding to Captain Singer in the same clumsy language, "All of her three children being delivered by me."

"I did not doubt it," replied Captain Singer.

Turning back to Zari, she asked, "The babies' dummy still being used?" Struggling through a few more sentences in Persian, she finally tired of it and carried on in English. But Zari was too distracted to understand, even though she had studied at the English school and her late father was considered the best English teacher in town.

It was really Singer who captured her attention, and although Zari had heard about his transformation, she refused to believe it until she saw him with her own eyes. The present Captain Singer was none other than Mr Singer, the sewing machine salesman who had come to Shiraz seventeen years ago, and who treated anyone buying his sewing machines to ten free sewing lessons delivered by himself in his barely understandable Persian. He would squeeze his enormous bulk behind the sewing machine and teach the girls of Shiraz embroidery, lattice-work and pleating. It was a wonder he didn't laugh at the ridiculous figure he cut. But the girls, including Zari, learned well.

Zari had been told that overnight, as soon as war broke out, Mr Singer had donned a military uniform, complete with badges of rank. Now she could see that it really suited him. It must have taken a lot, she thought, to live as an impostor for seventeen years. To have a fake job, fake clothes—to be a fraud in every respect. But what an expert he had been! How cunningly he had persuaded Zari's mother to buy a sewing machine—Zari's mother, whose sole fortune was her husband's modest pension. Mr Singer had told her

2

that all a young woman needed for her dowry was a Singer sewing machine. He had claimed that the owner of a sewing machine could always earn her own living, and had said that all the leading families in town had bought one from him for their daughters' dowry; as proof, he had produced a notebook containing a list of his influential customers.

At this moment, three Scottish officers, wearing kilts and what seemed like women's knee-length socks, broke Zari's train of thoughts as they came forward to join them. Behind them came McMahon, the Irishman, who was Yusef's friend. McMahon was a war correspondent and always carried a camera. He greeted Zari and asked her to tell him all about the wedding ceremony. Willingly she described all the details of the vase, the candlesticks, the silver mirror, and the reasons for the shawl, the ring wrapped in silk brocade and the symbolic meaning of the bread and cheese, the herbs and the wild rue.

Two large sugar cones, made at the Marvdasht Sugar Refinery especially for the wedding, were placed one at either end of the ceremonial table. One cone was decorated as a bride and the other as a groom, complete with top hat. In one corner of the room stood a baby's pram lined in pink satin and piled high with coins and sugar-plums. Zari pulled back the silk brocade cloth covering the traditional saddle and explained to McMahon, "The bride sits on this so she can dominate her husband forever."

A few people around them chuckled loudly and McMahon clicked away busily with his camera.

Just then, Zari's glance fell on Gilan Taj, the Governor's younger daughter, who seemed to be beckoning to her. She excused herself and went over to the young girl. Gilan Taj was no more than ten or eleven, the same age as Zari's own son, with honey-coloured eyes and sleek, brown shoulder-length hair. She was wearing ankle socks and a short skirt.

"Mother says would you please lend her your earrings," Gilan Taj asked Zari. "She wants the bride to wear them just for tonight. They'll be returned to you first thing tomorrow morning. It's Khanom Ezzat-ud-Dowleh's fault for bringing a length of green silk for the bride to put around her shoulders. She says it will bring good luck, but my sister isn't wearing anything green to match it." The young girl could have been repeating a lesson by heart.

Zari was dumb-struck. When had they spotted her emerald ear-

3

rings, let alone made plans for getting their clutches on them? In all the bustle, who could have spared the time to fuss over such minor details of the bride's dress? She said to herself, "I bet it was that woman Ezzat-ud-Dowleh's doing. Those beady eyes of hers constantly keep track of what everyone has." Aloud she replied nervously, "Those were a wedding present—a special gift from Yusef's poor mother."

Her mind flashed back to that night in the bridal chamber when Yusef had put the earrings on her himself. He was sweating profusely, and in all the hustle and bustle he had groped nervously under the women's scrutiny to find the small holes in her earlobes.

"They're playing the wedding tune," Gilan Taj prompted. "Please hurry. Tomorrow morning then . . . "

Zari took off the earrings.

"Be very careful," she warned, "make sure the drops don't come off." In her heart she knew that the likelihood of ever seeing those earrings again was very remote indeed. Yet how could she refuse?

At this point the bride entered on Ezzat-ud-Dowleh's arm. "Yes," thought Zari, "that woman is never slow to become confidante and busybody to every new governor of the town." The bride was followed by five little girls each carrying a posy of flowers and wearing frilly dresses, and five boys in suits and ties. The room was now full, and the ladies started to clap. The British officers who were still there quickly followed suit. Clearly all the pomp and formality was for their benefit, but to Zari the wedding march seemed more like a mournful procession out of a Tazieh passion play.

The bride sat on the saddle in front of the silver mirror and Ezzat-ud-Dowleh rubbed the sugar cones together over her head to ensure sweetness in the marriage. Then a woman holding a needle and red thread pretended to sew up the tongues of the groom's relatives. This raised a loud guffaw from the British officers. Next, a black nursemaid carrying a brazier of smoking incense suddenly appeared out of nowhere like a genie.

"All the villains of the Ta'zieh are here," Zari mused to herself. "Marhab, Shemr and Yazid, the farangi, the unwanted Zeynab, the rapacious Hend, Aysheh, and last but not least Fezza!" And for an instant it occurred to her that she was thinking just like Yusef.

The crowded room was noisy and stifling. The smell of incense mixed with the strong scent of tuberoses, carnations and gladioli

4

which were displayed in large silver vases around the room but glimpsed only from time to time between the whirl of the ladies' dresses.

Zari missed the moment when the bride gave her consent. Suddenly she felt a hand on her arm.

"Mother is very grateful," whispered Gilan Taj; "they really suit her . . ."

The rest of her sentence was drowned in the commotion and blare of military music which followed the wedding tune. A booming which pulsated like the beating of battle drums . . .

Now it was Ferdows, the wife of Ezzat-ud-Dowleh's manservant, who came in, threading her way past the guests to give her mistress her handbag. Ezzat-ud-Dowleh took out a pouch full of sugar-plums and coins which she showered over the bride's head. To save the foreign officers the trouble of scrambling for a coin, she handed one to each of them and one to Khanom Hakim. Until that moment Zari had not seen Ezzat-ud-Dowleh's son, Hamid Khan, in the wedding room, but she noticed him now speaking to the British officers.

"My dear mother has the Midas touch!" she heard him saying. Turning to her abruptly, he said, "Zari Khanom, please translate for them."

Zari ignored him.

"Not on your life!" she retorted silently. "My former suitor! I had more than enough of you and your ways that time when our history teacher took us sixteen-year-old girls to your home on the pretext of visiting an eighteenth-century house. You looked us over with your lecherous eyes, supposedly showing us the baths and the Zurkhaneh, boasting that your ancestor, the famous Sheriff, built the hall of mirrors and that Lutf-Ali Khan had done the painting on the mirrors. And then your mother had the nerve to come to the Shapuri public baths on our usual bath-day and barge her way into our cubicle just so she could size up my naked body. It was lucky Yusef had already asked for my hand, otherwise my mother and brother might well have been taken in by your extravagant life-style."

The ceremony over, celebrations got under way in the garden and on the front verandah. All the cypresses, palms and orange trees had been strung with light bulbs—each tree a different colour. Large bulbs lit the larger trees, while small ones had been used for

5

the smaller, twinkling like so many stars. Water flowed from two directions in a terraced stream into a pool, cascading over the red glow of rose-shaped lamps set inside each step. The main part of the garden had been spread with carpets for dancing. Zari assumed the wiring for the waterfall lights ran under the carpets. Around the edge of the pool they had alternated bowls full of different kinds of fruit, three-branched candlelabra and baskets of flowers. If a gust of wind blew out one of the candles, a servant would instantly relight it with a short-stemmed taper.

The Governor, a tall, heavy-set man with white hair and a white moustache, was standing by the pool welcoming even more guests. An English Colonel with a squint, walking arm in arm with Zari's former headmistress, was the last to arrive. Behind them came two Indian soldiers carrying a basket of carnations in the shape of a ship. When they reached the Governor, they placed it at his feet. At first the Governor didn't notice the flowers as he was busy kissing the English-woman's hand. But the headmistress must have drawn his attention to them because the Governor shook hands with the Colonel again before extending his hand to the Indian soldiers. They, for their part, merely clicked their heels together, saluted, about-turned, and withdrew.

Then came the hired musicians. One played the zither, while his plump friend accompanied him on the tar and an attractive young boy sang a song. When the song was over, there was a dance followed by another song. The musicians then changed to a rhythmic beat and a group of men and women dressed as Qashqais did a sort of tribal dance. Zari had seen a lot of fake things in her time, but never fake Qashqais!

Now it was the turn of the hired musicians brought over especially from Tehran. The noises sounded confused to Zari; even the sight of all those dishes piled high with sweets and dried fruit and nuts nauseated her. The sweets had probably been sent by the Confectioners' Guild and the fruit and the nuts by the Grocers' Guild, she thought cynically. The five-tiered wedding cake flown in by air had, she knew, been presented by the Supreme Command of the foreign armed forces. They had displayed it on a table on the verandah. On the top tier stood a bride and groom hand in hand, with a British flag behind them, each crafted skilfully out of icing.

To Zari it felt like watching a film. Especially with the foreign army in full regalia: Scottish officers in kilts, Indian officers in turbans ... If she hadn't lost her earrings, thought Zari, it would have been possible to sit back and enjoy the show.

The bride and groom led the dancing. The bride's long train with its glittering rhinestones, sequins and pearls swept over the carpet like a trail of shooting stars. She was no longer wearing the length of green silk or her bridal veil, but the earrings were still there. The British Colonel had one dance with the bride; so did Captain Singer, in whose large arms the bride skipped about like a grasshopper. He even trod on her toes several times.

Then the foreign officers sought out the other ladies. The Shirazi women in their colourful dresses danced in the arms of strangers while their men, perched on the edge of their seats, kept a nervous eye on them. Some of the men seemed particularly restless and agitated. Was it the light-hearted tempo of the music, or an inner fire kindled at the sight of strangers holding their wives so closely? It was impossible to know. At the end of the dance the officers carefully returned the ladies to their chairs, as if they were incapable of finding their own way back. They clicked their heels and kissed the lady's hand, at which the woman's own escort would nearly jump out of his seat and then settle back to try to compose himself. Not unlike a jack-in-the-box. The only person who didn't dance was McMahon. He took pictures instead.

Captain Singer came over to Zari. He clicked his heels smartly and said with a bow: "Shall we dance?"

She excused herself. Singer shrugged and moved on to ask Khanom Hakim. Zari looked over at Yusef who was sitting a few chairs away. His eyes were fixed on her, those eyes that seemed to her deeper in colour than the azure of spring skies. He winked at her, and she felt a pang in her heart. A faint teardrop always seemed to lurk in the depths of Yusef's eyes, making them glisten like two moist jewels—like the emeralds of her earrings.

Now the Colonel and Singer, either together or singly, began to accompany some of the men on a brief walk to the bottom of the garden. After a few minutes they would return and head straight for the bar, where they drank each other's health. Zari saw Singer whisper something in Yusef's ear, at which Yusef rose and set off with him down the garden path, with its border of illuminated cypresses and orange trees. But they were back almost immediately. This time they did not visit the bar. Zari saw Captain Singer make a sign to the Colonel, whose expression reflected his

7

annoyance. Yusef came and sat next to Zari, his face flushed and his fair moustache trembling.

"Let's get up and leave quietly," he said.

Flicking her hair forward to cover her bare ears, Zari said: "As you like."

She was getting up to leave when McMahon appeared, drink in hand, and sat down next to them. He had drunk so much gin he could barely keep his eyes open. He spoke in English:

"You're at loggerheads with the big tailor again, Yusef?" he asked. "I must admit, it's even more difficult for you Persians to deal with the British than it is for us Irish . . . Did you like my poem that I recited for you earlier tonight? You did, didn't you? Now I'm thinking of composing a poem for your town . . ."

Pointing to the slice of lime in his drink, he said: "The lime with its light green delicate peel, its fragrance combining all the perfumes of the plain, and the cypress tree with its strength and restraint—these are the things which grow in this region. People usually resemble the nature surrounding them; in this case, delicate and restrained. They've sent me to ask why you're not delicate and restrained, Yusef. I'm doing well you know, even though I'm blind drunk. Look how easily I've accomplished my mission!" He turned to Zari. "Cheers!" he said, draining his glass and putting it on the table.

"Let's go and sit on the bench near that ship of flowers," he suggested. "Zari, you come too—the presence of a lovely woman is always inspiring. That warship laden with flowers is a gift from our Supreme Command." They moved across to the bench. "That's better. Where's my glass? Zari, please pour us another drink.

"We are related, aren't we?" he carried on, with a faraway look in his eyes. "Iran and Ireland. Both lands of the Aryans. You the ancestors and we the descendants. O ancient, ancient ancestors, console us! Here am I a Catholic Irishman, a patriarch, a drunkard, bound to end up dying in a ditch one foul, rain-sodden day, or wandering around poor houses looking for some old woman to claim as my mother. I can see her now, knitting woollen socks with little patterns for her son at the front . . . like the ones I'm wearing. You see, my father was on air-raid duty; he knew that the planes were bombing our area, he knew that at any moment they would wipe out our home, and he knew that mother was there knitting patterned socks for her son at the front. When they pulled her out from underneath the rubble, she was still clutching the knitting needles—and now my father has written me a letter. He has written to me to say he's sorry ... he's sorry that ... "

McMahon's speech was becoming slurred and he broke off for a moment. Then he raised his hand in a grandly drunken gesture:

"Why did you, you home-loving Catholic family, wrapped in your traditions, with your confession and such nonsense ... why did you uproot yourselves and move to London? If you had stayed to help put right and free your own poor, blighted Ireland you wouldn't have had to pay so dearly for that move.

"Away from home," he paused, "I remember making up tales of Ireland, boasting to others of her countless poets, and sighing for my impoverished land. I remember saying that in our land the youth were innocent, uncorrupted, and people would ask me if I thought they were corrupt in London. We were all fooling ourselves. We'd forgotten Ireland's alcoholics. We'd forgotten the ships which arrived every week and loaded up their cargo—the youth of Ireland—and set sail for America. We ignored the fact that the convicts among them would be sent to the colonies—like our tailor here. That big tailor has surely got it in for you, Yusef. He can't stand the sight of you; nor me, for that matter. I told the Consul yesterday to count you out. But the big tailor won't let him ... "

He half-drained his glass, then continued:

"Some people are like rare flowers; others resent their existence. They imagine that such a flower will use up all the earth's strength, all the sunshine and moisture in the air, taking up their space, leaving them no sunlight or oxygen. They envy it and wish it didn't exist. Either be like us, or don't be at all—that's what they say. You Persians have the occasional rare flower among you, but also a lot of oleander to keep mosquitoes away, and then some plain grass which is only good for the sheep. Well," he rambled on, smiling, "there's always a branch on every tree which is taller and leafier than others. And this taller branch has its eyes and ears open and can see everything clearly. But no one likes it that way. So they send the drunken Irish poet, the war correspondent, to mollify you, Yusef, and this reporter carries his father's letter here in his coat pocket; his father who'd written to say he's sorry that ... well, if you give in, Yusef, it's all over." He took a long gulp. His eyes were barely open. Then he continued sorrowfully:

9

"O Ireland, O land of Aryan descent, I have composed a poem for a certain tree which must grow in your soil. The name of this tree is the 'Tree of Independence'. You must nurture it with blood, not with water. Yes, Yusef, you were right. If independence is good for me, it's good for you too. And that story you told me turned out to be so useful when I began to write. You said that in your folklore they talk of a tree whose leaves, when dried and put on the eyes, make you invisible, allowing you to do whatever you want. I wish there was one of these trees in Ireland and one here in your town."

McMahon fell silent. After a while he lit a cigarette and continued:

"All this mumbo-jumbo was just to keep you listening. When my father's letter arrived with the news ... I sat and wrote a story for your Mina—for your twins. Where's my story?" He searched in his pockets. "I thought I put it with my father's letter ... you see, I want to build an airplane which drops toys for children ... or else pretty stories. Ah, here it is!"

He took out a notebook and began to read.

"Once upon a time there was a little girl called Mina. She always cried for the stars when she couldn't see them in the sky. When she was smaller, her mother would pick her up in her arms, show her the sky and say: 'Little little moon, pretty pretty stars, come to Mina' or something like that, which is why Mina fell in love with the stars. Now whenever it's cloudy at night, Mina cries for the stars. If only the maid would sweep the sky—she's slapdash and brushes the dust away here and there, so on the nights she sweeps, at least some of the stars can be seen. But alas, if mother sweeps, she polishes the sky clean and gathers up all the stars and the moon and puts them in a sack. Then she sews up the sack, puts it in the cupboard and locks the door. But Mina found out what to do. She plotted with her sister to steal their mother's keys and now they sleep hugging the keys tightly. If they don't have the keys, they don't sleep a wink. I've never seen a little girl so in love with the stars, and I've never seen a town like yours where you can hide stars in its cupboards ..."

He took another sip of his drink and said: "That's the end of Mina's story. Say bravo, Yusef! See what a yarn I've spun from odds and ends you've told me about your twins. You say the people of your town are born poets: well, the Irish are like that too ..."

Then he became silent.

10

Zari was deep in thought when she noticed her brother-in-law, Abol-Ghassem Khan, approaching. McMahon stood up, picked up his glass and left. Abol-Ghassem Khan took his seat.

"Is that whisky?" he asked.

"No, it's gin," Zari answered. "Shall I pour you a glass?"

Abol-Ghassem Khan said quietly to Yusef: "Listen brother, you're being as stubborn as a mule. After all they're guests in our country. They won't be staying here forever, you know. And if we don't give them what they want, they'll take it by force. They won't be put off by the locks and bolts on your store-rooms either. Besides, you know they'll pay. I sold the entire contents of my store-rooms in one go . . . I've already taken a down payment for the wheat before it's even sprouted. After all, they're the bosses."

"I'm all too well aware that they're unwelcome guests," Yusef told his brother dryly. "But the worst thing is the feeling of inferiority that's taken hold of everyone; overnight they've turned all of you into their lackeys, go-betweens, and errand-boys. Why don't you let at least one person stand up to them so they can say to themselves that they've finally come across a man?"

Before Abol-Ghassem Khan could reply, dinner was announced. The guests filed inside the house. Zari, her husband and her brother-in-law pretended to be on their way too, but lingered.

"Sister, say something," said Abol-Ghassem Khan, turning to Zari. "Your husband is downright insulting to his elder brother."

"What can I say?" Zari challenged.

Turning back to Yusef, Abol-Ghassem Khan said: "Now listen, brother, you're young and you don't understand. You're gambling with your life with this stubbornness of yours, and creating trouble for all of us as well. These foreigners have to feed a whole army. You know very well an army that big can't be kept hungry."

"But our own people can be!" Yusef replied sharply. "The peasants who have been expecting to survive on the provisions from my store-rooms can be kept hungry!"

"Listen, last year and the year before you got away with not giving them anything and somehow we covered up for you and made up the amount. But this year it just won't work. Right now provisions and petrol are even more valuable to them than guns and ammunition."

They were still arguing when Gilan Taj came up to them and said: "Mother says please come in for dinner."

11

As they walked in, Abol-Ghassem Khan whispered in Zari's ear: "I hope he doesn't take it into his head not to come to their party tomorrow evening. They've even invited Khosrow. I'll pick you all up myself."

"But tomorrow's Thursday; it's a holy evening and I have a lot to do. You know the vow I made."

"Sister, I'm counting on you!" Abol-Ghassem Khan pleaded.

When they reached home, Zari sat on the bed. She only took off her shoes. Yusef was straightening out his trousers on the bed, ready for the hanger. When he had put on his night-clothes he went into the children's room next door. Zari could see him from where she was sitting, standing by the twins' bed watching them. Then he moved forward out of sight, but Zari knew he would be smoothing out their pillows, taking the keychain which they liked to hold at bedtime. She knew he would be kissing them and murmuring endearments to them. Then she heard a door open, and knew he had gone into their son Khosrow's room. He would be tucking him in, and whispering a few words of prayer for his future.

Yusef came back to their bedroom. Zari had not moved from the bed.

"Aren't you going to sleep?" Yusef asked, handing her the keychain, adding with a laugh, "The little twins are so funny!"

He sat down next to his wife. "I suppose you want me to undo your buttons. I'm sorry I didn't remember."

Without turning her back, Zari said: "McMahon wrote such a pretty story about them."

"Did you understand all of it?"

"Yes, I've got used to his Irish accent by now."

"Do you know what Mina told me today when I tossed her in the air and hugged her? She asked, 'Daddy, did mummy give you two stars? I can see them in your eyes'."

Zari laughed. "The child is right. There always seem to be stars twinkling in your eyes."

Yusef began to undo the buttons of his wife's dress.

"My goodness, what are all these buttons for?" he said. "Early this evening I said some things to McMahon, and if ever Singer gets to hear about them I'm done for." He undid the buttons and Zari's dress fell around her waist. He began to unhook her bra.

12

"I told McMahon that the people of this town were born poets but their poetry has been stifled; their heroes have been castrated. There's no room left for them to fight back, so at least there could be some glory, or the honour of an open challenge. They've made this into a land with no heroes and this town into a graveyard; the liveliest neighbourhood is the Mordestan district."

Yusef unhooked Zari's bra, and putting his hands over her breasts, said: "I feel sorry for your breasts; you bind them so tightly."

Zari felt her breasts responding. Her nipples gradually hardened. Yusef put his lips on his wife's shoulder. His lips were warm.

"Didn't he ask what the Mordestan district was?" Zari asked.

"Yes, he did. I told him it's the neighbourhood where the residents are mainly pathetic women who earn a livelihood from painting up their faces, and whom those Indian soldiers are sent to. The officers are much better off in that respect. I told him, 'You've killed the poetry, but instead the cab-drivers, prostitutes and go-betweens have picked up a few words of English.' McMahon said there was no need to tell him any of this, he was heartily sick of the war himself."

Yusef reached forward and stroked his wife's hair. He was about to kiss the back of her neck when Zari turned around and, throwing her arms about his neck, began to cry. Yusef asked in surprise: "Are you crying because of me? You know I can't be like the others. I can't see our people go hungry. Someone has to be man enough to stand up . . . "

"Let them do whatever they want, but please don't let them bring this war into my home. What do I care if the whole town has turned into a red-light district? My town, my country is this household . . . but they're going to drag this war to my doorstep too."

Yusef held his wife's face in his hands and kissed away her tears.

"Go and wash your face," he said soothingly. "It's not the time for this sort of talk. I swear to God, you're a thousand times prettier without make-up. Your face is like one of those they paint on tiles. Come on, my love. I want you tonight."

Zari undressed, and put out the light. She didn't want Yusef to see the 'geography map' on her stomach, as she called it. Even though Yusef always kissed the scars and said, "You've suffered this for me." It was Khanom Hakim who had disfigured her belly with stitch-marks and puckered scars.

13

She climbed into bed, and when Yusef's warm, hairy legs touched her cold ones, and his large hand caressed her breast moving lower and lower down, she forgot everything—the earrings, Captain Singer, Khanom Hakim, the bride, the military music, the drums, and the beady-eyed, squinting, bald wedding guests ... she forgot it all. Instead, in her ears was the sound of water flowing gently over red flowers; and before her stood the image of a ship full of flowers, a ship that was not a warship.

2

When Zari woke up on Thursday morning it was still half
dark. She crept quietly out of the bedroom, and when she
had finished washing, she joined her sister-in-law at the
breakfast table in the parlour. Ameh Khanom was sitting behind
the boiling samovar. The twins, Mina and Marjan, were chattering
like two little sparrows as they hung around the breakfast table. It
was for their safe delivery, and also in thanks for the birth of their
brother Khosrow, that Zari had vowed to take bread and dates to the
prisoners and the patients in the asylum.

Because of her slender build and narrow hips, Zari had had a
difficult time at childbirth. With each pregnancy she had hoped for
a home birth, making all the necessary arrangements with the best
midwife in town, but in the end she found herself resorting to
Khanom Hakim and the Missionary Hospital on the one hand, and
to vows and prayers on the other. And of course, Khanom Hakim
was a great one for the scalpel. She loved to cut and sew. Delirious
with pain at the first delivery, Zari had pleaded with God, vowing,
as an act of charity, to take home-baked bread and dates every week
to the mental patients. Then, when she became pregnant again five
years later, she was so frightened, she made a vow in advance to do
the same, but this time for prisoners.

Ameh Khanom poured her a glass of tea. "Well, how was last
night?" she asked.

"You should have been there! I'm afraid there was yet another
quarrel between the two heads of the family."

"I know my brother Abol-Ghassem, I know Yusef too. Abol-
Ghassem Khan isn't straightforward. And since he's taken it
into his head to become a parliamentary deputy, he's even less
so."

"He made me promise faithfully to go to the foreigners' party. I don't know how I'm going to carry out my vow."

"Don't worry about that. I'll ask Haj Mohammad Reza, the dyer, to go to the asylum with Gholam. I'll go to the prison with Hossein Agha, the grocer. Sakineh is here stoking up the oven, and the dough has already risen. I looked in after finishing my prayers. I think the bread is setting. You go to the party, sister. I don't want any more quarrelling between those two."

At that moment Khosrow came into the parlour.

"Here's Khosrow!" Mina shouted gleefully, clapping her hands together. "He'll let me ride his horse, won't you, Khosrow?" Marjan, who was a quarter of an hour younger, imitated and followed her sister in everything. She clung to Khosrow's leg and said to Mina: "First you play with him, then me, all right?"

"No time to play, I have to go to school now," Khosrow said, patting them both on the head hurriedly. Mina pulled at the table-cloth. The samovar tipped and nearly fell over, but Ameh Khanom steadied it just in time.

"They can really drive you mad with their mischief," she said, as she handed them each a sugar lump.

Khosrow reached for the sugar bowl. "Mother, may I? They're shoeing Sahar this afternoon," he said, taking five lumps and putting them in his pocket. Then he took some tea from his aunt, and reached out for two more lumps. As he put them in his pocket, his aunt said, "Don't you want any sugar in your tea?"

"No, I'll be late for school."

"Abol-Ghassem has sent Seyyid Moti-ud-Din, the mullah, a sackful of sugar and twenty packets of tea belonging to his own peasants and workers," Ameh added to Zari with a laugh. "I've heard my dear brother stands right behind the mullah when he leads the prayers in the mosque. Abol-Ghassem, who's never in his life known which way to face when he prays!"

"Auntie, I've seen Seyyid Moti-ud-Din, the mullah! I saw him the day we went to the bazaar with Gholam to buy Sahar a saddle," Khosrow exclaimed. "He was riding a white donkey. He brought his hand out from his cloak and held it up like this in the air . . . like this . . . " He waved his hand in imitation of the mullah, sitting astride his chair and rocking himself back and forth as if he were riding a donkey. "Everyone who passed by kissed his hand; Gholam and I kissed it too. He had to bring it lower down for me

16

because I was shorter."

Suddenly there was a knock at the garden gate. Zari's heart leapt. Perhaps they had brought her earrings back from the Governor's house! But so early in the morning? The sun was just rising. She went out to the verandah. There she saw Gholam in his nightshirt, coming out of the stables at the bottom of the garden. As always he was wearing his felt hat to cover his baldness. He opened the gate to let in Abol-Ghassem Khan who walked in with a brisk air. Disappointed, Zari thought to herself, "What if they send them back so late that Yusef is up and finds out . . . oh, how silly I am! What earrings? Who on earth is going to remember my earrings!"

She returned to the parlour and sat down. When Abol-Ghassem Khan walked in, Ameh said: "Talk of the devil. I was just singing your praises."

"You must have been saying that with all this running about, I'll finally make it as a deputy," he said. "And I will. I've seen the Colonel and the Consul. The Governor has promised, too. Only the mullah is putting his spoke in my wheel. He flatters me in the mosque one day, and takes it all back the next."

"Maybe the sugar and tea you sent him didn't go down too well!" Ameh remarked.

"Sister, what are you talking about? What tea and sugar?" Abol-Ghassem Khan retorted sharply, throwing a look in Khosrow's direction.

"I'm the eldest amongst you, and I'm entitled to give you advice," Ameh said quietly. "You have not chosen the right path, brother. And besides, Khosrow is not a stranger."

"So you think the path your precious brother Yusef has chosen is the right one?" Abol-Ghassem Khan replied angrily. "Taking sugar and clothing coupons from the government with one hand and passing them on to his peasants with the other? Well, what's the young fool getting out of it for himself? Whenever he goes to his village he takes medicine for the peasants. God alone knows that all the medicine in the world won't cure our peasants."

As Khosrow stood up to say goodbye, Abol-Ghassem Khan asked, "Where's Yusef now?"

"He's getting up," Zari replied. "He'll be here soon." She busied herself making fresh tea.

"Always sleeping, always sleeping!" Abol-Ghassem Khan complained. "In his village too, he's either asleep or sitting under the mosquito net, reading a book. My heels are cracked, my face scorched and wrinkled from the sun, but his Lordship keeps himself wrapped up in cotton wool." Then he added emphatically: "Peasants have to be afraid of their landlords. You must stand over them with a whip, like an elephant driver. You have to use the cane and the bastinado. Remember the old saying: peasants must be kept living from hand to mouth." He took some tea from Zari before going on.

"Yusef doesn't know about winter crops or the summer harvest. He can only keep his eyes glued to the sky, watching for rain. And if it doesn't rain he gets really upset; not for himself, of course, but for the peasants and their sheep. And when you try to set him straight, he only comes up with his favourite saying, 'What the peasant reaps belongs to him, even if the land doesn't'."

Ameh interrupted, "It's his way of being charitable. If he can't ensure his lot in this world, he will at least have his salvation hereafter. Besides, brother, why is it any of your business? It's not your money he's giving away."

Zari could hear Sahar, Khosrow's horse, neighing in the garden. She knew Khosrow must have gone to the stables before leaving for school and set Sahar loose in the garden. When he heard the neighing, Abol-Ghassem Khan stood up and looked out of the parlour window. His eyes followed the colt carefully.

"What a beauty he's become," he said. "Glitters like gold! Look at him rolling on the cool grass! Now he's standing again. Wide-set eyes, broad forehead, good ears—a perfect creature! Look at that golden mane and arched tail. He holds his head high too, just like his mother."

Sahar neighed again, revelling in his freedom. Abol-Ghassem Khan returned to his seat.

"Thank God you approve of one thing in this household," Ameh Khanom said with a sigh.

Abol-Ghassem Khan laughed: "Everything he does is so fanciful. Who keeps horses nowadays? Apart from my brother, that is, who's got three in his stables . . . " Mimicking Yusef, he said, "I like to go to the village on horseback. I ride the bay mare myself, my steward rides the roan, and the colt belongs to Khosrow."

At that moment Yusef came in. He was wearing a light cloak over his shoulders. He greeted everyone, and looked with surprise from his brother to his sister. Then he threw Zari an enquiring look, but

18

she merely shook her head.

"Has Khosrow gone?" he asked.

"Yes."

"Where are Mina and Marjan?"

"They're watching Sakineh bake bread and probably chattering away as usual," Ameh replied.

Yusef sat down. "Has something happened, God forbid?" he asked his brother.

Abol-Ghassem did not answer. Instead, he took a small book from his pocket and put it solemnly on the table. "Swear on the holy Quran," he said, "that you'll come tonight and that you won't stir up any trouble with your usual comments. Now, if you don't want to sell the surplus provisions from your village to the foreign army, don't. But you don't have to say so to them in so many words. Stall them somehow, until harvest time. You have to go to the lowlands in a few days anyway—tell them you'll give it to them after the harvest. Who knows what'll happen tomorrow? Maybe they'll be defeated by then and good riddance to them. They say Hitler is having a bomb made that will wipe out the world . . . now swear!"

Yusef sighed. "I never said I wasn't coming this evening," he said. "There's no need for swearing. But as far as fooling them goes, I'm a straightforward person. I won't lie to save my skin."

"For God's sake, swear," Abol-Ghassem implored. "I've never said this before, but now I will. Our father Haj Agha, God rest his soul, spent a great deal of money on your education, but not much on mine. When he was dividing his wealth he gave us equal shares even though I'm the older brother. Did I say anything then? Even when it came to marriage, you were the one who ended up winning the hand of Zari Khanom, Razieh Khanom's attractive daughter. Now that there's an opportunity for me at last, let me make something of my life too." He quoted a line from a Hafez poem: "Of strangers I have no complaints. Alas, what I've suffered has been at the hands of my own kith and kin . . . "

"Brother," interrupted Ameh, "one thing I know for sure is that neither your father nor his father before him ever begged a favour of anyone. Not from the unclean foreigners, nor from our own social climbers. Haj Agha never once took off his mullah's turban. He remained a recluse all his life. In that assembly—I forget the name . . . who cares what it was called, anyway—he didn't vote for the man they'd all been told to vote for. If Yusef was his favourite, it

19

was because they had a similar temperament and believed in the same things."

"Now I'm getting it from you, too!" Abol-Ghassem Khan shouted angrily. "If our Haj Agha had had a brain in his head, we would be rolling in money today. He spent everything he had on that Indian dancer, Soudabeh. My mother died heartbroken in a foreign land because of her. If he had had any brains at all he wouldn't have married you off to that imbecile, Mirza Miyur's son, who got himself killed on purpose, and you wouldn't have ended up as a servant in the house of . . . "

Zari cut her brother-in-law short. "Abol-Ghassem Khan, Ameh Khanom is the eldest among us and the most respected. If it weren't for her, I could never manage such a large place by myself. Besides, this house is her home."

"Yes, I know," he said. "She manages well enough for herself, and stirs up trouble for everyone else besides." He got up and added in a surprisingly gentle tone: "I hadn't intended to mention the dead and speak badly of our past first thing in the morning. On such a nice day, too. Well, it just happened. Don't take it to heart, sister. Goodbye."

Zari accompanied the two brothers to the garden gate. Sahar was grazing, but the moment he smelt a stranger, he stopped and lifted his head. His pink nostrils flared. Abol-Ghassem Khan stopped in front of him. The colt stepped back and neighed. His mother answered from the stable. When Yusef approached, Sahar nuzzled at his cloak and lifted his head, sniffing the familiar odour. Yusef caressed his neck and mane. Later, when husband and wife returned from seeing Abol-Ghassem Khan out, they found Sahar cantering from one side of the garden to the other.

"Zari, look! He's chasing the butterflies," Yusef said.

Sahar must have been getting hot, because he rolled over several times on the shaded part of the grass. Then he got up, and all of a sudden charged after a brown and yellow butterfly.

When they reached the verandah, Yusef paused and looked at the garden.

"Your town is looking pretty," he said. "It's a pity that it's summer again, and I won't have so much time for you or your town as I'll be at the village."

"My town?" Zari asked.

"Didn't you say last night that this house was your town?"

20

Zari laughed. "Oh yes," she said dreamily. "This is my town and I love every inch of it. The hill behind the garden, the verandah all around the house, the two streams on either side of the footpath, the two elms, the orange trees you planted with your own hands. That fruit tree to which you grafted a new fruit each year, the scent distillery next door, with its mounds of flowers and herbs in season, flowers and herbs whose very names make you happy . . . citron, willow, eglantine; and more than anything the orange blossoms and the scents which waft into our garden from over the wall. The sparrows and starlings and the crows, too, have made this their home. But the sparrows make me cross, you know. They build their nests above the windows, or in the trees, and their eggs are always falling and breaking all over the place. They're so careless, those birds."

"Your voice is as soft as velvet," Yusef said with a smile. "Like a lullaby. Go on."

"What shall I talk about?" Zari said. "About the people in my town? About you? About the children and Ameh and our neighbours?"

"About Haj Mohammad Reza, the dyer . . . " Yusef added with a laugh.

"About Haj Mohammad the dyer, with the colourful fabrics he ties on sticks, and leaves in the street to dry in the sun; with his arms dyed purple up to the elbows. About Gholam and Hossein Agha the grocer around the corner, and Hassan Agha the corn chandler . . . about Khadijeh . . . that's enough now! You're not letting me get on with my work."

She was interrupted by the sound of tinkling bells. She knew it would be the donkeys arriving at the neighbour's.

"They've bought orange-flower blossoms next door. What a scent!" Yusef exclaimed.

Zari couldn't tear herself away. She waited until the donkeys entered the neighbour's garden and unloaded their perfumed bundles. Only yesterday morning she had taken the twins to see the pile of orange-blossoms. Mina had clapped and said, "Oh look how many stars there are!"

And Marjan had laid her head on the heap of flowers and said, "I want to sleep right here."

Zari meanwhile had been engrossed in the actions of the old distiller and his three sons. The old man had knelt before the

21

orange-blossoms and piled them into baskets that the boys put on their heads to carry into the store-room. The old man had nick-named Marjan 'Nargessi', and Mina 'Narengi'. Zari had no idea why. And when his work was finished, he made Nargessi and Narengi a toy water-mill from an apple and four pieces of thin wood. He put the water-mill in the stream so that the running water turned it. The children were so happy—as if they owned the greatest water-mill in the world. And Zari kept on wondering why the old man hadn't married his sons off. It was high time they were married.

Then she thought to herself: "Why should people who live with so many beautiful flowers need to get married anyway . . . "

3

When they had cleared the table, Zari brought the hookah for her husband. Khosrow had been restless at lunch and became more so as time passed. It even looked as though there were tears in his eyes which he was fighting back. Zari put the twins to bed for their afternoon rest and then returned to the parlour to take the pipe away. Khosrow was pacing around the room. His father's eyes followed his movements.

"Tell me, why have we gone through all these preparations?" he asked his son.

"So he wouldn't be afraid," Khosrow answered sadly.

"It wasn't only for that," Yusef added.

Khosrow sat down next to his father. "Every time the blacksmith comes, I lift Sahar's foot myself," he said. "In the beginning he was very frightened and he shied, especially when the smith put the nails in. Of course, he hammered very lightly at first but yesterday he hit very hard."

"Well," reassured Yusef, "he did it so that when Sahar is being shod, he won't be frightened or pull away which might cause a nail to go into his foot. Now today, I'll hold up his foot myself, just as I once helped to deliver him." He turned to Zari who had come to sit by them. "You've put the hookah in front of you, as if you wanted to smoke it yourself," he said.

Zari took a puff but gave up the moment she began to cough.

"Father, may I come and watch?" Khosrow asked.

"Of course. Weren't you there when he was born?"

"Yes! Do I remember! Sahar stood up right away. The mare chewed off the cord and began to lick and smell him. You threw your cloak on him so he wouldn't catch cold and you rubbed his body to keep him warm while Gholam fetched a blanket ... But

23

he's really naughty now, isn't he?" he added laughingly. "He bites his mother, then he changes his mind and licks her." Khosrow paused, then said, "Father, why do I love Sahar so much? I want to talk about him all the time. When I'm sitting in class I keep praying for the bell to ring so I can rush home and play with him."

"There's nothing wrong with loving, my son. Loving lightens the heart, just as malice and hatred darken it. Learn to love now, and then when you grow up you'll be ready to love what's good and beautiful in the world. The heart is like a garden full of flowers in bud. If you water them, they'll open; if you feed them with hatred, they'll wither. Remember that malice and hatred are not for the beautiful and good but for the ugly, the dishonourable and the unjust. A hatred of these things means a love of justice and honour."

"Father, you're talking above my head again," Khosrow complained.

"Didn't you understand what I said?"

"I think I understood. You said that there is nothing wrong in loving Sahar. Then you said I must water the flowers . . . "

"We must have been miles away while father was lecturing!" laughed Zari. "If you ask me, you should go to your uncle's and visit your cousin Hormoz, and come back when they've finished with Sahar."

"No Zari," Yusef said. "Khosrow has to learn that if Sahar is to be shod, he must put up with a few nails. He has got to realize that there's pain and suffering in this world."

"Father, will it hurt him very much?"

"No. The important thing is to learn to endure things. We've trained him to stop playing around for a few minutes, long enough to put up with the shoeing. Whereas other horses . . . "

"But father, that herd of wild horses you told me a story about," Khosrow interrupted, "they didn't have bridles or shoes."

"What was the story?" Zari asked.

"I don't remember it myself," Yusef said.

Khosrow sprang up, exclaiming: "Don't you remember? You told me the story the night Sahar was born. Afterwards, Gholam and I talked a lot about the herd of horses. Gholam said you made it all up so I'd stop crying."

Stifling a laugh, Zari asked, "What was the story?"

"Father, let me tell it . . . It was when father was invited to stay

24

with the Qashqai tribe. One night when there was a moon and the air was as clear as can be, with the sky full of stars, they went hunting. Suddenly, in the middle of a very, very big plain, they saw a herd of wild horses. The stallions were standing in a really wide circle facing outwards, their backs to the centre, where a mare was giving birth. The stallions were too embarrassed to look, because a baby comes out from a very bad place. Father and the others didn't go any closer because the horses would have charged on them ... well, I mean the stallions were standing like that to reassure the mare, otherwise she would have been scared. After all, some wild animal could have attacked the foal. And, oh yes, I forgot to say that an older mare stood by as a kind of midwife."

"Did I say the baby comes out from a very bad place?" Yusef asked.

"No, father, Gholam said that."

At that moment Gholam came in, wearing his faithful old felt hat.

"Is the blacksmith here?" Khosrow asked.

"His wife is here. She says he's got a fever," he replied, and turning to Yusef, "he won't be coming."

That evening Gholam came back with two porters who could carry loads on their heads. Two copper trays, piled high with bread and dates covered with a calico table-cloth, had been put out by the pool in front of the house, ready for collection. Ameh, wearing her veil, was sitting next to one of the trays. Haj Mohammad Reza, the dyer, was pacing up and down outside the gate. But Hossein Agha, the grocer, had come inside and was admiring the orange blossoms in the grove.

Zari herself went to the prison and asylum on alternate weeks. But there was always someone who could help her out with her vow and go to the place she wasn't visiting that week. And when there was no volunteer, there were Hossein Agha and Haj Mohammad Reza to turn to—they were good neighbours who would never leave a friend in the lurch.

Zari, Ameh and Khadijeh the maid had been busy all afternoon putting dates between pieces of bread. Now Zari stood in front of her dressing-table, applying a touch of make-up. From her bedroom window she could see the garden and listen to what was going on.

25

She could hear Ameh asking one of the porters, "Well, how much do you charge?"

"Where do I have to go?" he asked.

"The Karim Khan prison—the dungeon," Ameh told him, to which the man replied, "God bless you; I don't want any money. Give me some home-made bread instead."

"Where do I go?" the other porter asked.

"You go to the mental asylum," Ameh told him.

"Pay me in bread too," he said.

Zari patted her face, smoothing out the powder. Then she walked on to the verandah.

"Sister, they're asking for bread instead of money," Ameh explained to her.

"All right," Zari replied. Turning to Gholam she said, "Give them each ten loaves."

"I have further to go, but it doesn't matter," the first porter said. "This fellow's child is ill. It's this disease they say the foreign army has brought with them. I've heard that the water in the Vakil reservoir has been contaminated."

"God protect us!" Ameh exclaimed.

"As if their presence alone wasn't enough, they had to bring their diseases as well," Hossein Agha complained.

"You're giving charity to prisoners and madmen on the holy eve of Friday," the first porter said, "but no one remembers the needy standing right in front of them."

"May God repay them for their charity anyway," said the second porter. "Our God is generous too."

Gholam arrived with the bread. Both porters unwound the cloths they usually twisted into a tight coil to use as padding for their heads while carrying the trays. Then they carefully wrapped the bread inside these cloths and tied the bundles around their waists, bulging out in front like a pair of pregnant women.

"What will you carry on your head, then?" Zari asked.

"If we don't do this," the first porter explained, "someone may snatch the bread from us. Especially this home-made bread, so fresh and delicate. Just the smell of it makes your stomach growl! It's a good thing you've covered the trays with tablecloths."

"But you're taking a droshke. No-one is going to snatch the bread from you in the little way you'll need to walk."

"It looks like the lady isn't a native of this town!"

26

"Gholam, go and get the master's and Khosrow's waistcloths from Khadijeh," Zari said, "and coil them into pads. These men can't carry the trays on their bare heads."

As Gholam ran back inside, a car drew up at the garden gate, and sounded its horn. Zari saw Abol-Ghassem Khan and his son Hormoz come in. She thought, "Oh my God! I'm not ready yet," and dashed inside. There, she quickly took off her house-dress, pulled on a woollen sweater and a skirt, and started looking for her shoes.

"Hello, everybody!" she heard Abol-Ghassem say. "Will you be long?"

"Now don't rush her," Ameh's voice rose in reply. "This is the first time she isn't carrying out her vow herself, and all for your sake."

"It's a long way and we must be there at five o'clock sharp," Abol-Ghassem Khan insisted.

"Isn't it near Seyyid Abol Vafa's shrine?"

"No, sister, it's about four miles further on."

"Now why don't you do a good deed for a change and help these poor porters. While the others get ready for the party you can give the porter and me a lift in your car."

"What's the hurry? Will you be late for your opium?"

As Zari quickly combed her hair, she prayed that the two of them would not start a quarrel again. She could hear Hormoz trying to patch things up. "Auntie," he offered, "if you like I can go. I like talking to the prisoners. I've been there three times with Hossein Agha. Isn't that so, Hossein Agha?"

"What nonsense is this again?" Abol-Ghassem Khan turned on him angrily. Then he walked up to the edge of the verandah and called out jokingly to Zari, "Sister, how many hours have you been spending in front of the mirror? Where's my brother; where's Khosrow?"

Zari didn't answer; she was listening to Ameh who was saying: "Let's go. Hossein Agha, help him lift the tray to his head."

As he heaved the tray up, one of the porters said: "God give me strength!"

When they arrived at the open-air party, Captain Singer was there to greet them in person. Together they walked past the fields of summer crops to where the marquees had been set up. Zari was feeling hot, but she knew it would be cooler in the evening. She was walking ahead with Abol-Ghassem Khan while Yusef and Singer followed behind, and Khosrow and Hormoz brought up the rear.

They passed a field of lettuces, caked with dust and sand, standing in rows like soldiers on parade. As they walked on, they passed other fields where the entire crop of cucumbers, eggplants, tomatoes and melons—ripe and unripe—lay exposed to the relentless sun.

"They need watering," Abol-Ghassem Khan observed.

To the left of the fields large tents had been pitched, in which soldiers and officers were sitting or standing. Their army vehicles were parked nearby. Zari heard Yusef recite a familiar yet very apt line of verse: "Will this wine ever suffice to quench our thirst?"

"What do you mean by that?" Captain Singer challenged him.

Abol-Ghassem Khan stopped abruptly and turned to face them. Zari also stopped. Abol-Ghassem Khan blinked, and said to Captain Singer, "To be quite frank, your honour, what my brother means is that a glass of whisky wouldn't go amiss right now; even though a person can't get drunk on only one glass." After that he made a careful manoeuvre, changing places with Yusef, and falling into step with Singer.

The guests were ushered into the Supreme Command's huge marquee. Abol-Ghassem Khan had rushed them so much that they were now too early. They greeted Khanom Hakim and a Scottish officer. A map of Iran had been spread out on a table near the entrance. Khanom Hakim was pacing around the marquee looking as though she were trying to memorize something from a piece of paper in her hand. Zari glanced at the map; there were enough multi-coloured markers stuck on it to confuse even the expert. Yusef headed for the map with an agitated Abol-Ghassem at his heels.

Staring at the familiar outline of his country, Yusef murmured, "How they've disembowelled her!"

Abol-Ghassem Khan placed a hand on his brother's arm.

At that moment, Singer directed an Indian soldier who had just entered the marquee, carrying a tray of sherbets and various soft drinks, to the table where the map was displayed. Turning to Yusef, he said: "Let's have something to drink."

The three men each took a drink. Then Singer, raising his glass in

28

a toast, proclaimed in his usual broken Persian: "To Iran, so much bigger than France; and to Tehran, bigger than . . . than Vichy!"

Yusef raised his head from the map and looked straight at Singer.

"But unfortunately we didn't get a chance to fight!" he said.

Abol-Ghassem Khan mumbled nervously: "Actually, Vichy mineral water does wonders for indigestion . . . "

"Why say you unfortunately?" Singer asked, cutting him short and staring at Yusef.

"Because we're suffering the consequences anyway, without ever having tasted victory or even an honourable defeat," Yusef replied.

"Then why did you not fight, if you were able?" Singer demanded. "How to find right word? Straw? Yes, that's it, straw. We only found stuffed dummy when we come here. When we ripped him apart, there was no blood, only straw . . . stuffed with straw."

Yusef gave a hollow laugh and put his hand on Singer's shoulder.

"My dear Singer, you knew yourself what the score was, and that's what makes all of this even more ugly and despicable. We were deprived the chance of an honourable defeat . . . "

Singer raised a hand to stop him. "A-a-a-a . . . slow now, slow, so that I can follow what you say . . . "

Abol-Ghassem Khan, with an attack of his nervous blink, tried to mediate: "That's all water under the bridge . . . "

"You talk in proverbs and confuse me," Singer said irritably.

A number of other officers, English, Scottish and Indian, and McMahon the Irishman, entered the marquee. Hormoz, who had been following the conversation, whispered in Zari's ear, "If Mr Fotouhi, our teacher, were here, he would shake uncle's hand, and call him a real man. Mr Fotouhi's always bragging about his own background. If only he could see my uncle now!"

But Zari's attention was fixed on Singer who had taken Abol-Ghassem Khan's arm and was saying, in his stilted Persian: "Give your brother some good advice. God has given you so much resources in this country. Give some to us. It belongs to everyone, to all mankind. It is too much just for you. You don't need all."

"Just what British Petroleum is doing!" Yusef said with a laugh.

Singer looked taken aback. His face and neck reddened noticeably. He placed his drink on the map and blurted out, "You didn't know how! We don't need you. We can take it out ourselves and

29

give to those who need..." And suddenly he became amiable again. Lifting his glass, he said, "Cheers!"

The Governor, the Colonel and the newly married couple with Gilan Taj in tow, now made their entry. The officers stood to attention while the Governor nodded to all of them. The army commander, the town's newspaper owners and the heads of various civic departments, all began to drift in with their wives. The marquee was soon crammed full of people, and the sickly smell of feet, sweat, perfume and alcohol filled the air. Three Indian soldiers were busy serving drinks.

Zari signalled to Hormoz and Khosrow, and together they went over to Gilan Taj. Zari had decided to summon up courage to slip in a reminder about her earrings. First she introduced Khosrow and Hormoz. The girl extended a hand, and flashed a dimpled smile. Then the bride, wearing a wide-brimmed straw hat and green sunglasses, came up to them.

"Zari, darling," she cooed. "Thank you so much for your gift. I'll always treasure them, and when I wear them I'll think of you."

Zari looked at her in astonishment. Since when had she and the Governor's daughter become so intimate? In the three years since the Governor's posting to Shiraz, she had not seen the girl more than three times. Well, maybe four or five times, counting the wedding. Zari opened her mouth to say: "What gift? I only lent them, as your sister here knows full well!" But no sound escaped her lips. She cursed herself inwardly for her own ineptitude and cowardice. "Spineless women like me deserve no better!" she thought to herself.

The bride looked at Hormoz and Khosrow.

"Zari dear," she said, "I never knew you had such grown-up sons. You, so young and pretty! Tell everyone they're your brothers, not sons."

Khosrow was quick to chip in. "Four-eyed Hormoz here is my cousin," he announced.

Hormoz blushed and removed his glasses. But Zari knew he wouldn't be able to see a thing without them. She felt like scolding Khosrow there and then. Four-eyed Hormoz indeed! Talking like that to an older cousin, and in front of such uppity people as the Governor's daughter! But the bride was too quick for her.

"Master Hormoz, aren't you Mirza Abol-Ghassem Khan's son?"

she asked. "I have a great deal of respect for him. How kind he's been! What a sweet man he is, and so amusing! Please don't be shy, put on your glasses by all means. I wear glasses myself; even my sunglasses have prescription lenses. Last night I had a frightful time without them."

A sudden flurry of trumpets and drums announced that it was time to leave the marquee for other events of the evening. The Colonel and the Governor led the way, followed by the guests, and Zari felt as if she were being taken to an execution. They reached a vast, open space, where chairs had been arranged in a horse-shoe. Already thousands of soldiers, mostly Indian, were seated.

The officer behind the Colonel gave an order and at once, as all the soldiers rose to attention, there was a deafening scraping of chairs. Around a platform which had been made out of a couple of old boards and covered with a carpet, five flags waved of which Zari recognized only one—that of Great Britain. Khanom Hakim made her way across the creaking platform to the microphone. A hush ensued. Reading from the piece of paper in her hand, she greeted the guests in Persian. Her voice was a little unsteady at first until she gained confidence and warmed to her speech. In the light of the setting sun, her dull teeth looked decidedly yellow.

From what Zari could gather, the gist of her speech was that in order to amuse the fighting boys of Great Britain now on leave in Shiraz, that sweet city of birds and flowers—they had arranged some entertainment. This was to enable the soldiers to fight the monster Fascism with greater strength of spirit, sending that devil Hitler back to hell in the shortest time possible. She thanked the Iranians for their hospitality, for they had made the war against Satan—meaning Hitler—easier to bear. Then she finished by declaring that Hitler was like a virus, a cancer, which had to be torn out.

Now Khanom Hakim was not only a midwife, but also a surgeon quite keen on using the knife. And in addition to these talents, as she said herself, she "brought glad tidings and led the people to Christ". Every night, as Zari remembered, she had the pregnant women, and the ones she had already cut up, as well as their relatives, queuing up to watch a film. A silent film, of course. She would hold a long stick in her hand, and point out the characters in the film, explaining in broken Persian:

"This be Jesus Christ . . . this be Mary Magdalen . . . this be Judas

31

Escariot . . . " Afterwards, in that same irritating patois, she would preach a sermon about Satan and hell-fire.

"Why should a midwife, surgeon and missionary all rolled into one, suddenly appear in a place like Shiraz?" Zari thought to herself, as she continued to muse about Khanom Hakim. "Maybe her Satan has some connection with the 'Satan' the fighting boys are trying to send back to hell? The boys are mostly Indian, anyway. And, to use Abol-Ghassem Khan's phrase, 'they manage well enough themselves, and stir up trouble for everyone else besides.' Yet our people have started to call this devil 'the Messiah'. I've heard it many times myself."

McMahon took over from Khanom Hakim on the stage, his presence adding a note of gaiety. He had thrown a red cloak over his shoulders, and was wearing a pair of black boots. It made him look like a famous film star, though Zari could not for the life of her remember the name. It was a pity he was fat. He spoke in English, and Zari didn't understand all of his jokes, but after two or three sentences, the sound of the soldiers' laughter filled the air. Even the Governor and the army commander laughed occasionally, but it was one of the newspaper owners who laughed the loudest of all. Could all this laughter be out of politeness, Zari wondered, since despite her own good English, she hardly understood any of it.

Then, with all the appropriate gestures, McMahon told a story about a soldier serving abroad who seduced a girl, exploiting her for what he could get out of her. He wanted new shoes and a hat; he wanted this and that, until one day the girl said she was pregnant and he must marry her. He confessed then that he already had a wife and children back home. McMahon rocked an imaginary cradle, put his arms around an imaginary wife, and said, "I have a wife and little ones" in Persian. This time the audience laughed a little less heartily.

After the story, he recited one of his poems—the one about the Tree of Independence. It told of a strange tree nourished by blood and by the earth on which it stood, tended by a prophet-like gardener who loved his tree above all others. When it needed water, the gardener would call for blood and people would surge to open the veins on their arms, eager to nurture the tree beneath whose cool, shady branches they sat and unburdened their sorrows. If its leaves were crushed and powdered, and then rubbed on the eyes, it would endow the bearer with pride, hope and confidence,

32

triumphing over cowardice and treachery to create a people of strength and courage.

Then the show began. A bearded Indian, wearing a turban and dressed from head to toe in white, came and knelt on the platform. He lowered the microphone and began to play a pipe. From a hole in front of him, which Zari had not noticed before, a dark-skinned woman with a red dot between her eyebrows bobbed up her head several times. Finally, the woman emerged completely, all the while moving to the music and slowly approaching the man. She was wearing a yellow sari with a gold embroidered border. When she started to sing in her shrill, high-pitched voice, she could hardly be heard above the din of the Indian soldiers who were whistling and shouting to the music. Her bracelets jangled as she moved her arms.

At one stage of the dance, it suddenly seemed as though the woman had unlocked the muscles of her neck. Her head fell effortlessly on to her shoulders, and she kept rotating it to the left and right just like a snake. She also lifted her eyebrows one at a time, to the rhythm of the music. Zari was amazed to see the amount of kohl the woman had used to outline her eyes.

Gradually the dancer moved back to the hole from which she had emerged. Then, as the snake-charmer quickened his pace, a rubber hose with a snake's head glued on to it rose out of the hole, stiff as a rod. The woman reached down, and pulled out the rest of the hose. Then she coiled it like a long snake, in a corner of the platform.

At this point a thin man with bushy eyebrows and a mottled moustache, wearing top hat and tails and carrying an umbrella, stepped up on to the stage. The fluteplayer kept on playing. The woman reached into the hole and brought out some odds and ends—boards, sticks, McMahon's red cloak, a conical hat, a box, a hammer and an air-pump. Then she helped the bushy-eyebrowed man to make a dummy out of the sticks. Taking the rubber hose, the man wrapped it around the frame. After securing a kind of snake's head in place, he threw a cloak over the dummy's body. Next, he placed the conical hat on the serpent-head, glued on a long moustache and, taking a swastika from the dancer, pinned it on to the cloak. Then he went to the air-pump, attached the nozzle to the scarecrow's foot and, to the beat of the music, began to pump it up. Zari watched as it grew bigger and bigger. Its head, body, hands and feet became inflated, swelling to an unbelievable size. It took up so

33

much of the main part of the stage that the turbaned man had to step aside. A voice behind Zari murmured: "It's Hitler!"

Suddenly drums began to roll. A fat man, with a cigar in the corner of his mouth, rushed on to the stage, followed by another dressed as 'Uncle Sam'. Then various officers, some in kilts, some with hammer and sickle armbands, one and all invaded the stage. Armed with bows and arrows, they first began to tease the scarecrow. One of their number kept holding them back saying: "Nyet! Nyet!" Finally he too gave in, and yelled: "Good! Good!"

The drumming reached a crescendo. Arrows flew at the scarecrow from all directions. Slowly it began to deflate until it sank to the ground with a loud hiss. The crowd cheered and applauded. And then there were other shows . . .

4

On Saturday afternoon, Sahar was shod by a new blacksmith. Khosrow was at school so he wasn't there to witness it. When he came home, he looked reproachfully at his father, who said, "I had to do it, otherwise it would have been too late."

They then began talking of hunting and Yusef promised to take both Khosrow and Sahar along. From that moment until Thursday afternoon, when the riders actually set off, Khosrow's entire concentration was focused on hunting and whether or not Sahar would be able to manage it.

They had not been gone twenty-four hours when Zari began to miss them. She couldn't help worrying, thinking of all the things that might go wrong. Ameh finally scolded her: "They're probably thoroughly enjoying their ride, in spite of the fact that you keep imagining the worst."

Zari instructed Gholam to sprinkle water over the brick paving in front of the house, and to put out the cane chairs around the pool. She was sure they would be back before sunset on Friday. Mina and Marjan, meanwhile, played around the pool, dipping their hands in the water the moment Zari's back was turned.

Suddenly there was a knocking at the garden gate. Zari, certain it was the huntsmen, ran out to greet them. By the time she reached the gates, Gholam had opened them wide. A horse-drawn cab pulled in. Zari was taken aback; they had left on horseback! When the droshke reached Zari, it came to a halt. Two women stepped down. They were wearing heavy veils, drawn tightly over their faces. But what strapping women! They were wearing thick woven summer shoes, and their feet looked very large. They also seemed unusually tall and broad-shouldered beneath their veils. The women bowed their heads at Zari's greeting, and one of them extended a coarse, thickly-veined hand to pay the driver. Zari noticed she was wearing a man's watch on her wrist. Zari racked her brains to remember where she had seen them before. Maybe they were friends of Ameh Khanom, who at that moment was smoking opium on the verandah. "Could they just be masculine-looking women, or are they gypsies?" Zari wondered.

Her attention was suddenly drawn to Mina and Marjan, who had plunged their arms up to the elbow in the water. "Get away from there!" she scolded.

Indicating the chairs by the pool, she offered the strangers a seat. But they took no notice and walked towards the house. The shorter one was obviously laughing because her shoulders were shaking underneath the veil. Ameh, glancing at the women as she puffed away at her pipe, said: "I don't recall having had the pleasure ... "

The women, ignoring her remark, crossed the verandah, opened the parlour door and walked in. Zari was totally bewildered. They were certainly not inmates of the asylum where she usually took bread and dates. But neither was it normal behaviour to arrive at someone's house, walk right in without a by your leave and make yourself at home.

She followed the women to the parlour.

"Please take a seat," she said, "although, quite frankly, I can't remember having made your acquaintance."

"Where is Yusef Khan?" one of them asked in a husky voice.

"He's gone hunting with Khosrow," Zari replied.

It was a man's voice and a familiar one at that. Someone was playing a practical joke. At that moment, the two 'women' simultaneously pushed their veils aside. Thick eyebrows, dark eyes, long eyelashes and a hooked nose set in a longish sallow face—the spitting image of each other, except that one was younger, and the older one wore a moustache.

"Malek Rostam Khan!" Zari exclaimed in astonishment. "What kind of get-up is this? You half scared me to death!"

Malek Rostam put a finger to his lips: "Hush! Be quiet. I'll sit here and wait for Yusef," he whispered.

Zari went out on to the verandah. There was no one but the twins watching Ameh smoke her pipe. She returned to the parlour with straw fans for Malek Rostam and his brother Malek Sohrab.

"You really had me fooled, you know," she said laughingly. "Turning up like this after all these years."

36

"When is he returning from his trip?" Malek Rostam asked her anxiously. "Is there a chance he won't be back today?"

"I'm expecting him any minute now. But why?" Zari asked.

"I hear he's going to the village—to the lowlands tomorrow . . . Why isn't he back yet?" Malek Rostam asked again.

Zari brought sherbet drinks for the guests, and then fruit and some nuts. She opened the parlour door for more air. But they wouldn't let her put on the lights. She sat facing them.

"Well, how is it that you've finally come to visit us?"

"Oh, Sohrab has come on behalf of my uncle," Malek Rostam answered, playing with his moustache. "I came because I missed you both."

"I bet it was Sohrab Khan's idea to wear the veils," Zari said. "He's still the same mischievous child at heart. Do you remember, Sohrab Khan, what antics you were always up to?"

"How could I forget!" he said with a laugh. "But we wore the veils so we wouldn't be recognized. If they catch us they will tear us to bits."

"Gone are the good old days when nothing used to worry us!" Zari sighed.

Her mind went back to one such day; a day in the first year of her marriage. In that same year the government had captured the head of the Qashqai tribe and taken him to Tehran. The tribe itself was breaking camp to move on. When Zari and Yusef arrived, a group of them came out to greet them. They even cheered for them, but it was an empty cheer, as Yusef said. They were dusty and depressed, and clearly not their usual selves. By the time Yusef and Zari reached the chieftain's large tent, most of them had scattered. Malek Sohrab was sitting in the tribal chieftain's place. When he saw them, he declared, "Welcome to this, our mobile capital!"

Zari had never seen a more beautiful tent in her life than that wandering capital. What carpets and rugs! The inside was painted with designs of legendary Shahnameh heroes such as Rostam, Ashkabus, Esfandiar, Sohrab and other characters whom Zari didn't recognize. It was funny; Malek Sohrab had seemed both childish and mature at the same time. He had got up, showing Zari the picture of Sohrab, and said, "This is me!"

"God forbid!" Zari had replied, because Sohrab was depicted with a dagger deep in his side. Then he had pointed to the picture of

37

Rostam and said, "This is Malek Rostam, the elder brother of our chief."

Zari had glanced at Malek Rostam who was busy whispering to Yusef. There was a wistful smile on his face. Then Malek Sohrab had pointed to the image of a severed head lying in a large basin full of blood. A black horse stood at the basin, smelling the tulips which grew all around it. Malek Sohrab had said, "This is my own little brother to whom my mother, Bibi, hasn't yet given birth!"

"You can't fool me," Zari had replied. "I bet you anything it's John the Baptist."

Malek Sohrab had laughed and said, "All right, let's have a bet."

"What do you bet?"

"A Brno rifle." Malek Sohrab called Yusef over and showed him the drawing.

"Your wife says this is John the Baptist."

"Please forgive her," Yusef had smiled. "My wife married straight from the classroom. Her head's still full of the Gospel stories she was forced to read every morning at the Missionary school."

"I know!" Zari had rushed to correct herself. "It's the beheaded martyr, Imam Hossein ... and that horse ... " But Yusef stopped her.

"My dear, don't embarrass me any more. That's Siavush."

Returning to the chieftain's seat, Malek Sohrab had said, "We number six thousand in this camp. Let them kill a hundred and fifty sheep a day ... And you, Zari Khanom," he said after a pause, "I hear you've brought your own bridal carpet as an offering to our chieftain. We cannot accept it. The very fibres of this carpet were a labour of love." And he asked eagerly: "Did you see the layout of the tents? Did you see the gunmen standing ready? Do you hear the horns and drums? This military march is being played in your honour."

The words had hardly left his lips when Bibi Hamdam, their mother, came in. After the usual greetings, she turned to Malek Sohrab and said, "Get up from that seat, child! Are you talking nonsense again? They've caught two hens. Run out and cut their throats before the sun goes down."

Angrily, Malek Sohrab stood up, made a face at Bibi, and stalked out of the room. When he returned, he threw the dead hens into his mother's lap.

38

Zari remembered it all as if it were yesterday.

"Zari Khanom, you're deep in thought," Malek Rostam observed, breaking the train of Zari's reminiscences. "Are we disturbing you?"

"Oh goodness, no!" Zari replied with a laugh. "I was only thinking back to the first time I came to your chieftain's tent. It was the first year of our marriage." Turning to Malek Sohrab she said, "Do you remember what you did to your poor mother in front of me, a newly-wed bride?"

"I remember it well," he replied.

"You were a child, then," Zari said.

"I was not a child. I was stubborn and rebellious," Malek Sohrab replied.

"I remember Bibi Hamdam had to change her skirts," said Zari. "I counted, she had eight of them on. Bibi had caught a cold . . . and you, Malek Sohrab, kept saying that a hardy tribal woman should never get sick."

"I remember very well. That same night I won a Brno rifle from you . . . and I'm still waiting for it," he added jokingly.

At that moment Khadijeh came in and took the keychain from Zari to give the twins so that they could go to sleep. She looked in amazement at the veiled men.

"You're sitting in the dark!" she exclaimed. "Shall I put the light on?"

"No," came the reply.

"I remember," Malek Rostam said, joining in the reminiscing. "It was the year I caught malaria and came to you for refuge. I was in bed for three months in your house, at a time when nobody even dared say hello to us in the street. A friend of a Qashqai was an enemy of the Shah. Yet you nursed me like a sister. I'll never forget. Once the washerwoman didn't come and you washed my clothes with your own delicate hands. Yusef even helped me with the bed-pan himself." Turning to Sohrab, he said, "Sohrab, I'm going. I shouldn't have come here."

Sohrab answered him in Turkish, and for a while the two brothers spoke together in their native dialect. Since Zari couldn't understand a word, she started to think, and that led her to worry about Khosrow again.

At the sound of hooves on the gravel, Zari once again rushed outside. The lights were on in the garden. They had shot two deer,

39

and a live fawn was tied to the saddle of the chestnut horse which their steward, Seyyid Mohammad, was riding. The riders dismounted.

"A good day's work!" exclaimed Ameh Khanom, who had also come out to greet them.

Khosrow couldn't tell his mother fast enough what had happened on the trip.

"Mother," he babbled, "Sahar has been really naughty. He chased after the fawn and bit it on the back. Of course he fell down himself. He's hurt his knee and now I have to treat it with burnt hazelnut oil. Mother, do you have any hazelnuts?"

"There's some on the table in the parlour," Zari said, adding quickly: "but don't go in there now. We have some important guests."

Yusef, meanwhile, had gone over to the wooden bed on the other side of the pool. The twins were sleeping there under a mosquito net.

As they went into the parlour, Zari quickly warned Yusef about their unexpected visitors. He switched on the lights.

"I was expecting you," he said to Malek Rostam, "but not today. Your visit is not only too late, it's badly timed as well. Today, I can't even say I'm pleased to see you. Why you of all people? Why should you have agreed to such things? After all those discussions we had . . ."

He sat on the sofa and Zari knelt in front of him to remove his boots. Malek Rostam bent his head and chewed his moustache. Sohrab rolled up his veil, threw it in a corner, and sat bolt upright. Yusef continued:

"You've taken out your rusty, broken guns from the cracks and crevices in the mountain-side, oiled them and taken to looting and killing your fellow-men again. What more can you and I have to say to each other?"

"Zari Khanom isn't a stranger," Sohrab said, "and I'm not afraid of saying in front of her that we had to take our revenge. How long can we take it from the government? With that general pardon of theirs, which they later broke—and how! What they promised us on the one hand, they took away with the other. There was only bribery, excuses, hatred, and executions. Their forced settlements turned out to be a total waste of money. They built a couple of mud-huts in dried-up areas, and told us to go and live in them.

40

Instead of books, teachers, doctors, medicine and health care, they sent us soldiers armed with bayonets, guns and hostility. It's only natural that we've gone back to our old trade and taken revenge on them."

While Sohrab was talking, Khadijeh brought a hookah and placed it in front of Yusef. Zari whispered to her, "Take the boots and give them to Gholam for cleaning. Bring some tea, too."

Drawing on the pipe, Yusef said, "What can I say, Sohrab my friend; you've put your finger on it yourself. You say you've gone back to your 'trade'. In other words the tribe has become a kind of business for you. You use it to make deals."

"Believe me," Malek Rostam protested, "they acted entirely without provocation at the beginning. I'm personally in favour of the idea of settlements. You know that yourself. But it's as if they themselves don't want us to prosper. Certain forces are at work against us. They want us either to rot away from the inside and ultimately destroy ourselves, or else to stay in our present state."

Yusef lifted the pipe to his lips again. "You yourselves prefer this present state of affairs," he said. "If you had been more willing, the settlements might have worked. But my friend, you tribal chiefs have become too accustomed to exploiting your tribesmen. For you they aren't human beings; they're no different from your sheep— you sell them both in one go."

"Don't speak to me like that, Yusef," Malek Rostam retorted angrily. "You're a close friend, we've been classmates and we've shared each other's hospitality many times, but . . ."

"I don't know how to say what I have to say any other way," Yusef interrupted. "You know me well enough. I don't stand on ceremony with anyone—especially not with my closest friends."

Malek Rostam replied quietly, "I know, better than anyone, that tribal life with all its excitement and adventure is not the right way to live. You know that I would prefer to be a settled Qashqai rather than a nomadic one. I know it's not right for thousands of men, women and children to be led by their herds, wandering from the top of the Gulf to the other side of the mountains in search of grass and water. I realize that the lives of so many people should not be tied to cows, sheep and grazing land. But do you think it's up to me alone? Am I the chief? What can one person do?"

Yusef put his pipe aside. "If that one person really wants to," he said quietly, "he can easily sway others. There are a great many

41

people who are capable of understanding what's right and fair, and recognizing it when they hear it. But these people are scattered and you must join forces with them ... Even if you don't do it yourself, your children and the children of others will do it in their time. They will pass through towns and villages, they'll see schools, mosques, public baths and hospitals. They'll grow to understand and want these things and finally do something about their lot."

"You know it's too late for that," Malek Rostam replied wearily.

There was a pause when Khosrow came in to take hazelnuts for Sahar. After he left, Yusef asked, "What was all that about the Malek Abad Pass? I've heard a few things, but I want to hear about it from you."

"I swear to you, it wasn't anything much," replied Malek Rostam. "The Ezhdehakosh clan disarmed a group of soldiers, chopped off a few heads, took a dozen rifles or so, some ammunition and about twenty horses—that's all. And what's more, they did it without permission. The Farsi Madan clan brought it to my uncle's attention. My uncle doesn't agree with this kind of pilfering."

Malek Sohrab, who had been silent for a while, spoke up: "Brother, tell Yusef about the incident with the captain's pups."

When Malek Rostam remained silent, Sohrab began to tell the story himself.

"The dog belonging to the captain in charge of the tribal settlement had just whelped," he began. "A couple of mischievous kids from the Ezhdehakosh clan threw stones at it—a purebred wolfhound, no less. Anyway, afraid that they would be found out, they stole the dog and got rid of it. Again the tell-tale Farsi Madans gave them away, and the captain forced three women from the Ezhdehakosh to breast-feed the puppies."

Zari felt sick, but Yusef merely smiled and said, "My dear Sohrab, that story must be at least ten, twelve years old. And it's the third time you've told it to me."

"Then why let me tell it a fourth time?" Malek Sohrab countered indignantly.

"I didn't recognize it at first, but it came back to me as you went on. Anyway, what do you think I am, some sort of saint? I'm a human being, like everyone else." Turning to Rostam, Yusef continued, "Well, what do you want from me? We've been talking about this and that; let's get to the point."

42

"Please believe that I don't agree with everything my uncle does," Malek Rostam said. "I was even against his sending me to you. I don't want to ruin our friendship. But in these sensitive times, I can't turn my back on him."

Zari could have sworn Malek Rostam had told her it was Malek Sohrab who was there on behalf of their uncle, and he himself had just come along for the visit.

"You still haven't said what you want of me," Yusef reminded him.

Malek Rostam lowered his head, seemingly lost in thought. But Malek Sohrab stepped in.

"Help," he said, after a moment's silence.

"What sort of help?"

"Sell us whatever provisions you have. We'll even buy the un-harvested crop. You just name the price."

"Who has put you up to this?" Yusef asked suspiciously. "Singer? Up to now there's only been talk of surplus crops. Now it's the whole lot!"

The two brothers exchanged a glance. Suddenly Yusef raised his voice: "You want the provisions to sell to the foreign army in exchange for arms, so you can go on fighting and looting your fellow-countrymen and brothers! Don't you realize that if you give them an inch, they'll take a mile? Haven't you any brains? Those 'mysterious government forces' which you claim have prevented you from prospering in the settlement could've been used to your advantage at a time like this ... So where's that spirit of adventure, that fight and dignity now?" Yusef's moustache trembled in anger.

"Do you know government men stopped the tribe in Kam Firouz?" Malek Sohrab pleaded. "Do you realize they refused permission to migrate this summer? All around us we face the guns and bullets of our own countrymen. The green grass on the slopes of the mountains is drying up untouched, and our sheep are starving and dying of thirst."

"Now look here, Sohrab," Yusef retorted angrily, "don't give me this nonsense, you young fool. You sold most of your sheep to the foreigners. They're frozen now, and being dutifully guarded in the cold-storage of the Ahwaz-Bandar Shah railway."

Rostam's eyes were glued to the designs on the carpet.

"If we hadn't sold them," his brother answered, "they would

have died on us. Believe me, our sheep couldn't even walk at the end. They had to be carried away in trucks."

"What did you do with the money—buy weapons? Golden pitchers? Golden jars? Did you sew royal crowns on to your hats, and get a thrill when they started calling your uncle 'His Highness'?" Yusef snapped.

Malek Sohrab, unable to contain himself any longer, jumped to his feet.

"Yusef Khan, our friendship is all very fine, but everything has a limit!" he shouted. "What right have you to call me a young fool? To say that we have no brains? You are the one with no brains, because right now you should be the deputy, not your brother . . . "

"Deputy for whom—Singer? I spit on the deputation for which you, Malek Sohrab, have to act as go-between!" Yusef said, his voice shaking with anger.

"What on earth are you talking about!" Malek Sohrab shouted even more angrily. "You say whatever comes to your mind without pausing to think that you may be the one who's wrong. Who uses me as a go-between? Why are you so self-righteous? Who on earth do you think you are? And besides, what mistakes? What do golden pitchers have to do with us? Why do you blame us for what Davoud Khan may have done? Why? What right have you got?"

"You're all the same," Yusef sighed wearily.

Malek Rostam turned to Sohrab, trying to calm him down. "Sit down, boy," he said. "I made you promise you wouldn't insult my friend." Then the two brothers started talking in Turkish. Rostam's voice gradually became harsher as Sohrab's tone softened, until he finally sat and apologized. Yusef pulled the hookah towards him.

"The charcoal has gone out, let me go and light it again," Zari said.

"There's enough fire within me," Yusef sighed, as he drew on the pipe.

"I didn't mean to offend you; I apologize again," Sohrab said, forcing a smile.

"My dear Sohrab, for once you've discovered my weakness and see what a fuss you made! But I like that, you have guts. Only you still don't see very far." He put the pipe aside and continued, "You know, I was never happy about your playing around with the Germans, nor am I happy now that you've made a deal with their enemies. You're the ones who've turned Hitler into a 'Messiah'

44

among our people. These tricks don't really work with us, and your political flirtations only gave these foreigners an added excuse to come here."

"Well brother, after all it's a war," Malek Sohrab said gently. "They don't give out sweets in a war. These people have to stay around to protect the oil and the access to the Gulf. They would have come in any case, even if we weren't here. And anyhow, they only come to the town on sick leave or on holiday. The main camp is at Khorramshahr . . . they have no other alternative."

"Now you're defending them too, my friend?" Yusef asked in a fatherly tone. "Their war is their affair. What does it have to do with us? Hitler is from their continent. They created him themselves. Let them pay for that. Let them pay for everything, even the unhappiness they've brought on the ones who, according to Singer, 'have resources they don't know how to use'. The English never ask who's to blame for this ignorance."

Malek Sohrab glanced at his watch. "It's getting late," he said. "I've got a headache. Do you have any aspirin? Make sure it's Bayer."

Zari got up and took away the hookah. When she returned with the Bayer aspirin and a glass of water, Yusef was saying, "I assure you that it's so. In order to discourage their ally from the plan I just mentioned, they'll arrange a few skirmishes and manoeuvres with your aid, and quite a number of our people will be slaughtered at your hands. The British never say no to an ally. They simply confront him with a fait accompli so that he abandons his original plan himself. Mark my words: they will stain your hands with blood, while they themselves just sit and watch. A real massacre will take place amongst us."

"We must be going soon," Malek Sohrab pointed out anxiously, "so let's get back to the point. You still haven't told us whether you'll sell the provisions or not."

"He hasn't said? Must he spell it out for you? He went to such lengths . . . " Malek Rostam laughed, but still Malek Sohrab bargained: "Please believe that we don't want to sell all of it. Our men are hungry; they're falling like flies from sickness and hunger."

"I'll take Rostam's word of honour," Yusef answered. "If he promises to buy just enough for your own men, and to use my provisions for your people only, then I will agree. Tomorrow I'm going to Kavar ... I know you've been stopped there too. Bring camels to load the provisions. But, remember, only for the tribe's use. Band Bahman is just a kilometre further away, and there you'll find water. I'll also provide the pasture for free."

"I can't cheat you," Malek Rostam said dejectedly.

"I know you can't." Yusef paused, then said with feeling, "Rostam, try to turn away from this path you've chosen for yourself. Why don't you try, at least, to create a spark of faith somehow, somewhere. Teach your people skills. How many times have I told you! My unused lands are there just waiting for houses, schools, public baths, hospitals, mosques, pastures ... "

Malek Sohrab cut Yusef short. "These things you talk about are not in our nature," he said. "We've lived free. Nature has always been within our reach. We've ridden horses in the mountains, rested on the plains, camped under the skies. We can't be imprisoned in houses."

"But it seems it can be done to us Khans," Yusef said bitterly. "We used to have the best gardens in town, the best houses ... and where are they now? At the disposal of the Supreme Command, that's where!"

Malek Sohrab, knowing what Yusef was about to say, stopped him gently. "I promise you our people love the kind of life they lead. If they settle down their spirit will be broken."

"Because it's the only life they've ever known," Yusef argued. "But Sohrab, my friend, when a man cultivates a piece of land, labours over its soil and reaps its harvest, he becomes attached to that land. In a village, nature is still within reach. When you're settled ... "

Sohrab finished the sentence for him: "You become stupid, helpless, petty and cowardly." Then, as if to change the subject, he said, "May I ask you a question? What will you do with all your corn and grain and dates? It's harvest time now in the lowlands. What will you do after the harvest? Will you hoard everything?"

"I'll give my villagers their share to the last grain," Yusef replied. "The rest I'll bring to town. Unlike those traitors who sold both their villagers' share and the food for the town to the foreign army. There are five of us who'll do this, and we're landowners of considerable means. Two of us are on the city council, and we've all sworn to take control of the town's provisions. We have the mayor on our side. I know you're not the sort to reveal this to anyone. I also want

46

you to know that it's not in my nature to hoard. The hoarders have sent their own people's provisions to North Africa and . . . "

Malek Rostam interrupted him. "Majid is probably with you too," he said sadly. "God willing, I hope you manage to accomplish something."

"What will you do about the Governor?" Malek Sohrab asked.

"The Governor is a human being," Yusef replied. "He'll agree to end the food shortage in order to have this part of the country quieten down."

"I think the outlook is bleak," Malek Sohrab commented. "It's a dangerous plan. So long as you only talk about it, they'll leave you alone. But the minute you put your words into action, they'll stop you by whatever means they can." He stood up and put on his veil.

"We'll do our utmost," Yusef assured him, adding: "Stay for dinner."

"No, we'd better go," Malek Sohrab replied. "They'll be worried about us; they may think we've been caught. Please ask someone to get us a droshke."

Malek Rostam got up then and put on his veil, inside out. Zari laughed.

"You have it on the wrong way round," she said. "The seams are showing."

"You stay," Yusef said, turning to Rostam. "I'll take you back myself tomorrow morning before sunrise."

"All right," he agreed.

They went into the garden together, and sat on the cane chairs to wait for Sohrab's cab. The verandah lights were on. Zari, standing at the edge of the verandah, saw Khosrow squatting by Ameh's opium brazier. He was roasting hazelnuts in the frying pan while she ground more nuts on a flat stone. Sahar was on the verandah, with his bridle tied to a door handle. Zari heard Yusef say, "Why didn't you take the bridle off the poor creature? Why did you bring him on to the verandah? Child, the animal is tired. Take him to the stables and leave your treatments till the morning."

Khosrow got up. "Father, please let me. The hazelnut oil is ready now. I'll rub it on his knee-cap and then I'll take him to the stables. I brought him to the verandah because he was playing around. He was chasing the fawn, who kept waking with a start and throwing himself against the branches and bushes out of fright. So I brought Sahar here with me."

Ameh burned herself taking the hot hazelnuts out of the frying pan. Dropping the nuts, and blowing on her fingers, she said:

"Brother, tell Gholam to kill the fawn tomorrow. First of all, not everyone managed to get meat from the hunt and they're grumbling. Secondly, keeping deer brings bad luck. Come to think of it, I wish the men in this family would put hunting out of their minds once and for all. Only last year you shot a pregnant deer. The minute they opened her up and I saw that little one sleeping there in her mother's womb, I beat myself on the head. I knew it was a bad omen . . ."

"Put your veil on. Those women in the garden are really men," Zari informed her sister-in-law quietly.

"God protect us!" Ameh said, jumping up in astonishment. "Heaven have mercy!" Frenziedly she covered herself with her veil.

When the droshke arrived, Malek Rostam stood up too.

"Allow me to leave also," he said to Yusef. "I have to reach my uncle as soon as possible. I think you're right. My uncle has blindly worked himself into a tight corner."

Yusef only asked, "Blindly?"

5

It was ten days now since Yusef had left for the lowlands. Zari wandered about the garden with her gardening scissors, looking unsuccessfully for flowers to cut. To her, the heat there felt every bit as oppressive as in the lowlands. Summer always seemed to rush upon them in this way, brushing away the last signs of spring. Mina and Marjan followed their mother around from one rose-bush to another, chattering and giggling, while Gholam watered the brick paving in front of the house to cool off the garden. Along one border of the stream that ran by the brick paving were some tired-looking amaranthus, while along the other side a variety of snapdragons stooped under layers of dust, side by side with the humble-plants sleepily closing their petals to the approaching dusk. Zari's only hope lay in the tuberoses that Gholam had said would bloom with the full moon. The orange blossoms were scattered now, brown and withered like so many burnt stars beneath the trees. At least in winter the narcissi bloomed gaily by the small stream, surrendering their image to the water only to be carried away, unseen and lost forever, as the water tumbled into the pool. Even spring brought with it white and purple violets that coyly greeted the passing stream, nodding cheerfully at their own reflection. But nothing seemed able to resist the heat of the summer.

"When is father coming to throw me up in the air?" Mina asked her mother. "You never do that to me!"

Marjan pouted. Her lips were like little buds that seemed to Zari more beautiful than all the flowers in the world. "We won't ever talk to you again," she said, adding her voice to her sister's. "So there!" And she pleaded, "Now why don't you throw us in the air, just once?"

49

Zari picked Mina up and tried to throw her into the air.

"You're too heavy—I can't do it," she complained, slapping the child's chubby thigh.

"Father's hands are big and he can do it. Your hands are too small, so you can't. We'll wait till your hands grow up," Mina told her mother.

At that moment, Ameh came through the garden gate. She had been to the public baths and was holding a paper bag dripping with water. Mina and Marjan ran towards her, shouting: "Auntie, what have you brought us?"

"Fresh walnuts."

"Give us some then."

"I hope you enjoyed your bath," Zari greeted Ameh, taking the paper bag over the children's heads, so that she could go and wash the walnuts. When she returned, Khadijeh had brought in the bag that Ameh used for her trips to the public baths, and put it down on one of the cane chairs. Ameh took out her towels and hung them on the line. Mina was dashing about chasing Marjan, but when Zari put the plate of walnuts on the table, the children rushed over excitedly.

"Well, talk about having your prayers answered!" Zari smiled.

"This town has turned into a zoo," Ameh complained. "Everywhere you go, those dark little Indian men follow you about saying, 'Need woman, need woman!'" She dipped her hand in the pool as if to wash away the obscenity of their suggestion. Holding out her wet hand, she sat on a chair and continued:

"The children in the street tried to chase away the pathetic Indian who followed me; they were teasing, and singing some nonsense at him. Then suddenly the man brings out this chain he had with him, swings it around in the air, stamps his foot, and shoos them all away in no time."

Khadijeh appeared then, carrying Ameh's opium brazier with all the accessories, as well as some fresh tea. As Zari and the twins joined her on the verandah, Mina asked: "Auntie, did the Indian cut the children's heads off?"

"Oh yes! He put them over his knee and sawed their heads off, didn't he?" Marjan said with rounded eyes.

"Our Khosrow's late," Ameh commented. "Perhaps that difficult final exam didn't go too well, and that's why he's not home yet. I think we should send Gholam to fetch him, sister."

Before Zari could answer, they spotted Abol-Ghassem Khan coming up the garden path towards the verandah. He was muttering to himself and gesturing with his hands. Zari's heart sank at the sight of him. Lately she had begun to feel as though she were facing the prophet of doom every time she saw him. And each time he blinked, she imagined he would blink her whole life away. As he reached the edge of the verandah, Zari stood up.

"Please come in," she invited.

"No, I'll just stay here."

"Greetings!" said Ameh Khanom, between two puffs on her opium pipe.

She put the pipe down next to the brazier and poured some tea, which she handed to her brother. Zari's eyes were on Abol-Ghassem Khan who put a lump of sugar in his mouth, then poured some tea into the saucer to cool it.

"Has something happened?" she asked.

Abol-Ghassem Khan put the saucer down on the edge of the verandah and asked: "Any news of my brother?"

"No, not yet."

"I don't really know how to tell you this," he said. Zari suddenly felt dizzy. She sat down and said faintly, "God forbid, has something happened to Yusef?"

"Out with it, let's hear the worst!" Ameh cried out.

"This morning they called from the Governor's house," said Abol-Ghassem Khan. "They told me: 'Miss Gilan Taj has heard a great deal about Khosrow's colt, and she's decided she would like it, so we're offering to buy. Send us the colt and we'll gladly pay any price you like.' God knows I've been in a state since this morning; I'm so distracted, I can hardly think."

Zari's eyes filled with tears. She looked at Ameh, with her braided hair and red scarf, flushed and tearful by now, hardly able to fix the piece of opium on her pipe for the trembling of her hand. Sure enough, the opium slipped from her grasp into the blazing brazier, raising a lot of smoke.

"A curse upon their household!" she said. "I'm so furious I could take this brazier with its burning charcoal and smash it over my own head! You didn't happen to mention, I suppose, that the boy's whole existence revolves around his horse? They cut off your tongue, did they?"

Mina sidled up to Ameh and tried to offer her the one remaining

51

walnut which she had held tightly in her little fist.

"Have it, auntie," she urged, as if to comfort her. "I was saving it for Khosrow."

"Khadijeh!" Zari called out. "Come and take the children to Haj Mohammad Reza's house and show them the snake he caught yesterday."

"Has he taken the teeth out?" Marjan asked. "Has he?"

"Yes, dear, don't be afraid," Zari reassured her.

Mina took Marjan's hand, saying: "You play with him for a minute, and then I'll play with him for a minute, all right?"

"They play with snakes?" Abol-Ghassem Khan asked incredulously.

"No, she won't let the children touch the snake . . ." Zari replied distractedly.

"Seeing that everything is done backwards in this house, I thought perhaps . . ." Abol-Ghassem Khan began with a laugh, but he never finished his sentence. Instead, he asked gently: "Did you find the snake here, in this house?"

Zari, distraught at the thought of Khosrow parting with Sahar, felt the more she talked about the snake the better.

"Yes," she answered. "Yesterday as we were sitting on the verandah, a female snake fell from the windowsill on to the paving in front of the house. Gholam happened to be watering at the time and he smashed the snake over the head with his watering-can. But it kept moving so Gholam had to finish it off with the shovel. He told us that the male snake would eventually come after its mate. So he called in Haj Mohammad the dyer who went to the roof, found the nest, and caught the male snake."

"Now I've dropped all my precious opium in the fire!" Ameh complained.

In the end, it was Abol-Ghassem Khan who returned to the main issue.

"Please don't imagine that I want to hurt Khosrow," he said. "I swear on my son Hormoz's life that Khosrow is very dear to me. I told the Governor's secretary over the telephone: 'This child is very attached to his horse; he doesn't leave its side for a minute. I'm prepared to go to the village and bring my best horses for the Governor's daughter,' I forget her name—Gilan Taj, Milan Taj, or whatever. She said, 'Well, Miss Gilan Taj has had typhus . . . she's just recovering . . . and she's been hankering after your nephew's horse.'"

Ameh Khanom prepared her opium pipe again. She drew on it long and hard.

"Didn't you tell them his father had gone to the lowlands and to wait until he returned next week for his permission?" she said. "Don't you know that my sister-in-law doesn't move without Yusef's permission?"

"As God is my witness, I did. The Governor's secretary said: 'Your brother's wife would refuse you a worthless horse? They'll pay for it, they don't want it for free, you know.'"

Putting the opium aside, Ameh poured tea for Zari and herself.

"I know this mess is all your doing," she said to her brother. "To become deputy, you'll stoop to anything. How did that little minx find out that Khosrow has a horse? You've engineered this whole thing. And now you're stuck with it."

"By God Almighty and all the holy prophets!" Abol-Ghassem Khan protested. "I swear on the Holy Quran that I never mentioned the horse. Don't you know about Ezzat-ud-Dowleh? She's at their house from morning to evening, plotting and scheming behind everyone's back—a right old busybody . . . Anyway, I tried to ignore the whole thing, but just before I left, the Governor himself called me to ask about the horse. I said: 'Your honour, my brother is away in the lowlands.' He said: 'Come, come, my daughter has just recovered from an illness. Send the horse over for a few days. When she gets tired of it, we'll send it back.'"

Zari thought that maybe he was telling the truth. She looked at Ameh, who was poking the ashes with the tongs. There were tears in her eyes. "This town has gone mad," Ameh said. "I'm getting out of this place. I'll go and live in Karbala, the holy city, as my poor mother did."

"What will you do for a passport?" Abol-Ghassem Khan shouted, his temper rising. "And what about an exit permit? No wonder they say women are bird-brained! And all of this with a war going on . . . You think it's going to be easy to leave?" Turning to Zari, he said: "Tomorrow morning they're sending for Sahar."

"When you've given in once, they expect you to give in every time," Zari said, remembering the earrings. "It's my fault, I've been too weak. But this time I'll stand up to them." Suddenly she felt something awaken in her. "I'll go to the Governor myself," she declared. "I'll tell him there's a limit to everything. Is his daughter the only one who's allowed to hanker after a horse? Can't he bear to see anyone else in this town with something precious? Mine, mine, mine, everything always mine!'"

Abol-Ghassem Khan couldn't believe his ears.

"Sister!" he exploded. "I would never have thought it of you! Now you're sounding like Yusef!"

"If only more people were like Yusef, things would be very different," Zari said. "Our men must learn to stand up for themselves. And if they're away, their wives should do it in their place. If more of our people had the courage to stand up for their rights, maybe one day we could achieve something."

Abol-Ghassem Khan put his head between his hands.

"I swear to God, you've all gone mad!" he moaned. "That one says she's going to up and leave . . . this one says she going to stand up to them. See what kind of a corner they've worked me into! And all for a miserable horse . . . "

At that moment Khosrow came out of the stables with Sahar. Zari watched as he let the colt loose in the garden, then walked on towards the verandah. His eyes travelled from his uncle to his mother; then from his mother to his aunt.

"What's happened?" he asked, seeing their sullen expressions.

Abol-Ghassem Khan laughed. "I'm going hunting, and I'm taking you with me. Don't listen to what women say. They're all cowards."

"How did your exam go?" his aunt asked.

"It went very well, auntie. I think I'll get top marks," Khosrow replied. Turning to his uncle, he asked, "Can I take Sahar?"

"No, son, we're going a long way. Captain Singer is coming too. I want to show them what fine young men you and Hormoz have become. You can ride all kinds of horses, you can shoot well . . . "

"It's not possible," Zari interrupted. "Khosrow's got exams."

"But mother," Khosrow replied in astonishment, "you know very well my exams finished today. Please let me go." Turning to his uncle again, he said: "If only I could bring Sahar along . . . "

"Sister, let him come and see something of life, become a man, outgrow his fears. He'll be in good hands, I promise you."

Ameh, who had been deep in thought till now, interrupted him:

"The man you want to make out of him is a far cry from what Yusef has in mind. Leave the child alone. All this lying and pretence—"

"Auntie, mother, please let me go! I'm old enough now,"

54

Khosrow begged.

"Go on, son, get ready for the trip. I'll let you use my own Brno—that is, if it's not too heavy for you," Abol-Ghassem Khan said cheerfully.

"I have my own gun," Khosrow answered as he hurried off.

"Do you imagine it's possible to stand up to the Governor?" Abol-Ghassem asked gently. "Yusef is risking his life with the kinds of things he's been doing and saying lately. At least let me cover up for him. I've heard that Malek Rostam has been listening to my brother's high-flown nonsense and he went and pulled a gun on his own uncle. Now he's taken refuge with Yusef. They're even saying that Yusef has handed out provisions to thirty tribal families. Malek Rostam, who's even more out of his mind than my brother, and that demented Majid, have joined forces with him to build houses for these families, filling their heads with all sorts of dangerous ideas." Abol-Ghassem Khan paused.

"For instance," he sighed, "they're building thorn-houses out of star-thistle. Pipes take water to the roof, the water drips down on to the walls, and the wind cools the place. Of course our dear Yusef is sitting there, whistling away, thoroughly enjoying himself! Doesn't the young fool realize that these tribal people don't need provisions? That they don't need thorn-houses? As far back as anyone can remember, they've been content with their acorns, mountain almonds and their own shelters. Why should they need houses? Their black tents are more than enough for them. These people are rebels against the government. Just a few days ago they disarmed a gendarmerie regiment in the Takab Pass. And Yusef has joined up with a bunch of dreamers like himself to take over the unlawful distribution of the town's provisions." Abol-Ghassem Khan paused again. "So you see," he concluded, "there's no harm in giving the Governor a small bribe now and again to soften him a bit and make him better disposed towards Yusef. I tell you, it's fatal to fall out with the Governor."

"You can't oppose the Governor," said Zari dejectedly, "and you can't oppose Singer. They've become sworn brothers. This town becomes more and more like the Mordestan red-light district every day."

"By Almighty God!" Abol-Ghassem Khan lashed out. "More of Yusef's nonsense! Look Zari, don't argue with me. Don't I have any rights at all over my brother's worthless horse? I swear on my dead

55

father's soul that I won't let Khosrow suffer ... I'll take him hunting. I'll keep him in the village for a few days. Whichever of my colts he chooses, he can have. Get a receipt for the horse when they come early tomorrow morning to take it away. When we return, just say the horse died. It's the only way. While we're in the village, I'll find a way to tell Khosrow that the horse is sick. I'll say he mustn't let himself be so attached to worldly things if he's going to suffer so badly when he loses them."

Ameh raised her head. "Why don't you practise what you preach?" she said bitterly.

Before Abol-Ghassem Khan could reply, Khadijeh came to take away the opium brazier.

"Where are the children?" Zari asked.

"They're with Gholam watching some tribal men and women do a dance. These beggars from the tribes are in such a sorry state, poor souls!" Khadijeh sighed.

"Good gracious!" Abol-Ghassem Khan said with a laugh. "Why does every member of this household have to be so concerned with the welfare of tribesmen, peasants and porters? I just don't understand it."

"Khadijeh, go and light a hookah and bring it here," Zari said. As Khadijeh walked out, Khosrow came on to the verandah.

"Mother, will you give me the key to the cupboard?" he asked. "I want to get my gun ... Have you seen my hunting trousers?" he added. "I can't find them."

"Come without them, boy," Abol-Ghassem Khan said cheerfully. "We have so many pairs of hunting trousers there, you wouldn't believe it!"

Zari felt a lump in her throat. She took out the chain from her house-dress, and placed it on the rug on which she was sitting. When Khosrow left, she started to cry. "So this is how they manage to corner you," she thought to herself. "By making all their deals behind your back. But there's still time. Tomorrow morning when they come from the Governor, I can refuse to give the horse. I can tell the Governor's servant that Sahar died and that will be an end to it."

"Sister, as God is my witness, I can't bear to see you cry," Abol-Ghassem Khan began. But he stopped short because Khosrow walked back in just then carrying his travelling clothes, his rifle and saddle-bag.

56

"I'm ready," he announced. Zari, struggling to hold back her tears, bent her head. Khosrow kissed his aunt, then turned to his mother and put his arms around her neck. Kissing her wet face, he said, "I'm not going away to China, you know ... Mother, ask uncle to let me take Sahar with us."

"Come along, son," Abol-Ghassem Khan urged. "Gholam will take care of Sahar." And he said goodbye and walked away.

"I can't refuse to go," Khosrow whispered in his mother's ear, "because uncle will think I'm afraid of the shooting."

Sahar was standing quite still under the orange trees. He didn't move when Khosrow approached him. The boy took the colt's face between his hands and stroked his mane. Then he called over his shoulder: "Mother, don't forget to give him some sugar lumps. Gholam knows the rest. He'll muck out the stable, give him clean hay and groom him."

Sahar lowered his head and dug at the soil underneath the orange tree. After Khosrow had gone, he came near the verandah and neighed loudly. His mother answered him from the stables. Zari looked at him through her tears. "You poor beast!" she thought. "What sweet eyes you have. Why don't you look straight at me? Why lower your gaze? Why don't you call me a helpless woman who'll betray you tomorrow?"

"I for one am leaving this place," Ameh Khanom announced. "Why do I need a 'dashport', 'pashport' or whatever they call it? I'll get myself smuggled out. I'll buy gold coins with my money, and sew them into the lining of my coat. I'll just take one suitcase, get myself to Ahwaz, and it'll be easy from there. I'll go through the date-palm plantations, then find some Arabs, give them each a gold coin, and they'll put me in one of their boats to cross the Tigris. Then I'll be rid of all this. From then on, I won't be a burden and I won't let anyone impose on me. And it won't be my own country so I won't have to worry all the time about what happens to it." She clenched a fist to her bosom, praying:

"O Imam Hossein! Allow this poor creature of yours to come to you in Karbala!"

"Did you want the hookah, Khanom?" Khadijeh came in to ask, bringing one with her.

Zari took the pipe from Khadijeh, and drew deeply on it. It made her cough. Then she drew on it again and again. It made her feel sick, but she kept on inhaling.

57

"They can drive you to addiction, sister," Ameh warned. "You mustn't smoke if you can help it. A habit is a terrible thing." She looked up at the sky and said with bitterness, "O Lord, I'm not ungrateful, yet I've never known anything but sorrow in this world of yours. They hounded and harassed my husband to death. He couldn't take it any more, and smashed himself, on horseback, against the pillars of the British Consulate building. My only son died young. A boil grew in his throat, and he withered away before my very eyes. In all of this godforsaken town no one could give him the medicine he needed . . . O Lord, maybe you brought me all these sorrows to see whether I have the patience of Job. Well, I haven't, I haven't! Grant my only wish now. Let me make my pilgrimage!"

Zari was in tears again. She brushed them away with the back of her hand. "Ameh Khanom," she pleaded, "don't make me so unhappy. Where do you want to get up and go to? At least this is your homeland. Your husband and son are buried here. Whenever you feel lonely, you can visit their graves. Whom will you turn to there?"

"To Imam Hossein."

"It's hot there. The climate won't agree with you. There's a big garden here. My children are like your own. We live like sisters. Besides, how will they send you money?"

"I'm only one person. I'm willing to live on bread and water. What makes me more special than Bibi, my mother?"

Before Zari could reply, Khadijeh came out to the verandah: "Khanom, the children are making a fuss. No matter what I say they refuse to eat their meal. They're driving me out of my mind."

"I'll come," Zari said, getting up and going to the parlour. She found Marjan sitting on the table, rubbing her eyes. Mina was standing by her, looking frightened and staring anxiously at the door. Catching sight of her mother, she laughed and stretched out her arms. Zari sat next to them and tried to put a spoonful of food in Mina's mouth, but the child pushed the spoon away. When she tried to feed Marjan, the same thing happened.

"I don't want any rice-pudding!" Marjan cried.

"Why not?" asked Zari.

"I don't like it!" she shouted.

"All right, then just have some bread," Zari offered.

"That child who threw a stone at me said, 'Gimme some bread! Gimme some fruit from your tree!'" said Marjan, rubbing her eyes.

58

"Which child?"

"That child who didn't have any shoes. That one whose mama danced. The papa sat down and said: 'Ouch!' His foot was hurt bad," Marjan explained.

"See, that poor child had no bread to eat. But you won't even have your rice-pudding and honey."

"Gholam went and hit him," Marjan said.

They drove Zari to distraction before taking a few more spoonfuls. As she was taking them to bed, she saw that Ameh was still sitting quietly next to the opium brazier.

The children, unable to get to sleep, tossed about restlessly. Obviously, Abol-Ghassem Khan's disturbing afternoon visit had affected them too.

"If you close your eyes, I'll tell you a story," Zari promised.

"I'm scared," Mina whimpered.

Zari didn't know why she should suddenly think of McMahon and the story he had written for Mina and Marjan. That night, the night of the wedding, when she had gone to the dinner table, McMahon had managed to find a plate and cutlery for her, despite his drunken state. The room was so crowded, with everyone rushing to find a place at the table. No one moved away, and late-comers were not given a chance. Those people didn't know the meaning of real hunger, Zari reflected, but they certainly behaved as though they did. Their children didn't have to go around barefoot, begging for a lump of bread . . .

Zari remembered thanking McMahon. "I really enjoyed your story," she told him. McMahon had laughed. His eyes were like slits in his face. She remembered him saying, "I'll polish it up, and send it to a publisher of children's books."

The Governor had come out then, and invited McMahon to sit at an empty table reserved for foreigners only, where they would be served roast pork. But McMahon wasn't tempted, choosing to stay with his friend's wife. Again, Zari thanked him.

"I hope you succeed in building that airplane which drops toys to little children!" she said.

McMahon sighed. "But who will ever build an airplane which will shower consolation over sorrowful men . . . men who've lost their mothers . . . "

Yusef made his way to them, bringing a plate of rice spiced with pistachio nuts and raisins.

59

"For all three of us," he had announced.

McMahon went on talking to Zari. "When I think about it," he said, "I realize that all of us, all our lives, we're just children who get our happiness from our toys. The day, alas, they take away those toys, or don't let us have new ones—our children, our mothers, our philosophies, our religions—we crumble."

"Have some of this now," Yusef had laughed. "I've never seen anyone so blind drunk and so philosophical at the same time!"

"I promise you I couldn't swallow a thing," McMahon replied. "Anything more, and I'd burst!"

Marjan brought Zari back to the present. "I'm scared!" she cried out. "Snake!"

"Go to sleep, dear," Zari said reassuringly. "There's no snake around. It's in Haj Mohammad Reza's yellow box. They've taken its teeth out, too, and the box is locked."

Then she started to tell a story.

"Once upon a time there was a man who built a big plane. The plane carried only toys, story books, fruit, food and sweets for children . . ."

"Mummy, was there a snake in the plane?" Mina asked.

"No, dear," Zari answered, "there wasn't a snake; the plane was loaded with things children like. This plane would fly over the towns to drop whatever toys the children wanted."

"But they'll break!" Marjan exclaimed.

"No, the plane flew low over the houses, and the children held out their skirts underneath the plane. Then the pilot dropped whatever they wanted into their skirts."

"What about Khosrow?" Marjan asked. "Khosrow doesn't have a skirt."

"You're right," Zari smiled. "But the pilot also gave toys and things to boys even though they don't wear skirts. Sometimes he stopped his plane on the roof and . . ."

"Would he give toys to the child who was throwing stones?" Marjan interrupted.

"Of course," said Zari.

"Oh good."

"Now where was I?" Zari continued. "Oh yes. The pilot stopped the plane on a rooftop and picked up the good children and took them to the sky with him. They flew past the stars, past the moon. They flew past them so closely they could reach out and gather the stars and put them in their lap."

"Tell him to bring his plane on our roof," Marjan piped up again, "and give Sahar to Khosrow ... all right?"

"All right," Zari promised; "now go to sleep." It occurred to her that if the twins were developing a memory even for recent events, they were no longer babies.

As soon as the children were asleep, Zari went out on to the verandah. Ameh was still sitting there, with her hand under her chin, staring at the cold brazier in front of her.

"Are you thinking of your journey?" Zari asked.

Ameh lifted her head. Zari was taken aback to see tears in her eyes.

"Yes, sister," Ameh answered. "Even if my heart is sad and heavy, it doesn't mean that's all there is in the whole world. Now that it's too late for happiness in this life, I want at least to prepare for my peace afterwards. They say whoever is buried next to the Imam won't have to answer to Nakir and Monkir. There's no inquisition of the dead either. First the Imam Ali, and then Imam Hossein come to you. If you're a woman, Hazrate Fatemeh comes to you. Hand in hand with these holy ones, the dead are taken to God ... "

"It's strange," commented Zari, "how Abol-Ghassem Khan disturbed us all with his news! Even the children felt it. They saw Haj Mohammad Reza's snake yesterday and they weren't afraid. But tonight they were frightened and couldn't sleep."

"You're right," Ameh said. "It's been a long time since I went over the untimely death of my loved ones in my mind. Tonight all of them passed again before my eyes."

"I've been in your family for many years now," Zari said, "but I'd never heard you mention your late husband or your child before. Tonight ... "

"I know. I've always kept my grief to myself," Ameh replied. "I've never told anyone what I've suffered."

Zari sat down and took her sister-in-law's hand. "You've always said yourself that a sorrow shared is a sorrow halved. You used to say that the Imam Ali would lean over a well and tell his sorrows to the water deep down which he couldn't see."

Ameh nodded. "Should I sigh for you in sorrow?" she recited, as if to herself. "Then as Ali I look into a well."

"Am I not as good as a well?" Zari asked.

61

"You're young. I don't want to destroy your hopes in life with my unhappy tales."

"I've had my share of sorrows."

"I know." And so it was that Ameh began to tell all she had kept locked away inside her; stories which Zari had never heard before.

6

That night, Ameh began, I was sitting right next to this very brazier, in the same wretched darkness, stirring the ashes with these tongs. I was gazing at the brass figurines, holding hands all around the edge of the brazier. That night I counted thirty-two of them. They're still intact, those featureless little figures.

It was the night my child died. Soudabeh, my father's mistress, sat with me till dawn, shedding tears as I cried. When he died . . . at the grove . . . all alone . . . I knew he was dead, but I held him, my six-year-old, and ran to Sardazak. If I hadn't lost him, I wouldn't be obsessed with veils and religious modesty now, nor with opium and convulsing at the mere thought of not getting any.

I rushed to my father's house. He and Soudabeh were sitting in the room with the sash windows next to this very brazier. Grief-stricken, I wished I could breathe out fire and turn everyone around me into ashes. Soudabeh stood up and took my child from me. She was shaken, but trying hard not to show it. What a woman! She went out and came back without the child. I asked her what she had done with him. She said, "Who knows, maybe my brother, Mohammad Hossein, can bring him back to life with his healing touch." I said, "Don't blaspheme, woman! Only God brings to life. It says in the Quran: I breathed life unto him of My Spirit." But Soudabeh wanted to give me hope.

I had studied Arabic and Persian with my father, and geography and geometry with Mohammad Hossein, Soudabeh's brother. When my father came back from Tehran after completing his religious training, he shut himself up at home. He didn't go out to lead prayers anymore. He was forced to give up teaching at the Khan seminary too. He only taught at home, in the main room with

63

the sash windows. Men would come in, kiss his hand and bring him questions on jurisprudence or theology. I used to sit in the next room and listen. When my father returned from his pilgrimage to holy Najaf, everyone in town went all the way on foot to Baj Gah to welcome him. That first day he led the communal prayers, and all the mullahs in town—even the Imam Juma—followed him as a mark of respect. When he spoke at the Vakil Mosque there was a packed audience.

Oh Lord! And I was quite a woman in those days too! I remember being daring enough to carry my father's secret anti-government letters in my bosom to the Shah Cheraq shrine where I would deliver them to someone waiting there. I can remember it as if it were yesterday ... the meeting place used to be between the two lion statues at the front of the shrine.

Then my father, of all people, fell for an Indian dancer. Mohammad Hossein and his sister Soudabeh had recently arrived from India. Despite my father's courtship, to the last Soudabeh refused to marry him. She used to say they were better off the way they were. Of course she broke up our home and caused Bibi, my mother, no end of grief. But what a woman she was! And what a dancer! I'll never forget the day my father asked Soudabeh to dance for his guests at the Rashk Behesht Gardens. She wasn't really pretty, quite short and very sallow. She had a dark beauty spot on her upper lip, and used to outline her large brown eyes with a lot of kohl. When she wasn't laughing she looked like an owl, but when she smiled it was as if the heavens had opened.

At that gathering, everyone—men and women—stood around the paving of the garden to watch her dance and to clap. I'd never seen her perform before. It was certainly out of the ordinary. She seemed naked at first glance, except for a few bits of jewellery. But in fact she was wearing a jewel-studded brassiere and a flesh-coloured body-stocking. She managed to move each and every part of her body: not only her shoulders, belly, eyes and eyebrows, but even her chin, nose, ears and pupils. First, she pretended to do a ritual dance over the corpse of a man. For the second dance, she wore a blue silk dress with a gold border, and had two live doves with dyed feathers perched on her breasts. She moved slowly and gently, as if afraid of disturbing the birds. When the dance was over, she let them fly away. By the end of the third dance, she was looking hot and flushed, so she went and sat by the pool, dressed in her pink satin dress. As she dipped her bare feet in the water, I saw my father, my Haj Agha—the high clergyman of the town—sit down before Soudabeh and meekly fan her.

So it came about that my father asked Mohammad Hossein to teach me at home. I used to study geometry and geography with him, drawing endless charts and maps. I was so wrapped up in my studies, I was often unaware of what was going on around me. Just imagine, the first day an airplane came to this town, everyone packed their rugs and took off at dawn to Baq Takht to watch its arrival. I was sitting on the roof of our house in the sunshine, drawing a map of India. The airplane flew right over my head and I didn't even lift my eyes to look at it. Oh God, a person like that shouldn't become an opium addict!

Mohammad Hossein was quite a character. He was a sun-worshipper. Every morning and evening he'd go on to the roof to watch the sun rise or set, until finally sunlight ruined his eyesight. He could also do conjuring tricks. He fried eggs in a felt hat floating on the pool. He could produce gold coins from bits of paper. He would swallow my Haj Agha's fob-watch and bring it back out of Abol-Ghassem's pocket. He dabbled in palmistry, too. Once he told my fortune, and said I would have twelve sons, all of whom would become ministers. I remember thinking that my family would make up the entire cabinet! My father used to say that Mohammad Hossein had spiritual powers. But the townspeople thought he dabbled in witchcraft and black magic. Whatever he was, the man took great pains over my lessons, God rest his soul.

That terrible night it was Mohammad Hossein who washed and buried my child. For a whole week he would make me sit in front of him, gaze into my eyes, and repeat, "I shall put you to sleep, and in your sleep you will see your child, see how well and happy he is in his new place." But I couldn't be hypnotized. He said I resisted too much. He even painted my thumbnail black and told me to gaze at that. "Your child will appear right now," he said. "Can't you see him? Here he is. Here he is. Ask him what he wants. He wants something to eat." But no matter how hard I stared, I didn't see anything.

His sister Soudabeh, however, had charmed my father. She never did become his wife, but she had him under her spell. What a woman she was! The kind who could draw people to herself as if by magnetism . . . once seduced, you could never be free of her. It had nothing to do with beauty. It had more to do with charisma. Everyone around Haj Agha was amazed at his behaviour. Perhaps they even cursed him behind his back. One sly fellow—we never found out who it was—commissioned several lengths of hand-printed cloth from Isfahan, picturing the proverbial Sheikh San'an going to Europe with his followers. The Sheikh was shown as a besotted-looking old man, wearing a turban and cloak just like my Haj Agha. There was a train of followers behind him and a lewd woman languished in an upper chamber of the house. Those days wherever you went, they seemed to have hung up one of these cloths. People certainly know how to be vicious when they want to.

As for Haj Agha himself, he would say, "They've taken away my teaching and preaching from me. Far be it from me to interfere in other worldly affairs. I gave it a try and suffered the consequences. After all, a person must do something greater in life than just the daily business of living. He must bring about changes. Now that there's nothing more left for me to do, I'll abandon myself to love." "Love hath done more than steal your faith," he used to quote, "A Sufi it can turn to Christian." And sometimes he would add, "The pilgrim's destination is but the starting place for love." The mullahs in town even spread a rumour that he had turned into a heretic and a Babi. But since my father was always a generous host, and continued to solve their problems by telephone, he was never officially excommunicated. Besides, the clergy had lost much of its power, and most mullahs had exchanged their religious turban for the civilian hat.

Our Haj Agha felt the time hadn't come for his beliefs. So he decided to retire. But he was never one to put up with injustice either. During the fighting between the police-chief and Massoud Khan, almost every household hung up a British flag to show their loyalty to the police-chief and to prevent raids on their homes. My father not only refused to put up the flag, but he even helped, side by side with the chief Rabbi, to carry the Jewish wounded from the poorest quarters to a doctor. He did his best, too, to prevent the armed men from plundering the Jewish quarter, but to no avail. Those men had been well paid.

They had shot a Jewish mother as she was nursing her baby. The baby was still suckling when she passed out. When Haj Agha arrived on the scene, he quickly tucked the baby under his cloak and rushed straight to Dr Scott, the European doctor at the Missionary Hospital. And who was this Dr Scott? None other than the special physician to the police-chief and his family, who refused to visit those wounded by the police-chief's cronies. Single-handed, my father had the hospital closed down that day, forcing Dr Scott and several Armenian nurses to visit the wounded mother and other casualties in the Jewish district. The mother recovered. Do you know who she is? Our very own Tavuus Khanom who still comes to see us regularly and brings wine for Yusef.

I remember Felfelli, a drummer with Musa's musicians, had been among the wounded. They brought him to our house and stretched him out at the entrance on the doorman's bench. Blood was gushing out of the wound in his thigh like an open fountain, covering the entire entrance. My father happened to be away and Bibi, my mother, fell sick at the sight of all that blood. I grabbed my veil and ran to Dr Abdollah Khan's office in the Arab quarter. I didn't stop for breath until I got there. Between you and me, they hadn't put up the British flag either.

Dr Abdollah Khan's father was the well-known Haj Hakimbashi, who was still alive then. He had four sons, three of them doctors and the youngest a pharmacist. They owned a pharmacy too. God rest their souls. Only Dr Abdollah Khan is still with us. In his office that day you could hardly move for all the wounded and dying. I resorted to tears and pleas before the doctor agreed to come with me. They used to say he was quite a healer, despite his youth. But as fate would have it, Felfelli was already dead by the time we arrived, and he had been covered with a bedspread. His relatives were crowding into our house and raising the roof with their wailing and mourning. Bibi had fainted. And now where do you think our house was? Right opposite Ezzat-ud-Dowleh's father's house. Ezzat had just married, and her husband—none other than the police-chief's son-in-law—had actually moved into her parents' home. All the trouble had been started by this very son-in-law. Now what if they had heard the din in our house?

Of course, Ezzat-ud-Dowleh and I had taken an oath to be sisters, but in those troubled times people hardly thought of their real sisters, let alone their sisters by oath. No, it was respect for Haj Agha that prevented them from raiding our house, especially since they were afraid he might decree a holy war. All this happened well before my father became a recluse, you see.

I'm sure Haj Agha had the kind of power it took to hypnotize

67

people, if he wanted to. He would stare right at the space between your eyes, and who could resist him? Imagine a man like that letting himself be enslaved by an Indian dancer and break our Bibi's heart! Oh Lord, don't put us to the test! Bibi knew what was going on, but she never said a word. It's all over with now, but she never even confided in me, her own daughter. Haj Agha and Soudabeh were the talk of the town, but my mother, the only one that mattered, remained silent.

At least my father had the decency not to bring Soudabeh and Mohammad Hossein into the house until all the family had moved away. I was married first, then Abol-Ghassem Khan found a wife. Finally Bibi went off to Karbala. My husband was a textile merchant who traded with Egypt and India. He and his father imported a delicate fabric known as 'miyur'. It was even finer and more beautiful than silk, and quite often used for underwear or babies' clothes. Nowadays you can't find it anywhere. But my husband was an unhappy man and he committed suicide. One day, at sunset, he dashed himself on horseback against the pillars of the British Consulate building. Because of our son, and because of an unjust society that made life unbearable for him. You see, Haj Agha could retire when he felt the time wasn't right for his ideas. But my poor husband was still a young man. Just like Yusef, God forbid. Yusef is ahead of his time, too. That poor soul used to say, like Yusef, that we had to change the times. But he was just beating his head against a stone wall—as he literally did in the end. Let's face it, these are times for double-dealers like my brother Abol-Ghassem Khan. When will it be time for people like Yusef, I wonder?

I'll never forget, after my husband and child died, Yusef wrote me a letter telling me to stand on my own two feet. He said if I fell, no-one in the world would bother to help lift me up. One could only rely on oneself, he said.

Thank God Bibi was not around to see my unhappiness. When she made up her mind to leave, she invited the entire family to dinner. That night she kept staring at us as if to engrave our faces on her memory. Only Yusef wasn't there because he had been sent abroad for two years to finish his education. Actually, when Abol-Ghassem Khan complains that our father never spent any money on his education, he isn't telling the truth. Haj Agha wanted to send both of them away together and Abol-Ghassem Khan turned it down of his own free will. He asked my father to give him what his education would have cost in land, and that's what Haj Agha did.

Anyhow, Bibi bid us farewell that evening, supposedly to go on a pilgrimage to the shrine of Hazrate Massoumeh in Qom, and from there to Mashad. She said she would be away for a month or two. But unbeknownst to us, she had arranged to have herself smuggled over the Iraqi border to Karbala. All she had in the way of worldly possessions was some money Haj Agha had given her, and some women's trinkets, a suitcase and her ewer. Her emerald earrings she left in my care, in case something should happen to her on the journey. I was to keep them for Yusef to give to his wife on their wedding night.

A month later a letter arrived from her telling us not to worry, that she was in Karbala where she planned to stay permanently as part of a religious vow she had taken. Only much later did we discover—and please don't let this be known—that she had ended up being a maidservant there—to a Khanom Fakhr-ol-Sharia. All the time she was in Karbala, Bibi never asked for money, nor did my Haj Agha offer to ... no, perhaps three or four times on our insistence he did send her some in one way or another. Whether she received it or not, I never found out. She wouldn't write, you see. In that first letter she stipulated that we were not to write to her, since she wanted no distractions from her religious calling.

But I've been digressing. I was talking about that dreadful night, wasn't I? Yes, I was sitting right here by this brazier, prodding the ashes with my tongs. There wasn't much of a fire left. I was counting my sorrows in the dark, with Soudabeh sitting next to me the whole night. What a woman she was! A pity she broke our mother's heart.

That night I asked Soudabeh, "I never understood why you, with a thousand admirers, should have chosen my father, driving my mother out of her own home?" She said she couldn't help it; she knew she had ruined the reputation of a Shi'ite clergyman of the highest order, and made an innocent woman homeless. But it was out of her hands, she claimed. "Sometimes, in a previous life," she said, "you've lost a person you've been very close to. Once that has happened, you keep coming back to this world to find him. You bear the waiting, the separation. But when you finally find the person again, how can you possibly let go of them? It's like two intertwining plants at first, where one withers and dies, then in a

69

later life they happen to be two migrating birds, who return once again as two loving deer—and perhaps one is shot by a hunter—and so on. They could be father and daughter, sister and brother . . . who knows? And when they find each other at last, they can no longer be separated." She often used to say things like that. She would say these things and yet she never agreed to marry our father. She just stayed with him until they grew old.

After my husband's untimely death, I decided, as Yusef had advised me, to stand on my own feet and run the estate I had received from Haj Agha as my wedding gift. I'd straddle my horse in my breeches, cover the poppy fields from one end to the other on horseback. How old do you think I was then? Twenty-eight. I even used the bastinado on my peasants, God forgive my sins! Bibi had been gone then for about three years. The poor woman was only forty-four when she died. One day, Fakhr-ol-Sharia telegraphed my father to say Bibi was ill. To his credit, Haj Agha made every effort to get exit permits. He cabled Yusef to go to his mother at once, but decided not to say she was on the point of death. Which is why Yusef only arrived after we had buried Bibi in the shrine tomb. Abol-Ghassem Khan had gone to great lengths, paying quite a bit out of his own pocket, to get permission for the body to be placed in the shrine, even though we knew the moment our backs were turned they would take the corpse out to a public graveyard. Still, even one night in such a holy place was quite a blessing, and Bibi's wish had been fulfilled.

O merciful Lord, what a tragedy it was! My Bibi in the throes of death in a room two feet square, on a torn straw-mat covered by a ragged quilt . . . she cried out from the heat, but there was no cool basement, no iced water for her. Fakhr-ol-Sharia would call on her for service, for a hookah, for this or that without the least consideration or respect. Oh Lord, no Khanom, no title! My mother's name was Fassih-ol-Zaman, meaning 'eloquent one'. An eloquence which never uttered a word of what had happened to her! Even the story of her becoming a housemaid was told us by Fakhr-ol-Sharia herself, who talked about Bibi as though she came from a long line of devoted servants. I've never said a word of this to anyone. Not even Yusef. There was no point. He was only twenty years old, he couldn't have taken it. Is he ready to bear it now, at forty? I doubt it.

We never did find out how Bibi got herself to Karbala. We merely heard that when she arrived, she fell into the clutches of a certain

Sheikh Abbas Qomi who used to disguise himself as an Arab and frighten illegal pilgrims by threatening to denounce them to the authorities unless they bribed him. When he confronted my mother, she was so panicked she dropped her suitcase, grabbed her ewer and ran away! As it happened, her birth certificate was in the suitcase. With the hundred tomans Haj Agha had given her, she managed to obtain a dead person's birth certificate from a worker at the mortuary.

Khadijeh came out to the verandah to ask: "Aren't you having any dinner tonight?"

"We'll call you when we're ready," Zari answered.

"No, that's enough for now," Ameh intervened. "I've talked too much and I've given you a headache. Let Khadijeh bring us a bite to eat, then we can go to sleep and see what tomorrow will bring."

7

Early next morning, Zari instructed Gholam to tell anyone coming from the Governor for anything that Khanom was not at home, and that nothing could be given away in her absence. If the person still insisted and mentioned a horse, Gholam was to feign ignorance and say they had come to the wrong house—they used to have a horse, but it died. At a pinch, he was to give them the chestnut horse.

It was watering-day for the garden, and Zari went outdoors to watch the trees and the grass thirstily drink in the water, sharing their refreshment and feeling revived herself by breathing in the smell of moist earth. Gholam and the gardener, shovels against their shoulders, trouser-legs rolled up, crossed the garden barefoot from one end to the other, opening or closing the flow of water in the narrow irrigation canals. Mina and Marjan wanted to stay around, but kept getting in the way. Finally Zari had to coax them into building a mudhouse under the big elm near the stables. She told them they could plant flowers in it, and have a wedding for their dolls. But she warned them that if they didn't stay in the shade, the sun would scorch their lovely soft skin.

Mina started to draw a plan for the house, making room for a little pool, a cupboard, and a cold furnace. Marjan completed the plan by adding the stables. Then, with a lot of squealing and fuss they caught a toad which they put in the stables, but it soon leapt away. Still, there were plenty more in the garden.

Gholam directed the flow of water towards the elm trees, and before long the children's mudhouse was flooded. Water ran into pools around their feet, and they squatted down in it. Zari called them away, all the while listening for a knock at the door so she could hide in time from the Governor's messenger. Mina shouted

72

at Gholam for having ruined their mudhouse:

"You meanie!"

"It was just a flood, sweetheart," was his reply.

All that day and the next there was no messenger from the Governor, and Zari felt reassured, thinking that they must have changed their minds. Even Ameh commented, "Thank God! So much needless worrying. They must have just mentioned something in passing, and Abol-Ghassem Khan made them a promise to curry favour, as usual."

But early in the morning on the third day, Zari had just got out of bed when there was a knock at the door. Gholam went to answer while Zari kept watch from her hiding-place. She saw a gendarme greet Gholam and embrace him, handing him an envelope. Gholam brought the envelope to Zari.

"It looks as though you know him," she said.

"Yes, he's from my village," he replied. "From Bardeh. He always wanted to become a gendarme, and now he has."

Zari went to the verandah and waited until Ameh Khanom had ended her prayers before opening the envelope. Then she read out loud the neat handwriting addressed to herself:

My dear Madam,

If I were not certain of Shirazi hospitality and of the generosity of your respected family, I would never make the following request of you. Recently, my daughter Gilan Taj was so badly afflicted with typhus that the doctors had given up hope. But God's mercy was with us, and my child has recovered. My daughter enjoys horse riding, and despite carefully searching this town, we have not been able to find a horse gentle enough for her use. I assure you the general sent us two of the best horses from the army stables, but they were large, headstrong animals not suited for a child who has just left the sick-bed. Our honoured friend, Abol-Ghassem Khan has promised to send us your son's colt. I hear he is away on a trip. I humbly beg you to loan us the young horse belonging to your respected son for a few days by means of this messenger. The moment Gilan Taj tires of horses and horse riding, we shall return it.

Yours sincerely

Since the signature of the Governor's wife differed from the rest of the handwriting, Zari decided the letter must have been written by someone else.

"Now what am I to do?" Zari turned to Ameh.

"They've taken us by surprise," she replied. "We can't give the colt away, and yet we can't refuse either. If we give them the colt I know Yusef and Khosrow will be up in arms. If we don't, well, you remember Abol-Ghassem's outburst the other day? There will be endless quarrelling. If he isn't made a deputy one of these days he'll blame it on us and our pettiness."

"And now that they've stated their request clearly," Zari added, "I can't even send them the chestnut. What should I do?"

"Just sit in a corner and think, I suppose," said Ameh with a sigh.

They asked the messenger to come in and sit on a chair by the pool. Khadijeh brought him some breakfast which she placed on another chair. The gendarme took off his hat and put it on his knee. Zari watched him empty the sugar-lumps from the bowl into his pocket and gulp down his unsweetened tea on top of huge mouthfuls of food. Gholam was sitting opposite him on the edge of the pool.

"Are you the guard at the entrance to the Governor's estate?" Zari asked him.

"Hmph!" grunted the man with his mouth full, and then he quickly swallowed his food.

"Do you have a wife and children?"

Grinning widely, he answered in a thick accent: "I wed me cousin last New Year's."

"When will you return the horse?"

"The lieutenant gave me a mission," he said. "His honour said I'm a good lad.. But he didn't say anything about bringing the horse back." And again he grinned from ear to ear.

"But it's not mating season yet, brother," Gholam intervened.

The gendarme dug a hand into his tunic pocket and produced an envelope which he presented to Zari, saying: "Agha Mirza, the governor's secretary, gave me this. He said it's eighty tomans."

Zari took the envelope, opened it and began to count. It really was eighty tomans. She whispered to Ameh: "They imagine they've paid for it, too."

"Let him take Sahar away for now until we think of something,"

74

said Ameh.

"Gholam, go and bring Sahar out of the stables," Zari ordered.

"Khanom, I swear what they're doing is wrong," Gholam protested. "Mating season is over now. Besides Sahar is too young . . ."

"They don't want him for mating," Zari explained wearily, "the Governor's daughter has taken a fancy to Sahar . . ."

Gholam took off his felt hat. His bald head was flushed and sweaty. He said, "Khosrow Khan has left Sahar in my care. Now you ask me to give him away to someone else? Never!"

"Gholam, can't you see they've sent a gendarme?" Ameh said.

"What makes you think this poor fellow's a gendarme?" said Gholam. "He's just a simple, honest lad." Turning to the gendarme, he continued, "Listen brother, go and tell your master that the horse was dead. Khanom here will give you your tip."

But the gendarme was insistent.

"Aren't we from the same village?" he pleaded. "Don't make it so hard for me. The lieutenant ordered me to bring the horse back by whatever means. He gave me a mission. He said I'm a good lad. He said if I don't bring the colt back with me, I can resign my post and go straight back to Bardeh, back to my mother's apron! He said that himself."

Gholam put on his hat and said: "Whoever wants to take Sahar has to go and bring him out of the stables himself—if he dares. I'll knock him over so hard with my shovel, he really will have to run straight back to his mother's apron!"

"I give the orders here," Zari intervened authoritatively. "I'm the mistress of this house. Go and bring Sahar from the stables."

By now Mina and Marjan had woken up and come outside to the verandah, with Khadijeh trailing behind asking them to wash their faces first.

"Khanom, if you ask me, you shouldn't do this. Think of tomorrow when your son comes home— he'll be heartbroken. Think of later on when the master gets back . . . don't be afraid of these people. Just refuse, that's all. What can they do to you?"

The gendarme started off towards the stables. "Aren't we brothers, from the same village?" he appealed.

"Where do you think you're going?" Gholam asked.

"To the stables."

"We may be from the same village," Gholam threatened, "but if

75

you dare set foot in those stables . . ."

"I haven't brought my gun," countered the gendarme, "I'm going to get it now."

Gholam grabbed him by the collar and shouted:

"Now you're showing off to me with your gun? Aren't you the same miserable urchin who used to sneak off at night to steal chickens? Did your lieutenant tell you to come threatening me with your gun too?"

The man shook himself free and muttered: "No, I swear it! But he said I could resign my post and go back to the village if I failed. How can I go back there?"

Ameh Khanom called Gholam over.

"Gholam, don't be stubborn," she said quietly. "Abol-Ghassem Khan has already made them a promise. Let him take Sahar away for the time being. I've had a good idea. I think I can get him back before Khosrow returns."

Gholam fetched Sahar from the stables and gave the reins to the gendarme. As he tried to mount, Sahar gave a mighty kick, reared up on his hind legs, and neighed loudly. Both the mare and the chestnut horse answered from the stables. The man fell back and let go of the bridle. Sahar turned to Gholam and sniffed at his rolled-up sleeves. The gendarme made several more attempts to mount, sweating profusely all the time. He tried stroking Sahar's mane and patting his neck. He brought out a sugar-lump and held it in front of the horse's mouth. Finally he managed to grab the bridle. Zari handed him the money.

"Take that for yourself."

The gendarme's eyes shone. Putting the notes in his tunic pocket, he dragged Sahar away.

The twins watched in horror, ignoring all Khadijeh's pleas for them to have breakfast. To Zari, it felt as if the garden had been robbed of its life and lustre. Ameh Khanom roundly cursed the universe, before turning on Zari: "Now why did you have to go and tip him?"

Gholam stood there, watching his mistress whose eyes had filled with tears.

"Khanom, may the men return safely from hunting," said Khadijeh appeasingly. "That's all that matters. The mare is young, and soon she'll give birth to another Sahar."

"I bet I shall have Sahar back in three days!" said Ameh. "It's

76

just as well you returned their money."

Zari was not convinced, however. She ordered Gholam to dig a mock grave down by the stables. She told him to pull out the weeds, smooth over the soil and arrange some stones in a rectangle with a few pots of petunia around it.

"Take my word and be patient for a while," Ameh advised.

But Zari merely turned to Gholam and warned him not to breathe a word of what had happened to Khosrow.

When they went into the sitting room, Ameh Khanom went straight to the telephone and invited Ezzat-ud-Dowleh for lunch in three days' time.

When the day of the luncheon invitation came, Zari went to great lengths to receive Ezzat-ud-Dowleh, although she had never liked the woman much. When she arrived, Zari took her guest's head-scarf and white gloves and dark glasses and wrapped them neatly in a bundle. Then she gave her a fresh peach-coloured chador to replace the dusty outdoor one. Even though Ezzat-ud-Dowleh had brought along her favourite maidservant, Ferdows, Zari sent the girl to rest in Khosrow's room. And even though Zari had cooled the parlour since early morning by closing the windows and letting down the straw blinds to keep out the sun, she still provided Ezzat-ud-Dowleh with a fan. Trying to make herself pleasant, she complimented her guest, "What a beautiful head of hair you have."

"God bless you," responded Ezzat-ud-Dowleh.

Although it was well before lunch-time, she refused any sherbet drink or fruit. She asked for tea which, when she tried, she did not seem to like. She merely remarked: "Ration tea is always stale."

At lunch she didn't eat much. She toyed with a few spoonfuls of rice and kebab which she then pushed aside, asking for sour-grape juice instead. To that she added some grated cucumber and bread-crumbs and onions, saying it was good for her leg pains. Unfortunately the sour-grape juice was last year's, too, like the tea.

After lunch, Zari spread out a thin cotton sheet in the parlour and brought a pillow and a delicate coverlet for her guest's afternoon nap. Ezzat-ud-Dowleh stretched herself out, fan in hand, while Ferdows the maid massaged her legs. Ameh Khanom lay down on another cotton sheet beside her. Zari left the so-called sisters by themselves, and went to her own bedroom, leaving the door

77

slightly ajar so that she could overhear their conversation. If Ezzat-ud-Dowleh was willing to cooperate, she was the one person who could get Sahar back. She could even have Zari's earrings returned, so Zari's pains would not have gone unrewarded.

Ezzat-ud-Dowleh's voice could easily be heard through the door: "God bless you, Ferdows. Rub harder. That's better. Have you said your prayers yet? No? Then get up, child, go and say your prayers ..."

Zari could tell Ferdows had left, because Ameh was chatting and laying the groundwork for the favours she wanted to ask later. It was a pity Zari could not hear every word. But Ezzat-ud-Dowleh, lying closer to the door, could easily be heard in a loud and flowing monologue.

8

Now I understand, she was saying. When you called I asked myself, why has my sister suddenly remembered me after all this time? We only see each other on holy days or funerals. So you have some sort of problem, and I may be able to help.

Did you say horse? No, as God is my witness I had no idea your nephew had a colt called Sahar. I had heard about your brother keeping horses. I thought, well, talk about showing off . . . but as for giving the Governor's daughter the idea of harping after your nephew's colt—upon my word, never!

True, I can't stand the sight of your brother. And if Zari hadn't become your sister-in-law, I wouldn't have hesitated to destroy her entire family. Yes, the whole thing goes back thirteen or fourteen years. But can I ever forget? A distinguished lady like me going to their slum to ask for her hand for my son! Their smoky little living-room the size of our prayer-chamber at home, and her mother like a living skeleton! I'd be ashamed to have my own servant looking like that, with her white hair and yellow complexion, her front teeth missing, wearing an old crumpled dress. I had to hold my breath for the smell of her sweat. You would've thought she could at least get some false teeth, comb her hair and dab a spot of rouge on that wrinkled face. After all, I'd come to ask for her daughter's hand. Such a distinguished lady as myself, too! It was a great stroke of luck for her that my innocent boy had chosen her daughter of all the girls available to him. A hundred times I asked my Hamid, "Son, isn't it beneath you to marry the daughter of Mirza Ali Akbar Kafar, that unbeliever of an English teacher at the Shoaieh School?" . . . Now don't you be offended, sister, I'm only telling the truth. Anyway, Hamid would say to me, "I'm looking for something I don't have myself." I said to him, "What does this girl

79

have besides a nice pair of eyes?" He said, "She has gentleness, virtue and education." I'd say, "But my love, my son, you can't live on gentleness, virtue and education." To cut a long story short, they turned down that piece of luck themselves. I sent Kal Abbas, the doorman, to their awful house for an answer and all they said was that they had consulted the Quran for an augury and the outcome was unfavourable. Since when had Mirza Ali Akbar Kafar's family believed in consulting the Quran?

But Hamid had set his heart on marrying Zari, and there I was having to lower myself to go to that ramshackle house again—not once, but twice, three times! Until finally the mother admitted you had taken their daughter the customary shawl and ring, and they'd promised her to you. I thought of coming to dissuade you, telling you that the mother had cancer, telling you that a beggar will always remain a beggar at heart. But you had long since turned your back on our oath and sisterhood. Now, now, how quickly you take offence! It's true isn't it?

No, as God is my witness I didn't give the Governor's daughter the idea of taking your nephew's horse. And now ... all right. I'll do what I can. I'll tell them it's a real shame, the boy is utterly heartbroken, and they should give the horse back to him. You did say you've sent back their money, or haven't you? Maybe I'd better persuade her to ride the horse—it's sure to take off with her and gallop right back to its old stable. That will put riding out of her mind for a while! But as for talking to them about "oppression" and "cruelty" and saying that everyone is cursing the Governor behind his back, that I can't do. Unlike you, I won't hurt my friends. You insist? Well, all right. Just for your sake I'll do it. You know me. I bear grudges, that's true. But I also understand friendship and sisterhood.

I'll tell you the truth about those emerald earrings of Zari's. The minute I walked into that wedding and set eyes on your sister-in-law looking so pretty and prosperous, I decided to get my own back by making her suffer the loss of her precious earrings. What, you didn't know? How's that? You mean she hasn't let on about them? Well, I could have told you she wouldn't be particularly honest, coming from that family! ... Now it's no use getting offended, I'm only telling the truth. Yes, it was my doing. I sent Ferdows off at top speed to the haberdasher's bazaar to buy some green silk. I threw it around the bride's neck, and told them to go and borrow the emerald earrings belonging to Yusef Khan's wife, knowing full well they're not the sort to return earrings. Why are you getting in a state about it now? Let Zari do the worrying. Come now, sister, please don't look so upset. Well yes ... I did know they were a special token ... very well, I'll try to get the earrings back, too. You don't need to tell me how to do it; I know myself.

Let's be sisters again like we used to be. Do you remember that celebration we had when we were children, and we brought over a mullah to swear us to sisterhood, and then they showered us with sugar-plums? But then you changed. Ever since you lost your little boy and your husband killed himself, you seem to have changed into another person altogether. Do you remember, when we were a bit older we both fell in love with Dr Marhamat Khan? He'd just come from Tehran, and they said he'd studied in Europe. I can't forget that day when we made ourselves up so no-one would recognize us, and went to the doctor's office. We counted eleven other girls there—some from the town's best families—who'd also made themselves up and were pretending to be ill. Like us, they were really there to show off their faces and bodies to the doctor. Do you remember Etrat, who later became Etrat-Saltaneh, wearing her fancy starched kerchief? Oh Lord, those were the days! You'd pulled out a handful of your hair to say you were going bald, and I'd made up a story about a lump in my right breast which was sometimes there and sometimes not. He dabbed some tincture on your bald spot, and told me I was imagining things. He never married any of us, either. He went and brought a wife from Abadeh.

Then each of us went our separate ways. I was married first, but we both met with tragedy. Maybe you were better off in the beginning, but your happiness didn't last. And I couldn't bring myself to confide my troubles to anyone, not even to you, my sworn sister. They say every ill-starred woman has at least forty days' grace in her husband's home, but I didn't even have that. Imagine my large dowry, my parents' house and wealthy life-style all falling into the hands of that no-good husband of mine! And a distinguished lady like me, the police chief's granddaughter ... and he was a man whose forefathers had ruled our province like sultans, generation after generation ...

You see, we'd only been married three days before we began to quarrel and my husband said, "Don't play the police chief's granddaughter with me; all your ancestors were traitors. Even your great-grandfather was a close aide to that ruthless Agha Moham-mad Khan Qajar in return for a piece of cold-blooded treachery." He said, "Don't you show off to me with your ancestral home either. Every one of its stones and bricks was laid over the body of an honest, hard-working person. Its clay plaster was mixed with the blood of our wise men ... " What, sister! Are you saying my husband was right? I'll show all of you what right is! Anyway, that same evening when my brother turned up, my husband was all sweetness and light again. You should have seen him with his yes-sir no-sir!

It was during the first month of our marriage that he fell in love with Nim-Taj, the wife of Massoud Khan. "Major" Massoud had been appointed by the government as chief of police here, if you remember. My uncle and my brothers didn't want the town to fall into his hands. From the day he arrived they gave him trouble, and finally they set off that famous riot. I watched my coward of a husband suddenly change and become the driving force of that fight, turning my house into a sort of headquarters for my uncle's armed men. I said to him, "Didn't you say my brothers, fathers and ancestors were all traitors? How is it that now you're fighting their battle for them?" I'd just found out that he'd fallen for Nim-Taj. May he never rest in peace!

Eventually Major Massoud realized he had no chance of surviv-ing. Early one morning he ran away on foot to Seyyid Abol Vafa's shrine so he could take sanctuary there. My disgraceful husband chased him on horseback and caught up with him before he ever got there. He shot him in the back, and left the poor wretch rolling on the grass crying out for water. A crowd gathered to watch him in his death-throes. No-one dared give him a drop of water for fear of the armed men. Haj Agha, your father, appeared on the scene and took control of the situation. He shouted at the armed men, and told them they'd gone out of their minds, just like their master. He said they'd do penance for this killing right here in this world, and they'd always be haunted by the memory of the poor man's death-agonies. And he carried Massoud off in a droshke, but apparently the young man died then and there in your Haj Agha's arms. My husband was afraid of your father, you know. Several times they were about to raid your house but my husband stopped them, saying that Haj Agha would call for a holy war, and Solat the

Qashqai chief would join him—and no-one could resist that combination.

But I was impressed by Nim-Taj. That very night she went to Agha Sheikh Razi, and wouldn't budge from the house until they arranged to get her back to her parents. When my shameless husband went for her, the bird had flown.

May your soul never rest in peace, man! He never deserved a well-born lady like me! Whenever we quarrelled, he would say that I was cross-eyed, and he'd been forced to marry me. He would say he didn't love me but wouldn't leave me either because he didn't want people to insult our son by saying that his mother was a divorcee. And I, pathetic fool that I was, loved him to distraction. He knew exactly what to do to get his own way with me. I was always finding strands of blonde or black hair or sequins from women's dresses on the collar of his coat. Eventually he had the nerve to bring his women to the house. First he only brought them as far as the outer courtyard, and then he even brought them to the inner rooms.

Towards the end, he loved to have "hundred toman" whores. He'd say it was too demeaning for a "hundred toman" whore to be taken to the outer courtyard. So they would sit on the wooden bed we placed over the pool in the inner courtyard while I sent them trays of drinks. I would soak his tobacco in spirits and prepare his hookah. That hypocrite! First he would say his prayers, then he would settle down to his drinking. "Don't perform the holy prayers after imbibing drink," he would quote from the Quran. I would watch them through the stained-glass windows of the sitting-room till dawn.

In the morning he would kiss my hand, he would kiss my feet. He would say, "What can I do, that's how I am. The minute I see the flutter of a woman's veil, any woman, I lose my senses." And I would cry floods of tears and tell him, "Take my marriage portion and set me free, go away, leave me alone. This house and everything in it is mine anyway. I don't need a useless effigy to call a husband." I would swear by my one and only son, threaten to go to Haj Agha your father or to you, my sister, and take sanctuary. Haj Agha wasn't the kind of man whose word people took lightly. But he was always ready with an answer. "Whose house did you say you're going to?" he would sneer. "Haj Agha himself is one of the great lovers of our time. He keeps a mistress living under his own

83

roof!" He declared he didn't care a hoot what the Almighty said, let alone Haj Agha. Believe me, he meant it; he had turned away from God. Around that time he stopped bothering to say his prayers altogether. When he rode on horseback and people greeted him, he wouldn't return their greetings. He would signal to the outrider to answer them. Yes, my sister, this is the first time I'm telling you all this. You see, when your husband and son died, you forgot about me, your sworn sister.

The incident with my maid Ferdows and her mother? I suppose you heard rumours about that and now you want to hear the truth from myself? Well sister, I have nothing to hide from you.

One night after my evening prayers, I was coming out of the door of the New Mosque, when I saw a little girl crying by the door, with a bundle next to her. The sight of her was so pathetic, it would have melted a heart of stone. When I asked her why she was crying, she said, "My mistress threw me out of her house where I was a maid and I don't know how to get home to Baj Gah." I took the child in as an act of charity. The next morning I sent for the midwife to examine her. I thought someone might have taken advantage of her and then the blame would fall on my poor, innocent son Hamid.

To cut a long story short, sister, within a week either my husband or my son managed to take advantage of the girl. It never occurred to me that they wouldn't even pass up a wretched little peasant girl. Of course, I didn't find out which of them had done it. I scorched the girl with a hot iron but she wouldn't confess; her screams pierced me to my very bones, but there was no way I could ask Hamid himself. A mother can't talk to her son about things like that.

Ferdows grew into a woman in our house. When she got her period, she bloomed into a rosy-cheeked, dimpled lass, with such a twinkle in her eye! I was worried all right, and I looked around desperately for a solution, but sure enough before I could do anything her belly was out there and I didn't know who to blame—my husband or my son?

Anyway, I was forced to latch her on to Kal Abbas, our doorman. Before that, his mother used to go to the Jewish quarter once a month and buy him a little girl for three tomans, dress her up in pink satin and bring her home. By the time the dress had worn out, so had Kal Abbas's interest, at which point she would take the girl back to her family. But do you think Ferdows would consent to my

84

plan for her? I locked her up for three days in our chilly basement in the middle of winter. She had no food but her own thoughts and tears ... I said to her, "You shameless wench, what do you want from me? Should I be sending you back to Baj Gah with your belly full like this?" She said, "I can go to the police station to lodge a complaint against you, and then your family's reputation will be ruined." That half-size peasant wench certainly knew how to play her cards! "I'll give you whatever you want," I promised, "just get out of my house!" Obviously she had fixed all her hopes on that bastard in her belly. She said to me, "The child is yours; his inheritance and wealth will be worth piles and piles of money." Finally I beat her as hard as I could. Fortunately she started to bleed and Khanom Hakim got rid of that loathsome thing in her belly. With the baby gone, she gave up all her trouble-making. She just settled for having her mother brought over from Baj Gah and I had her start work for me on six qaran a day. Nana Ferdows, the mother, is an able woman. She's hard-working, but too bold as servants go ...

85

9

Khosrow was back from his hunting trip, covered with sweat and dust. His gun was still hanging from his shoulder, and a few dead partridges dangled from his hand. He went to the howzkhaneh which had a small pool in it and which Zari was preparing for use during the hot summer days. He held up the partridges before his mother's eyes as she was smoothing out the carpet.

"Look, I shot them myself!"

"I can see," Zari replied, without looking up.

"Aren't you pleased to see me?" Khosrow asked.

"Of course I am," said his mother.

"I'll give one to Sahar. He won't eat it, he'll just play with it." Then he added, "No-one's happy to see me back. Gholam was sitting in Haj Mohammad Reza's shop; he almost ducked when he saw me. I came to you first and you didn't even kiss me. It doesn't matter."

Zari bit her lip and said, "Take the partridges to the kitchen and give them to the cook to pluck. It's warm weather and they'll spoil. Tell him to serve them with rice tonight. Raisin rice, your favourite."

As soon as Khosrow had gone, Zari cursed the whole universe—she cursed herself and her ancestors and her fears; she cursed her English schooling and her cowardice and Ezzat-ud-Dowleh. When she said goodbye Ezzat-ud-Dowleh had promised Ameh Khanom to send Sahar back to his old stable within three days. So what had happened? Zari sat by the small pool and turned on the fountains. At first the water came out in short, muddy spurts, then it cleared and rose higher. Soon after, the twins came in. They both sat down by the pool and held their hands underneath the fountain while their mother reminded them for the thousandth time not to tell Khosrow who took Sahar, but to say instead that he was dead.

When Khosrow came back he didn't even notice Mina and Marjan.

"Mother, where's Sahar?" he asked.

Zari didn't answer. Instead she busied herself washing the children's faces with water from the fountain.

"My uncle was saying Sahar had caught the glanders disease," Khosrow blurted, "and that glanders is dangerous. Is that true? Captain Singer said glanders has become epidemic. Mother, he even imitated father. I nearly hit him when he said to me, 'This disease is yet another gift from the foreign army, as your father would say!'"

"Singer was with you all the time?" Zari asked, carefully skirting the issue.

"No, only for the first few days. There was a woman with him, too, who spoke good Persian. But she was just like a man. She even had a small moustache and wore boots. She rode well. Now tell me where have you sent Sahar?"

"Well, why did they leave?"

"Who?"

"Singer and that old woman."

"How should I know?" Khosrow complained. "Why are you interrogating me? Now you're probably going to ask me what we had for dinner, what we had for lunch . . . aren't you going to tell me where Sahar is?"

"You went off and left us for so long. After all, you were the man of the house. Now that you're back, won't you tell your mother where you went? Who was with you? Whether you had a good time?"

"Well, we went hunting," Khosrow answered impatiently. "On the third day when we came back after sunset, another foreigner wearing dark glasses arrived and took Singer and the woman with him. Uncle sent three armed men and one of his guides along with them. They headed for the mountains. Four-eyed Hormoz said, 'You can be sure they're off to see the tribe.' Now tell me where Sahar is."

Zari bit her lip. "God help us!" she exclaimed.

Mina got up from the edge of the pool. "Sahar was hurt and died!" she blurted out.

87

"Died!" Khosrow shrieked. "But why? Is it true, mother?" he asked through his tears. "I guessed it myself. I saw the flowerpots on his grave."

"What could I do, my dear?" Zari said with a sigh. "It was his fate. Your uncle took you to the village on purpose so you wouldn't see him die. At least he had a peaceful end. We buried him at the bottom of the garden just for your sake."

Khosrow squatted by the pool and said, "I knew inside me right from the start that something was going to happen. I could tell from the way my uncle talked. He went on about how a person should be patient, and what you should do when you lose someone you love. And after that he kept talking about the glanders disease. That's funny, you know, I dreamt last night that I was riding after game. Uncle and Singer were there too. Singer had spread a map on his saddle, and at the same time he was looking through his long binoculars for game. The first day of the hunt he was doing that, you see, and my uncle kept saying, 'Look how these foreigners do everything with calculation, even their hunting' . . . "

"Yes, especially when they're hunting people . . . " Zari commented sadly.

"But I was riding Sahar, not uncle's horse. We were coming down the mountain. Suddenly Sahar reared up. His front legs and mane froze in 'the air, and there I was hanging in space on horseback. The earth looked like a nutshell under my feet. In the morning I told uncle my dream. He said, 'It probably means something has happened to Sahar. Now don't you get upset! It's not worth it. Pick out whichever of my colts you like.' I said, 'Uncle, that's impossible. When we left Sahar was perfectly healthy. How could it be? No other colt will ever take Sahar's place for me.'" Khosrow broke off, sobbing. "Now I remember. When we were leaving, Sahar was stamping his foot and digging at the soil with his hoof. Poor animal knew he wouldn't see me again, but stupid me, I didn't know. Mother, why is my stomach turning so? I feel as if someone's choking me."

Zari hugged and kissed her son.

"Wash your face with some cold water, my dear," she said, "you'll feel better." Her own heart was brimming with sorrow. "Why don't you invite your schoolfriends over this afternoon to a mourning ceremony for Sahar? I'll bring out some tea and sherbet drinks for you."

"Will you make some halva too?" Khosrow asked.

"Certainly, if you want some." She paused and added, "Yes, I'll make some halva. As soon as the smell of halva rises, Sahar's spirit will know we're thinking of him."

"Can we come too?" Mina asked.

"No," Khosrow answered, kissing each of his sisters in turn. "The ceremony is for men only."

That afternoon, Sahar's all-male 'mourning ceremony' really did take place in the garden. At least twenty children of various ages poured in. Gholam had swept over the make-believe grave, and covered it with a carpet. Watching from the verandah, Zari could see the children squatting silently by the grave. She noticed a small boy wearing a black mourning shirt, staring fixedly at something. When she looked more carefully, she realized that he was staring at his thumbnails. Probably to stop himself laughing. But finally he started to giggle and then burst out laughing. All the other children, besides Khosrow and Hormoz who was sitting next to him, joined in the laughter and the ceremony broke up. Zari couldn't bear it anymore. She went to the parlour. Seeing a lot of flies buzzing around, she took a fly-swatter and attacked them, killing them left and right. She could hear the children playing in the garden and looking out from the parlour window saw that they were going at the unripe fruit on the trees. But Khosrow and Hormoz were still sitting on the carpet while Gholam walked toward them with some coffee and Khadijeh put the trays of halva on the ground. Hormoz whispered something in Khosrow's ear and Khosrow slapped his forehead with a grown-up gesture, then covered his eyes.

When the children had gone, Khosrow and Hormoz came to the parlour. Khosrow's eyes were red and Hormoz's glasses all fogged up.

"Cheer up, my dear," Zari comforted, "it's not so bad after all. As Khadijeh says, the mare is young, she'll give birth to another Sahar for you." And she thought to herself, "If, as Ameh Khanom said, he ever sees that wench riding Sahar, then all hell will break loose! How we end up lying to our children!"

"I'm trying not to cry," said Khosrow, "but I feel so unhappy . . ."

Hormoz took off his glasses. He took out a handkerchief from his pocket and wiped them. His eyes were puffy.

"I keep telling Khosrow this is just the beginning," said Hormoz. "We have a lot of ups and downs ahead of us. We mustn't give up so easily. Besides, look how many people die of typhus or starvation each day. What's a colt next to all these people?"

Zari looked at Hormoz. She wasn't sure whether they were his own words, or he had learned them from someone else. In any case, he was four years older than Khosrow. She thought with bitterness, "The real death of humans next to the fake death of a colt! Certainly there's no comparison."

Suddenly her mind went back to that evening in the Missionary Hospital where her mother was spending the last hours of her life. Zari had had no idea how near the end it was, even though Khanom Hakim had told her, "Now the cancer be overtaking the whole body, and there be nothing more the knife can do."

Her mother had looked at Zari out of the corner of her eye.

"Stay with me tonight!" she had said.

But how could she stay? Khosrow was only three years old and would not eat unless she fed him nor sleep unless she were next to him. Besides, they had guests. Yusef had invited a number of people.

"I have to go," she had said. "We have guests. I'll be back tomorrow morning."

"Tomorrow?" her mother had echoed. And didn't insist anymore. She merely asked for some sacred soil to be brought her by Ameh Khanom. By the time Zari had gone home and Ameh Khanom had finished her prayers and her opium-smoking, put on her outdoor dress with the long sleeves and her gloves and her scarf, the evening had drawn on and she was unable to go all the way to the hospital by herself. In any case, no-one would have thought a person who seemed so alert one minute would die the next.

Abol-Ghassem Khan had arrived before all the other guests and when he found out about the situation, offered to accompany Ameh Khanom. But he had no car in those days, and they couldn't find a droshke. They managed to get there, nevertheless, though it was after eleven by the time they returned. Zari was serving dinner and Khosrow had not been put to bed yet. The guests were playing with him, taking turns holding him and listening to his sweet baby-talk. Zari didn't even get a chance to ask Abol-Ghassem Khan how her

90

mother was. As for Ameh, she went straight to bed. Later, at dinner, Abol-Ghassem Khan drank so much vodka that he became completely drunk. Tears streamed down his face and he babbled on about his own mother. He smashed several glasses against the wall and then threw up violently, upsetting the other guests. Finally they took him to the bottom of the garden so he could vomit as much as he liked. When the guests had left, they told Zari her mother had died, that alas, she hadn't received the sacred soil she asked for, that no-one had been at her bedside, except a foreign nurse who didn't speak her language . . .

At that moment Mina and Marjan barged into the room, bringing Zari abruptly back to the present. Each of them was holding a doll.

"Uncle gave me this," Mina said.

Abol-Ghassem Khan followed them into the parlour with Gholam in his wake, carrying two loaded sacks.

"It's our first picking of lemons," Abol-Ghassem Khan announced. At a sign from Zari, Gholam took the sacks to the storage-room. Abol-Ghassem Khan embraced Khosrow and said, "Shall I send for that colt of mine you liked in the village?"

"No, uncle, I don't want a horse at all."

Mina, still holding her doll, put a hand on her brother's knee.

"Have you seen my doll?" she asked. "Do you want to have it?"

10

That week Zari finished early at the asylum, for typhus had reduced the number of patients to slightly over half compared to the week before. The warden, a short fellow with a dark complexion who received her every alternate Thursday, would only allow her to distribute bread and dates among the inmates after taking adequate payment for himself and his nurses. This week he told her that the epidemic had hit them hard and that his patients had been refused admission to the town's hospitals. "He doesn't look too well himself," thought Zari, as she handed over his payment. Not that he ever looked particularly well, dealing as he did all the time with mental patients. His eyes had sunk into their sockets.

When they entered the men's ward, Gholam put the tray of food on the floor, but unlike other weeks, no-one seemed to show any interest. Zari looked around at the men, with their shaved heads and soiled white gowns, sitting silently in the room. They seemed to be listening to sounds only they could hear and to which one or other of them would occasionally mumble a reply. They took the bread and dates from Gholam absent-mindedly. Zari felt depressed. It was as if today her vow had not been fulfilled since she hadn't made anyone happy. Downhearted, she began to distribute cigarettes and matches. One patient who claimed to be the Chief Commander of the World and who always asked for the Homa brand of cigarette, took an Oshno this time and without striking a match, listlessly put the cigarette to his lips. The sun poured in through the shutterless windows, and flies buzzed sleepily around the room, exploring every nook and cranny, as well as the untouched food in the patients' hands.

"Ali!" summoned the head nurse loudly. Ali was Zari's favourite patient, a tall, German-looking young man who had attempted three times to escape from the asylum. Twice his relatives had found him, each time in the neighbourhood of the high-school where he had finished five grades. The last time Gholam had found him on the hill overlooking Yusef's garden. Apparently Ali had followed Gholam like a lamb, allowing himself to be led back quietly to the asylum. Hunger had taken its toll. He had told Gholam:

"They tricked me. They whispered to me that the airplane is ready; please get inside it and go to Europe to your uncle. I came out and no matter how hard I searched, I couldn't find the airplane. Maybe it left without me. I have many enemies, you see." Later he confessed, "I've been drinking water from the gutter and stealing bones and bread from dogs. Yesterday I grabbed a piece of raw meat from a dog, and ran away with it. I washed the meat in the gutter and ate it. My stomach turned, and now I have diarrhoea. There's blood in it too. I really looked everywhere, but I just couldn't find our house. I know my father made our house get lost on purpose so I wouldn't find it."

From that day on, they chained Ali in the asylum basement. Zari would visit him there and take him bread and dates. He always smiled when he saw her. Once he had asked her for 'Essential English, Part III', and Zari had brought him one. Thereafter, he refused to speak a word in Persian, talking instead in a language no-one could understand.

Ali came in. He had lost so much weight that Zari felt distressed at the sight of him, and he did not recognize her. He threw her a blank look and, without using his invented language, proclaimed in Persian, "An attack of pliers equals typhus + famine + cheating in an exam. O madmen of the world unite!"

The Seyyid from the Arab Quarter was also sitting silently in a corner. Usually when he saw Zari he would reach under his belly and start scratching himself, saying, "Burning, burning, I am burning!" And then he would add, "It's me Eilan-ud-Dowleh, it's me Veilan-ud-Dowleh." In exchange for Zari's gifts, he would give her bits of imaginary paper with prayers of love and affection on them, or magical and occult charms or talismans.

"Our account is clear," he would say, "but do wash your shirt with water from the morgue. Spread it out on a deadman's grave

93

then have him wear it the next morning. Tiger's whiskers and the brain of a black mule ... "

Then there was another patient who tied his imaginary leg wounds with whatever bits of material he could get hold of, and would stretch out the leg and fan it. But today the fan had fallen away from his hand.

As Zari and Gholam, accompanied by the warden, were passing through the dried-up yard of the asylum, they saw a young woman stretched out on an old mattress under a pine tree. Hearing footsteps, the woman flicked open her eyes. Zari recognized her, even though her face had been drained of colour until it blended with the dust on the ground. It was the same woman who sometimes claimed to be the wife of God, and at other times God himself. Occasionally she would smear her cheeks and lips with some red petals from the Marvel of Peru flowers in the garden and say she was waiting for God. Apparently she would stare at the sky and repeat some mumbo-jumbo in a language resembling Arabic, saying God was waiting for her on the roof. But she herself wouldn't go to him; she was a woman, and a woman could never take the first step.

'God's wife' was now stretched out under the pine tree, her face twitching and her lips blistered. "She seems ready to join Him at any time," Zari thought. "If only she would intercede with Him for the rest of her fellow sufferers ... "

A sound escaped the woman's lips. "Water!" she moaned, as her blankly staring eyes slowly closed. Gholam ran for some water.

"Why is she lying here?" Zari asked the warden.

"She's got typhus," he replied.

"Well, all of them catch that at one time or another ... "

"All the better! It will be a relief for them. Their relatives pray that they'll be released from their suffering. What's the use of keeping them like this?"

Gholam came back in a rush, holding a glazed bowl full of water. He lowered the edge of the bowl to the woman's lips. "Drink, sister," he coaxed, but she couldn't swallow. Zari took her handkerchief from her handbag, soaked it and rubbed it on the woman's face and lips. Then she wet it again and placed it on her forehead.

They walked on. The warden followed alongside, offering explanations, "Three of our nurses caught typhus," he said, "and are now sitting comfortably under the Tuba Tree in paradise. 'God's wife' will be on her way there too tonight." Then, seeing Zari looking at him disapprovingly, he continued in a different tone, "It's amazing. When their fever goes up, their madness seems to disappear. If only we could save them from this second disease, maybe they'd be cured of their madness too! But what's the use? If they ever came to their senses, it would only be the beginning of their troubles. Their families have become used to their absence, and they would have no room or patience for them."

In the women's ward, Zari noticed the crippled woman who always managed to frighten her. "You fucking whore," she would say, "are you back again? What do you want from my life?" This woman blamed Zari for her paralysis and Zari felt guilty at heart about it too. When the woman had had healthy legs, she had asked Zari for a pair of old slippers, or a sturdy pair of second-hand givehs.

"I'm a respectable woman," she had said, "and I can't go to the toilet barefoot." Then, "May God strike Khanom Essmat dead! If she had spent my marriage portion and inheritance on me instead of on that goddam cuckold who sleeps with her, I'd never be grovelling for your droppings, you whore from Mordestan!"

But the following week Zari had been due to go to the prison, and the week after that she had forgotten all about it. By the time she remembered to buy the woman her new shoes, it was too late—she was already paralysed. Of course everyone knew her paralysis had nothing to do with the givehs. But every time after that when she saw Zari she threw unspeakable insults in her direction. Still, the nurses said she hugged the new shoes tightly each night as she went to sleep.

Zari glanced around for the young teacher with the glass eye. This one wasn't particularly fond of her, either, and wouldn't let her come close. Zari always left her share of bread and dates on the sill. Sometimes when the teacher was in a good mood she would say things like, "Look how much perfume this harlot's used! Ugh! How lucky you are, my little servant, to have got this far. You remember you were the daughter of our dressmaker? I knew you'd finally give in. With that cab driver who had a wife in every town . . . " And she would put a finger under Zari's chin and say, "You little coquette!" Then suddenly she would get angry and shout, "You've put rat poison inside these dates! You've taken out the pip and put ratsbane instead. What an offering!"

95

Apparently she used to teach first graders. One day, sometime after the veil was banned, the school was inspected by the Governor, the army commander and the minister of education. The minister had found out that this teacher would punish children by squeezing a pencil between their little fingers and laugh when they hopped with pain. He had made quite a fuss, but only about the issue of corporal punishment, yet the young teacher had fainted from humiliation at the sight of all those important people. She was immediately hauled off to the principal's office where they revived her, but the shock had been too much. She had stared blankly at everyone, then calmly taken out her glass eye, holding it out in the palm of her hand for her bewildered audience to behold.

One day in the asylum she played the same trick on Zari. Until then, Zari hadn't known that the woman had a glass eye, although she had noticed that the right eye didn't move in its socket. The young teacher was agitated that day. When Zari came into the room she went over to her, reached out her hand, and said, "Take it!" Then she opened her fist into Zari's hand, and there was Zari holding a large, shiny glass eye.

Now, on inquiring, Zari was told that the first fatality from typhus had been this very girl.

"At first we didn't know she had typhus," the warden explained. "Of course her fever was very high and she was delirious. She imagined she was putting on her shroud. She tied anything she could find around herself saying it was her shroud, and began reciting the Quran by heart. She was superb. But instead of cursing the Devil, she cursed the Cardboard Man. I believe the Cardboard Man was that same minister of education who fired her from her job. Finally, she said her last prayers and threw herself into the pool. She died that night."

At the end of her rounds, Zari went to Khanom Fotouhi whose bed lay next to a window where she could constantly watch the yard, in the hope that her relatives would come and take her to the 'hundred and twenty-four thousand metre garden'. Zari knew the Fotouhi family. They were well off. At the beginning of Khanom Fotouhi's illness, they kept her at home. But when she finally drove them to desperation, they gave up hoping for her recovery, and passed her on to the asylum. Before the war, she had had a private room where she was visited regularly by her mother who would even take her home for a week or two sometimes. When she had

had enough, she would drag her daughter back to the asylum, leave her in the reception office and disappear. But the mother had died years ago.

Khanom Fotouhi's brother was the well-known history teacher in town and something of an idol for its youth. The most he could manage was to visit his sister once in a blue moon. Now it looked as if they had all really abandoned her at the asylum. But Khanom Fotouhi never despaired. She was still waiting for them to come and take her to the 'hundred and twenty-four thousand metre' garden.

She was a sallow-looking girl with thick eyebrows that joined in the middle, protruding teeth, and grey hair. She never accepted food from Zari, as if it were too demeaning to show interest in something which others would grab at with such greed. When the fruit in her garden ripened, Zari usually took woven baskets piled high with apricots, sour apples, cherries, peaches and pears to the prison and asylum. But Khanom Fotouhi wouldn't even look at these.

On several occasions Zari had prepared a special fruit basket for her and left it on the windowsill. But the nurses later said that the minute she had stepped outside, the other patients raided the basket. When they got to the sour apples they would split them in half, ask for some salt and sprinkle them until they were well 'seasoned' in the Shirazi way. It was enough to make anyone else's mouth water. But Khanom Fotouhi would merely stare out of the window at the yard, waiting for her relatives to take her away to the 'hundred and twenty-four thousand metre garden'. The other patients didn't even spare the apricot pips which they would either split open with their teeth or bang with stones on the floor to get at the little kernels. After all, as the warden said, how could any of the patients get real sustenance on their pitiful daily allowance? Most of them had gone mad from poor nutrition in the first place.

When she had finished dividing the food, Zari would sit next to Khanom Fotouhi's bed and listen to her complaints. Khanom Fotouhi hated all the other patients and never spoke to any of them. They, in turn, had nicknamed her 'Princess'. The kinds of things Khanom Fotouhi used to ask for included the large-format *Iran* newspaper which was mailed to Yusef twice a week from Tehran, lined notebooks and pencils which she would accept from Zari, saying, "I have allowed you to contribute to the world of science

97

and literature." She loved all the serial articles in the *Iran*, and the notebooks she would use for writing her autobiography—or so she claimed.

Each time she finished a notebook, she would hand it ceremoniously to Zari. "Rent a safe deposit box in the National Bank," she would say. "Take the money for it from my brother and store my works there. We could have a fire here someday, and I don't want to have my works destroyed."

The first time Zari had believed her, and tried to read one of the notebooks only to discover that it was filled with some incoherent ideas written out in a language of the occult sciences. Wherever the handwriting became legible, it described a 'hundred and twenty-four thousand metre garden' with man-made waterfalls and lakes, blooming water-lilies, acacias and ash-trees. In one part she wrote about a well-built man with a wide forehead and white hair around the temples who hid behind an ash-tree while she herself, wearing a loose white chiffon dress which fluttered in the wind, stepped gracefully into the open air. Her shapely breasts and erect nipples showed through her dress, and the well-built man rushed out from behind the tree, capturing her in his arms and hugging and embracing her. At the end of her notebook she had written, "Thus endeth the sorrowful tale of the Fotouhi maiden in the Nai prison," and underneath this sentence she had added, "Some verses by the Fotouhi maiden:

I was a fledgeling my mother died
The wet nurse took me, but she too died
They raised me on cow's milk
I was so ill-starred, the cow then died."

Zari was quite certain these lines were not composed by the 'Fotouhi maiden' because Ameh Khanom had hummed them herself from time to time. Actually, in the days when the 'Fotouhi maiden' was in her right mind, she had been a good writer, producing articles in local papers about women's rights, and the injustices of male domination. She also brought out a magazine which aimed to raise women's consciousness.

In the days before her mental breakdown, Khanom Fotouhi was a woman to be reckoned with. She had been the first to abandon the black veil—or black shroud, as she called it—in favour of a roomier, more attractive blue veil. The lifting of the veil had not yet been announced officially before she even gave up the blue one also. On a good day, she would complain to Zari that it was too bad she had not been appreciated. "A pity," she would say, "that our men were not ready to accept a woman like me. At first they thought I could be taken advantage of, like a pot of honey you could dip your finger into. But when I smacked them on the fingers and sent them off packing, they humiliated me or ignored me." Then she would suddenly shout with tears in her eyes, "They drove me mad! They drove me mad! I told them I wouldn't give in! I won't give you what you're after! And that's that! When will other women—those silly little dolls—ever understand who I was and what I stood up for!"

Zari sat down by Khanom Fotouhi's bed and greeted her. Khanom Fotouhi turned her gaze from the yard to Zari and said hello. Zari reached into her bag and brought out four issues of *Iran* for her, at the same time catching sight of a pillow next to which all the previous newspapers had been neatly stacked. Khanom Fotouhi opened the new issues one by one. She frowned at the changes in detail and the recently introduced small format.

"Didn't you give the newspapers to the other patients to read this time?" Zari asked.

"No, most of them have been freed from prison," she replied nervously. "Ali took two of your newspapers and ate them." Then she looked Zari up and down. She didn't seem to like the long, wide sleeves of Zari's shirt. "You've wasted a hundred metres of good material just on those sleeves, haven't you?" she asked. Then she crumpled up the new newspapers and threw them down beside the bed. She turned her attention to the old newspapers and started counting them. Then she rolled one up and suddenly hit Zari very hard on the head with it. "They say Afsar Khanom, the daughter of the commander, is dead!" she shouted. "And she didn't even have a shroud!"

11

A Shirazi woman, trained as a midwife in Tehran, had recently opened an office in town. She had more patients than she could handle, but Zari had managed to get an appointment for seven o'clock Thursday evening after her rounds at the asylum. As soon as she was finished, she sent Gholam away and headed for the doctor's office, thinking all the while of the futility of her charities. She remembered Yusef's words, "What's the use of your charity and goodwill? This society is rotten at the core." But no matter how hard she thought, Zari did not seem to come up with any ideas on how to improve a society at its core. The solutions which Yusef suggested always seemed so dangerous that they sent shivers down her spine.

At six o'clock, she arrived at the midwife's office. She was feeling queasy. There were two donkeys standing at the door with their bridles tied to the door knockers. In the small courtyard next to the office, two women were huddled on a bare wooden bed, with another stretched out behind them. One couldn't tell their age because the expression on their faces was so strained. A sick man was tossing about on yet another bed. Right next to the door of the waiting-room a woman was stretched out stiff as a rod. Her bare, henna-dyed feet protruded grotesquely from underneath the blue polka-dot veil with which she was covered. Her black trouser-legs had been pulled up to her knees. Zari was taken aback. Surely the woman was dead. Zari had seen enough in life to recognize death when she saw it. But it would seem the woman had no-one, since she was obviously abandoned even in death.

Inside the waiting-room all the seats had been taken. Only five of the patients were pregnant women—recognizable by their round bellies and blotchy skin—the others were either male or elderly. A

100

young girl with blistered lips leaning her head on the shoulder of an older woman entered the waiting room just then. "Oh, my heart! My heart!" she moaned. A pregnant woman stood up and gave her place to the young girl, opening the window above her. But only a blast of hot air came in. The door of the doctor's office opened, letting out a pregnant woman, who slowly crossed the waiting-room as if the weight of her nine-month burden made it impossible to move any faster. A nurse with dishevelled hair followed her and announced:

"Forty-eight!"

Zari managed to reach the nurse as she scanned the patients for number forty-eight.

"Forty-nine!" the nurse said loudly.

"I have an appointment for seven," interrupted Zari.

"It's no use getting an appointment these days, dear. All sorts of patients are crowding in on us. Even the courtyard is packed. Didn't you see for yourself?"

"Yes, I did. One of them was dead."

"I know," said the nurse coolly. "By the time they're brought here on donkey from the villages, they've taken their last breath." Then turning to the other patients she shouted, "Forty-nine isn't here? Fifty!"

An old hunch-backed woman got up. Clutching her veil tightly across her face, she walked over with an odd shuffle. The nurse opened the office door for her. Zari reached into her handbag, and the nurse followed her movements with her eyes as she groped for a handkerchief. Finally she grew impatient.

"If there's nothing wrong with you and you're here only for pregnancy, I suggest you leave it for another time." And with that she disappeared into the inner room.

"She's right," Zari thought to herself. "After all, I'm in no hurry. In any case, I'll probably end up at Khanom Hakim's yet again." She decided to go home and wash thoroughly, even boil her clothes. She wasn't going to let those delicate children touch her before she had disinfected herself. On the way home she stopped at the pharmacy and bought anti-flea powder, alcohol, soap and sulphur.

By the time Zari reached the garden-gate of her home, the sun had

101

already set. A dark little boy with curly hair opened the gate. As soon as he saw Zari, he grinned widely at her. Zari recognized him.

"What are you doing here, Kolu?" she asked.

"I've come back with the master."

"Is he back then?" she exclaimed, rushing past him towards the house. Yusef, still dressed in his dusty travelling clothes, was sitting on the cane chair by the pool, smoking a hookah. His face lit up at the sight of his wife.

"Where have you been till now?" he asked. "I was waiting for you. I came all the way to . . . why are you standing so far away?"

"You're back so early," Zari answered, "but I'm glad you've returned. You mustn't touch me, though. I have to take a bath first. I'm full of germs. Oh, when you're here everything seems so much brighter!" And she hurried inside.

Bathed and perfumed, she came back into the garden, but by that time it was nearly dark. Yusef was holding his head in his hands. She went to him and lifting his head, kissed him on the hair.

"Don't you feel well?" she asked him.

Yusef pulled his wife on to his lap and the chair creaked beneath them. He kissed her neck and face and bare arms with soft, tender lips. Zari got up.

"Let me go and put the lights on," she said.

"Leave it," he said, pulling her by the hand.

"It's a heavy sky," Zari observed, glancing up. "But it won't rain either to let us breathe."

"Not unlike my heart . . . "

"Well, it's midsummer," said Zari. Her mind was on Sahar and how to prevent her husband from asking after the horse.

"The house felt really empty when I arrived. Where are the children?"

"Ameh Khanom took them to Mehri's house for the Rowzeh," replied Zari. "Khosrow has gone out with Hormoz."

"You really shouldn't be sending the children to the Rowzeh."

"They insisted on going," said Zari. "Besides, they don't pay any attention to all the mourning. They play with Mehri's children. Ameh Khanom has made them chadors, and they say their prayers standing next to her . . . " she stopped in mid-sentence. "Why are you back so early?" she asked. "And why did you bring Kolu with you?"

"Send him to the baths tomorrow and give him some new

clothes. I've adopted him as a son," Yusef said quietly. "I killed his father, so I couldn't stay at the village any longer."

Zari's heart sank. "I don't understand," she said. "You killed Kolu's father? Our shepherd? You? Nonsense!"

Yusef buried his head in his hands. "Don't talk about it anymore," he said. "My head is about to burst."

"But won't you tell me what happened?"

"Well, that's why I came back so early. I just dropped everything I had to do and rushed back so I could confide in you, but you weren't here."

Zari took a seat next to her husband and let his head rest on her shoulder, stroking him soothingly.

"My love, how was I to know you would suddenly arrive? Tell me about it now and I'll listen. You'll feel better if you talk about it."

"Our shepherd was supposed to take the last of our flocks up to the mountains. Before he went, he killed two of our sheep, cured the flesh and stored it in a sheepskin. I don't know what suddenly possessed him to do such a thing. He's never been dishonest before."

"Well, you told me yourself that people are panicking because of the famine."

Yusef got up and started to pace about.

"Nothing escapes the notice of the village headman," he continued, ignoring Zari's comment. "When I got there, he had to come out and tell me all about it in front of everyone. I wanted to ignore the whole thing, but the headman had no intention of dropping the matter. When the shepherd brought the flock back at sunset, the headman reminded me again. I was forced to interrogate the shepherd and ask him why two sheep were missing. He swore that a wolf had eaten them. The headman then told him to take an oath, and swear by the holy prophet Hazrate Abbas that he was telling the truth."

Yusef paused. Then he went on, "I could see the poor soul shaking at the knees as he stepped forward to take the oath. There I was watching him, stupid fool that I am, and I did nothing to stop him. That night he came down with a stomach-ache. I went to his house—or rather hovel. He looked at me with dumb eyes—like a lamb—and begged to be forgiven. I nearly shouted at him that I'd forgiven him all along. I told him that he should know me well

103

enough. But it was no use. Tears were rolling down his face on to his dirty pillow. I tried giving him sweetened warm wine, but he refused it. He kept saying that he'd sinned more than his share and the holy prophet Hazrate Abbas would take his due. 'But I'm the owner of the sheep and I forgive you, man,' I said. And still he wouldn't listen. He just repeated, 'The prophet has struck me down. You can't do anything for me anymore. Give the flock to my brother and he'll care for them in my place.'"

Yusef sat down by his wife and went on, "He motioned to Massoumeh, Yarqoli's wife, who disappeared for a moment and came back with two sheepskins full of cured flesh. She threw them in front of me. I wanted the ground to open up and swallow me . . ."

"My love," Zari said calmly, "you know very well it wasn't your fault. It was that cruel headman who didn't know any better. The shepherd took a false oath, or maybe he'd just eaten something bad. Besides, why must you think the worst? He could have caught typhus. We know nothing of God's will. Perhaps his son was meant to get an education and have a bright future. How do we know?"

Khadijeh came out to the verandah and put the light on. Then she went to the garden to lay out the beds. She fixed up the twins' bedclothes on a wooden bed on the far side of the pool. Then she arranged the mosquito net over it. When she got to Khosrow's bed, she laid out the mattress but then it seemed that she had lost something when she got to the bedclothes.

"Khanom, have you put Khosrow Khan's blanket somewhere?" she asked Zari.

"No. Maybe you used it for the ironing yourself," Zari replied from where she sat.

"I didn't, Khanom."

"So what's happened to it?"

"Well, I don't know. Maybe the same clumsy thief who stole the clothesline, stole Khosrow Khan's blanket too."

Suddenly Zari was filled with anxiety. Could it be that Khosrow was behind the disappearance of both items? But what for? Very early that morning, even before prayer-time, Zari had been woken up by a light footstep next to where she slept on the roof terrace. When she opened her eyes, she had seen Khosrow, looking stealthily all around him, tiptoe to the clothesline and untie its knot from the hook on the wall. Then he had gathered the entire length of rope around his arm and sneaked into his room with it. When he

104

returned he crawled silently under the mosquito net and pretended to be asleep.

Khosrow had been acting very strangely these past few days. His mind seemed to be elsewhere and from time to time Zari had caught him staring blankly into space. When he first heard of Sahar's death, he seemed heart-broken, the tears springing to his eyes at the slightest excuse. He hung around most of the time at the bottom of the garden by the grave, digging out the weeds and watering the flowerpots with his own hands. But recently he had changed. He didn't even glance at the grave anymore. He avoided his mother's gaze, and gave only short, confused answers to her questions.

Zari got up. She had a feeling he had also taken his gun, even though she remembered having locked it away in the cupboard and taken the key with her. Yusef's voice brought her back to herself. He was saying, "Why are you standing like that? Sit down. Say something."

"What did you say?" she said, as if roused from a daydream.

"I know I've upset you. You're disappointed in me too."

"You're wrong," Zari answered absently. "It's not at all your fault. I saw the sick they brought in from the villages to Khanom Massihadem, the midwife. One of them was dead. Typhus has spread in all the villages; the town is full of it too."

"What were you doing at Khanom Massihadem's office?" Yusef asked in amazement. "Are you . . . "

Zari felt completely flustered. It was as if they had been inhabiting two different worlds. How little one knows of what goes on in the mind of another person!

"Oh I just went to buy some anti-flea powder from the pharmacy and I passed by there," she said. "The door was open so I took a look. Well, maybe that patient wasn't really dead . . . I was probably imagining it . . . " She didn't know what she was saying anymore, so before Yusef could pin her down, she hurried to the bedroom. Without switching the light on she found her bag, took out her keys and groped around for the keyhole in the cupboard. Her hand was shaking and her stomach turned. No, thank God, the guns were still there. To reassure herself, she touched their long, cool barrels, the breech-blocks and heavy butts, leaning tall against the cupboard wall. She locked the cupboard door, closed the windows and doors of the parlour and went to the telephone. She asked the operator

105

softly to connect her to Abol-Ghassem Khan's house. She couldn't be heard, so she had to ask a second time. Abol-Ghassem Khan himself answered at the other end. She asked whether Khosrow was there. He said no, and Hormoz wasn't either. She could hear Abol-Ghassem Khan asking around from others in the household. Apparently Hormoz had said he was having dinner at his uncle Yusef's house. He had said that Zari had invited him ... "Now why weren't we invited too?" Abol-Ghassem Khan complained jokingly. "Do you think we would have turned down a treat?"

Zari's throat constricted. She mumbled something about God willing next time, and hung up. She was terrified. Both boys had lied, so there was no doubt they were up to something. They had also taken a rope and a blanket with them. She must go and tell Yusef everything.

As she was leaving the parlour the telephone rang. She went over and picked up the receiver. It was Abol-Ghassem Khan. He had been thinking about the boys and had become worried too. Zari pulled herself together and managed to say, "Don't worry. I think they've gone off to the cinema or somewhere together. They'll come here for dinner, it's not too late yet. As soon as they're here, I'll tell them to call you."

She opened the doors and windows of the parlour again. She heard Mina's voice. The children had arrived. She went out to the garden. Both children were sitting on Yusef's lap, and he seemed a little more relaxed. Mina was saying, "Mother won't let us. She says we'll get all burned on our skins and we'll have to stay inside."

Ameh Khanom was sitting there, with her veil still on.

"Sister," she said, "Mehri sends her regards but says she's cross with you because you didn't call in for the Rowzeh. She won't forget it, she said."

Mina clapped her hands together from where she was sitting. "She's cross with you! She's cross with you!" she chanted.

Then she turned round to kiss her father under the chin, and struggled to climb down from his lap. Yusef hugged both children tightly. "Well," he said, "what else are you going to tell me about, my little dolls?"

Zari, staring at the verandah lights and listening to the sounds in the garden, could not think where to begin. Like the patients at the asylum that afternoon, her mind was all in a jumble though she

106

seemed composed on the outside. Mosquitoes, tiny moths and various kinds of dragonflies flitted around the verandah light, got stuck to it, and finally dropped off. In the garden, the crickets and the frogs were having a contest. There was no other sound or movement. If the boys were heading home, she would easily have heard their footsteps. She had to tell the others now and rouse them to some kind of action, make them comb the town to find her son. What if this were the shepherd's vengeance? What if the Lord had sent them the shepherd's son in exchange for their own son? She felt sick. The trees seemed to slumber under the heavy blanket of the sky. If only there was a breeze, or if she could, like a furious wind, whip the trees and everyone around her into action. If only the sky would clear so the stars, like a million eyes, could scour the earth for Khosrow, and the trees could whisper his whereabouts to her.

"Let's go and sit somewhere else," she said involuntarily.

Yusef was holding up Marjan's hair and kissing the nape of her neck. He laughed and said, "What better place than right here?"

"Let's go and find Khosrow," said Zari.

"Sister, Khosrow has gone to Abol-Ghassem Khan's with Hormoz," said Ameh Khanom.

Zari was unable to contain herself anymore. "But he's not there!" she sobbed. "He's gone off with a rope and a blanket, though his gun is still here."

Yusef put the children down in amazement. "What for?" he demanded. "Where could he have gone to?"

"I don't know where he's gone," Zari replied through her tears. "Let's go and find him. I know something has happened to my son. I realized it when I saw Kolu. It—it must be God's revenge. God has sent Kolu to replace my son." And she broke down into loud sobs.

Yusef got up and held her by her shoulders. "Your nerves have been under strain," he said. "It's my fault for telling you everything that happens. Put these superstitions out of your mind. Call Abol-Ghassem Khan's house. Maybe he's there."

"I've already called."

"I'll put the twins to bed," Ameh Khanom volunteered. "Go over the hill to the Governor's house. I've a feeling Khosrow and Hormoz are there."

"What's all this, sister?" Yusef asked with a look. "Have you turned clairvoyant?"

"The sooner you leave the better," Ameh insisted. "I'll call Abol-Ghassem and ask him to get there as soon as possible."

"I don't understand it at all," Yusef said wearily. Then he had an idea. "They could have gone to Fotouhi's house. Hormoz's history teacher. But then Fotouhi's in Isfahan. I know he's not back yet."

"Come on, leave right away," Ameh Khanom urged. "Zari will tell you everything on the way."

Zari and Yusef went out by the small door in the back wall of the garden which opened on to the foot of the hill behind their house. They headed towards the hill.

"What have you been up to, woman?" Yusef demanded. "What have you led Khosrow into? Maybe it's my own fault for not controlling my tongue . . . walk faster . . . " He took such long strides that Zari had to run over the rocky terrain to keep up with him. By the time they reached the top of the hill, Zari had had enough. The Governor's estate, on the other side of the hill, looked wide awake with all its twinkling lights. Zari, panting hard, collapsed on a rock.

"Wait a minute," she said.

Her pulse was racing, her stomach heaved. She retched and then vomited so violently she thought she would bring up her insides too. Yusef took her by the shoulders and massaged her neck.

"You're driving me mad!" he begged. "Why don't you tell me what's happened, for goodness' sake? What has brought us all the way here to look for the boys?"

"You go on," Zari replied. "I'll sit right here. If you don't bring Khosrow back with you, I'll die on this very spot. I'll lay my head on this rock and die. Abol-Ghassem Khan forced us to send Sahar for the Governor's daughter. I guess Khosrow's now gone to steal Sahar back from the Governor's house. That place is surrounded by gendarmes and guards! They've probably killed my son!" And she sobbed hysterically.

Yusef slapped Zari. It was the first time he had ever done such a thing. Zari didn't know it would be the last time also.

"Shut your mouth!" he said quietly. "In my absence you're no better than a stuffed dummy!"

He let go of her roughly and headed downhill. He was wild with rage. Zari got up despite herself, wiped her mouth on her skirt and began to run. She stumbled, and got up again. She had to reach him and calm him down. She could see his looming silhouette in the darkness approach the wall of the Governor's estate and stop.

Thank God he had stopped. Somehow she managed to reach him with her last ounce of energy. By now she was fighting for breath. She grabbed his hand, but he only peered around, listening for noises.

"We'll go to the guard-post by the gate," he said. "If we hear the boys' voices we'll go in. God help them if there's so much as a scratch on either one of the boys!"

"Promise me you won't make a fuss if they're all right," Zari pleaded.

They knocked at the gatehouse and went in. Yes, the boys were there. A young lieutenant was sitting casually on a desk, the smoke curling up from a cigarette dangling from his lips, in imitation of movie-star officers. When he saw the husband and wife, he asked, "What can I do for you? I suppose you've lost the way too?"

On the desk was a half-eaten tray of food, and in front of it stood Khosrow and Hormoz. Two armed non-commissioned officers—one of whom Zari immediately recognized as the man who had come to take Sahar away—were searching the boys' pockets. Khosrow looked as if he had been crying. When he saw his father, a smile broke across his face, and Zari felt as if she could breathe again.

Gholam's friend extracted a few lumps of sugar from Khosrow's pocket. He put them on the table and stood to attention.

"Sugar-lumps, lieutenant!" he announced.

"On what charge have my boys been brought here?" Yusef demanded angrily.

Disregarding his question, the lieutenant said, "To be included in the file."

"Sir," Zari interrupted as calmly as she could, "these boys go on scientific expeditions in the afternoons." Her eyes took in the rope and blanket on the table and the sack Hormoz was holding, inside which something seemed to be squirming. "They collect stones and ... and ... " she hesitated, unable to guess what was inside the sack. So she said, "They collect insects, butterflies, field mice. They dry them later. They take a blanket to sit on and rest. Sometimes they take a rope and pretend they're Tarzan ... or if they find suitable trees, they make a swing ... "

The young lieutenant was clearly becoming interested in Zari's face and voice. Zari continued, "Tonight they were late, so we came to fetch them."

109

"It's true, sir," Hormoz confirmed. "We've sworn it to you. We'd gone on an expedition, lost our way, and when we saw the lights we came here."

The lieutenant squashed his cigarette butt in the ashtray.

"Then why did you whistle?" he inquired.

"We whistled so some kindly person like yourself could hear us and come to our rescue," answered Hormoz.

Yusef lost his temper again. "What possible harm could these two defenceless young boys do with a couple of sugar-lumps in their pockets?" he shouted.

Zari grasped her husband's arm. "Please don't get angry, my dear," she pleaded. "You can see the boys are perfectly safe and sound. There's just been a misunderstanding which we'll soon clear up."

"They're treating my children like criminals," Yusef shouted more angrily than before. "Do you know why they came here . . . "

Zari knew that if Yusef told the truth, there would be no end to the matter, and none of them would be allowed to leave. "My husband has just returned from a journey," she interrupted, explaining to the lieutenant, "he's very tired . . . "

The lieutenant suddenly noticed the sack Hormoz was holding. "What's in this sack?" he queried.

"A snake, sir!" Hormoz answered coolly.

"A snake?" the lieutenant exclaimed.

Zari instantly realized that it was probably the snake Haj Mohammad Reza had found in their house. She remembered that the snake's fangs had been pulled.

"I told you they collect reptiles. This time they found a snake. But it's probably harmless."

"Would you like to see it, sir?" Hormoz asked. And he emptied the contents of the sack on the floor.

A brightly-spotted snake crawled out. At first it held its head high, looking straight at the lieutenant's shoe. Then it flashed its tongue and slithered under the desk. The lieutenant hastily lifted his feet out of the way.

"Kill it!" he cried.

Gholam's friend went for the snake with his rifle butt, but it escaped.

"Threatening the life of an officer on duty with a snake . . . !" shouted the lieutenant. But he never finished his sentence.

Jumping down from the desk on which he had taken refuge a few seconds ago, he inadvertently stepped on the head of the snake. Meanwhile Gholam's friend was about to attack the snake again when the lieutenant suddenly stood to attention and did a military salute.

"Good evening, your honour!" he said.

Zari turned to discover Abol-Ghassem Khan in the doorway. "Sister," he chuckled, "is this where you bring your newly-arrived husband?"

The young lieutenant was stammering in confusion. His foot was still on the snake's head, while at the other end the tail wriggled grotesquely.

"Your honour," he said, "I had no idea the gentleman was your honour's brother. Even though the resemblance of nobility can be detected in every feature . . . if I have given offence, please forgive me, I apologize . . . " And turning to Yusef, he bowed and said, "Why did you not inform me, sir?" Indicating the other graded officers he added, "I shall have these bastards thrown in jail." Giving the man closest at hand a slap across the face, he barked, "Imbecile, you bring the son of the most respected man in town to this sentry post?"

"Forgive them this time," Abol-Ghassem Khan said with measured coolness and dignity. "My regards to His Excellency, the Governor. It's too late, otherwise we would have gone to convey our regards in person."

Yusef, Abol-Ghassem and the boys were climbing back up the hill, joking and chatting. The sons were telling their fathers all about it from the beginning. They took no notice of Zari. She no longer had the strength to follow them uphill so she turned into a side-street which led up to the main road, and walked off alone as quickly as possible. A few Indian soldiers were sitting by the stream along the road, another one urinating at the foot of a tree. When Zari passed him, he turned and flashed his naked body at her, saying, "Need woman!"

Zari quickened her step. A gendarme and a night-guard turned to look at her as they walked past. Deep down she was hoping that either her son or her husband would follow her, but when she turned into the small road that ran alongside their garden, she saw

111

no one on her trail and felt it was just as well they hadn't even done her that favour.

As she went into the garden, she was surprised that the others had not arrived yet. The twins were sleeping peacefully under the mosquito net. Zari sank on to her knees by the pool and immersed her face in the water. Then she sat on the edge of the pool and soaked her feet in the surrounding overflow. The water was luke-warm. She placed her hand on the head of the stone figure by the pool. Whenever they needed to use the well for watering the garden, the cistern supply flowed out of that open stone mouth. Hossein Kazerouni, the labourer, would arrive with a little cushion which he placed on the ledge behind the treadwheel, and from morning till dusk, from that cushion-seat he would work the wheel with his feet, filling the water-bucket and bringing it up to the surface. His hands were free, except when the brimming bucket appeared. Then he would detach the bucket and empty it into the little reservoir which led in turn to the cistern. Alone, from morning till dusk, that was all he did. When he went to other houses, he did the same thing. He never even sang, and Zari used to think it was a wonder his mind didn't wither away. In order to keep him entertained, she would send the twins to watch him and talk to him. But how long could they be expected to stand there and watch?

Suddenly Zari thought, "That's the way I'm spending my whole life! Every day I've sat behind a wheel and made it turn. The wheel of our lives, nurturing my children, my flowers . . . "

Ameh Khanom called her from the roof, interrupting her thoughts. "Did Abol-Ghassem Khan arrive on time?" she asked.

Zari lifted her head and said, "Ameh Khanom, please come down. I'm not in the mood for arguing with them by myself."

There was loud knocking at the garden gate. Gholam, lantern in hand, dressed in a nightshirt and his usual felt hat, opened the gate. They all came in. But Khosrow followed Gholam straight to the stables and stopped in front of Sahar's make-believe grave. Zari could only see his legs in the light of Gholam's lantern and she stood up despite herself to get a better look at what he was doing. The feet kicked over the flowerpots one by one, and then all of Khosrow could be seen squatting to dig out the stones arranged around the grave. He flung them around the garden, disturbing the birds in the trees. The others came to join Zari and sat on the cane

112

chairs. By this time, Ameh Khanom had come down too. Her head was bare and she was wearing a long white nightdress.

"Sister, which way did you come?" Abol-Ghassem Khan asked. "Halfway up the hill, we realized you weren't with us. We followed you to the street . . . " He took off his hat and wiped the sweat from his forehead. "I suppose there's no whisky to be had in this house? Spare us a bottle of Tavuus Khanom's wine then, will you? As there's no Dutch cheese to be found either, we'll put up with some goat cheese and thyme. I'm not an ungrateful sort, after all!"

Zari didn't move, watching for Khosrow as he approached them by the garden path. His footsteps could be heard on the gravel, but his body was enveloped in darkness. He walked up to his mother and flung the bundle he had in his hand at her feet. It was the sack, the rope and the blanket.

"Mother, why did you tell me so many lies?" he shouted. "Why?" And turning to his father, he added, "Father, you ask them why they all got together to fool me? Would they do something like that if you had been here?"

"I've decided," Yusef sighed, "that I'm incapable of changing anything. If I can't even influence my own wife . . . "

"We were afraid you might do something rash and endanger your life to try to get Sahar back," Ameh told Khosrow, interrupting Yusef, "which you did . . . and now don't shout so much, you'll wake the twins."

But Khosrow stubbornly raised his voice louder than before. "Either the children are sleeping, or the ladies are afraid!" he shouted. "Women are either worrying or lying. All they can do is to dig graves, or sit around and cry!"

"Sister, how about that wine?" Abol-Ghassem Khan asked, blinking.

Zari looked at him; she looked at all of them. How strange and unfamiliar they all seemed! Abol-Ghassem Khan bit his lip and turned to Khosrow. "I told you it was my fault, my boy, now don't argue so much with your mother . . . " And to Zari he said, "Sister, give us your wine, I want to drink the boys' health."

Zari walked off like a robot. She went to the cellar and fetched the wine. Khadijeh followed her with a tray of drinks and snacks. Zari could hear Ameh Khanom telling Hormoz, "You're the older one, you should've had the sense to tell us. Poor Zari nearly died of fright tonight."

"But if we told you, you would've tried to stop us," said Hormoz.

"If they had seen you climbing that wall, they would have shot you!"

"Well, they didn't, and no one shot us," said Hormoz. "Our plan was to have me climb the wall first, then pull Khosrow up by the rope tied around his waist. We wanted to throw the blanket over Sahar's head and bring him out through the back gate. We were going to let the snake loose in the garden as our revenge . . ."

Abol-Ghassem Khan poured three glasses of wine. He handed one to Hormoz. "Cheers!" he said. "Drink this stuff from now on and try to enjoy the world! I hope you won't turn out like your uncle who ruins life for himself and everyone around him by taking on a whole nation's burdens. Brother, why aren't you drinking? Lord knows this world isn't worth it; all your pleas for justice, your frustration and your self-destructive attitude. A man of the world like myself is clever enough to have his smuggled whisky always at hand! One must take advantage of these foreigners, you know. Besides, they're having the time of their lives behind your back and a good laugh at your expense. Actually, why don't I break the good news to all of you now? I've finally made it as deputy in parliament and my appointment has just been confirmed! The telegram of approval arrived from Tehran today."

And he got up and did an absurd little dance of joy.

"Uncle, you'll probably go to Tehran and take Hormoz with you," Khosrow said sadly. "We had so many plans together . . ."

"Yes, my dear boy," Abol-Ghassem Khan replied, "I'm certainly taking Hormoz. He's very lucky too. Here the two of you have been taken in like so many idiots by that man Fotouhi. The fool's gone to Isfahan to get a permit to start a Communist party here, and he's persuading the seamen down south in Bushehr to join him. Pah!" Turning to Yusef he added, "I hear his highness came to you first to try to enlist you, but thank God for once you had the sense to refuse. I don't believe in these political parties one bit. They'd invited me to join that Anglophile Baradaran party too. I didn't refuse, though, I just put them off for the time being." Then he chuckled and added, "Actually, it wouldn't be so bad, would it? One brother flirting with the Russians, and the other with the British. When the going gets tough, one brother could come to the rescue of the other. Still, I guess you're not the kind to help out your own flesh and blood when it's needed . . ." He lifted his glass again and said, "Cheers!"

114

There was a pause while he carefully rolled some meat patties, pickled eggplant and fresh herbs in a piece of bread and gave it to Khosrow. Then he continued, "I was there when the man reported to the Governor about you and Fotouhi, telling us how well you'd spoken and stood up to them. I said well, don't take my brother here too lightly! It's not for nothing that he has a doctorate in agricultural economics from Manchester or Massagussets or whatever university it is . . . " He laughed heartily at his own joke. Then he added, "Actually, I'm making up these names right now. At the time I didn't mention the name of your university. I don't even remember the name. Anyway, our man said you told them you don't like being a slave—either to an individual or to a group. You'd said you despise party discipline. Even though laziness was probably behind it all, I'm still proud that, for once in your life, you came out with the right thing . . . "

Yusef shook his head bitterly. "That person was obviously a bit of a hypocrite, and hadn't understood most of what I said, or didn't repeat it all because you were there . . . "

"On the contrary," Abol-Ghassem Khan interrupted, defending the man. "From the report he gave the Governor, it was clear he had been keeping his eyes and ears open."

"The main thing I said was that it wasn't as easy as they thought," explained Yusef. "I said Marxism or even socialism is a difficult school of thought which requires careful training and education. I told them that adapting those ideals successfully to our way of life, attitudes and social fabric, requires a great deal of maturity, open-mindedness and sacrifice. I said I was afraid they were about to stage a play with inexperienced actors; that because of its novelty the play would draw large crowds for a while, but that soon both actors and audience would tire of it and despair. To achieve something for the people of this country, we need enlightened minds, intellectuals, and no outside interference."

"And what actors these are! Gorbeh Shah Cheraq, Masha Allah Qari, Fotouhi, Seyyid Agha with the long face, the son of Ghavam's wet-nurse . . . Hah!"

"I didn't mean to insult anyone," Yusef replied sadly. "These people are worth ten times the rest of the so-called Actors of our Golden Age . . . "

Hormoz laughed uproariously. Abol-Ghassem Khan threw him a ferocious look. Hormoz lifted his glass clumsily to his lips, grim-

115

acing as he swallowed.

"My uncle is right," he opined.

"Who asked you to air your views, you young parasite?" his father retorted.

"Brother, let him have his say," Ameh Khanom interceded. "Don't shut him up like this in front of everyone."

Hormoz stammered, "This—this very Masha Allah Qari has so far sold two of the houses he inherited in the weavers' quarter, and distributed food among the poor with the money."

"Don't tell so many fibs, boy!" Abol-Ghassem Khan snapped. "I've had enough of this nonsense. Let's go now, it's getting late. I was in such a rush, I forgot my night-pass. We'll be lucky if we don't get stopped under the curfew." He stood up and told Yusef, "Do you imagine that the British are just going to sit quietly and watch while others carry on as they like down by the Gulf? You just wait and see how they'll buy off all these upstart Communists in one go. If they can't do that, they'll bribe the big shots and the leaders. Then all the pious, gullible, freedom-loving idiots better start watching out!"

After Abol-Ghassem Khan had left, Yusef turned to Khosrow. "How many times have you been to Fotouhi's house?" he asked.

"Four times."

"Did he give you the idea of stealing the horse?"

"No, he said, just like you did tonight, to try and find the solution to the problem on my own. Hormoz said let's do a sit-in and protest. I said no, it's better if we just steal him."

"You should have told your mother where you were going."

"Told my mother?" Khosrow sniggered. "I'm not a baby anymore, I'm a man. Mother likes to cover up and stop you from doing things. The first thing Mr Fotouhi taught us was to burn the bridges behind us so there would be no way back. He said we were to memorize those words like a lesson."

"Well, bless my soul!" Zari exclaimed angrily. "You've got to have a reason to be burning bridges behind you! What reason do you have? What have you ever had but love and affection from your father and me? Have we neglected your lessons, your schooling, your clothes or your fun for an instant? If Fotouhi is at all sincere, he should look after his pathetic sister at the insane asylum, who's glued to the window, waiting for him to come and take her to some imaginary garden!"

116

"But Mr Fotouhi says when society is reformed, no-one will go mad, and every place will be a garden!" Khosrow said innocently.

"I'm certain a Fotouhi-type is just what we need to reform our society!" Zari snapped back sarcastically.

"Can't he, father?" Khosrow turned to Yusef.

"If Fotouhi and others like him can't," Yusef answered, "at least they've offered our people the opportunity of sharing an important experience."

"I don't understand, father," Khosrow said helplessly. "You're talking above my head again." Suddenly he grimaced at his mother and said, "In any case, Mr Fotouhi doesn't lie, and he defends your rights behind your back!"

"If I lied about Sahar," Zari said in a calm and motherly tone, "it was on your uncle's orders. At any rate, I don't want you children to be brought up with fighting and quarrelling around you. I want our home to be peaceful, so . . ."

Khosrow finished his mother's sentence, "So, as Mr Fotouhi says, we can all be blind calves who never see when we turn into cows. Just like . . ."

"That's enough now," Yusef stopped him authoritatively.

"No, let him talk," Zari said with bitterness. "He probably means a cow like me. Now listen here, the two of you, do you really want to hear the truth? You remember the day of the Governor's daughter's wedding? They came and took my emerald earrings as a loan, and never returned them. On the day of the foreigners' party, the Governor's daughter had the nerve to thank me for the present I gave her. Then they started talking about the horse. I'd decided to stand firm and not give in this time, in spite of Abol-Ghassem Khan's insistence. I knew myself that eventually I'd have to stand up to them. But I was afraid. Yes I was afraid of that gendarme who came to get the horse . . ."

"But that stupid idiot was Gholam's friend!" Khosrow broke in. "You could've tricked him somehow, you're good at that!" Turning to his father, he explained, "He was that same man who followed us half-way up the hill after we left the guard-house and said I could come and ride Sahar in the mornings. He said the little mistress wouldn't mind. He said the poor animal had lost a lot of weight and wouldn't let the girl ride him at first, but now she can take a few turns around the garden. She doesn't dare go outside with him yet . . . he said he'd taught Sahar to trot. He said Gholam

117

beat him up . . . " His lips puckered and for a moment he became the same little boy whose plaything had been snatched away and given to another, not the lad burning with desire for manhood.

"That night I wanted to tell you about my earrings, Yusef," Zari continued, "but you were already so angry, I didn't want to make things worse :.. it's always like that, to keep peace in the family . . . "

"I always tell lies," Khosrow finished her sentence for her.

"When I said enough, I meant enough!" Yusef reprimanded sharply. And he added thoughtfully, "It's not your mother's fault. It's the way things work in this town; the best school is the British school, the best hospital the missionary hospital, and when a girl wants to learn embroidery, it has to be on a Singer sewing machine with Singer for a salesman. The teachers who've trained your mother have always tried to steer her away from reality, filling her instead with some etiquette and coquetry and embroidery. She can only talk about peace and quiet . . . " And suddenly turning on Zari he shouted, "Woman, what use is this peace and quiet when it's based on deception? Why shouldn't you have the courage to stand up to them and say those earrings are a wedding present from my husband, a keepsake from his late mother? After all, the poor woman died in poverty but she was still thinking of the bride her son would choose . . . How could you have given them up so easily? It's not their value that matters. It's the memory and the love behind them." He paused for breath. "Woman, think a little bit. When you become too soft, everyone will bend you."

Ameh Khanom who had been silent for a long time, decided she had had enough. "What's all this about?" she said. "Why are father and son taking it out on this poor soul? Giving away the horse was not at all her fault. I was a witness. I even told her to give it away. As for the earrings, when I first heard the story from Ezzat-ud-Dowleh, I was very upset too, but after I thought it over, I decided she couldn't have refused them. What can you do when there are people who govern your possessions and your life, not just your town? Now do you want to know the truth, brother? She is soft, she gives bribes, so they leave you alone. And that's enough for one night. Eat your dinner and go to bed. Tomorrow morning it will all be water under the bridge. As for me I'm going to bed." With that she got up and left.

"I'm going to show you what I can do," Khosrow said, standing

118

up. "I'm not my father's son if I don't get Sahar out of their clutches. First I'll write a letter to the Governor himself and if he doesn't answer, I'll go to see him. My father and Mr Fotouhi are right. I have to solve my problem myself. If the Governor refuses to see me, I'll do my best not to get upset. No one's ever going to see me cry again. Mother, when they caught us, I was really crying for your sake because I knew you'd be worried about our being late. I hated crying in front of Hormoz, in front of the officers, but I couldn't help it because I know how afraid you are about me or father . . . Comrade Fotouhi . . ."

"Yes dear," Zari said, "according to you and your father and your teacher, I'm a coward, I'm helpless, I'm soft. I'm always afraid something may happen to one of you . . . I couldn't bear it. But when I was a young girl I too had a lot of courage . . ." And turning to Yusef she asked, "Wasn't it a mark of courage to walk off with you that day in the middle of a street riot . . . you, a total stranger . . . which girl would've . . ." she bit her lip and tried to change the subject. "But you're right about the rest. Our English headmistress constantly harassed us about manners and how to live. Singer was always doing us a favour by teaching us to sew, and Khanom Hakim had us convinced that our cures and medicines lay in her hands alone. I knew in my heart there was more to it than they were willing to tell. Something was wrong somewhere. I knew all of us, all the time, were losing something . . . but I didn't know what it was . . ."

"And that was why I married you," said Yusef. "Why have you changed so much?"

"I've already told you; must I repeat it a hundred times? You're too outspoken and deep down I know it's dangerous to say the things you do. If I wanted to stand firm and put my foot down, I'd have to do it right here with you first, and then what kind of battle of wills would we have at home? Shall I tell you one more thing? You are the one who took my courage away from me . . . I've obeyed you for so long that subservience has become a habit with me."

"Me?" Yusef shouted. "Stand up against me? No matter how fierce I am outside this house, you know well that once I'm within these four walls I'm as meek as a lamb before you! I think your courage has been all show. Prompted by pure, unrefined instinct."

Zari thought silently that if she carried on any longer, they would have a real quarrel on their hands. She hesitated and then said,

119

"Who knows, maybe I was a coward from the start and I didn't know it. Time and again I stood up to that headmistress of mine without stopping to think whether I was committing an act of courage or rebellion. That day in Ramadan when she forced Mehri to break her fast . . . all the other girls abandoned the poor soul out of fear, but I stayed with her. I don't know, maybe in those days I had nothing to lose . . . and now . . ." Without knowing quite what happened she lost all her patience and composure. She got up from her chair and slapping her belly hard, cried, "I hope this one in my stomach will miscarry tonight . . . I've gone close to death and back for your sakes. Khanom Hakim has carved up my insides . . . etched a map on my belly and here I am on trial for courage!"

She collapsed on the chair and burst out sobbing. It felt as though nowhere in the whole world was there a person as lonely and as tired as she. Yusef went to her and clasped her head in his arms. He kissed her hair and wiped her tears away with his fingers. He lifted her chin and looked her in the eye, fighting back his own tears.

"Don't cry, my love," he said. "Why didn't you tell us all this earlier? I was completely taken by surprise."

"Today I damn well wanted to get rid of this one," she moaned, unable to hold back the tears. "Wasn't I brave to keep it? When you bring a child into this world with such agony as I go through, you can't bear to lose him so easily. Every day I . . . I turn the wheels in this household to nurture you, my precious flowers. I can't bear to see people trample you. Like Hossein Kazerouni I don't do anything with my hands for myself . . . I . . . I have no experience, I don't know much of the world . . ."

"My love," Yusef smiled, "instead of going to the mental asylum and getting tired and nervous, you should go to the new Anglo-Iranian Council here and teach Essential English II! Can you believe Singer sent me this message via McMahon?"

"You're making fun of me!" said Zari from between her tears.

"You know I can't bear to see you cry," Yusef said gently. "I wanted to make you laugh with the suggestion . . . But my love, if only you'd told me the truth right away, we wouldn't have gone on at you like this. You said you went to Khanom Massihadem's office, but you quickly covered up the real reason behind it. Why did you keep it a secret from me? Now I feel guilty about the way I jumped at you." Khosrow had sat down at his mother's feet. He was holding on to her leg and listening silently to her words.

120

Zari wiped away her tears. "You had just got home from your journey," she said. "You were tired and unhappy. I didn't want to make you feel even worse." She asked wearily and at a loss, "What can I do to please you two? What can I do to become brave, as you say?"

"I could teach you," Yusef said with a laugh. "Your first lesson in bravery is this: whenever you're afraid to do something, if you feel you're in the right, then do it even if you're frightened. My sweet little kitten!"

"For one thing I'm a person, not a sweet little kitten," Zari said pensively. "What's more, you give a first lesson to someone who has to start from scratch."

In bed under the mosquito net, despite Yusef's cool hand caressing her warm abdomen, despite his kisses, Zari seemed to have forgotten all sexual response. Instead, she kept thinking about her past, and wondering whether she had always been a coward or whether she had become one. Was Yusef really to blame? For one instant she even concluded that marriage was wrong at its very basis. Why should a man be tied for a lifetime to a woman and half a dozen children ... or conversely, for a woman to be so dependent emotionally and otherwise on one man and his children that she couldn't breathe freely for herself? It had to be wrong. Yet she knew that all the joys of her own life stemmed from these very attachments.

She couldn't sleep for remembering those carefree days of her girlhood. The memory of that day in Ramadan when the headmistress broke Mehri's fast came back to her as if it were yesterday.

That year Zari and Mehri were taking their sixth-grade exams. Four months before the final examinations a letter from the Ministry of Education arrived at the school stipulating that sixth-graders must be taught the Quran and religious laws. Zari realized that her mother's petitioning had finally worked. Because she couldn't afford a private teacher to instruct her daughter in religious matters, she had been pressing to have these taught as part of the school curriculum. Letter after letter and notice upon notice from the Ministry arrived on the headmistress's desk, upsetting her considerably. But Zari knew that behind this pressure lay her mother's insistence ...

121

Those days every lesson in 'Ethics' turned into a nagging session about the Ministry of Education. The headmistress would complain that the Ministry had agreed from the start to maintain a policy of non-interference. She went on about the impossibility of suddenly producing a suitable teacher in the middle of the scholastic year. She nagged about finding extra hours to fit in these lessons . . . and so on. She would say, "Why don't you girls find an old mullah-baji somewhere on Sundays when the school is closed and learn your Quran and religious laws from her . . . or better still, ask your people to teach you at home?" She would use the idioms correctly, since this one knew Persian well.

Mehri, whose uncle was the head of the Sufi dervishes, was well versed in both the Quran and in religious law. Unbeknownst to the headmistress, she agreed to give her classmates lessons in these subjects when they came back to school after the lunch-break. Zari struggled to pronounce the Arabic word "Fassayakafikohomo'-allah" correctly, but she didn't always succeed. Still, Mehri was patient, being a year or two older than the rest. And then came the month of Ramadan. She had just been teaching them the Ayat Prayer for use in times of natural calamity, when that memorable incident took place. It seemed like yesterday.

Fasting was forbidden in the school, but Mehri was doing it anyway. When the headmistress found out, she stormed into the classroom and demanded that Mehri end her fast there and then by eating something. Mehri refused. The headmistress gave her a shove which sent her sprawling all over the classroom floor. Then she kneeled by her and holding the girl's head with one hand, roughly opened her mouth and attempted to pour some water down her throat. Mehri bit the woman's hand, at which the headmistress shouted at her and called her a pathetic wretch. Mehri sat up. "The dirty hand of an unbeliever in my mouth was enough to break my fast," she said. "Give me the water and I'll drink it to the last drop. The sin be on your head."

The headmistress slapped Mehri across the face, and again sent the girl on to the classroom floor. She then left Mehri and turned to the class to rebuke them. But the other girls were whispering anxiously and no-one paid attention. Even their Indian teacher was just standing, staring round-eyed at the scene.

"In this school," the headmistress shouted, "there is no room for superstition. Leave fasting and religious mourning to your aunties and grannies! Ask your nursemaids about religious rules on menstruation and childbirth. Fasting weakens the body. Why did I buy parallel bars, a vaulting horse, and a basket-ball net? To strengthen your bodies, that's why! Now you want to ruin all my efforts by fasting? You don't deserve any of it !" Then she barked again at the top of her voice, "The bell has rung—why don't you leave the classroom? Mehri's punishment is to stay right here on the floor till this evening. Come along now, girls! No-one is allowed to remain with her."

The headmistress marched out, and the Indian teacher, tossing her braid over her shoulder, followed her. The other girls filed out too. But Zari felt she could not leave. She bent over Mehri and gave her a hand to stand up. She dusted her off and sat her on the teacher's chair. Both of them searched for a handkerchief to wipe away Mehri's tears but neither of them had one. So Zari dried her friend's face with her fingers, and kissed her, saying, "I don't think your fast is broken. You were forced to drink the water."

"There were only two or three hours left to the end of the fasting day," Mehri cried, "and I had managed to fast for twelve days. I'd even fasted two extra days. This year I was determined to fast all thirty days of the holy month, because by next year I'll have my period and I'll never be so lucky again."

"Oh it's a long way to next year! Besides, you said yourself that a woman in her menopause doesn't get periods anymore. When you get to that age, you can fast all thirty days again."

Mehri laughed at that, and Zari was pleased to have made her laugh.

"I know who's been telling tales—it must have been Taji. That stupid girl has turned Christian. I know my saviour Imam Ali will strike at her and she'll fail her exams! Tonight the dervishes are holding a chanting session for the Imam Ali and I hope my uncle curses her."

That night, they went home together. As they passed the Sufi monastery, they heard the rhythmic chanting of the dervishes, "Ya Hu. Ya Haq. Ya Ali!", as it drifted through the open doors of the house of Imam Ali.

12

All the quarrelling, reconciliations, and anxieties of the past days faded into insignificance when that very Friday morning Sahar walked back to the house on his own feet. It all began like this.

They were sitting on the verandah at the back of the house which was protected from the morning sunlight, and which looked out on the hill Zari and Yusef had climbed with such fear and anxiety the night before.

Zari was using the breakfast table as an ironing board. The rugged hill lay bathed in sunlight, so still that it seemed hardly touched by the tread of human feet. Khosrow was sitting across from Zari, and had put a pen, paper and several books on the table in front of him. He was leafing through a book called *Principles of Letter-Writing* and reading out loud: "Write a letter to the head of an office and ask for a job. Write a letter to your uncle and ask him to ... Write a letter to your friend and invite him for the Mab'ath holidays. With fondest regards and compliments ... what joy to receive your latest missive ... with reference to your letter of ... " He put the book down on the table and said, "As Mr Fotouhi says, nothing more than begging and flattery!" then took another and started to flip through its pages.

Though still early in the day, it felt hot and there was no breeze to relieve the heat. Sweat trickled down Zari's spine, and she longed for a cool, refreshing drink like willow-water or betony, or perhaps a piece of crushed ice to crunch between her teeth. She remembered how in each of her pregnancies Ameh Khanom had gone to great lengths to provide her with whatever she craved. From Hassan Agha the grocer she would order Indian magnesia, which was crunchy and white as snow, and reputed to be good for the baby's

124

bone structure. Other days it would be lamb's rumen, which Ameh would buy fresh and clean out herself, cooking it with nutmeg and making Zari take it because it tightened the belly. If a single raisin proved too sweet for Zari, Ameh would ply her with tamarind sherbet, and if one sour grape was too acid, she made hot syrups for her. But ever since Ameh Khanom's decision to follow her mother's footsteps to Karbala, she had become listless and depressed. She had no patience for anyone, not even the children. It was very noticeable, but Zari had decided not to say anything.

Khosrow put down his book. "What rubbish!" he exclaimed. "There's not a word in here about how you should ask for your rights!" He took another book and leafed through it. "I think I've found it . . . " he said, "what good sentences!" He raised his head and asked Yusef who was facing the hill in his armchair, reading a book, "Father, what does this mean? 'His deep-toned voice resembled that of a violoncello.'"

"It means like the mooing of a cow," Yusef answered, without raising his eyes from his book, "it won't do for Sahar. Listen, why don't you just write what comes into your mind?"

Ameh's voice could be heard ordering Mina to put down her coins, which were unclean from being passed around hundreds of hands. Ameh was sitting on a rug with her back to the hill, leaning against the verandah railings, sewing gold dinars into the lining of her coat. This had been her sole activity over the past few days and now she had started on her second coat.

Gholam came out to the verandah. "Khanom, are Kolu's clothes ready?" he inquired.

"They'll be ready in a minute."

"I know it's not my place to say this," Gholam commented, "but why bother to iron them? Last night he only dreamt of cows and sheep. He kept waking up with a start to look for his kid goat. He kept me awake all night with his sighing and moaning. This morning he sobbed for an hour, asking for his mother, his sister, his brother . . . I don't see how he can last here."

Khosrow chuckled as he laboured with his letter, and Marjan tried to build towers with Ameh's gold dinars which Mina would immediately scatter with a fling of her hand. As always, the initiative came from Mina who behaved as if she knew she had a headstart on her sister, having arrived fifteen minutes earlier into the world.

125

"Run along now!" Ameh Khanom shouted at the twins. "Money isn't for playing! Call Kolu and tell him to come here. Gholam, take the girls to the stables."

The twins pretended to cry and crawled under the table.

"Why don't you put on the chadors your aunt made for you and show your father," Zari said.

Mina emerged from under the table. "Auntie, can we have a prayer-stone so we can say our prayers?" Whenever Ameh stood up to say her prayers, they would also put on their chadors and bend or stand in imitation of her. When Ameh pronounced the 'amen' in Arabic, they would quickly put their foreheads to the ground to ask God for what they wanted. God alone knew what these little souls could be asking of Him . . . They would try hard to pronounce the Arabic 'Wala-z'alin' but they couldn't, so they would turn to Ameh and say, "Now you say it."

Zari finished ironing Khosrow's old trousers and shirt which she had let out for Kolu and handed them to Gholam along with some socks, a vest and underpants. "Put anti-flea powder on all of these," she said. "Buy him a pair of givehs too." And she sat down on a chair. She was feeling parched, perhaps from all that ironing in the heat.

"The powder is finished," Gholam told her. "I mixed the whole lot with water in the ewer to splash around the stables. They're infested with lice."

"Send Kolu here," Yusef ordered.

"Let him have his bath first," said Zari.

"Agha, he won't come," Gholam complained. "This morning he was like a wild animal. He wanted to run off into the hills. He kept saying he was going to walk all the way back to his mother."

After Gholam had gone, Ameh Khanom said, "Brother, you can't keep the boy here. He's like that wild fawn we finally had to get rid of . . . still, it's none of my business. I'm only a guest in this house for a few more days."

At heart Zari agreed with her sister-in-law about Kolu. When she had seen him the day before, his eyes had looked to her just like those of the wild fawn—large and outlined, with a shocked expression. Even though he had smiled at his mistress, deep down in his eyes lurked the fearfulness of a trapped animal.

"It really is too soon to take him away from his home," Zari observed. "It's no use being kind to him. We're only making him

126

unhappy, and his relatives angry . . ."

"Once he's lived here comfortably for a few days, he'll feel at home with his new surroundings and he won't even mention his village anymore," Yusef said impatiently. "Next year I'll send him to school."

Khosrow stopped writing and giggled. "Not unless you send him there with his hands and feet tied inside a sack," he said, "he's too wild. And he's too old, anyway; they may not accept him."

"In a sack?" Yusef asked absently, folding his newspaper.

"Yes, father. I saw Davoud Khan's son when they brought him to school from the tribe. They'd brought him straight there. I think I was in the second grade. At break-time we saw this tribal man with a big moustache arriving at school on a mule. He was wearing a felt hat and a slit tunic with a shawl wrapped around his waist. On his saddle was a big canvas sack tied up carefully at the top, with something wriggling inside it. The man got down from his mule and tied the bridle to the same tree I always use when I take Sahar to school. All this time he was holding the sack firmly with his other hand. He was being very careful with it. Then he hoisted the sack and brought it into the schoolyard. When he put it down and opened it, the Khan's son jumped out, wearing nothing but long black trousers! He did a few somersaults—I don't know what for. Then he started to run all around the schoolyard. As if anyone could catch him!"

Zari picked up her ironing and went to the pantry. She checked the cupboards. They'd completely run out of flower essence. In the kitchen she found Khadijeh, frying egg-plants on the stove. She was working stripped to the waist in the furnace-like heat, exposing sagging breasts and hairy armpits, while below the waist she wore her loose, flowery-patterned trousers. On seeing her mistress, Khadijeh grabbed her veil to cover herself.

Zari decided to pay a visit to her neighbours, the distillers. Maybe they could supply her with some essence. She went out the garden gate with her purse and two large pitchers. The neighbours' garden door was open, so she went in without knocking. There wasn't the usual pile of flowers on the paving in the middle of the garden, and the old distiller himself was nowhere in sight.

"Is anyone there?" she shouted.

She approached the house, knowing that the distillery store-rooms were in the basement. She had an uncontrollable urge to fill a

127

china bowl with betony extract, add syrup to it and mix in some crushed ice ... she would stir the ice in her drink with her fingers and with a ladle that had a carved handle ... ah, how refreshing that would be! Even if the distillers weren't there, she could go to the store-rooms, fill her pitchers and leave the money somewhere in sight.

Inside the house, she called out again, "Anybody there?"

Suddenly the head of the old distiller appeared behind one of the basement windows. He peered at her through the ornate stone lattice. Then he came out to greet her, dressed only in his drawers.

"Khanom, why go to the trouble of coming here yourself? You could've sent one of the servants ... " And then he added, "Please come to the store-rooms. Take whatever you want. We were waiting for the last picking of eglantine which hasn't arrived. The flowers will wilt. They say the whole town's been blocked because some horse has taken off with the Governor's daughter. They're not even letting goods deliveries come through."

Zari put the pitchers down.

"I'll be going down to the garden door," said the distiller. "I've sent my sons to fetch the load and I want to see if they're here yet. I just know those flowers are going to wither. This town is turning into bedlam. Why does the girl have to go about riding a horse and getting herself into trouble? How can you make those fools understand that flowers don't have the patience of human beings? Especially eglantine. They have to be picked at dawn and piled inside the store-rooms by early morning. Flowers can't be kept waiting in this blazing sun!"

Zari didn't know whether to be glad or upset. She felt for the child's mother: she was, after all, a mother herself. She knew Sahar was a noble horse and wouldn't throw his rider. But how terrified the girl must be! And how anxious the mother!

She took the pitchers and went to the basement. An intoxicating fragrance permeated the cool air of the cellars. The covers of the stone vats made especially for boiling flowers had been removed and leaned against the walls. The bamboo pipes leading from the vats to the tank were dry and, unlike the last time she had brought the twins to watch, were not dripping with thin streams of fragrant essences. Of the two tanks, one was full and the other half-full with rose-water. Flasks of rose-water were stacked neatly around the store-room. She opened a small door and went to an adjoining cellar. She dipped her pitcher in the first tank there and filled it with betony extract. How she longed to lie down right there on the cool, moist earth of the store-rooms, next to the sweet aroma of those tanks!

On her return home, the first thing she noticed when she went to the verandah was the noise in the distance. The others were seemingly oblivious to it, Khosrow still writing his letter and Yusef leafing through his book, chuckling. The noises, however, seemed to be coming closer, a mixture of the sounds of a crowd and the hum of car engines. Zari glanced towards the hill. Not a soul in sight.

"Where are the twins?" Yusef asked.

No-one answered.

She could see two cars now, one following the other at an angle to the slope. A voice rose, saying, "He's heading for the hill!" Several people started in the same direction.

"There! I've finished my letter," said Khosrow. "Father, will you listen while I read it to you?"

Yusef shut his book, got up from the armchair and looked out. "What on earth is going on over there?" he asked.

Khosrow stood up too and went to the edge of the verandah. "Look how many people there are at the foot of the hill!" he exclaimed. "Four . . . five cars!"

A voice in the distance shouted, "Did you see? Right there!" And another voice commanded, "Don't shoot, you idiot!" Someone screamed. The crowd at the foot of the hill was growing by the minute. A policeman and two gendarmes arrived. Two more cars passed by the slope. The first car was sounding its horn like an emergency siren, and raising a great trail of dust and gravel as it drove forward.

"Is there a war, father?" Khosrow asked. Before Yusef could answer, another voice shouted, "He's going up the hill!" Other voices were lost in the din of the crowd, and the revving of car engines.

"I think it's to do with Sahar," Zari said. "The distiller next door was saying that a horse had taken off with the Governor's daughter."

Yusef clapped a hand to his stomach and laughed heartily. "What a war!" he said, catching his breath. "All this to catch a colt! There he is! Look, it's Sahar all right! He's standing at the summit. She'll be lucky if he doesn't throw her!"

Ameh Khanom, still sitting with her back to the hill, didn't even turn round. She was struggling with a thread and needle. "It's just like threading a needle," she observed. "If you aim the thread exactly at the needle's eye and your vision is good, then you get it right the first time. But if your eyes are like mine, on the blind side, you have to keep wetting the thread in your mouth, and guessing at the eye. The thread goes back and forth so many times until finally, by accident, it goes through the hole. Now Khosrow, your horse has come to you on his own feet by accident too. Go out there and let's see how well you thread your own needle."

Yusef put a hand on his son's shoulder. "Your aunt is right, son," he said. "Go ahead."

Khosrow jumped down from the verandah and ran off. Zari, understanding Ameh's hint, knelt down and threaded her needle for her. "But it can't always be helped, you know," Ameh commented. "In life you're not always allowed to follow the right path, so only after a great many battles and a lot of failures do you finally make up for your mistakes."

"Sister, ever since you've decided to leave for the Holy City, you've become quite a philosopher," Yusef observed.

"Just a wise old owl," Ameh sighed.

At that moment Zari noticed a car struggling noisily up the hill. Sahar, at the summit, neighed and shifted nervously from side to side. The girl grabbed at his golden mane, shrieking above the noise of the crowd. The mare and the chestnut horse neighed in response from the stables.

"I knew the first day they tried to ride him outside the four walls of their estate, he'd head straight back home," Yusef said.

"A credit to that noble beast," said Ameh, still busy with her sewing.

Suddenly a long black limousine drew up. The policeman saluted and the gendarmes presented arms. The driver jumped out to open the door, but the man in the back seat opened it himself and stepped out. Zari recognized the Governor. Then another limousine drew up behind the first. Singer stepped out, followed by two Indian soldiers. He and the Governor shook hands.

The crowd kept parting and re-assembling to allow for the random movement of the cars. The car which had driven up on to the hill backed down noiselessly as if afraid of causing Sahar to shy again.

Zari couldn't see her son as she strained to pick him out in the crowd. This was the time to act, so where was he? By now, the army commander's car had drawn up as well. Out stepped the commander and three more officers, slamming the door loudly. The car moved on, veering closely past the other two limousines. The army commander took in the scene around him. The officers, with swords dangling at their sides, headed straight for the hill. The Indian soldiers saluted and Singer started to do the same, but the army commander prevented him as if to emphasize their warm relations. Then the commander turned and saluted the Governor.

Yusef had meanwhile fetched his binoculars, and he and Zari took turns surveying the scene on the hill. Sahar neighed several times. The girl was clutching at his mane, lying full-length along his neck. Sahar slipped several times on the rocky terrain, veering first to the left and then to the right. The army commander, holding a short, thick baton in his hand, left the Governor and Singer behind, and headed uphill.

"Gilly dear," he shouted at her, "take your feet out of the stirrups, sit sideways and try to jump down."

"I'm scared! I'm scared!" came Gilan Taj's voice.

"What an ass!" murmured Yusef.

Zari couldn't tell whether he meant the army commander or 'Gilly dear'.

Sahar seemed to notice the gendarmes all of a sudden. One of them uncoiled the rope he was carrying and threw the noose at him, in an attempt to lasso the horse and its rider. Sahar backed off, the girl screamed, and both disappeared down the other side of the ridge. The crowd surged towards the hill. The drivers of those cars who had room to manoeuvre, jumped behind their steering wheels, revved their engines and drove away to the other side.

"Get back, you half-wits!" yelled the army commander. "You've frightened the horse. He was standing perfectly calmly . . . "

"If there was an ounce of brain in their heads," Yusef said, "they would all go away and let Sahar bring the girl safe and sound back here."

Suddenly Zari caught sight of Khosrow clambering up the hill. Her stomach began to churn. "Ameh Khanom, pray for him, pray

131

for him!" She turned to Ameh and begged her. Ameh looked towards the hill, and her lips moved in prayer: "God's protection upon him; He is the most merciful of the merciful."

Khosrow had nearly reached the top. He put two fingers in his mouth and let out the long whistle he always used for Sahar. Whenever he heard that sound, no matter where he was in the garden, Sahar would come to Khosrow and sniff at his sleeves. The crowd fell silent. Zari looked at her husband. Yusef's face was radiant with smiles and his green eyes were shining like two stars. Again Khosrow whistled. Sahar's head appeared in sight, looking to left and right.

"Here I am, Sahar!" Khosrow shouted. "Don't be scared," he reassured the girl, "he won't throw you." The crowd was so silent, it was as if there had never been an uproar. Sahar neighed and slowly approached Khosrow. When he reached the boy, he lowered his head, as tamely as a household pet. Zari knew he would be sniffing at Khosrow's sleeves and pockets, taking in the familiar odour. She knew how closely the animal's existence was tied to familiar smells around him. Khosrow hugged Sahar's head, kissed him and patted his mane. Then he held his hand to Sahar's mouth, and Zari knew Khosrow had not forgotten the sugar-lumps.

Khosrow helped the girl dismount. She was wearing riding boots and jodhpurs. As she touched the ground, she collapsed. Khosrow held the bridle as he bent over to tell the girl something. She sat up and screamed. Khosrow stood in front of the girl and was obviously talking to her. Finally he gave her a hand and lifted her up and the three of them descended the hill. Sahar had brought his ears forward, as if to listen to Khosrow's words. Near the foot of the hill, the girl left her companions and threw herself into the arms of her father, who had come forward to meet her. As the boy and his horse reached the crowd, people stood aside to make way for them. Then Khosrow mounted and galloped back home.

13

The mare was ready, saddled and bridled. Yusef was about to mount when Kolu dashed out of the stables and threw himself at his feet, begging to be taken back to the village. He was so altered after a haircut, a bath and some second-hand clothes! Or had he got thinner in the past few days? His dark eyes seemed sunken in his haggard face. Yusef tried to reason with him. "Listen son," he said, "you'll be staying in town, going to school, really be making something of yourself. You can learn a thousand things from Khosrow."

But Kolu was deaf to the master's words, uncomprehending, pleading only to be taken back to his mother and brother. Finally Yusef lost patience and boxed his ears. "I'm not going to your village just now! I'm going to Zarqan." And he mounted. Kolu burst into tears and threw himself into the bushes, kicking and howling like a trapped animal. When Yusef bent over from the saddle to kiss Zari, he noticed tears in her eyes.

"Would you like me to take him back?" he asked.

"No, I expect he'll settle down eventually," Zari answered. "He can't know what's good for him, can he? Just remember, this time you're the one who's being charitable! What's the use of helping this one out and adopting him when there are thousands of other peasant children like him?"

Over Yusef's departing footsteps, Ameh Khanom splashed the customary water and orange blossom leaves from the crystal bowl she was holding, before going off to recite the An'am Surah for his protection and blowing it towards him with a symbolic gesture. What a curious creature a human being is! How easily a ray of hope or a happy event can renew his will to live! But when all around is oppression and despair, a person feels no more than a used-up shell, abandoned by the wayside. Ever since Sahar's return, Ameh had connected her life with the family's again and had stopped repeating that nothing concerned her anymore.

Zari went over to Kolu who had rolled away as far as the middle of the garden path. She knelt beside him and stroked his hair.

"Now look how you've dirtied your new clothes . . ." she scolded him gently.

Kolu sat up and tore his shirt off angrily, screwing it up and throwing it in front of the master's wife.

"Listen," said Zari, "if you're a good boy, I'll ask Khosrow to give you lessons from tomorrow. When you can read and write, I'll send you to your village to see your mother and show her you can read their letters and write letters for her, too."

Kolu had calmed down. Either he was paying attention or he had tired himself out. "But no one writes my mama letters," he said.

"Get up, child," Zari urged, patting his sweaty back. "Go and wash your hands and face. Shake the dust off your clothes and put them back on."

As Kolu didn't budge, she asked, "What do you want me to buy you?"

Kolu burst out crying again and sobbed, "Send me home, mistress! I beg you on your children's lives, send me back to my mother and brother. My brother's sitting right now by the stream playing his flute. My mother's putting oil in the lamp. I'd laid some traps to catch a few goldfinches, and now they must be trapped and there's no one to get them out . . . I put my slingshot on the shelf—my sister Massoumeh will take it and lose it. If I was there now, I'd have pinched a few walnuts and I'd be cracking them and eating them."

"Maybe the goldfinches will chirp a lot and someone will hear them and let them loose. I'll send someone to buy you some walnuts: and you can sit right here and crack them. I'll even get you some elastic and you can make yourself a slingshot."

"You make slingshots with leather cord, not with elastic," Kolu said with an unhappy smile.

"All right then, I'll send out for some leather."

Kolu's lips quivered again. "No-one will go to the goldfinches. The traps are far away from the village."

Zari tried to distract him. "Look," she began, "the master is going to the village. Maybe he'll pass by the place you set your traps. He'll

134

hear the chirping. He'll get down from his horse and take the goldfinches out of the traps and set them free."

"But the master isn't going to our village."

Khadijeh's voice came from the verandah. "Khanom!" she called out. "Telephone!"

Zari stood up. "Who is it?"

"Khanom Ezzat-ud-Dowleh."

What could she be wanting, Zari wondered. Probably the woman wants to say what a huge favour she did us, and that she was the one who sent the horse back! When Zari came to the parlour, she saw Khosrow sitting idly by the window, staring out at the garden.

"For heaven's sake, Khosrow," she said, "go and play a bit with that poor orphan boy . . ."

He didn't move. "Mother, don't even think about my giving Kolu lessons," he said.

Zari went to the telephone. It appeared that the very minute Ezzat-ud-Dowleh had set foot in her own home after their luncheon together, she had come down with a bout of her usual leg pains, confining her to the house. She had heard about her sister's intended pilgrimage, and she longed to see all of them—including the twins—in the near future. They owed her a visit after all. In fact, fresh water was being brought for her private baths the next day, and Ezzat-ud-Dowleh wondered if they would honour her with their company for a bath and luncheon on Wednesday. Zari's many excuses and protests were firmly turned down, and the date was set.

On Tuesday morning, Kolu went down with a fever. Zari darkened the pantry using reed blinds, and set up a bed in there so she could have him close at hand. Kolu would open his eyes wide and hold his fingers in front of them, straining to see. You could tell he was trying to focus, but wasn't able to. Khosrow, Gholam and even Ameh Khanom were of the opinion that he should be sent to hospital. There was little doubt he had typhus, and that put them all at risk. But which hospital would take him? Even the town's best doctors were down with typhus, and rumour had it that Khanom Massihadem and the three head-nurses at the Nemazee Hospital were in a grave condition. Khadijeh had heard from Sakineh, the woman who came to bake bread for them, that Dr Abdullah Khan, the town's most skilled physician, refused to leave Khanom Massihadem's bedside. He would soak two large white towels in ice-cold water, wring them out, and continuously cover the patient's naked body with them. Sakineh, who had gone to visit Khanom Massihadem, had thought that she was already dead and they had spread a shroud on her. Before anyone could stop her, Sakineh was beating her head and searching for mud in the garden to smear over her hair in mourning. When they finally calmed her down and explained everything to her, she had rushed to the shrine of Seyyid Mir Mohammad to light ten candles in thanksgiving.

Nor was Sakineh the only one so concerned with Khanom Massihadem's fate. Large numbers of men and women had covered their heads with the Quran at Mehri's Rowzeh as a mark of urgent prayer for the sick woman, and had recited the Amman Yujib prayer for her deliverance. Akbar Khordel had circumambulated her bed with a sheep which he then slaughtered for her sake and distributed the flesh amongst the poor. The skin he had taken to the well-known mountain dervish, Baba Kouhi, so the old man would pray for her too.

Ameh Khanom made Zari call Khanom Hakim for a hospital bed. But Khanom Hakim merely said, "Unfortunately the beds of the Missionary Hospital be for the foreign officers and soldiers only and all the beds be full and even there be no place in the corridors."

Zari hung up without saying goodbye. "Obviously the hospital was built for their own needs, not for the townspeople," she told Ameh who was waiting to hear what the doctor would say.

They put their heads together and began their nursing. They gave him manna of Hedysarum, and they wrung towels in cold water and wrapped them around him. They plied him with watermelon juice which he accepted eagerly, being parched from the fever. They moistened fleawort, sewed it up in some thin cloth, and kept it immersed in cold water, to be dabbed from time to time on his blistered lips. Ameh Khanom resorted to the traditional rite of placing some item blessed at the Shah Cheraq Shrine next to the patient. In this case, she cut two hand-lengths of braided white cord from the shrine, tied it around Kolu's neck, and sat by his bedside to recite the Hadith-i Kasa prayer. But despite all these measures, it was clear Ameh Khanom's spirits were sinking again.

"Obviously the poor boy's had a fever for several days and we hadn't noticed it, putting it down as we did to homesickness," she

136

had begun to criticize as soon as Zari noticed Kolu's high fever that morning. "Yes, nothing can replace a mother's loving care."

Despite trying all day, they could not even get a doctor to visit Kolu, let alone a hospital bed. The boy was now semi-conscious and delirious. "Goldfinches in the trap ... chirp, chirp. Chirp, chirp. Beak down and feet up ... in the air ... no water ... no seeds ..."

At sunset, Zari pleaded with Khosrow to go with Gholam to Khanom Massihadem's and persuade Dr Abdullah Khan to drop by for a minute to visit their patient. But Khosrow refused. "I want to take Sahar out for a ride, and then go to Mr Fotouhi's with Hormoz," he said. "Father didn't say I couldn't go."

"What a stubborn child!" Zari snapped, losing her temper. "Fotouhi is as crazy as his sister. All he does is to mislead other people's children!" She was about to say that he was a paedophile, but stopped herself in time. Instead, she lodged a silent complaint, "May God forgive you, Yusef! Look what trouble you've landed me in! What'll I do if this poor child dies on my hands?" And she vowed to send Kolu back to the village as soon as he recovered, whether Yusef liked it or not.

Meanwhile, she felt she had no choice but to turn to Abol-Ghassem Khan for help. Gholam had returned without much success from Dr Abdullah Khan who had said he was getting old and hoped the townspeople would allow him to retire. Zari resolved to go back to Khanom Massihadem's herself and beg the doctor to attend to their patient if Abol-Ghassem Khan was unable to help. Surely a doctor couldn't take refuge by one patient's bedside and tell all the others that he's stopped practising, even if that particular patient is very young and has served the townspeople.

Abol-Ghassem Khan was at home. He picked up the telephone himself. "Well, to what do we owe the honour, sister?" He was in a chatty mood and didn't allow Zari to get in a word edgeways. "I hear Sahar came back to Khosrow on his own feet! I wasn't in town that day. I had to escape to the countryside, away from my honourable constituents. Can you believe they actually think I'm about to represent them? They've already started with their petty requests. One of them wants to have a patient hospitalized; another wants to obtain his rights in a court of justice; one fellow wants to have his daughter registered at the Mehrain School for free, and so on. For heaven's sake, this position as deputy cost me all of seventy thousand tomans! Anyway, it seems Sahar's escapade was quite a spectacle. Singer said my nephew charged into the middle of the crowd like a real hero wearing nothing but a pair of givehs and his shirtsleeves. Now sister, why wasn't he dressed in some respectable clothes? Anyhow, Singer was saying that as soon as the horse spotted Khosrow, he came forward like a long-lost lover and started kissing and sniffing at the boy, nuzzling into his arms."

With an effort, Zari forced herself to say, "Abol-Ghassem Khan, I beg you to help me. Kolu has come down with typhus, and I have him on my hands. I can't get a doctor or anyone to come to him. All of them are so busy."

"Which Kolu? Why does this brother of mine bring the village sick into town? And in his own house too! Has he no thought for his delicate children? Didn't he always say that things must be changed at the root and our charities were of no use? I heard him say that to you myself."

"That's right, but this Kolu is our shepherd's son and his father died recently. He didn't have a fever when he first came. He's fallen ill now." Zari knew if she said anything about Yusef adopting Kolu she would receive a one-hour lecture on how another man's son will never behave as one's own.

Finally Abol-Ghassem Khan consented. "For your sake, sister, and for the sake of the children, I'll arrange to have him admitted at the Missionary Hospital."

"I've already called the Missionary Hospital. They didn't have any room."

"They'll have room for me," Abol-Ghassem Khan said grandly.

It was eight o'clock in the evening when Khanom Hakim called. "Why haven't you tell me it be Abol-Ghassem Khan's patient?" she complained at first. Then she added, "There be an empty bed ready in the corridor and this be separated from an Indian sick man by a screen. And the Indian man also be sick with typhus. I be setting aside some pills for the family of Abol-Ghassem Khan which those who contracted . . . contacted the patient must be taking."

At the hospital, tents had been put up in the grounds to house extra beds. A strong smell of phenic acid penetrated the nostrils. Most of the patients were fair-skinned and fair-haired. They could not have been typhus cases because they were either sitting upright in bed with bandages around their heads or their arms in slings, or else lying down with their legs in traction. Four men were sitting around a table playing cards. Their fair hair shone under the light of

138

a lantern which hung from the tent-pole. They did not seem to be ailing or suffering in any way.

Gholam held Kolu all the way in the droshke and carried him to the bed prepared for him at the hospital. From behind the screen, the Indian patient could be heard crying, muttering words Zari couldn't understand. "Seri rama! Seri rama! Krishna!" The crying became louder and he repeated names which Zari guessed must be those of his relatives, "Sandra! Sandra! Kitu!"

When Zari got home, Khosrow was still not back. At first she wanted to call Fotouhi, give him a piece of her mind and vent her anger. But she soon thought better of it. Why blame Fotouhi? These young boys were looking for a way to express their manhood. Fotouhi was merely a vehicle. She decided to wait until her son returned, and then interrogate him. She would be gentle at first, then give him a scolding, and finally raise such hell, he would have something to remember.

But when Khosrow came back, he was at his most charming, pre-empting any efforts at remonstrating or questioning. The minute he arrived, he threw his arms around her and kissed her, saying out of the blue, "Mother, you're not an aristocrat, are you? I mean, your father was a worker from a ... something class ... oh no! I forget what you call that class ... anyway, your father was a worker, right?" The questions tumbled out of his mouth.

"Why do you ask?"

"Well, the comrades were feeling sorry for Comrade Hormoz and me because we're branded as aristocrats, and it takes so long to get rid of that label."

Zari burst out laughing when Khosrow confessed that the comrades were even against well-ironed trousers, so he and Hormoz had decided to smear their trousers with dirt and rumple them up before going to the meetings. As for ties, well, they were completely out. Then he admitted to having cut a hole in his new grey trousers and fraying the threads around the hole to make the trousers look old and worn. He told her he had boasted to the comrades about his maternal grandfather who had been very, very poor. "Mother," he said, "I told them my mother's mother had nothing but dry bread to eat in the morning, which is why she had a broken front tooth. I told them my mother now takes bread to prisoners and mental patients every week in memory of the dry bread that broke her front tooth ... "

139

"You've learnt to lie, too," Zari interrupted.

"The comrades really liked it. Now tell me about the day you stood up to your English headmistress. You had quarrelled, I mean struggled, with her many times. You said so yourself the other night. Those struggles are very important to me."

Zari felt depressed. What struggles!

She remembered the day when a group of Englishmen, newly arrived from London, were due to visit the school on a tour of inspection. Classes had been suspended in the morning so that Nazar Ali Beg, the Indian janitor, could sweep out the classrooms. The headmistress had sent the girls home and told them to come back in the afternoon looking absolutely spick and span, insisting that they all wear a spotless white shirt under their uniforms. Zari's father had recently died, and she owned just the one black shirt which she wore in mourning under her black-and-white check school tunic. All the girls who went into mourning did the same: it wasn't against the rules. But how on earth was Zari to produce a white shirt in the two or three hours she had, and with no money?

Her mother was ill in bed, complaining of sharp pains in her breast and little lumps the size of lentils in her armpit which she wouldn't let Zari touch in case they were contagious. Zari couldn't let her mother pawn the silver mouth-piece on her hookah, nor the family silver plate, at Deror's the Armenian silversmith. She couldn't sell them either, to buy white material for Zari. Besides, even if it were possible, how could the blouse be made up in time? Those were very hard times, the first few months after father's death, as her mother used to say. They weren't getting a pension then. Later on, the head of the Shoa'ieh School gave them the idea of writing a petition. He had called Zari's brother into his office and quietly made him understand that his family could apply for a pension, giving suggestions on how to write the letter and to whom it should be addressed. When Zari's brother had come home and related the incident, their mother had prostrated herself and kissed the ground in thanksgiving.

On the day of the inspection, Zari decided to take a risk. She washed and ironed her blouse and went to school. They wouldn't kill her for it, after all, she decided. But when the headmistress spotted her, she was so upset, she nearly hit her. "You ugly little runt!" she shouted. "You've become quite disobedient, haven't you?" Of all her compatriots, this one had learned Persian well.

140

"I'm in mourning," Zari replied. "My father died less than a month ago."

"And you answer back, too! When did your father ever believe in such superstitions?" Then she calmed down and said, "Too bad your English is so much better than all the other students and I need you to welcome the guests in English, otherwise I would expel you. Perhaps I was wrong to exempt you from paying tuition fees."

Now it was all out. Until that day none of Zari's classmates had known she didn't pay fees. How could she ever hold up her head again?

Somehow within fifteen minutes, the headmistress had found a white blouse Zari's size which she handed to her and ordered her to wear.

But Zari decided to be stubborn. "I'm in mourning," she insisted, "my father has just died."

The headmistress got down to it herself. In front of all the other girls, she carefully removed Zari's uniform, then yanked off the black shirt, ripping a sleeve in the process. The white blouse she put on again with care.

Singer arrived before the others and assembled all the girls about him in the garden where they were scattered. Most of them knew him since they had bought sewing machines from him. He looked them over critically, saying, "Like so. They enter the hall, you pretty girls bow. These people pay money for school from own pocket. For the sake of Jesus they give large school." Then he called Zari over. "Zari, you say welcome. Lady stretch hand to you. You kiss hand!"

The assistant headmistress rang the bell and all the girls lined up and filed into the assembly hall of the school to wait for the guests. Singer walked in after a while followed by an assortment of ageing ladies and gentlemen, some stooped over, others stiff as a rod, some of average height, others short. Zari counted sixteen of them. Singer was being particularly respectful to one of the old women who was sporting a large hat with what looked like two sparrows buried in it. One was perched with open wings, ready for flight, the other's head merely peeped out.

Zari stepped forward and spoke her welcome. The headmistress had a smile on her thin lips. Singer's eyes were fixed on the old woman with the sparrow's nest. When the woman stretched out her hand, Zari shook it. Singer frowned, but it was too late.

141

Then Zari joined the other girls in singing the hymn "Christ in Heaven", ending with a resounding "Hallelujah!" Their Indian teacher opened the Bible, tossed her braid over her shoulder, and began to read St Paul's letter to the Corinthians: "Though I speak with the tongues of men and of angels . . . " But when it was Zari's turn to recite a poem, she involuntarily launched into Milton's "Samson Agonistes" instead of Kipling's "If":

"O dark, dark, dark, amid the blaze of noon . . . "

When they were filing out of the hall, the headmistress squeezed Zari's arm hard, whispering, "You little wretch!" This one knew Persian well. She even knew expressions Zari and her friends had never heard of.

14

Kolu's illness and the confusion that went with it, caused Zari to forget all about Ezzat-ud-Dowleh's lunch invitation. But Ezzat-ud-Dowleh herself had not forgotten. That distinguished lady had probably gone to great lengths to make preparations, because she rang bright and early on Wednesday morning to double check, reminding them of the invitation. Now it was Ameh's turn to grumble.

"Why don't you all go, sister. I, for one, am not going. I went to the baths only the day before yesterday. And sister, you didn't say a word to stop me. Besides, I'm not in the mood for Ezzat-ud-Dowleh's fuss and ceremony. She spreads a feast from one end of the room to the other, but her crossed eyes follow your every mouthful. She watches the sugar-bowl to count the sugar-lumps you take! And probably sees double, too."

Zari had never felt so tired in all her life as she had over the past few days. "Ameh Khanom, the lunch is in your honour," she said. "In any case, Ezzat-ud-Dowleh is your friend." She nearly added, "She is your sister-by-oath and your crony," but decided against it. Instead, she said, "You know, lately you've been cutting yourself off from us, and I was thinking perhaps it's because you're preparing to leave us altogether."

"You're quite right. When I leave here on my pilgrimage, I don't want to feel your absence all the time. Besides, I don't want these poor children to keep asking for me as soon as I go away."

But finally Ameh Khanom consented. They took a droshke through the avenues, but walked the narrow back-streets. Khadijeh carried one twin while Zari gave a hand with the other, who was walking, helping her over the rock-strewn alleys. They passed the narrow Qahr-o-Ashti street, and on the right-hand side, just before

143

Sardazak, they stopped in front of the enormous gates of Ezzat-ud-Dowleh's house. Khadijeh was out of breath. Ameh Khanom read the Quranic inscription on the mosaic over the gate: "Lo! We have brought unto ye a great and glorious victory." She glanced at the house opposite Ezzat-ud-Dowleh's, the house in which she had grown up. "What a ruin it's become!" she commented.

The gates of Ezzat-ud-Dowleh's house were open. As they passed through the large, shady octagonal porch, the doorman was sitting idly on his wooden bench. He jumped to attention, as if roused from a dream. Taking off his felt hat, he greeted them and invited them in. At the entrance to the outer courtyard, an old black maidservant held out a crystal bowl. She removed the lid of the bowl and invited them to help themselves. The two women each took a jasmine-flavoured almond sweet. The black maid bent down to serve the twins, and then came round to Khadijeh. At the entrance of the inner courtyard, which was an orangery, Ezzat-ud-Dowleh's personal maid Ferdows, wearing a blue silk chador, offered them a platter of fragrant melon. She served them as the black maid had done. Zari placed the cool melon against her face, inhaling its mild scent as if every refreshing aroma in the world was to be found right there.

In the large, cool basement, the fountains of the indoor marble pools had been turned on. Ezzat-ud-Dowleh was dominating the room from her position at one end where she was sitting on a folded blanket. She apologized for not rising to greet them, explaining that her chronic rheumatism plagued her even in the middle of summer. She then welcomed them profusely.

Ferdows re-appeared carrying a square bundle of cashmere brocade which she placed before Ameh Khanom. Then Ferdows helped her take off her black outdoor chador which she carefully folded while Ameh Khanom unwrapped the bundle and examined the pile of different chadors, choosing a plain navy one. Ferdows opened it up and draped it on her. Then she wrapped up the bundle of chadors again, including Ameh's black one, inside the cashmere brocade and took them away.

After this, they were brought fresh lime juice in a decorative china bowl with a matching ladle. The bowl was placed carefully before Ezzat-ud-Dowleh. On a silver tray, the old black maid brought some finely-cut crystal glasses and Ezzat-ud-Dowleh served the lime juice with deliberation and ceremony. Turning to

144

Ameh she said, "You're so fortunate, Qods-ol-Saltaneh. If I didn't have this rheumatism, I would have dearly liked to become a pilgrim to such an imam ..."

Zari had long forgotten Ameh Khanom's title.

"First of all, tell them to turn off those fountains," Ameh said. "The damp does your leg pains no good." Ezzat-ud-Dowleh ignored this. Zari concluded that the leg pains were merely pretence and wished that she would get to the point, in other words, the reason for all the hospitality. In an effort to make conversation, Zari once again complimented Ezzat-ud-Dowleh on the colour of her hair. Ezzat-ud-Dowleh smiled and passed a hand over her garish hair.

"Acquaintances," she said, "even the Governor's wife, kill themselves to get me to reveal the ingredients of this hair-dye. But I've refused to tell anyone so far. Everyone who sees me says, 'What beautiful hair!' And I say, 'Beauty is in the eye of the beholder.' But Zari dear, I'll tell it to you. You're like my own daughter. Your mother, God rest her soul, and I were like one soul in two bodies. I so wanted you to become my daughter-in-law. My poor Hamid singled you out from amongst all those girls. Well, it was not to be. That is, you played hard to get. But your own chestnut shade is also very pretty. It hasn't turned grey yet, so it's a shame to dye it. When you dye hair, it starts to go grey before you know it."

"God bless you for your kindness," replied Zari, and to herself, "Thank God I didn't marry your lecherous son!"

"I'm going to tell it to you, but you must swear never to divulge it ..." confided Ezzat-ud-Dowleh, staring cross-eyed at her guests, "it's been a family secret. Henna, coffee and cocoa, that's what it is! I added the cocoa myself. It softens the hair. Take one soup-spoonful of henna, cocoa and coffee at a time, add some chamomile and rub all over the hair. Then cover this with fresh walnut leaves and wrap your hair overnight or from morning till afternoon ..."

Zari had no interest in hair-colour secrets. If her poor mother had been alive, it might have meant something. Her mother had vowed, if she ever recovered from her illness, to take a set of silver dishes as a gift to the shrine of Hazrate Abbas and then come back and dye her hair just like Ezzat-ud-Dowleh. She used to say that she would get the secret ingredients out of Ezzat-ud-Dowleh by whatever means. But her mother was away from all this now. She began to pray that Ezzat-ud-Dowleh's breathtaking generosity was not building up to some impossible favour in return.

When they went to the changing rooms outside the bath, the black maid was squatting there next to a His Master's Voice gramophone with a conical horn which she switched on the moment they walked in. "You left me and broke your pledge . . . " The lower half of the changing-room walls was made of marble, while the upper half and the ceiling were covered with frescoes. Zari had seen this very hammam and the Zurkhaneh behind it, on that school trip when the teacher had brought all the girls of marriageable age to Ezzat-ud-Dowleh's place on the pretext of visiting a historic old house. The building was one of the town's landmarks, nevertheless, and no important foreign visitor left Shiraz without seeing it.

It was easy to understand why Hamid Khan himself had taken on the role of tour-guide to the school visitors. The large reception room with sash windows did not have electric lights yet, and Hamid Khan had tried to show the girls the paintings on the ceiling with the aid of a kerosene lamp which he held high above his head. The reception room ceiling was lined from one end to the other with portraits of men and women next to each other. The women were depicted with tiny, pea-sized mouths, doe-like eyes, and long, wavy locks. The men were identical to the women, only they had forelocks and no earrings.

That day Zari had not really noticed Hamid Khan's ogling. But the following week, when Ezzat-ud-Dowleh intruded into their private cubicle at the hammam, squinting curiously at her naked body, Zari suddenly realized what was going on. The woman's stare sent shivers down Zari's spine. It was as if something was being stripped away from her. How impudently Ezzat-ud-Dowleh had tilted Zari's chin upward to catch the sunlight in the cubicle, muttering to herself, "God protect her, never seen such a fair and delicate body! Just like fine porcelain! Eyes the colour of mahogany . . . never seen eyes this colour. God created you for His own heart. By all that's perfect! God knows if we weren't in a bath I would've thought it was make-up or something . . . "

Zari had wanted to shove the woman's hand away from her chin. But after two hours of Etiquette and one hour of Conduct every day at school, how could she possibly do such a thing? Of course they always ended up reading the Bible instead of Conduct, but Etiquette was about manners . . . and Ezzat-ud-Dowleh was not going to give

146

up. "Pearly teeth, such a beautiful neck you'd think it's carved out of marble, what eyelids . . . "

The twins brought her back to the present with their refusal to undress and their fascination with the paintings on the ceiling, especially one of a man on horseback staring at a naked girl combing her long hair. Zari remembered that on the day of the school-trip, Hamid Khan had purposely kept the girls for a long time in the changing-rooms to explain in detail about this very picture which was a scene from the famous Khosrow and Shirin love-story. The naked woman had huge breasts and was sitting next to a stream, combing her long, black hair. Some kind of screen separated the woman from the rider, who sported a thick moustache and a royal hat, and although the screen should have hidden the man's anatomy too, every detail of his body and that of his horse was visible. And the woman had nothing covering her genitals, either.

Zari promised the twins that if they let Khadijeh undress them, she would send them in the afternoon to see the Zurkhaneh next door which had pictures of the ancient warrior Rostam with his parted beard and tiger-skin garment, torn off the body of the monster, Akvan. They could also see Akvan being slaughtered and skinned.

In the bath, Ameh Khanom did an ablution, rinsed her body quickly and left. She couldn't bear the noise of the scratchy records. But Zari tried to linger as long as she could. She sat on the lowest step of the warm-water pool and let the luke-warm water engulf her body. Soon every part of her was feeling limp and relaxed. She closed her eyes and leaned her head against the edge of the pool. When she got out, she sat on a shiny white tray, and wrapped a large white embroidered cloth around her body. The black maid came in at that moment. She was stark naked, and brought in the water-melon on a tray which she set down on top of one of the empty copper bowls. The water-melon had been neatly cut with a zig-zag pattern along the edge. The twins gaped at the sight of the negress. Marjan was about to cry out in fear, but was stopped by Mina's loud question, "But mother, this one has a skin! Didn't you say they've skinned her and that bearded man is wearing the skin?"

Zari laughed, and the black maid said, "God bless you, my sweet child! I'll go burn some incense to protect you against the evil eye."

Nana Seyyid, the best bath-masseuse in town, came in holding a

147

shiny pitcher with prayers engraved all round the rim. She was taken aback to see Zari, but she greeted her politely. She was naked except for a red loincloth tied between her legs and held up at the waist with a thin red band. On that day too, this same Nana Seyyid had been in their cubicle at the Shapuri Hammam. She had come to wash Ezzat-ud-Dowleh but was ordered to wash Zari first. Chatting away pleasantly, Nana Seyyid had first washed Zari's right arm, but had given the left one such a harsh rub that Zari was forced to say, "Gently!"

Nana Seyyid had quickly taken offence. Removing her bath-glove, she had placed it in front of Zari and said, "Do it yourself, if you know how." And how pleased Zari had been about that! They didn't have any money to hire or tip a bath-masseuse, anyway.

Now Nana Seyyid went over to the warm-water pool with the pitcher which she filled and then emptied over Zari's shoulders. She sat on the floor in front of Zari, pulling forward the raised tray containing the bath-glove and other items for the bath. She took a pinch of salt from a small copper bowl and rubbed it on Zari's heels. Then she began to gently massage the heels with a delicately fashioned pumice-stone which had a silver cap. It tickled, but Zari didn't make a sound. Again, the black maid came in and circled around each one of them—even Khadijeh and Nana Seyyid—with a fistful of incense. Shortly after she left, the smell of burning incense from the changing rooms filled the bath.

Zari sat on the outside step of the warm-water pool while Nana Seyyid massaged her scalp with a shampoo mixture of mud and rose petals. It occurred to her that it was a pity to stain the shiny whiteness of the marble floor with mud from the shampoo. But she surrendered herself to the gentle kneading of the masseuse, thinking of all those wonderful fragrances still lingering in her senses: melon, jasmine, lime, incense, rose-petal . . . and she wished this euphoria could go on for a long time.

15

But Ezzat-ud-Dowleh did not get to the point till late that afternoon. Even then she built up to it with much preamble, explanations and beating about the bush. It was early evening and her guests were sitting around cross-legged on a large, twelve-segment wooden takht placed over the pool for cool air. The takht was covered with layers of carpets over which soft, striped sheets had been spread. Carpet-covered cushions had been arranged against the tall latticed railings of the takht. Ezzat-ud-Dowleh had taken up her usual place at the head of the takht, fanning herself. Ameh Khanom and Zari were seated on either side of her, but were not using fans.

The air had cooled. The blossoms of jasmine bushes, in large flower-pots around the pool, seemed to twinkle like so many stars at the reluctant sun, unwilling to set over the orangery. Ezzat-ud-Dowleh had managed to send Mina and Marjan off with Khadijeh, Ferdows and her children, to the police-chief's garden to watch the Pahlavan Kachalak puppet show.

Zari didn't even quite realize how the conversation turned to her charities at the prison and the asylum. She found herself explaining about the women's prison. "It's not too crowded there," she said. "They're not too restricted, either, because the crimes are generally not more serious then stealing a ewer. Yes, I'm allowed to sit privately with the prisoners on the little rugs their relatives bring them and listen to their complaints. But I don't see the men. I just take their food to the Karim Khani citadel, and deliver it at the warden's office. What happens to it after that, is a matter between God and the warden! But there's a belief among prison wardens that whoever steals from rations will be stricken with leprosy." She added, "One day I insisted on taking the food to the male prisoners

149

myself. That day they were cleaning out the Dosagkhaneh latrines which are in the hallway. The stench makes you want to die."

Then the conversation turned to the madam of a 'hospice' who had recently been imprisoned.

"I wanted this woman imprisoned myself," Zari said, "but I wasn't the one who reported her. It was the regional officer who'd accompanied us. Mahin Khanom and I had been on an inspection tour of the houses in the Mordestan District, on behalf of the Women's Society. No matter how long we knocked at this woman's house, no one would answer. The regional officer started kicking the door. Finally the madam herself let us in. It was getting dark. We inspected all the rooms. Mahin had them open up some of the beds and she ordered fresh pillow cases and sheets for the mattresses. In the end, when we had gone to the madam's room to give her a supply of anti-flea powder and disinfectant, I saw something wriggling under the sewing-machine stand in the corner of the room. First I thought it was a cat. Only a black little head was visible. I reached out and switched on the light, motioning for the regional officer to take a look. Sure enough he pulled out a seven- or eight-year-old girl from underneath the sewing-machine table. The little girl was wearing a glittery, wrinkled dress, and her breasts hadn't yet fully developed. She was shivering like a sparrow in snow. Despite my quiet nature, I lost my temper. I shouted at the madam and asked whether she wasn't ashamed to use children of this age for work like that. At first she swore frantically that the girl was her niece who was staying with her for the night, but then she broke down and confessed. 'Well, what can I do, Khanom?' she said. 'There are too many customers. One Indian sergeant major has been waiting some time for a young girl. You can't let the customers down. We're constantly being ordered from above to keep our customers satisfied, and now you're here criticizing us? What brings you here, anyway? Isn't it to clean up the place to ensure the satisfaction of the foreign customers? After all, I've been in this business for many a year and no one has ever come to inspect us for anything else.'"

Zari stopped talking. But when she sensed her hearers' eagerness to know more, she went on.

"Later it transpired that the madam had had ten or twelve of these children working for her and that day she had sent them off to escape over the roof—all except the little one who hadn't been able to get away in time. But what bracelets the madam herself was wearing! She had on at least ten pairs of gold bracelets."

"Shameless woman!" exclaimed Ezzat-ud-Dowleh. "May she pay hereafter for what she did to those innocent children!" Then she added, "They've got our maid Nana Ferdows in prison too. I expect you'll see her tomorrow when you go there."

"On what charge?" Ameh asked.

Zari suddenly understood. She realized the favour needed of her somehow related to the women's prison and Nana Ferdows. She waited. But Ezzat-ud-Dowleh was taking her time.

"What I suffer because of this child of mine! My husband—may he never rest in peace—had no idea how to raise a child. He didn't even let Hamid do his compulsory military service. He faked the medical certificate by slipping pebbles in the boy's urine sample and bribing the doctor to diagnose a kidney stone condition. If they'd taken him for military service, maybe it would have done him some good. May he never rest in peace, my husband! He would go whoring with a fifteen-year-old boy, and my poor Hamid caught gonorrhoea at sixteen. His wife isn't capable of making a man out of him now. How I wished he'd married Zari! It was not to be, I suppose. Like father, like son. May he turn in his grave, my husband, may he never rest in peace!"

"But I heard Hamid has given up his extravagant habits and settled down," said Ameh Khanom.

"Settled down? With all the money he throws away and that shrew of a wife? I kept insisting that he should do up this big house and come to live here, but he wouldn't listen. Or rather, his wife wouldn't think of it. The woman kept repeating that she would get depressed living in these back alleys and nothing would do but that she had to live on a main street."

Ezzat-ud-Dowleh fell silent for a while and fanned herself.

Then she went on. "There's an old saying that only children turn out either mad or crazy. When my boy was five, all he did was to fly kites with coloured paper-lanterns. At seven or eight, he became obsessed with pigeons. When a person is born under an unlucky star . . . even now as a grown man all he does is play with pigeons. He's made three hundred nests on his roof-top for them. Every evening he flies his pigeons, and he claims that when the birds fly up and away, his heart flutters to the rhythm of their wings, and only comes to rest with them when they've returned."

151

Ameh sighed. "He was playmates with my poor son," she said. "When my child died, I couldn't bear to see your Hamid. But now, time has taken care of all that. I miss Hamid."

"He'll come to see you in a little while. I told him his aunt would be here and he said he'd come early this evening to pay his respects. He misses you very much too ..."

The black maid appeared just then, carrying a tray of afternoon refreshments which she placed in the middle of the takht. There were all sorts of seasonal fruits as well as a variety of imported biscuits. She also brought in a brazierful of hot coals standing in an ornate copper tray. This she put in front of Ameh for her opium-smoking. She made tea in a red china teapot with floral designs which matched the china bowl of the opium pipe. The flowers on the design were white poppies. The tongs and the pipe-rod gleamed like gold.

Ezzat-ud-Dowleh went on. "How I've suffered because of that child! You probably know that he sends foreign officers and soldiers here on the pretext of seeing antiques. In reality they sell us whatever extra bits and pieces they may have like biscuits, soap, shoes, stockings, silk, and so forth. I sell the goods in turn through Nana Ferdows ..."

Ameh interrupted her harshly, "Come now, Ezzat, do you think no-one knows? It's hardly a secret that you, a distinguished lady as you say, have turned into a smuggler! I didn't want to mention it today, but at our house I tried to give you some hints. You kept evading the issue and I didn't insist. Your son's driver told the story of your Jahrom haul in front of everyone at the Do-Mil teahouse. He said you and Nana Ferdows looked as if you'd put on quite a bit of weight overnight! He said you spent two whole hours wrapping up your body in silk to hide the smuggled arms. Apparently you also packed two big canvas sacks full of goods in the boot of a car which could have cost you a twenty thousand toman fine. Why have you become so greedy? A little bit of self-respect and dignity go a long way, you know."

Ezzat-ud-Dowleh controlled herself. Only the corner of her mouth twitched as she said, "That driver was probably the one who betrayed us. I kept telling Hamid not to dismiss him in this god-forsaken summer with all the sickness and famine around. But he wouldn't listen. What I go through because of that boy! But then you know, as I'm sitting here by myself of an evening, he comes along with a special rice dish, or a plateful of best quality apricots or some large tangerines . . . he'll say, 'Mother, I was thinking of you.' Then he'll kiss my hand, my foot, lay his head on my bosom and with all this pampering, I know that the next day he'll get anything he wants out of me."

Ameh Khanom opened the small jewel-studded case before her, took a piece of opium, and smelled it. "What good quality!" she said. She warmed the opium and stuck it to the pipe-bowl.

"Forgive me for being so bold," Zari said, "but you have a great deal of assets and property."

"May he never rest in peace that husband of mine!" Ezzat-ud-Dowleh exclaimed. "What assets and property? He would steal the title-deeds of my land, cover his sister with a chador and take her to Sheikh Gheib Ali the notary and introduce her as his wife. He would sell my land, and have his sister—well-hidden under her chador—thumb-print the foot of the sale transaction as signature. All the money was spent on his women . . . and on that bedroom! His private room where he took the prostitutes, with that double-bed he brought over from India. He bought every pack of old playing cards to be found in this town so he could paste all the aces, queens and jokers on one wall of that room. He hired a painter to illustrate another wall with every imaginable kind of love-making position. Whatever money was left over, at the end when he was confined to the house, he smoked away in opium."

Ameh Khanom took a puff and said, "He left enough for your family to live on respectably for several generations. But if you're hinting at my addiction, too, let me just say I don't smoke away anyone else's money . . . it's my own. Besides, I've vowed to give it up the instant I set foot in the shrine of Imam Hossein. Right then and there, I'll break my opium-pipe in two. O Lord, please give me the strength to do it!"

"Sister, why have you become small-minded?" Ezzat-ud-Dowleh asked. "And why so touchy? I swear by my only son that I meant no offence to you. As for giving up opium, I'm certain that you'll be able to do it. You're one of those people who can do whatever they want."

Ameh Khanom took a long puff. "What good opium! Where do you get it? It brings the scent of the poppy-fields right to my nostrils! How often I used to ride around those fields! Field after field of poppies, and each one a different shade . . . the scent of it at sunset intoxicated both me and my horse. When the flower-petals have fallen, the yellowish, moss-green seed-heads nod in the breeze as if to talk to you, and you're certain they're alive. They have something no other flower in the world has. At sunrise, they come to cut them. The dew is still sparkling on the seed-heads, and drop by drop the pretty sap oozes out."

"Since you like it so much, I'll tell them to prepare some more pieces from the same batch for you to take with you on your trip. You can think of me when you use it."

"Curse the devil! Even if it kills me I'm going to give it up. The beauty of the poppy-fields is quite a different thing from its poison."

Zari was beginning to feel anxious. She had planned to visit Kolu in hospital earlier in the evening, but it was too late now. She was worried about Khosrow, who had gone to join Hormoz so the two of them could go to Fotouhi's together in the evening. Khosrow had inadvertently mentioned the night before that although they might not be accepting him at any party branch because he was under-age, Mr Fotouhi had generously allowed him to join Hormoz and his friends as an 'independent observer'. This was the same group whose members pitied those with aristocratic blood.

Zari turned to Ezzat-ud-Dowleh and said, "I'm beginning to understand now. Nana Ferdows was caught red-handed smuggling."

Ezzat-ud-Dowleh sighed. "I wish it were that simple," she said. "This time she was actually smuggling arms."

"By Allah, the Almighty!" exclaimed Ameh, putting her pipe down next to the brazier.

"Yes. Two Brno guns, ten revolvers and a box of ammunition. God knows we were very careful, very cautious. Four times previously Nana Ferdows had delivered the same load safely to its destination. But this time she was caught. I'm certain it was the driver who gave us away and was probably paid well for it too. A curse upon him! Nana Ferdows was supposed to take the load at sunrise before the women's public baths opened, to the Khani Hammam and deliver them to the Mirza Agha Hennasab."

"Which Mirza Agha? The son of your own wet-nurse?" Zari asked.

"Oh no. No-one knows where my wet-nurse's son is. They say he's joined the Communists . . ."

154

"I see. Go on."

"Yes, she was supposed to deliver the load to the Mirza Agha Hennasab and tell him, 'Mirza Agha, these are Khanom's bath things. I'm leaving them in your care. When it's the women's hour at the baths, give them to the bath-keeper's wife.' And Mirza was supposed to call out casually to one of the errand boys and ask him to take the bundle to the back of the hammam for safe-keeping. I'd wrapped up the 'bath things' myself in the dead of night. Even Nana Ferdows didn't know what was in it. I packed the guns end to end and wrapped them tightly inside a small rug. And even though my fingers were pricked till they bled, I pinned both ends of the rug so the guns wouldn't slip out and the fringes of the rug would cover up any parts that were showing. I placed the rolled-up rug on the porter's tray myself and put the large copper bowl which had the box of bullets hidden inside, next to it. The revolvers I rolled up in bath towels and carefully wrapped that in a cashmere brocade. These I put inside the large copper bowl as well, with part of the brocade cloth showing. I even sat down and prayed for the safe delivery of the load."

"What things you pray to God for!" muttered Ameh Khanom.

Ignoring her, Ezzat-ud-Dowleh continued. "At dawn with the help of Kal Abbas, Ferdows's husband, we managed to lift the tray and put it on Nana Ferdows's head. It was very heavy, but she didn't have that far to go. Again I prayed and blessed the load and Nana Ferdows. I made her leave through the door of the inner courtyard. Kal Abbas had checked the street to see if the coast was clear."

"How did you find out she'd been caught?" Ameh asked.

"I was saying my morning prayers when there was a knock. My heart sank. Apparently, just before reaching the public baths, Nana Ferdows had come across a policeman and a gendarme. I imagine they must have stopped her and searched her load. They asked her who it belonged to and where she'd got it. Kal Abbas says when she came home and he opened the door to her, it was obvious she'd been beaten up and had been crying. Anyhow, she had spilled the beans, and brought them to my doorstep. But see how clever and loyal Kal Abbas is. At the door, the policeman asked him whether he knew Nana Ferdows. Kal Abbas replied, 'No sir, I do not.' Nana Ferdows instantly burst out crying, saying, 'I spit on you! My own son-in-law! You don't know me? Has the world come to an end?

155

Have you lost your eyesight that you don't know me?' And Kal Abbas said, 'Listen you shrew, why make up such lies at this time of day? How should I know you?' "

"What a mess you've got yourself into!" Ameh said, between puffs.

"Well, by this time I was glued to the door of the outer courtyard, eavesdropping and trembling from head to toe. No-one should ever live through such a thing! Nana Ferdows was wailing and screaming, swearing by the Quran that the goods had been brought from our house. 'I had no idea there were guns and things like that in it,' she was saying. 'And this bastard here is Kal Abbas, my son-in-law, who's siding with them and won't help me out, his own mother-in-law! I shut up once when they dishonoured my daughter, but now they want to dishonour me too! I spit on you, Kal Abbas! You're a traitor, you help them. You helped them the other time too ...' She sobbed her heart out, and cursed with such bitterness that my hair was standing on end. She kept saying, 'O Lord, where are You? Are You blind?' "

Ezzat-ud-Dowleh fell silent for a while, fanning herself. Ameh Khanom and Zari kept quiet the whole time. Zari was biting her thumbnail. She thought silently, "And now what is it I can do for you?"

Ezzat-ud-Dowleh went on. Obviously she was not going to get to the point until she had recounted all the details.

"Either the gendarme or the policeman shouted at Nana Ferdows to stop blaspheming, and ordered Kal Abbas to wake the master of the house so he could be questioned. Kal Abbas told them the master had died a long time ago, at which point the policeman asked to see the mistress. By this time I was feeling so faint I had to sit on the ground. Kal Abbas said, 'The mistress is away on a pilgrimage to the shrine of Imam Reza.' The policeman shouted at Nana Ferdows, 'Didn't you say these were Khanom's belongings that you were taking to the Khani Hammam?' Kal Abbas didn't let Nana Ferdows answer. He laughed and said, 'Sir, we have a private bath in this house. The mistress never uses the public baths. I can show it to you if you like.' Then he said, 'Please go and have your fight elsewhere. I have a thousand things to do.' When the policeman started to hustle her away, Nana Ferdows pleaded with them, 'Where are you taking me?' The policeman said to her, 'First to the lieutenant, who's going to lock you up.' The foolish woman kept

156

screaming, 'Let me see my child first, and I'll go wherever you want.' But they took her away. It was a stroke of luck that Ferdows and her children were sleeping far away from the entrance and didn't hear all the noise. As for me, well! No one should ever have to live through such a thing! I was shivering as if I'd been struck down with a fever. I couldn't breathe. I sent Kal Abbas at top speed to the Mirza Agha Hennasab to inform him."

Then turning to Zari, she said, "But Zari, my dear, you hold the solution to my problem. We've made the necessary investigations indirectly. We know that Nana Ferdows is in the women's ward. Now I beg of you, when you visit the prison tomorrow, go and see Nana Ferdows. Talk to her. Beg her on my behalf not to mention our name under any circumstances. You see, Kal Abbas managed to nudge her foot at the last moment and make her understand that she must keep her mouth shut. It seems she's either caught on or simply tired out, because she's stopped talking for the time being. My dear Zari, please tell Nana Ferdows to say at her trial that the mistress was on a pilgrimage; that Kal Abbas had bought the goods from a few Indians, wrapped them up in the mistress's bath things and given them to her to sell at the bazaar, and that the Mirza Agha Hennasab had offered to buy the goods. If she doesn't stick to this story, my whole family will be ruined. So will our long-standing reputation. We'll be utterly undone."

"Is it all right for Kal Abbas's family to be ruined, then?" asked Ameh Khanom cynically. "Why implicate that poor Mirza Agha Hennasab? I don't want to criticize you, but ... well, anyway, it's none of my business."

"Qods-ol-Saltaneh, this is no time to talk Zari out of helping me," Ezzat-ud-Dowleh pleaded with her. "Doesn't our sisterhood mean anything to you? I swear I'll repent and give this up. Besides, neither Kal Abbas nor Mirza Agha's family will suffer. We've notified Mirza Agha in good time and he's escaped to the tribe. And I've persuaded Kal Abbas to cooperate. Tell her I've persuaded her son-in-law to cooperate. We've made enquiries and found out that if an ordinary citizen smuggles arms just for money and nothing else, the sentence is no more than a year or two in prison. They confiscate the arms and levy a fine twice their value. That's nothing to worry about; I'll take care of all the fines. I'll give Kal Abbas five thousand tomans reward when he gets out of prison. And I've promised to take good care of his wife and children in his absence.

157

Tell her to ask for Mr Sharifabadi as her lawyer. I'll contact the judge and the public prosecutor for her. And I promise that this time I really will keep my word and send her on a pilgrimage to Karbala."

She reached under the cotton sheet and pulled out two envelopes and a small box which she handed to Zari. She shouted to the maid, "Bazm Ara, put the lights on!" The tall garden lights which looked just like carriage-lights were immediately switched on.

"Give her these two envelopes, my dear," Ezzat-ud-Dowleh continued. "The first one contains a written request for a lawyer, and the second one has the details that I've been telling you. She can read—she reads the Quran—but she can't write. Make her press her finger in this ink-box and fingerprint the bottom of the first letter. Then give the letter to the warden's office and ask for a receipt. You can say you wrote this letter yourself as a form of counsel or kindness to the prisoner. Since everyone knows you as a generous, charitable woman, no-one will suspect you. But make sure you take both letters from her . . . whatever you do, don't leave them with her. I beg you in God's name to do this . . . will you? I've thought of sending her daughter Ferdows to her as a visitor, but I don't trust the girl. There's a strange glint in her eyes these days. I'm afraid mother and daughter will get up to something and land us in a real mess. Should they decide to take their revenge, what better opportunity than this?"

Zari wondered which would take more courage: to accept or to refuse? Giving two envelopes to a prisoner, and talking and probably reasoning with her, having her finger-print the letter, waiting for her to read all that was written on the two sheets of paper with her minimal reading ability—all this in front of other prisoners, especially that madam who held Zari responsible for her imprisonment, demanded courage enough. But she could be adventurous and do it. What kind of justice, however, would that be? She would be shielding the real criminal and allowing her to appear innocent, while an innocent person took the blame for a crime. Besides, she wasn't afraid of Ezzat-ud-Dowleh.

But what if she refused to cooperate? Would she be showing the courage that her husband and son expected of her? After all, if Ezzat-ud-Dowleh didn't succeed in using her, she would merely find some other way, buying and safeguarding her reputation through whatever means. And it probably didn't make much of a difference to Kal Abbas whether he was imprisoned in the entrance of Ezzat-ud-Dowleh's house or in a real jail. Nevertheless, why should she be a vehicle for injustice? The right thing to do would be to encourage Nana Ferdows to tell the truth, undaunted by Ezzat-ud-Dowleh or anyone else's reactions or conclusions. But then, couldn't Ezzat-ud-Dowleh crush the woman with her money and influence anyway, and destroy her family? In any case, Nana Ferdows had long been an accomplice. She had accepted the life they offered for many years now.

Ezzat-ud-Dowleh broke her train of thought.

"Zari my dear, what a long time you take to weigh up such a small thing!"

Zari pushed the letters and the ink-box in front of Ezzat-ud-Dowleh and said, "No, I won't do it, I'm sorry."

"You won't do it? But why?" Ezzat-ud-Dowleh asked, stupefied.

Zari didn't reply. Ezzat-ud-Dowleh tried to cajole her like a child. "What if I get your emerald earrings back from the Governor's daughter?" she coaxed. "Would you still not do it? I was just about to do something about your son's horse when this whole situation came up . . . "

"My earrings are not that important to me anymore. It's better if you allow the truth to be known. You were saying yourself it was a pity Hamid Khan didn't do his military service. Well, this might prove to be a form of military service for him."

Ameh Khan laughed so hard that she was seized by a fit of coughing. Ezzat-ud-Dowleh forced a nervous titter and said, "You don't seem to understand the difference between Kal Abbas and Hamid. If Kal Abbas is convicted, his jail sentence is only for a year or two. But if our family name is mentioned, our whole livelihood will be at stake. They'll charge us with smuggling arms with intent to jeopardize national security. Sharifabadi was saying that according to article 171 of the penal code, the sentence for that would be execution, or at best life imprisonment. The maximum he can do is to settle the case on appeal for ten or fifteen years. No-one is going to believe that our living expenses are high and we did this for money."

Tears sprang to her eyes as she said, "When you're born under an unlucky star . . . so much for friends and avowed sisters . . . they abandon you in times of need." And she shouted, "Bazm Ara, bring me the drops for my heart." Then she continued, "I know why you're refusing. You disliked us from the start. I don't know what we ever did to you. Or maybe you regret now that we didn't press you harder to marry Hamid. A beggar like you played so hard to get! I know. Now you want to take your revenge on us. With that crazy, temperamental husband of yours, I don't blame you. He's made more enemies than he can count!"

At this moment Hamid Khan arrived. He looked plump and jolly, and greeted everyone effusively. He took his shoes off at the foot of the takht and stepped up in his socks. He hugged and embraced his 'aunt' over and over again. Zari noticed that Ezzat-ud-Dowleh hurriedly wiped away her tears and smiled at him. Her son literally bent down to kiss her feet. He kneeled down next to his mother and asked, "How are you, how have you been, what news?"

He went over to Ameh Khanom, leaned his head on her shoulder and touched her braided hair. Looking Zari over, he said, "Khanom Zahra, touch wood, you remind me of first-rate wine! You constantly improve with age."

He held Ameh Khanom's hand affectionately, then kissed it and said, "My dear aunt, how many years is it since we saw each other?"

Ameh Khanom didn't answer. She poured a cup of tea and placed it in front of him. Then she took up her opium pipe which she cleaned and prepared for fresh use. She asked him, "Will you smoke if I fix you a pipe?"

"What I've gone through in your absence, my dear aunt!" replied Hamid Khan, trying to ingratiate himself. Turning to Zari, he said, "I was never blessed with brothers and sisters, but God gave me two mothers instead."

He puffed on the opium pipe once, then several times, and became even more talkative, going over old times. He asked Ameh, "Do you remember I used to sit on your lap, and even though I was three or four years old, I'd try and fondle your breasts and then ask you to nurse me. I loved you like a mother because you always looked after me. I remember that time when the other children threw stones at my prize pigeon and broke its leg. You'd come to visit my mother, and I was hugging my pigeon, shedding tears like a river as my dear mother would say, begging people to do something for it. The poor bird was making the most pathetic noises. It was worse than all the moaning in the world to me! I remember you soaked some crushed peas and mixed it with egg yolk and myrtle to

160

make a sort of plaster for the pigeon's leg. When you finished, the pigeon was cooing peacefully again."

Zari felt as though she had nothing more to do there. She was restless and couldn't wait to excuse herself and leave. But Hamid was not ready to give up.

"Remember that night on the summer estate?" he asked Ameh again. "We'd all gone there for the day but ended up staying overnight. The musicians couldn't find a droshke to take them home, so they were forced to stay, too. When they spread out the bedclothes, there wasn't enough room for everyone. My mother never gave up the chance of sleeping next to my father if she could help it, so I was left alone. No-one else wanted to sleep next to me because I had some boils on my face and the one on my nose had become infected. Everyone knew those boils were usually contagious, especially since the garden buzzed with flies and mosquitoes which were carriers of that disease. I was left there wondering where to sleep, feeling really tired. It was very cold, too. Even though your own child was sleeping next to you, you called me over and said, 'Come my dear, come and sleep on my other side.' Then I cried and you wiped my tears. You even kissed my nose despite the infected boil. When your son died, I used to avoid you to spare you grief. One day in the Vakil bazaar, I saw a woman who looked just like you. I called her 'my dear aunt', and she turned around and slapped me one! 'Your dear aunt,' she said, 'I bet!'"

He looked at Bazm Ara bringing a tray containing a small bottle of medicine and a cup of water to his mother. "Mother dear," he asked, "why are you taking medicine again?" And he stole a meaningful glance at Zari.

"It's nothing," Ezzat-ud-Dowleh answered. "I'm having some palpitations again."

Turning to Zari, Hamid asked, "Khanom Zahra, I've heard you're going to the prison tomorrow. Will you be visiting our prisoner?"

Counting the drops she was putting in the water, Ezzat-ud-Dowleh said, "But not as we wanted." And she resumed her counting. Hamid frowned and looked a little nervous. He took the opium and began to smoke again.

"Why?" he asked. "I suppose you're afraid. Well, it is frightening for you." He put the pipe down clumsily next to the brazier and addressed Ameh affectionately. "But my dear aunt is as brave as they come. She'll kiss my boil this time again, won't she? I'm sure you don't want to see me on the gallows. Anyone but you carrying out a plan like this would be suspect, you know."

Zari saw Kal Abbas passing through the orangery and coming toward the takht. As he came forward and greeted them, Ameh Khanom pulled on her chador. Kal Abbas stood by the takht and called to Hamid Khan who bent forward while he whispered something in his ear. Hamid put his shoes on in a hurry and rushed off. Zari suddenly felt anxious. What if something had happened to her little girls! Ezzat-ud-Dowleh was capable of anything. She could even kidnap the children and keep them as hostages somewhere while she forced Zari to consent. Why hadn't she thought of that earlier? Why did she let the children go to the police-chief's garden in the first place? And she thought with bitterness that the real 'show' had been taking place right here! Only it was too complicated for the children.

"It's late. Why aren't the twins back?" she asked Ameh in a shaky voice. She was ready to give in to anything they proposed now. If she were to choose between courageousness and her children, she would clearly choose the children. Yes, Hamid would come now and make the first move. Ameh looked at her sharply and said, "Don't worry. They'll turn up sooner or later."

Zari thought, "I'll wait. I'm worrying needlessly. It was a good thing I sent Khadijeh with them." She remembered a line from a poem Yusef often recited, "From naught but a thought comes their fear and dread . . . " No, she had changed the poem. It really went like this:

"From naught but a thought their peace or war
From naught but a thought their fame or disgrace."

Hamid soon returned with a tall, well-built woman who was tightly clutching her chador. They came and sat on the takht.

"Mother, do you want a guest?" he chuckled.

Zari immediately recognized the 'woman'. She had received her wearing the same veil in her own house. "Malek Sohrab Khan!" she exclaimed involuntarily.

Sohrab sat down and took off his veil. His unshaven face seemed thin and haggard, and he was covered with dust. Ezzat-ud-Dowleh laughed so hard, tears ran down her cheeks. He turned to Zari with a faint smile and said, "I went to your house first. No-one was there." He held his head in his hands. "If only Yusef Khan was in town," he said. "I should have listened to him."

162

Bazm Ara came in, carrying a brightly-polished ewer and bowl which shone like gold. A thick towel with floral patterns was folded over the maid's arm and the soap she held was shaped like a pear. Zari's soap in the bath had resembled an apple. Was it for these items of luxury that Ezzat-ud-Dowleh had run such risks? But Malek Sohrab's presence there at that time of night seemed to shed a different light on the whole situation.

"Sohrab, we've just had the bath water changed," Ezzat-ud-Dowleh said. "Why don't you go and take a bath?"

"Maybe they'll call," he answered. "I'm hoping against hope that we'll be contacted and that the English haven't tricked us. I've come straight from the battlefield. I've been to that English Colonel who's just like the treacherous Yazid. He thinks this is the desert and he can play Lawrence of Arabia with us. He wouldn't see me. He sent a message saying he has a cold. A cold in the middle of summer? Then I went to that sly fox Singer who gave me a garbled answer about being too busy to receive me. The fool still hasn't learned Persian after all these years. If they've tricked us into fighting and looting without keeping their promise, we've shed our brother's blood for nothing. Still, he said he would call."

Ezzat-ud-Dowleh tried to signal to him, but since everyone else noticed, she merely said, "Did you go to them wearing the chador too?"

"No, I was wearing the uniform of a Captain Mohammad Kashmiri Kermani. His identity card was in the uniform pocket. First we stripped him down, then we put a bullet through his neck. It was ten against one. Afterwards I went over to Mirza Agha Hennasab's to change into the uniform."

Suddenly the children's voices could be heard from the outer courtyard and Zari sighed with relief. Hurriedly she excused herself, saying she must leave, and Ezzat-ud-Dowleh, happy to oblige, called out, "Ferdows, bring my sister's chador! Bring my prayer things too. Make sure your hands are clean."

"Have you heard anything in town about our fighting in the region?" Sohrab asked.

"No," replied Zari. "They haven't mentioned it in the newspapers."

"When do they ever write anything in the newspapers? There's been a rumour that the bodies of the officers killed in battle with our tribe are being brought to town for official burial." He added, "But we shouldn't be blamed for the bloodshed, because we only fought for our ideals. After the way the cunning English have treated us the past few days, I felt so guilty about the slaughter that the dead man's uniform seemed to be choking me."

Ferdows brought the brocade wrapper containing Ameh Khanom's black chador and Ezzat-ud-Dowleh's prayer rug. Zari could not help noticing Hamid's expression. When the maid bent over to put the prayer rug before Ezzat-ud-Dowleh, his eyes sparkled as they swept over her body appraisingly. Following his gaze, Zari noticed for the first time the shapeliness of Ferdows's figure. Her legs clad in sheer stockings looked as if they had been chiselled out of fine marble. Her light-blue chiffon chador moved tantalizingly over a flowery crepe de chine dress which barely disguised the firm, well-proportioned curves of her body. It was hard to believe she had had three pregnancies and a miscarriage.

But Ameh Khanom didn't open the brocade wrapper. "Khanom Ferdows," she said, "take some food for the children and keep them in the outer courtyard until we come. Tell Bazm Ara to come and take away the brazier."

Ferdows busied herself piling two small plates with fruit and biscuits, oblivious to what had been going on and not understanding why the mistress was darting such poisonous looks in her direction. Ezzat-ud-Dowleh pushed aside the cotton sheet on which she was sitting and performed a ritual dry ablution with the dust on the carpet. With some difficulty she adjusted the starched headscarf over her head to cover up her gaudy hair for prayer-time. Only her face was now visible. But what a face! She looked as if she had just swallowed some bitter poison. At war even with the deity to whom she was praying, she tugged angrily at the prayer rug as she spread it out, and began her prayers in a seated position.

Deep down, Zari was feeling quite pleased with herself for standing up to the woman. If only Yusef would hurry up and come back! She'd never had so much to tell him. Her experiences at the prison and the asylum were interesting enough, but not for Yusef. Often he would ask her to talk to him and cheer him up, and she had to rack her brains for something comforting or cheerful. It was a long time since she had been able to come up with things like that. She knew her stories had become quite repetitive of late, and Yusef seemed content just to be lulled by her voice. But now Zari had a chance to show her mettle and she couldn't wait to tell him about it.

164

She felt sure Ezzat-ud-Dowleh would prolong her communication with heaven just to annoy them, and that they would have to maintain a respectful silence for a while. But Malek Sohrab would soon tire of it and begin to talk. Her curiosity about the fighting had been aroused to such a degree that, if Ezzat-ud-Dowleh didn't actually ask them to leave, she knew she would wait until the whole story was told.

The black maid reappeared and took away the opium brazier. Zari broke the silence. "Sohrab Khan, you were telling us about the fighting . . . "

"Actually, I had decided to confess all the details of these recent events so that if I take off to the mountains and become an outlaw against the government, or if I disappear altogether from this place; if my tribal blood gets the better of me and I take my revenge on these foreigners, or even if everything is lost and me with it, my friends should know why I did the things I did. How I wish I had listened to Yusef Khan like my brother did! He knew. He's friends with McMahon. They translate poetry together—poems of a revolutionary poet who's changed all the rules of our verse." He shook his head and recited, " 'where in all the darkness of this black night, should I hang my shabby robe . . .' " Suddenly he said, "But Singer promised us! He told us to attack at Semirom, then at Shiraz, next at Isfahan, and finally Tehran. And what barbarities we committed! I'm the first to admit it—what mistakes our brothers made. What an ugly war it was!"

"Brother, maybe I'm the one who's confused," said Hamid, "but I don't understand a word you're saying."

"Mark my words, McMahon must have known their intentions. He's a war correspondent."

"Come now, don't take it too hard. Be grateful you're alive and in one piece. It's all over with now. I think you should smoke some opium and forget about the whole thing. Shall I tell them to prepare it for you?"

"I'm not the kind who can drown my sorrows with opium. If I can't atone for my sins, I'll do away with myself. Right now, I'm prepared to do anything."

Hamid baited him. "What if the English do call? Then you'd even forget the cardinal sins, wouldn't you?"

Zari thought that this was the only true thing he had said in his life.

165

Sohrab unwittingly confirmed Hamid's intended taunt with his next sentence. "If they were really going to call, they would have done so by now. They trust you and your mother." And he continued, "You see, the Russians had asked for thirty or forty Iranian soldiers, maybe more ... some say they had requested as many as five divisions for logistics service. Soldiers, that is, armed with guns alone to guard ammunition stores and roads, to help with transportation or unloading cargo, admitting patients to rural hospitals, that sort of thing. Although Russia and England are allies for now, the British are obviously very reluctant to allow the formation of a 'communist nucleus', as Yusef Khan calls it, here in Iran amongst its soldiers. So they made excuses about the lack of training of the Iranian army ... how worthless they are even in the face of a group of local upstarts. They staged our recent little skirmishes to demonstrate that point to the Russians."

"But if you knew all this, why did you go ahead and fight your own countrymen?" Ameh asked.

Hamid laughed and said, "My dear aunt, the Qashqai tribe loves to fight. Fighting gives them the same pleasure as hunting."

Ignoring Hamid, Sohrab answered Ameh. "Because I thought it was all rumours. Now I know better. You see, I've only just found out that there was a Russian inspector present at the Khoongah Pass to send back reports about the fighting. But the British were telling us to prepare our crowns as successors to the Achaemenid dynasty. They managed to get weapons to us by whatever means. For instance, twice we were instructed to raid their own shipment by previous arrangement. They had loaded our guns and ammunition in a civilian car and transported them as a shipment of coins from Khuzestan through the foot of the Bakhtiari mountains to the Shahi Bank in Isfahan. They did exactly the same thing during the First World War, only then they used mules. According to what we had been told to do, we ambushed the car, tied up and abandoned the driver and their agent at the roadside. The driver had been waiting for us, since he even signalled with his lights. But we took the car too."

"But I heard that you killed the manager of a bank and stole all the money," Zari said. "Was that the same incident?"

"No, that was another time. Well, it takes money to do things like this. Our friends helped too. Hamid and the others got weapons to us ..." Turning to Hamid, he added, "These last bullets really came in handy, even though you overcharged us . . . and the revolvers too, although they seem heavier in the heat."

Ezzat-ud-Dowleh, whose prayers had come to an abrupt end, turned to Malek Sohrab and said, "Must you say all this in front of strangers? The fact of the matter is, we've been caught too. They found out about Nana Ferdows. You can't rely on your sister for help . . . and you can't even trust your very own eyes."

"Who's Nana Ferdows?" asked Sohrab. "The mother of this pretty maidservant here?"

Hamid laughed and said, "She stole your heart, too? When I used to tell my dear mother that this girl literally sends off sparks which go straight to the heart, she wouldn't believe me!"

Ezzat-ud-Dowleh invoked God's name out loud and hurriedly clapped her hands over her ears. Either she was going to say her evening prayers, or she was paying penance for her previous debts.

Suddenly Sohrab remembered. "Mirza Agha Hannasab's wife did tell me that one of your people had been caught, but I didn't know her name was Nana Ferdows. She also told me her husband had managed to get away in time. Before we make any other decisions, we must send Mirza Agha's wife and children to him at the tribe. Hamid, go to Singer first thing tomorrow morning or even tonight and tell him that it was while helping to carry out their plans that you were caught. You can tell him from me that they have only twenty-four hours to keep their word. If they don't deliver, they'll be risking their very necks. As God is my witness, I'm going to round up a few of my bravest men, and they know what we can do . . . to think we've done all these things just to protect their precious oil pipe-lines!"

Zari was beginning to understand. If a crime was committed successfully, then it wasn't such a crime after all, but if it met with failure, it was a sinful thing and had to be paid for. She was about to voice her thoughts, but she stopped herself in time. Who would pay attention to her? Hamid had no interests in life besides women, whisky and pigeons. Sohrab was blind to everything but ambition. And Ezzat-ud-Dowleh was wrestling it out with God that instant. As for Ameh, all she dwelt on was her departure for Karbala or giving up her opium addiction.

So Zari merely advised, "Sohrab Khan, it's not too late yet . . . why don't you go and join Yusef now like your brother Malek Rostam?"

167

"Everyone has a different nature," replied Sohrab. "My brother has a settled farmer's disposition, but I'm a nomad. I don't like being patient and attaching hopes to the distant future. I want to seize the future right now. I want to die in combat, with bullets and axes, not in bed. I want to be the last person to surrender. But not on my own feet. I want them to drag me out and shoot me point blank and chop me up with an axe. I want to stare my executioners in the eye so they can envy me and wonder at my indifference to life or death!"

"It's his tribal blood again ..." Hamid said.

"You were always fearless," Zari said, "even as a child. But you were quite a poet too. I remember for your first wife ..."

"And what we need now is a fearless poet," Sohrab interrupted. Turning to Hamid, he asked, "I wonder if you've ever gone to Semirom from Shahreza in a south-westerly direction?"

"No, but if you remember, once we crossed the north-westerly foot of the Denna Range to Semirom," Hamid answered. "We were going to the wedding of Esfandiar Khan Khashkouli's son. I remember we stopped at the Semiron spring. A strikingly beautiful girl there gave the driver some water from her pitcher and poured some into the car radiator, too. The way she walked, that girl! Tall as a cypress, yet graceful as a deer ... she seemed to bless the ground with each delicate footstep ..."

"Is this the time for that sort of thing?" Sohrab asked.

"It's always time for 'that sort of thing'!" Hamid replied. Then he sighed and turning to Ameh, said, "My dear aunt, you really should not have sent Ferdows away. Call her. You call her. I'm dying for a glass of gin and lime." After a pause, Hamid looked at Sohrab and said, "You know, brother, your tribal ambitions can only lead you to more trouble and bloodshed. Personally, whatever I do is for money so I can possess the beautiful things of this world: women, wine, the most exquisite Fastoni cloth from Manchester ..."

"Just a minute!" Sohrab interrupted, placing a hand on Hamid's knee. "Isn't that the telephone?" He stood up. Someone must have answered because the ringing stopped and then Ferdows came into the garden. All eyes were on her. Sohrab was standing expectantly. Ferdows said, "Khanom Zahra, Khosrow Khan wants to know whether you will be home for dinner or should they go ahead and eat?"

"I'll be there right away," replied Zari, and turning to Ameh added, "Would you mind if we go?"

Sohrab sat down again on the edge of the takht and said, "Those sly foxes are not going to get away with it!"

"Now, now! A great man shouldn't bend under a straw," said Hamid.

Ezzat-ud-Dowleh shouted, "Ferdows, bring my sister's chador! Are you deaf?" She couldn't have dismissed her guests more obviously. Ameh's chador was in front of her in the wrapper.

"But the night is young," said Hamid. "Why are you going so soon? I know we've depressed you with all our talk about killings and war. Let me tell you the story about Sohrab's famous fox hunt, it'll cheer you up."

Zari felt too embarrassed to mention that she had already heard the story several times from Malek Sohrab himself. So she waited patiently while Hamid told it with gusto once again.

Apparently they had wanted to catch a fox that was attacking Hamid's hens every night, but each time the fox had outwitted them. One winter night they put a dead hen on a mound of snow so that Malek Sohrab could get a good aim at the fox when it climbed to the top of the mound, and shoot it. But the fox, sensing a trap, didn't head straight for the hen. Instead, it burrowed its way through the mound of snow and grabbed the hen from underneath. Of course they only discovered the creature's trick later, when they saw that the fox had disappeared along with the hen.

Zari wondered all the way home why Hamid had been so insistent on telling that story. Was he trying to remind Sohrab that he would never succeed in outwitting the clever British foxes? And it occurred to her that while Hamid made every effort to appear the pleasure-loving simpleton, he was in fact a very shrewd and cunning fellow.

When they reached home, Zari switched the radio on in the hope of hearing some news of the fighting. But although she kept trying until dinner-time, she was unable to tune into the Persian newscast of Radio Berlin. They had bought the radio recently, but because it was in the parlour where it was usually hot, they didn't listen to it very often. Besides, the set was too heavy to be moved about frequently. When Yusef was in town, he would always go into the parlour at this time regardless of the heat, and play around with the

169

radio, making some earsplitting sounds until finally he managed to find the Berlin station and the voice that carried on a stream of insults at the regime. The voice accused all influential people of being Jews and, as Yusef said, cursed them so whole-heartedly you thought it had a personal grudge against them. In the mornings, Yusef would listen to Shir-Khoda and enjoy his readings from the Shahnameh. On Fridays when Yusef was in the village, Zari tried to engage the twins in listening to Sobhi's stories on the radio. But they were too restless to stay still for half an hour.

That night after dinner, she tuned in to Iran and the World programme for international and domestic news. There was no mention of an incident in the south. She tried searching the local newspapers, but the most significant items seemed to be the obituaries. She turned to a stack of the newspapers which were sent to them from Tehran and which she collected to take to Khanom Fotouhi every other week. She opened the first newspaper. 'The Ministry of Provisions will be dissolved', it read. Then another headline: 'Lump sugar and sugar rationing . . . henceforth the ration for lump and granulated sugar will be as follows: three hundred grams of lump sugar, four hundred grams of granulated sugar . . .'

In the second newspaper there was only one item of news which vaguely interested her: 'The Fars Society will be composed of Fars residents in Tehran', followed by 'Shutdown of *Man of Today* newspaper' and many more such commonplace articles. But she didn't want to give up. So she continued to search carefully through the papers every day until finally, several days later, she came across a short news item on the third page of a recently published newspaper. It read:

'Reinforcement of the Semirom and Abadeh Garrisons: According to some reports, Boyer-Ahmadi and Qashqai insurgents have raided trucks carrying provisions, ammunition and clothing which were despatched by the army for the Semiron garrison. The garrison itself was attacked on 29 June, and a number of officers and soldiers were killed. The matter is currently under investigation in Tehran, and fortification of the Semirom and Abadeh garrisons is being considered.'

16

When Kolu left hospital, he was too weak to be sent back to his village as Zari had vowed. They had shaved off his hair, and hung a copper crucifix around his neck which now seemed barely strong enough to support his head. His eyes were deeply sunk into their sockets, and his legs wobbled. He had been discharged too early, so Zari confined him to bed at home.

Kolu kept talking about a bearded man with a long black robe who always carried a book with him, and who wore a 'charm' around his neck like the one he had given Kolu, except that the chain on his was much longer. He had appeared on the day Kolu's Indian neighbour was in the throes of death. He had passed by Kolu's bed, and then Kolu had heard him chanting out loud. Kolu understood neither the bearded man's chanting nor the Indian. Actually, there, no-one understood anyone else's language except—yes, except that woman with the fang-like teeth and the bearded man when he wasn't reciting verses, who both understood Kolu's language.

The Indian had walked over to Kolu one night, kissing him and crying over him as if Kolu were his own son and had kept repeating "Sandra! Kitu! Kitu!" In fact all he could say was Sandra or Kitu. Or did he think Kolu was called Sandra or Kitu? On his last night, Kolu had tiptoed over to him as he lay snoring, and saw the man moving his eyes and jaws in the same way his father had done before he died.

But the bearded man in black seemed to be living at the hospital because he appeared every day. At first Kolu had thought he was the prophet Hazrate Abol Fazl come to cure the sick. But when his Indian neighbour died, he was sure the man was not the prophet.

171

At any rate, it was he who gave Kolu the 'charm' and told him to kiss it every morning, and then to go and fetch his uncle from the village so that he could get a 'charm' too.

The man in black had read Kolu three stories from the book he always carried with him. Kolu only liked one of them, the one about a shepherd boy who played the reed, just like Kolu. That boy had been friends with the King's son and had killed a giant with a slingshot. The man in black kept repeating that Jesus was everywhere and he had paid for everybody's sins with his own blood. Then he had taken Kolu by the hand and led him to the house of Jesus, which was just a very big, dark room, and Kolu had been frightened. But no matter how hard Kolu had peered around, he had not found Jesus in the room. The man in black had shown him a picture of their host, and their host's mother. She was holding a baby in her arms and sort of looked like Goldusti, Kolu's aunt.

Kolu had really wanted to find Jesus. But when he discovered from the man in black that Jesus was a shepherd too and was looking for his lost lambs, he felt sure Jesus had gone off to the plains and it would take him an age to find those poor creatures!

Early on Wednesday morning Yusef returned from the village. When Zari heard the knocking, she never imagined it could be her husband at the door. But she remembered that just recently he had gone to great lengths to obtain a night-pass. As she stepped out of the mosquito net to welcome him, she saw him dismount and come towards her. He was not alone. There was a man sitting astride the chestnut horse, his eyes closed. Zari had to rub her eyes to make sure she wasn't dreaming. The man was wearing Yusef's coat over his naked body. At first he appeared to be dead, since they had tied him to the saddle with ropes. But after Gholam and Yusef loosened him and lowered him gently to the ground, it was obvious he wasn't since he opened his eyes and tried to focus with an unseeing look. Blood had clotted on his right temple and his unshaven beard was white with dust. His underpants had dark red stains on them.

"Is the bathwater hot?" Yusef asked.

"No, but we'll soon heat it up," replied Zari.

By the time Gholam was ready to take the stranger to the bath, Yusef had examined his wounds in the changing room, washed them with soap and water, and applied some tincture. The wounds were superficial, but the man kept his eyes closed all this time.

When they sat down to breakfast on the back verandah, Yusef explained to Zari how he had come across the man at dawn by the stream next to the Zarqan city gates. "There he lay naked, except for his underwear and a pair of torn socks. At first we thought he was an animal or something. But when I shone my torch, I realized it was a human being who'd probably been robbed by some bandit. I dismounted, and he immediately begged to be taken into town. He said he knew of me and was on his way to our house, but his legs had given way and he'd collapsed on the ground. I told him he could still travel to the house with Seyyid Mohammad, our steward, on the back of his saddle. Then he could leave for town when he felt better. But he kept on insisting that I should take him home myself. He said I would realize later why it was so important to take him to town myself, and that if I didn't want to do it I should just let him lie there until someone else would. Well, since I'd invited a few guests for this morning I agreed to take him. At first he galloped right alongside me. But by the time we got to Baj-Gah, he couldn't even hold the reins anymore and I had to tie him to the saddle. I think he's either very tired or very frightened. We'll be seeing a lot of this sort of thing these days. He kept talking about a truck which caught fire. Maybe he's a truck driver or something."

Kolu came up to greet the master and kiss his hand. His legs still seemed a little shaky, and Zari was hoping he wouldn't fall. Yusef absently patted him on the head, as if he didn't recognize him.

"This is Kolu," Zari reminded him. "He's had a narrow brush with the Angel of Death!"

When Kolu left, Yusef said, "I really didn't know him at first. He's lost so much weight! I guessed this child would catch typhus too because a messenger from Kowar told me all his family had caught it. You were right, Zari. Our shepherd had typhus. It's spread through all the villages in that area. Imagine it—in this heat ... The messenger said our village looks abandoned. But the people haven't gone away. They're just lying sick at home. As well as all the other things I have to do, I must get a doctor and medicine to them."

"I doubt if you'll be able to find a doctor," Ameh Khanom said.

"I'll get one of Dr Abdullah Khan's assistants," Yusef said. Then turning to Zari he said, "Go and wake the children, dear, I want to

173

see them. Bring the past two weeks' newspapers for me to read, too." As she was getting up to go, Yusef added, "Zari, we have a few guests today. When they come, don't let anyone disturb us. Tell Gholam to leave the garden gates open. They're coming by car."

Passing the pantry, Zari came across Gholam carrying a plateful of fresh pistachios and hazelnuts. The outer green skin of the pistachios had a rosy blush, while the fresh hazelnuts looked like little buds severed from their leaves. Gholam told her he had found them in the mare's saddlebag. She had guessed right away that Yusef was preoccupied, otherwise he would never have returned empty-handed from the village. Each time he would bring her a seasonal offering which, when he handed it to her himself, seemed to evoke the very scents of the village with its harvests, streams and orchards.

She could hardly wait for Yusef to ask her for news so she could tell him some of the stories she'd been saving up. She noticed that Yusef was cutting sections of the newspapers and putting them aside. Soon he would be coming across the 'Semiron and Abadeh garrison' news, and she hoped he would ask her something about it. But although Yusef saw the news item, he only cut it and put it aside, without asking anything.

On Yusef's instructions, Gholam took Mina and Marjan for a ride on the mare around the gardens of the Verdy Mosque, with Khosrow following on Sadar. Although Yusef insisted that Kolu should go too, Khosrow refused to make Sahar carry two riders, so Kolu, too weak to walk so far, was told to lie down on Gholam's bed in the stables and not come out unless he was called. Khadijeh was very busy that morning and was quite happy to let Khanom take care of the guests herself. Ameh disappeared into the howzkhaneh where she planned to finish stitching in the rest of her gold dinars inside her one remaining coat. As for the stranger, he was sleeping soundly in the pantry. From time to time, Yusef would look in and listen to the sound of his breathing or would send his wife to check on him. If he woke up, Zari was to give him some food and clothing and send him on his way.

Yusef was pacing about anxiously in the garden, glancing towards the gates at the slightest noise. Finally a green car drove up with its headlights on. Obviously the driver had forgotten to switch the lights off, for the sun had outstripped the guests and was already caressing the tree-tops. The car stopped in front of the

174

house by the pool. The driver stepped out, but went back to turn his lights off as soon as he noticed they were on. Zari recognized him. It was Majid Khan, one of her husband's sworn companions in the plan to take over the town's bread supplies. The other passengers were a man and two women with black chadors. Zari recognized the man as Fotouhi because of his resemblance to his sister. The 'women' she recognized as soon as they climbed out of the car to greet her. Malek Rostam and Malek Sohrab were relying more and more on the protection of the veil these days.

It looked as if they all had some important business in hand. As Zari was bringing them some tea in the parlour, she heard them shouting at each other, and she could tell from their expressions while she served them that they were not going to come to an agreement soon, either. At first all five of them paused while they took their tea pensively and without thanking her. Sohrab and Rostam had thrown off their chadors in a bundle at their feet. She picked up the garments and began to fold them with deliberation so as to listen to their talk, putting the chadors on one of the seats. Sohrab was saying, "Khanom Zahra was a witness. She knows what I went through that night. The massacre has turned into a real nightmare for me. Now I'm ready for anything. I'll pay for the blood we shed with my own blood. Isn't that enough? I'm prepared to go on a suicide mission and destroy one of their oil docks—I'll swallow gunpowder and blow myself up with gasoline next to it. I'm not afraid of death. I'm just afraid of our plan failing. Yusef Khan, why don't you devise a plan that has at least a thirty percent chance of succeeding . . . "

Turning to his wife, Yusef said, "Zari, will you look in on our new guest?"

Zari realized she was being politely dismissed, even though she very much wanted to stay. She went out, but stood behind the door to listen. Malek Sohrab's voice could be heard pleading, "My uncle is still hopeful. I'm even willing to trick him into giving us at least two hundred guns. But you, Fotouhi, you insulted me. You're just as dependent on others yourself. Otherwise why would you be so concerned about how they're getting on in Stalingrad and whether or not the Russians have received weapons?"

Zari felt discouraged. With three children on her hands and one more on the way, what part could she possibly have in these schemes to be standing there, eavesdropping? The children had barely been gone an hour, and she was already worried about whether they had fallen off the mare, or whether they were getting sunstroke despite the shady paths of the Verdy Mosque gardens.

While preparing the hookah for Yusef, she reflected that, regardless of her courage or cowardice, both her upbringing and her life-style made it impossible for her to participate in anything that would jeopardize life as she knew it. One had to be prepared, physically and mentally, for any action which smelled of danger. And she was ready only for those things which ran contrary to danger. She had neither the courage nor the endurance required. It might be different if she were not so attached to her husband and children. On the one hand were Yusef's caresses, the words and the loving looks; on the other, witnessing the miracle of her children ... no, a person like that could never take risks. True, she turned the treadwheel of her household, endlessly, every day; and it was no less true that from morning to night she laboured like Hossein Kazerouni with her feet and did nothing for herself with her 'free' hands—where had she read that "hands were the means to all other means"? But the smile, the look, the voice and feel of the people she loved was her reward. Each new tooth her children had, every new curl on their little heads, their voices chirping like birds, fashioning words which then trailed each other randomly into sentences; their angelic sleep, and the softness of their skin alone—all these had been her gratification. No, there was really nothing she could do. Her only act of courage would be not to hinder others who wished to be brave, and allow them to accomplish things with their free minds and hands—their means to all other means.

If only the world were run by women, Zari mused, women who have given birth and cherish that which they've created. Women who value patience, forbearance, the daily grind; who know what it is to do nothing for oneself ... Perhaps men risked everything in order to feel as if they have created something, because in reality they are unable to create life. If the world were run by women, Zari wondered, would there be any wars? And if one loses the blessings one has, what then?

She remembered the time when Abol-Ghassem Khan first bought a car and they all went on a hunting trip. It was before the war, and the two brothers had not fallen out yet, although Abol-Ghassem Khan occasionally complained about Yusef's methods of manage-

176

ment as a landlord and that he let his peasants get away with too much. The driver accidentally ran into a fawn. The poor creature lay there like a pile of broken bones. They stopped and got out to drag that wretched pile to the side of the road. Suddenly the mother appeared with another fawn at her heels. She circled her dead baby several times and then rammed herself against the car, unaware that it was made of metal. She kept charging at Abol-Ghassem Khan and Yusef and Zari, dazed and confused, staggering about on those long hind legs and appealing to each one of them with her large, dark-rimmed eyes, as if to ask, "But why? Why?" Abol-Ghassem Khan began to cry. The game had walked up to them on its own feet. But they turned back.

Zari put the glowing coals on the hookah, and took a puff herself before taking it into the parlour. On the way she looked in on the stranger, who seemed to be sobbing in his sleep. She thought of waking him, but decided against it. He was a well-built man.

In the parlour the argument was still raging. From outside she could hear Sohrab urging Yusef, "Now that I know what's going on and have decided what to do about it, why do you want to stop the others from helping me? Are you saying I'm ambitious and dangerous and you'd hate to see me succeed?"

Zari entered the room and placed the hookah in front of her husband. The air in the parlour was hot and stifling with all the doors shut, and she could see the sweat-beads on the men's foreheads. Majid had removed his coat and opened his shirt collar. She went to the cupboard and took out some fans which she placed on the table in the middle of the room. Then she took out some side-plates and knives and forks and set them noiselessly on the table.

"I'll be the only one facing danger in this plan," Sohrab continued. "I know my death will be just one step away. But if I don't do it, the nightmare of our massacre will drive me mad. You say this plan is yet another kind of show ... my dear fellow, don't you see I'll be courting death of my own free will?" He put a hand to his eyes and suddenly wept. Zari stared at him in amazement and offered him a fan which she put on his lap. Sohrab quickly composed himself and smiled at Zari, saying, "Otherwise I'd have to wait for you every Thursday to bring me bread and dates in the asylum!" Turning to the others, he added, "Khanom Zahra is like my own sister. I revealed my plans to her before I told any of you.

Unfortunately, apart from her and her sister-in-law, some undesirable people also heard. Still, it's too late for all that now. Even if you don't help me, I'll go ahead and do it. My brother will have to provide me with gunmen, and Yusef Khan must give us provisions. I myself have thirty reliable men who are willing to risk their lives."

Strangely enough, the two water-melons which Zari had just cut open were both yellow and unripe. She took this as a bad omen. The third water-melon wasn't too bad, and she was about to cut each slice in a zig-zag pattern when she decided that her guests were too preoccupied to notice. She placed the dish of melon slices next to the map of Iran which they had spread out on the table. They were all bending over it now and Malek Sohrab put his finger at a particular spot on the map.

"If we can reach Yasuj," he explained, "it's not too far to Basht. Then we can go on to Gachsaran ..."

"It'll take a long time to get the locals on our side," Yusef said, "but we have no choice. This is just a first step. Meanwhile Mr Fotouhi has to create some internal diversions ..." Then turning to Zari, he said, "Please don't make so much noise." Zari realized she was being asked to leave again. As she was going out, she heard Majid's voice, "I doubt, Fotouhi, if your army of comrades will approve of such a plan. If you agree to it yourself, that's a different thing."

On Yusef's instructions, she set the table for lunch in the parlour. They had all removed their coats and ties and were using their fans by now.

At lunch, Yusef asked for wine, and Zari brought out two bottles of red from the cupboard. She imagined they must have reached some sort of an agreement to be asking for wine in the mid-day heat. As she was pulling on the cork, half of it broke off and the other half fell into the bottle as a result of the pressure. Yusef must have been watching her since he told her not to worry and that the cork must have been rotten. She poured wine for everybody, and they all drank her health. But she could only think to herself, "What use is health alone?"

They were talking and joking together, ignoring her presence, her sole function being to pass the salt here, fill a glass there or make sure Majid got the giblets which she knew he liked best.

"It would've been easier for our fathers," said Yusef, "but if we

178

don't take action, it will be harder for our sons. Our fathers had to face one usurper who became Shah and unfortunately they gave in to him, so that now we have to face two usurpers. Tomorrow there will a third, and before we know it, even more the day after that ... and they'll all be guests at this table ..."

"If we achieve nothing more than showing the way to our children, we will have done enough," Malek Rostam said.

"Even if it's me against a whole army, I won't show them my back ..." put in Malek Sohrab.

"And for thousands of years, everyone's blood will rise in our revenge, brother!" Malek Rostam said, and added, draining his glass, "To the blood of Siavush!"

Yusef held out his glass to be filled, but Zari was seized with such fear of the things they were saying that the pitcher slipped from her hand and broke to pieces on the floor. As she bent over to clear away the glass, she felt her throat constrict from the tears she struggled to hold back.

"Oh Lord, what kind of men are these who know what they're doing is no use, but just to prove their existence and their manhood, and just so their children won't spit on their graves, go ahead and actually dig them—God forbid—with their own hands ..." She bit her lip.

And what odd things women remember at the strangest moments, Zari thought, as her mind jumped back to one night when Yusef had sighed in his sleep, and she had woken up and put on the bedside lamp, only to gaze for the longest time at the soft down on his earlobe which had looked just like pink velvet brushed the wrong way ...

The stranger slept until sunset, then came out into the garden wearing Yusef's pyjamas which they had given him that morning. He sat by the pool and washed his face, and then watched Majid and Yusef playing backgammon. The other guests had left earlier that afternoon despite the heat. It was obvious from the man's demeanour, his easy movements and his comments on the backgammon game, that he was no truck driver.

Khadijeh brought him some food. He ate voraciously. By the time Zari brought him the spirits he had asked for, he had already finished his meal.

The stranger stood up and looked at the garden, saying, "You have a nice life. But it's a pity you don't have any children. There should be at least ten or twelve of them running about in this garden."

"Do you have any children?" Zari asked.

"I have two sons," the man sighed.

It was a long time before the man got round to talking about himself, confessing that he was a lieutenant in the army. Only slowly did he warm up to his tale of the events that had befallen him. In the middle of his story, the twins arrived. The man fell silent and looked at them with envy. Yusef kissed the children and ordered Khadijeh to take them to Ameh on the roof terrace, but to watch out that they didn't fall or touch the hot coals in the brazier. The man took up his tale again, by now more involved than his audience, and then finally became so engrossed that by the time Khosrow and Hormoz arrived, he barely replied to their greeting.

17

I was the commander of a motorized convoy travelling from Shiraz to Abadeh. All in all, we had fourteen yellow provision trucks, forty-five soldiers and five non-commissioned officers for guarding the trucks. A third-lieutenant, just out of the academy, was my immediate subordinate. He was young—no more than nineteen or twenty years old. We were carrying provisions in three of the trucks, and soldiers' uniforms, gasoline, and weapons in the others. We also had an ambulance. I had verbal orders to lead the convoy to Abadeh and wait there—no one had given me any written instructions. In Abadeh I received a telegram telling me to clear the needs of the Isfahan division and then proceed to Tehran.

Among my men was a fellow called Rezvani-Nejad who had accompanied me on several other missions and whom I knew well. The poor man had fourteen mouths to feed, including his parents who were blind. His brother was with us too. Both of them were warrant officers.

We spent the night at Abadeh. Late at night when we were returning from a good time out on the town, I saw a light in one of the trucks. I got in and saw Rezvani-Nejad and his brother having a little tea and dry bread. I felt sorry for them. I gave them permission to go out together and have rice and kebab at the local inn. I told them they could get the best spirits there—so pure you could set fire to it. But the man said, "Sir, don't you think we'd thought of having a drink ourselves? We would have liked to have had a good time too. But we took on this mission just to earn a two-hundred toman bonus for our children, and take it home to them."

In the morning we started off again, and stopped on the banks of a river by noon. We were supposed to wait there for a tank. When I got out of the truck I noticed a few tribesmen nearby. They were

181

wearing their felt hats and cloaks. Their unsaddled horses were being watered on the other bank of the river. As soon as one of them saw us, he jumped on his horse and galloped off in the direction of the mountains. We went to a nearby orchard to eat our lunch. A few more tribesmen were there with their felt hats, but these men were wearing thin cloaks. We didn't realize they were spies. We only found that out from the tank commander. When he arrived, he told us to get into battle-formation since we would be passing through a gorge surrounded by tribesmen. Up until then we had all imagined we were on a simple mission of delivering provisions, weapons and gasoline to the Semirom garrison and returning home safe and sound.

I said to the tank commander, "But my friend, we have only a handful of men! How can we possibly traverse a route surrounded by tribesmen?"

"They won't attack in daylight, and that's when we'll be passing through. If we start off right now, we'll reach the garrison by late afternoon. We'll return then if we can, and if we can't, we'll just spend the night at the garrison and come back first thing in the morning."

So we started out. But we had no sooner taken the first bend to the left, than we realized the road had been sabotaged. Every twenty metres or so the trucks either fell into potholes and stalled, or else they got stuck in deep puddles. We weren't even doing five kilometres an hour. We didn't turn the headlights on and the trucks followed each other closely. Later we found out that the man responsible for planning the road obstructions had been one of our own officers. Sentenced to death by the government, he had deserted and taken refuge with the tribe. He had even drawn up their general strategy and combat-formation.

Eventually the tank engine overheated and after a few yards, it stalled. It was getting dark and we could see scattered bonfires high up on the mountain. Obviously they were Qashqai and Boyer Ahmadi entrenchments. We had just reached the Khorus Galoo Pass, and they were high up on either side of us, but they were leaving us alone for the time being. They only made shrill, frightening noises like a war cry.

We decided to open the hood of the tank to let it cool down. But as soon as we did, we realized the pump had sustained several holes. The decision was to repair it by the light of a lantern, so

182

while this was being done, I gathered up the men to dig trenches around the trucks as a precaution, with some of the soldiers on guard and others patrolling. I told everyone that we neither had the right nor the possibility of turning back.

All our truck-drivers were sergeants. The senior sergeant came over and told me the soldiers were new conscripts and had no combat experience. I ordered him to distribute their weapons among the officers and sergeants. Each of us received one rifle and fifteen bullets. We left three light machine-guns to guard the tank: two on either side, and one at the rear.

We spread out in the individual trenches which the soldiers had dug, cocked our weapons and sat ready for the attack. I had a revolver hidden under my tunic. We had no food or water, the weather was very cold, and we could neither turn back nor advance. The tank commander and a few others were working on the pump, but they never managed to repair it. Meanwhile the tribesmen kept up their shrill cries until ten o'clock that night. But they were still leaving us alone. When the tank commander—he was a lieutenant like me—gave up on the pump, he became so frightened he got the runs.

"There must be two thousand of them!" he said. "A thousand Qashqais on this side of the Khorus Galoo and a thousand Boyer Ahmadis on the other. They're going to tear us into pieces! If only we could leave the tank . . . "

I didn't let him finish his sentence. "You're ruining everyone's morale," I said. "Get inside the tank for now and keep the hatch shut."

It was well after ten, and darkness engulfed us. There was no light, no moon, no lamps. We didn't dare strike a match. All we could see were their bonfires, dotting both sides of the mountain. I ordered the sergeants not to waste any bullets but to wait until their target came well into range. Maybe help would arrive in time from Semirom or Shahreza. When the tank commander had first joined us, he'd talked of another mobilized convoy leaving from Shahr Kurd for Shahreza.

It must have been after eleven when, from behind us, I heard the sound of horses trotting. There must have been ten or twelve riders. The senior sergeant said, "Sir, here they are!" From the sound of the horses, I estimated them to be about thirty metres away. "Here they come!" said the sergeant manning the machine-gun at the rear

183

of the convoy. The darkness was vast, and so was the silence. They had come to test us—to see if we were awake. Three or four of them let out a whooping cry as they fired a few shots that rang against the metal of the trucks. Our machine-gun fire drove them away.

By dawn I could see some horsemen appearing and disappearing on the skyline. Suddenly they started down the mountain. The soil inside the trenches still felt cold from the morning air. Shots rang out against the body of the trucks. I ordered the men not to fire back. "Shoot only when they're all the way down the slopes," I told them.

The sergeant who drove the last truck was an old man. Suddenly he cried out and fell. I rushed to his side. An Isfahani sergeant called to me, "Sir! Get down! Lie flat! They're still shooting!" I dragged the old man towards the ambulance and stretched him out on the bed inside, hoping for the best. Three minutes later, another soldier was wounded in the shoulder, and then another in the stomach and in the thigh ... the men dragged those two to the ambulance and stretched them out on the beds as well. There were only three beds in the ambulance—it was one of those old brown Fords with the lion and sun emblem on it.

The tribesmen crawled and slid down the mountainside. They took up positions behind the brick wall of a garden about a hundred and fifty metres from our trenches. We in turn opened fire as soon as they came within range. One Turkoman sergeant who drove the first truck volunteered to take a short-cut up to the top of the mountain and check out the enemy's situation. I refused permission because it was too light. It must have been seven, seven-thirty in the morning.

From the top of the mountain came the sound of about sixty or seventy of them whooping and chanting: "Army men, weapons down! Hands up! Army men, weapons down, hands up!"

"They can go to the devil!" I said. "We will not surrender." By around nine-thirty, twelve of our men had been wounded. We heard the shrill cries again, followed by "Attack!" and then they swarmed down the mountain. We jumped into our trucks, and two of the drivers desperately tried to turn round. There was no other choice. The tank had to be abandoned so we could at least try to save the trucks carrying fuel and weapons. I'm ashamed to say that we had to leave the wounded behind, even though some of them were crying out ...

184

They charged. There were about a thousand, maybe more, of them. The Turkoman driver managed to slip out from behind the steering wheel in the nick of time, but the driver of the truck in front was shot so our way was blocked. We were forced to get out then. The tribesmen were crawling forwards on their bellies, firing away all the time. I had only one bullet left. Now they were just ten steps away. Rezvani-Nejad raised his head to shoot, and fell. He cried out, "Khandan!" as he rolled to the ground. I imagine it was his child's name. The poor man had fourteen mouths to feed. The bullet had blown his brains out—I saw the white of his brain with my own eyes. His brother ran to help him, but they shot him too. The bullets seemed to nail the two brothers together. I kneeled and aimed with my one remaining bullet at the man who had killed them. I got him in the middle of the chest. His friend ran to him, wailing, "Did he hurt you, Zargham?"

I crawled underneath the weapons truck, and gradually managed to pull myself into one of the trenches. The sergeant inside the trench was dead. I stretched myself out on top of the dead man like another bloodied corpse. The Boyer Ahmadis were coming at us at a gallop, and once or twice they jumped over my head, covering me with dust. Then the looting began. First they took our weapons, and then I could hear their women ululating and repeating the shrill war-cry. I heard that chant so many times, I learned it by heart:

"Up the pass, down the pass, there's a camp, Sohrab Khan, look ahead, look ahead, how many thousand are there?"

And:

"Drunken drunken through and through
I hold the army in my hand.
Drunken drunken through and through
I hold a rifle in my hand."

A Qashqai loomed over my head and dug his heel into my shoulder. "You dog, you're alive! Get up, I saw you lie down. Give us the new gun, get up, get up!" A short, dark Boyer Ahmadi arrived just then. As I handed my gun to the Qashqai, the two men began to fight each other for it until the Boyer Ahmadi killed the Qashqai and grabbed the gun. Again I stretched out on top of the dead man in the trench, close to passing out from thirst and fatigue, and trembling with anger. By this time the Qashqai and Boyer Ahmadi women had arrived and were throwing out the sacks of provisions from the trucks. They tore them open and poured the tea, sugar and rice, beans and peas into their own sacks. I saw a Boyer Ahmadi take the gun belonging to the third-lieutenant, the one who had just graduated from the academy, and make him undress. Stark naked. The boy grabbed a piece of canvas to cover his genitals, but one of the women immediately snatched the rag from him and used it to collect some onions. Finally the women and children of the nearby village arrived on donkeys and filled their saddlebags with whatever remained.

We had left three wounded sergeants in the ambulance which was clearly marked with the lion and sun emblem. But they didn't realize, and set the ambulance on fire. You could smell the burnt flesh for a long time. And then they set the fuel truck on fire.

Again a Qashqai came along to where I was lying and kicked me in the shoulder, saying, "Get up! Take off your jacket!" I gathered all my strength and threw him bodily on to the burning fuel truck. But almost immediately another rider came towards me. He was a thin, dark man, carrying a baton spiked with a knife. His gun was fastened to his belt. He too, wanted my uniform. He said he wouldn't kill me so the clothes wouldn't be bloodied. He took my uniform and gold medals and army boots. Then he ripped off my watch with his knife, and with the same knife cut loose the revolver at my waist. Finally, the tribesmen drove away in the two un-damaged trucks which contained military uniforms and ammunition. Later I heard they used those uniforms as disguise for a surprise attack on the Semirom garrison.

I ran off in the direction of the mountains. On the way, I heard a moaning in the distance. I decided I'd find the person and steal his clothes. It turned out to be one of our own sergeant-drivers. He was spattered with blood. I asked if he was shot, and he said he'd managed to escape in time by giving up his gun. "Get up and come with me, then," I told him. He pleaded, "Captain, I beg you, my suitcase, my souvenirs from Shiraz ..." I interrupted him, "From now on, we're equals." And we started up the mountain. We passed the tribesmen's entrenchments, made of white stone and each taking four people, but now littered with empty cartridge shells.

We were heading towards Abadeh by way of a side-track, and we had just passed the mountain ridge when we noticed a Qashqai rider approaching us at a gallop. We threw ourselves on the ground beneath a bush. Before long he was standing over our heads and

186

saying, "Hey you army dogs! Get up! I saw you." Eyeing the sergeant he said, "Is it you, Mirza Hassan, you bastard? Where's your gun?" The sergeant sat up, and started to undress of his own accord. Standing in nothing but his underwear, he took off his army boots and handed everything in a neat bundle to the Qashqai.

"How fat you've become, Mirza Hassan, you bastard!" said the Qashqai.

"You'll be wasting two bullets if you kill us," I told him. "Don't shoot us. On the other side of the mountain they're looting truck-loads of goods—rice, chick peas, beans, lump sugar, tea, onions, oil, military uniforms, ammunition and guns. If you hurry you'll get there in time."

"Is he telling the truth, Mirza Hassan?" he asked the sergeant.

"Yes, brother."

The Qashqai took out a pair of delicate women's slippers from his saddlebag and said, "This piece of softskin is for you, Mirza Hassan."

"Keep them, I can't use them. Give them to Sister Golabtoon and greet her for me."

"I'm taking a flowery tunic for Golabtoon. And a gold necklace and mirrors, I don't need these."

"Then hurry so you can take her some provisions too," I said to the tribesman.

When he had left, I asked the sergeant, "Are you related?"

"Yes, we're cousins. But my name isn't Mirza Hassan. That's the name they give to thieves."

By then I think it was almost two o'clock in the afternoon. A government airplane buzzed over our heads and circled around the remains of the convoy. There were a few retaliating shots from the Qashqais and Boyer Ahmadis, and then it roared away again. So much for aerial military reinforcement!

Now the two of us were left thirsty, hungry and barefoot, wearing nothing but underwear, and holding on to a pair of women's delicate sandals which didn't fit either of us. We made our way down the ridge of the mountain until we reached the valley where we found a spring and washed our faces in its muddy water. The sergeant announced that he couldn't go on anymore and lay down wearily right there. "As you like," I told him. "I'm carrying on without you." But I walked on very slowly. I hadn't gone a hundred metres before I heard him call me. "Captain," he said, as he caught

187

up with me, "I wanted to go to sister Golabtoon's tent. It isn't too far from here. But to tell you the truth I felt too ashamed." I didn't say a word. Soon we had left the valley and we could see several villages ahead of us, with crowds of people milling about.

We caught up with an old man, a pedlar, following a child riding a donkey. He had a small piece of bread, and gave us half of it, but no water. We said we were truck drivers, that bandits had raided us and had set our trucks on fire. He told us that the river was only a kilometre away but that we should be careful because the Qashqais and Boyer Ahmadis had taken to the mountains, and had been fighting government men on the other side.

It was early evening when we reached the river and drank some water. I told the sergeant not to drink too much because he would get bloated. We rested for about ten minutes, and then waded across the river. On the other bank we saw two Boyer Ahmadis sitting around a fire, having some tea. They asked us who we were and where we were going. We told them the Qashqais had robbed us and that we were truck drivers. The sergeant asked one of them who was smoking a pipe to give him a puff. When we gave the pipe back to him there was nothing left in it, and the man dumped it on the ground. He gave us a drink from his water-skin, and then sent us on our way.

We joined a few peasants headed towards the village. Again, we were asked who we were, and again we told them we were truck drivers. After a long trek, we finally reached Abadeh at eight o'clock in the evening. We found the police-sergeant who'd been left in charge of the garrison. He told us the deputy chief was at the teahouse, but the garrison chief himself had gone to Shiraz. We were taken to the deputy chief at the teahouse, and I told him how they had set up a fine trap for us—looting, killing and burning as they went. We had some sweetened tea before going to the garrison. There the deputy chief called his assistant and said, "This is the lieutenant. Come and listen to what he has to say. It's not as simple as we were told—it was worse than Judgement Day! Their soldiers didn't even know how to shoot, and they were crying from fear in front of their lieutenant." Then turning to me, he said, "When your convoy left Abadeh I was relieved, thinking that the poor colonel at Semirom won't be begging for help behind his wireless anymore. You'd be taking them reinforcements. But now . . . God help them!"

188

He instructed his assistant to bolt the tower door, issued orders for protective measures, and went behind the wireless himself to report the situation to the gendarmerie and ask for help. He was quite sure they would be attacked that night. They did their best to find some us clothes from here and there, and then scraped together some money to give us. Those old clothes and shoes felt like a great blessing to us. The deputy chief said, "Wash yourselves and then go to the village headman's house for the night, but whatever you do, don't tell them you're officers. If they find out, they'll kill you before morning." A gendarme accompanied us, past the local sheep-fold, to the headman's house. The headman, who had a red beard, came out of his room and led us to a bare, mud-built room. He took two old quilts from the top of a wooden chest in the corner of the room and spread them on the floor. He asked us if we'd eaten and we said no. So his daughter brought us some dirty-looking milk in a black bowl, and two loaves of brown bread which she took out from the wooden chest that was kept under lock and key. We slept like logs till the morning. They never found out we were officers. In the morning they gave us more brown bread and hot tea before sending us back to the deputy chief at the garrison. He was even kinder than the night before, allowing us to wait around until noon while he tried to get me permission to go back to Tehran. By then, five more people, wounded and half-naked, had straggled into the garrison at Abadeh with the aid of some peasants. They were patrols from the Semirom garrison. They told us that the real battle had begun only yesterday evening.

Finally the deputy chief managed to contact the gendarmerie. He was instructed to help us out, but we were all to return immediately to Shiraz. The deputy chief agreed to find us two or three donkeys so we could head off to Deh Bid, hitching a ride as soon as we found a car that would take us. We treated the wounds of the injured as much as we could, and the deputy chief found some civilian clothes for us to wear. He also gave me eighty tomans. Meanwhile our Turkoman driver showed up, riding a Qashqai mare. He was the only one to have escaped safe and sound. Apparently a Qashqai had taken his gun, then left his horse in his care to go off looting. As soon as the Qashqai's back was turned, the driver had jumped on the mare and galloped straight to Abadeh. He had spent the night in a safe place, and been given rice and stew and a yoghurt drink. He'd

189

even gone to the baths in the morning and been regaled with a massage and refreshments.

The injured rode on the donkeys while we followed on foot, taking turns on the Qashqai mare which the Turkoman driver had brought us like an unexpected blessing. We had some bread and cheese and a jug of water with us, and managed to reach Deh Bid by ten o'clock that night. At the town gate, we came across an officer with a riding crop and high boots. I looked him over and told him I was an officer too. His crop, shiny boots and officer's uniform were all brand new. I told him briefly what had happened to us and asked him for a car to take us to Shiraz. He said, "The whole area has been taken over by bandits. No cars can pass through." He took us to the gendarmerie, where their chief welcomed us and said he'd been expecting us since he'd had news from Abadeh. They served us roast chicken, yoghurt with cucumber, and spirits to drink. We had just sat down to our meal, and the chief had gone to use the wireless, when the tribesmen arrived. But this time they weren't Qashqais or Boyer Ahmadis, they were Doshman Ziaris. The chief was shot right there behind his wireless. If looting and raiding was profitable for two tribes, why not for a third too?

I haven't seen the others since then. I managed to escape on my own from the back of the garrison tower, running down the mountainside until I reached an open field. After a while I came to a walnut tree, and I wanted to lie down right there to sleep, but it was cold and dark, and I could hear shooting going on all around me, so I decided to pace about or jog to keep awake. There was no moonlight, no stars, no lamp. I didn't have any matches, but I had the eighty tomans that the deputy chief had given me. If I'd had matches, I would have made a fire with the bills and gone to sleep next to it.

In the morning two shepherds came along with their flock. I greeted them and told them I was a truck driver, I'd been robbed and I was hungry. The shepherds made a fire and one of them milked a sheep and gave me the milk in a dirty bowl. His son, a seven- or eight-year-old, showed up just then holding a loaf of bread. He told his father, "I ran all the way. It's still piping hot!" He was right, the brown bread was still warm. Suddenly we heard shots being fired and a bullet pierced the milk bowl. It was the tribesmen from the night before. Some of them went for the sheep which they herded off, shooting the two sheep dogs on their way

190

down the mountain. A few others came towards us and tied us up, though they left the child alone. They made us walk ahead of them all the way to their tents. The tribal chief was sitting on a chair in front of his tent.

On the way, I had whispered to the shepherd boy to throw himself, on our arrival, at the chieftain's feet and beg him on the life of his children to spare his father and uncles. I told him I'd give him a reward when they freed us. The boy did as he was told, and the tribesmen spared our lives, but we were held for six days and then they stripped us naked before letting us go. They had taken my eighty tomans the very first day, and again I found myself trudging along, on and on, until I managed to reach Zarqan, where you found me.

Just imagine what happened to those poor bastards in Semirom! That's where the real massacre took place—at the garrison and on the Semirom plain. Those patrol soldiers whom we bandaged at Abadeh, told us that they'd had only one day's ration for four days. I knew they weren't equipped to put up any kind of resistance for long. They had guns, but no bullets. And of course we never managed to get any to them. The same officer at the Deh Bid gate with the riding crop and the boots, told me that the Boyer Ahmadis and the Qashqais had sent a letter to the colonel at Semirom saying he'd been sentenced to death and that he should surrender. The colonel had written back that he would sooner die than do such a thing. The poor colonel had given up on the Isfahan division, and had resorted to the Abadeh garrison. Now the Semirom wireless was dead.

One of the fellows from Semirom, whose arm injury I treated myself, told me on the way to Deh Bid that they'd seen the approach of the tribesmen through their binoculars, spotting three mules carrying machine guns. I asked him whether he'd seen the military tank they'd stolen from us. He said, "They'd set the tank on fire, and we could see it burning as we ran away. We warned our poor colonel of their approach. He first made us pitch tents on four sides of the stream, so we wouldn't be hard up for water. Then we dug trenches all around the tents. He'd planned a circular defence, you see. The poor man kept urging us to resist. He believed we could mow them down with the crack of our machine-gun fire. He was certain help was on its way since the Abadeh wireless had said that the convoy had set off in our direction. To those of us on patrol, he promised a good reward for sighting the first vehicles of the convoy. He said to us, 'These people have no heavy arms and their firing range isn't more than four hundred metres.' When we told him the tribesmen were advancing with three machine guns on their mules, he paled. He realized then that the reinforcement convoy had been attacked. As soon as he lost all hope of your arrival, he was forced to change his defence tactics. Guessing that they would probably approach by way of a back-road following the Khorus Galoo Pass, he ordered combat formation, with the soldiers taking up positions on top of two high promontories on either side of the back-road. But those poor soldiers only had one bullet each. On the promontories there was a half-decayed brush made up of thorn-bushes, almond and lotus trees. The soldiers lay in ambush under this shelter. At the foot of the hills, we rapidly set up first-aid and food tents. But what food and what first aid! One day's ration for four!"

The fellow from Semirom described the attack for me. He said the tribesmen charged from three sides, with a blare of trumpets and drums which echoed awesomely in the mountains. The Boyer Ahmadis had headed down from the north-eastern parts of Semirom, while the Qashqais charged from the north-west, with another group descending from the heights of the Denna mountains. They had approached through the orchards and vineyards, gradually tightening their circle. "A mounted captain, the first lieutenant of the artillery, and some other non-commissioned officers as well as myself, had gone inside the Semirom garrison tower to dissuade the colonel from fighting back. We wanted him to put up the white flag. But the colonel was obstinate. He just sat behind his desk, hand under his chin, and after hearing us out, merely shook his head and asked if anyone had a cigarette. The captain begged him, 'This isn't a battle anymore; we're just waiting to be butchered.'

"'Maybe help will arrive at the last minute,' the colonel had said sadly.

"'But sir, you've been trying for ten days behind that wireless— where on earth can the reinforcements be? Why are you putting up such a brave front and getting us all killed in the process? For whom?'

"'I'm not forcing you to stay. I'm staying myself. But you must forget about the white flag.'"

No sooner had those men come out of the garrison tower than the shooting began. One of them, the same fellow who told me all this, was wounded in the arm. He tied a handkerchief around the wound and managed to get himself to the village of Semirom. There he was told by the villagers that groups of Qashqais and Boyer Ahmadis were turning up all the time, picking up military uniforms. Apparently, the plan was for the disguised tribesmen to penetrate right into the garrison and mingle with the soldiers, who probably rejoiced for one short instant that the long-awaited help had finally arrived!

When the lieutenant's story was finished, Majid stood up, yawned and said, "What a small world it is!"

"There is no escaping one's deeds . . . " Zari said pensively.

"My dear, you're beginning to understand quite a lot of things, aren't you?" Yusef observed with a laugh.

The next day, the stranger, who was no longer a stranger, left for the army headquarters, wearing Yusef's ill-fitting clothes. They heard no more of him until a week later, when his letter arrived from Tehran thanking them and telling of his forthcoming court-martial. There was a whole file of trumped-up charges against him and, he said, it was not unlike the story of the famous coppersmith in Shushtar having to pay penance for the crimes of the infamous blacksmith in Balkh. He was resolved to resign from the army and go to Switzerland by whatever means, with his wife and two sons. But he made no mention of the two hundred tomans he had borrowed from Yusef.

18

On Thursday afternoon Zari went to the asylum. The warden was not there, so she set out on her rounds with the head nurse. She knew Khanom Fotouhi would be angry when she saw that parts of the newspapers had been cut out. In the women's ward, only the paralysed woman, who hugged her givehs every night, and Khanom Fotouhi remained out of all the others. But there was no shortage of new patients. Four strangers were sitting on the other beds, and a folding screen hid another newcomer. In the middle of the room three patients sat around on a straw mat, playing a children's game called "Away flies the crow". As soon as Zari walked in, one of them said, "Away fly the bread and dates!" Zari smiled at them. Fortunately she had brought bread and fruit which Gholam placed on the floor. One of the women said, "Away flies the princess!" Then they started to fight amongst themselves and played another game.

The head nurse didn't let her go near the bed which was protected by the folding screen.

"This patient has already received a lot of flowers and fruit," she whispered. "Only she can't swallow any food. Right now she's on a drip. They're setting up a private room for her. Her relatives say it's all the strain and overwork in this heat, but the doctor says it's both from stress and typhus. May the Lord cure her!" She added, "There's a woman who comes here late at night after everyone's gone to sleep, does her ablutions and says a special prayer to Hazrate Fatemeh for her. Ezzat, the nurse who was on night-duty last night, said the woman stayed praying with her forehead glued to the ground for so long, she became worried. Ezzat went closer and was relieved to hear the woman repeating, "O Fatemeh save her! Save her!" She repeated it fifty, a hundred times, pleading with

194

God. The woman had to sleep here last night as it was well past the curfew. Now Dr Abdullah Khan has prescribed donkey's meat for the patient ... if they manage to find it, that is. They have to make her meat patties for dinner tonight; maybe she'll be tempted to eat."

When she had finished distributing the food, Zari went up to Khanom Fotouhi who was sitting with her back to the patients, staring out the window. Zari said hello to her, left the papers by the bed and stood a little distance away. She knew that the moment the woman opened the newspapers, the incident of two weeks before would be repeated. Khanom Fotouhi suddenly jumped up from her bed. "My brother!" she exclaimed. "I had a feeling my brother would come and take me to our hundred and twenty-four thousand metre garden!"

Zari looked out of the window, but could not see anyone. Khanom Fotouhi brushed past her and left the room saying, "The rudeness of it all! You stupid fools, I'll show you what I mean!"

Before long she was back in the room accompanied by her brother who had truly arrived this time. Khanom Fotouhi sat on the bed and started to cry.

"Why did you come alone, brother?" she asked. "Why didn't mother come? After all this time, you've come empty-handed!"

Mr Fotouhi greeted Zari who was about to go out and leave the brother and sister by themselves.

"Khanom Zahra," he said, "I have something to tell you."

"Tell her to get lost," shouted Khanom Fotouhi furiously. "Every week she comes here with a lot of fuss and bother to show off for me!" And she asked again, "Why hasn't mother come? Take me to the hundred and twenty-four thousand metre garden ... my heart is withering in this cage. What kind of brother are you? You should at least get a private room for your sister ... "

She clutched her brother's hand tightly, kissing it and rubbing her tearful eyes on the dark, veined skin, asking over and over again why her mother had not come. She worried about whether her enemies had confiscated their garden ... those enemies who constantly put electric currents through her body, her hands, her feet, her heart, making her heart beat backwards. She placed his hand on her heart and said, "You see!"

The head nurse and Gholam and all the other patients were staring, even those who had been playing "Away flies the crow" a moment ago. Fotouhi kissed his sister on her fair, tousled hair, and said, "My dear, you know very well our mother's dead. I've told you that a hundred times."

"But you see, brother, I know my mother isn't dead. She's tricked you. When you put her in her coffin, she slipped out quietly and went into hiding. All this time she's been hiding somewhere in the hundred and twenty-four thousand metre garden and you haven't even tried to find her." She swallowed and said, "I swear to God they came in the middle of the night last night and dug out my liver with a knife and stuffed some straw in its place. Since this morning my mouth tastes like straw."

"My dear, since when do we have a hundred and twenty-four thousand metre garden?" Fotouhi said impatiently.

"Take me away," Khanom Fotouhi begged. "I'll be like a servant to you. We'll live together, all by ourselves. We'll plant wheat in that huge garden. We'll plant mulberry trees and cucumbers, keep beehives, and I'll bake bread myself. We'll keep hens and a rooster and hatch chicks. We won't let anyone in, either ... we'll buy narcissus bulbs and wrap them in cotton wool in our Kashkouli pot ... "

A nurse came in and whispered something to the head nurse, who then said out loud, "All right, arrange the flowers around the room, and put the fruit on the table. No, come back. Help me take the patient out. Wait a minute, take the suitcases first."

The nurse went behind the screen and came out with two new suitcases. Gholam helped her with one of the suitcases, and they left the room together.

Zari and Mr Fotouhi went outside too. They stood under a dust-covered pine tree in the flowerless courtyard of the asylum.

"I came here to see you," Fotouhi said. "Yusef Khan probably told you I would come today to inform everyone of my decision using you as intermediary."

No, Yusef had not told her anything. Perhaps he had wanted their meeting to look as natural as possible.

"Since yesterday, I've investigated every aspect of the plan," Fotouhi said, "and this morning I discussed the matter at the party leaders' meeting. Of course without mentioning any names, and more as a suggestion of my own. Everyone opposed it." He seemed nervous, shifting from one foot to the other, and talking in clipped phrases. "You know we haven't officially announced the existence of our party yet," he continued; "we're waiting for the right moment. But how would it look if I were to leave the comrades and go south to Khuzestan with a group of like-minded friends in a plan the comrades oppose ... you realize I'm responsible for my students too. In my group ... with a group of young boys, what can I do?"

"So they were right," Zari said bluntly, "they shouldn't have asked you to join in their plan. You don't care about your own friends, any more than you care about your sister." She was amazed at her own harshness, although she had been harbouring resentment against Fotouhi for some time now. Yet Fotouhi answered her without the slightest appearance of being upset.

"We must build our society in such a way that no-one's sister ends up having a mental breakdown. My sister's condition is the symptom of a social disease. When we eventually organize the masses and come into power, we will see to it that justice is carried out." Then he added after a pause, "In my opinion the time is not ripe for their plan, and the only result will be chaos and anarchy. It's not as easy as Malek Sohrab thinks. I don't believe they should allow themselves to be led by a hot-headed fellow like him. And I'm sure they won't. After all, Yusef Khan has more experience than any of us, and even he said that without a forty percent chance of success, running the risks they have in mind is tantamount to suicide."

The words had hardly left his lips when Khanom Fotouhi appeared, coming towards them wrapped up in a white sheet which kept tripping her as she walked.

"Kill me and let me have some peace!" she shouted. "Take out your pen-knife from your coat pocket and kill me! I've put on my shroud and I'm ready!"

She let go of the sheet when she reached them, exposing her stark naked body underneath. The nurses immediately rushed to her, but she fought them off, hitting one nurse sharply with her elbow.

"You bastard!" she shouted, shaking a fist at her brother. "Meeting under the pine-tree, is it?" She held her own against all the nurses as they struggled to pin her down. "You stole my property! You sold my hundred and twenty-four thousand metre garden to pay for this whore ... " Then she ran around the empty pool in the courtyard, dodging everyone and screaming, "People, I want you to know I'm the greatest woman of this nation! I'm a

197

poet. I've composed fifty thousand verses. This whore has stolen my verses ... " She gasped for breath for a moment, then went on, "This whore has given my verses to the *Red Aurora* newspaper under her own name. I'm the Prophet's daughter, Hazrate Fatemeh ... I'm pure and chaste like Hazrate Fatemeh herself. My brother's stolen my possessions ... he executed my mother and father ... all these flowers you see ... springing from their blood ... put these flowers in a bunch on my grave—" And she cried with abandon. "Oh the fatherless wretch that I am! How wretched ... " she sobbed, and she went on and on until she started frothing at the mouth and collapsed. The female nurses covered her naked body with a chador and a well-built fellow came forward and picked her up to take her to the office.

Zari was tired and her head was aching. Telling the head nurse so, she began to take her leave.

"Thank goodness our new patient, Khanom Massihadem, is feeling much better," the nurse said. "We've transferred her to a private room, and she can have visitors now. Why don't you go and wait there while I bring you a pain-killer or something."

So the patient who was getting such special treatment was the new midwife! Zari knocked and went in. Khanom Massihadem was sitting on the bed and shaking her head from left to right, sending a mass of black curls around her head and letting them sweep her face from side to side. The room was filled with flowers. Some of the bouquets had obviously been arranged by the caring hands of a lady gardener, and some of the others were made up of rare wild flowers which someone must have searched for in distant fields or plains. Khanom Massihadem went on shaking her head from side to side, and paid no attention either to the flowers or to the crystal bowls arranged tastefully on the table in the middle of the room. The bowls were covered with lids, and Zari guessed that they must be filled with all kinds of home-made sweets, painstakingly prepared for the patient in that heat.

Eventually Khanom Massihadem tired of shaking her head. She noticed Zari for the first time. Zari said hello, while Khanom Massihadem stared at her with a vacant gaze. Despairing eyes, set in a young but skeletal face. Her collar-bones stuck out from underneath her thin white night-dress. Her breasts sagged, and her complexion had a jaundiced look, paler than the sunshine touching the last row of bricks on the opposite wall.

198

"I hear you're feeling much better," Zari said.

"I've heard this voice somewhere before!" replied Khanom Massihadem, biting her nail and staring at her hard. Then suddenly she burst out laughing as recognition came into her eyes. "I know you! I know you! You're Tal'at Khanom!" She clasped a hand to her heart as she said, "How frightened I was! So you're alive. I knew God would answer my prayers. I asked God to take six months off my life, but to keep you from dying at my hands. Come closer so I can see you with my own eyes."

Zari knew Khanom Massihadem was mistaken, but she kept quiet. If the poor woman could smile and her eyes brighten up at thought of some friend or sister or patient being alive, why should that joy be taken away from her? Zari sat next to her on the bed. Khanom Massihadem took Zari's hand in hers and pressed it. Then she explained in a surprisingly sane manner,

"When it's born, if its complexion is pink as a petunia, if it screams until the mother can hear it, or if it pisses—" she put her other hand to her mouth and suppressed an innocent giggle, "then all the tiredness seems to go out of your body. And you feel so satisfied, as if you yourself created the baby! But when your child came out, your first one too, dear oh dear, he had no colour. There was no blood in the umbilical cord. I hit him, I hit him hard, but he wouldn't scream. I felt the weight of a mountain on my shoulders. It was the first still-born child I had delivered. Suddenly I noticed you weren't bleeding either. I knew the blood would be running somewhere into your stomach, filling it up until it stretched out like a drum. I palpated your belly. But oh God, your eyes turned up, your pulse disappeared, your heart stopped. I heard the front door slam. Your mother had gone out into the street. Your husband came in and said, 'You killed them both? You murderer!'" And she pressed Zari's hand even harder, complaining, "But if you hadn't died, why were you pretending? Why?"

Zari didn't reply, and Khanom Massihadem continued, "You know, we doctors have to get used to death. We mustn't be afraid of the signs. But I panicked. It was as though a storm was raging inside my head, tearing out all the wires of my nerves and brain and jumbling them up in a heap. It was as if my heart had sunk down to my feet. These people think I've gone mad, but I haven't. I'm just very, very unhappy."

199

Zari tried to get up, but the young woman would not let go of her hand.

"I saw the ceiling part with my own eyes," she was saying, "and a black-robed, winged person came down and took you away under his wings. But they won't believe me. I begged that black-robed person to spare Tal'at and take away my life instead. But he said he was taking her to heaven, under the Tuba tree. 'Take me instead,' I said ... Now, for goodness sake, Tal'at, tell me how come he brought you back? Do you mean to tell me there was no room in heaven?"

She was squeezing Zari's hand very hard and carrying on rapidly, "Now, will you do something for me? You know that I've promised to go away in your place?"

"Of course."

"Buy a few grams of good opium," she whispered in Zari's ear, "and crush it well. Bring it to me before this evening, before the old man comes. But don't tell anyone anything. If the old man is here when you come, just drop it quietly in my lap and go. All right?"

Zari bit her lip. Khanom Massihadem burst into tears and said, "When the sun starts going down, I get so depressed ... it's as though they're piling a ton of steel on my heart."

Again she began to shake her head. The long hair brushed Zari's face as she tried to pull herself away and free her hand. But she couldn't manage it. And all this time, Zari felt her head was about to explode with pain.

Finally a white-haired old man leaning on a cane entered the room. Zari guessed with relief that it must be Dr Abdullah Khan. The old man went to the patient and placed a hand on her shoulder.

"But my dear, you've started it again!" His voice was not authoritative, but infinitely soothing. The patient stopped her head-shaking and smiled at him.

"I kept her here so you could see her with your own eyes," she said. "Do you see? There wasn't any room, so they sent her back ..."

"Has she been talking a lot of nonsense?" the old man asked Zari softly.

"On the contrary," Zari replied quietly, "she made a lot of sense."

"You see how the old man is going senile?" shouted Khanom Massihadem abruptly. "Why don't you ask Tal'at what goes on on the other side? What happens after the end? Because she's been

200

there and back, you know. I thought she'd disappeared into that pitcher of water and I was too frightened to drink. Or I'd think she's gone inside the flowers and I wouldn't look at them. It's all the rubbish you've been saying, you daft old man, and now my brain's out of order." Then she mimicked the old man, " 'Only death is true, the rest is a lie.' Tal'at, for God's sake tell him that Death had wings and took you away. He keeps telling me I've tired myself out and I'm just imagining things."

"I have to go now," Zari said.

The old man accompanied her to the door. "I've brought a pair of scissors to cut her hair," he whispered; "she can't stand to see her mother and relatives, and won't let them near her. Do you know how to cut hair? It really gets in her way."

"I know how to do it, but it's getting late and I'm expecting guests tonight."

"Can't you spare five minutes?"

Maybe the patient heard the old man's whisper or had guessed what he was saying. "Have you gone mad?" she screamed, clutching her hair tightly with both hands.

"Your hair will grow out thicker than ever in less than a month, my dear," he said. "By then you'll be healthier yourself and have a little more weight on you. I want to throw sugar-plums over your head with my own hands at your wedding. But hurry up and get well, my dear. I'm an old man."

What a soothing voice he has, Zari marvelled. He could tame anyone with that voice—a person with delusions, a person in a hurry . . .

Khanom Massihadem motioned to Zari, saying, "Come closer, I want to tell you something in your ear."

Turning to the old man, she said, "You go to the end of the room and shut your ears."

Zari was forced to bring her head close to the woman while she whispered, "When you cut my hair, plunge the sharp end of the scissor into my artery, will you?"

Then she sat obediently while Zari wet her hair, combed it, and cut it short like a boy's. When she'd finished, Zari handed the scissors back to the old man. For a minute their eyes met; Zari looked into his bright and lively gaze which belied his age. The old man nodded knowingly and Zari realized he had guessed her secret. The old man put the scissors back in his pocket and Zari said

201

goodbye, not certain whether the sparkle in those eyes was somehow a reflection of the snowy-white eyebrows or whether it was from his new-found knowledge. Khanom Massihadem, who had been staring at them, suddenly shouted, "Get lost! Go drown yourself. Go to the other side . . . " And again she started to shake her head.

Zari was about to step out of the room when the head nurse arrived with a pill wrapped in some paper. She gave it to Zari.

"I had to go out and buy it for you," she said. "The warden went to the Department of Health this morning for our supplies of medicine, and he's not back yet. We've no drugs at all. If we don't get some by tonight, with all these lunatics . . . " She didn't finish her sentence, but walked over to the pitcher of water in the corner of the room. She took the glass from the top of the pitcher while Zari unwrapped the paper to take out the pill.

"Wait, Khanom Zahra. Pain-killers are not too good for pregnant women," said the doctor.

"Do you know me?" Zari asked in amazement. After a pause, she said, "I recognized you too. You're Dr Abdullah Khan."

And again she stared at him. The man looked as if he had knowledge of all the secrets in the world. "If only his fingers would touch my forehead . . . " she thought, "this is a man who's healed people all his life; he has comforted them, guarded their secrets and only brought them to their attention for their own good."

But Zari was in a hurry. She had to get home as quickly as possible. Her headache was getting worse, and her heart felt no lighter than Khanom Massihadem's. McMahon was coming to dinner, and she kept praying he hadn't arrived yet so she could at least rest for half an hour in a darkened room.

Outside, Gholam was sitting in the droshke next to the driver, smoking a pipe. When he saw her, he jumped out, emptied his pipe, and helped her to get in. The droshke seemed to move along so slowly, the horses shying each time they passed a car, and Zari began to feel as if they would never get home. But they did, finally.

Yusef and McMahon were sitting in the cane chairs on the pavement in front of the house. Mina and Marjan were sitting on McMahon's lap, leaning over the table. With one hand he was holding the children and with the other he was turning the pages of a book they were looking at. When Zari reached the twins, they laughed and clapped their hands. The men and the children seemed

202

very cheerful. But Zari knew that if she sat down next to them, some of the sadness in her heart would infect them too. With her splitting headache, she hadn't the strength to smile and put on a pleasant face. When McMahon saw her, he carefully lowered the children to the ground and rose to his feet. They shook hands.

"I'm sorry I'm late," Zari apologized. "I'll go to the kitchen for a minute and then I'll be with you."

She went straight to the bedroom and threw herself on the bed fully dressed, burying her head in the pillow and with it the pain that was radiating from her eyes, ears and left jaw. "If this pain doesn't go away," she thought, "I'll ruin their evening." She decided for a moment to take two aspirins, then she remembered Dr Abdullah Khan's words and changed her mind. The old man had not spent a lifetime treating people for nothing! He was wise, and held the key to many a secret. How quickly he had managed to guess her condition with those bright eyes of his!

Someone came in and switched on the light.

"Put it off!" Zari ordered.

"Are you sleeping?" It was Yusef's voice.

"Please turn the light off."

Yusef did as he was told and went to her side, sitting on the floor.

"Has something happened?" he asked.

"I have a headache," said Zari.

Yusef removed his wife's shoes and put them quietly on the floor. Then he came closer and massaged her neck and her temples.

"Would you like me to get you some vinegar to smell?" he asked gently.

"You go to your guest. When I feel better I'll come too."

"I can ask him to leave."

"No. But I'll feel more comfortable if you go to him."

Yusef left, and it was a while before he came back again. Switching on the bedside lamp, he said, "Turn your head towards me so I can begin my treatments. I bet you'll feel better."

Zari turned around. Yusef was holding a tray which he placed on the vanity stool. On the tray was a bowl of steaming hot water. He dipped a small towel into it, wrung it and put it on his wife's face. He repeated that several times, then holding her head in an embrace, tried to make her take some hot lemon and honey. He kissed her forehead, her eyes, her ears, and said soothingly, "Close your eyes and go to sleep now." He put two cotton wool swabs

203

moistened in rose-water on her eyes, and said, "Why do you tire yourself out like this?"

Zari suddenly burst into tears. "Why should there be so much unhappiness?" she sobbed.

Yusef picked up the wads of cotton wool which had fallen on the pillow, dipped them again in rose-water, squeezed them and placed them on Zari's eyes. "You're not responsible for all the unhappiness, you know," he said.

Zari sat up abruptly and the cotton wool swabs fell into her lap again. "And you're not, either!" she exclaimed. "So why do you put yourself in danger?" And after a pause, "I saw Fotouhi. He's decided against collaborating with you."

"Now I understand. That frightened you, and it gave you a headache."

"That wasn't all. His sister attacked me, Khanom Massihadem took me for one of her patients who died in childbirth . . . Oh God! So much misery! So much loneliness!"

"Someone has to do something . . ."

"If I beg you not to be that someone, will you agree?"

"Listen my love, if you start getting restless and impatient, it will distract me from what I'm doing."

Zari threw herself into her husband's arms and said, "We have three children and one more on the way. I'm so frightened, Yusef!"

"Would you like me to read you a Hafez poem and see what he predicts for us?"

"No!"

"Would you like me to bring the radio in this room and play you some music?"

"No. Just promise me you won't be the one person to change things. I know you people want to go down to Khuzestan and do something dangerous there."

"I have a good idea. McMahon's story has been published. I'll ask him to come here and read it to you. I know it will make you feel better."

"All right," Zari agreed. "Prop up the pillows behind me. I'll sit up. I feel better already." But she was only pretending.

Khadijeh came in first. She had come to take away the tray. "May all your troubles be on my head!" she exclaimed. "The master was frightened out of his mind, thinking you'd caught this disease that's going round the town." She went away for a few minutes

204

and reappeared with a small round table from the parlour on which she arranged some glasses and drinks. Zari had given her instructions for everything that morning. She had even prepared the stuffing for the chicken herself that afternoon before going to the asylum, telling Khadijeh to leave it in a basket over the cistern to keep it cool.

"Ameh Khanom hasn't returned yet?" she asked Khadijeh.

"No, she hasn't," Khadijeh replied, adding with a sigh, "If only it were God's will for me to go on a pilgrimage too! Perhaps she might think of getting me a fake dashport or whatever they call it, from that fellow. I'm not about to go to Karbala yet, but I would hide it until the Imam is willing to receive me, his humble and sinful servant." She paused, then continued, "I broke an egg as an augury to find out who had fixed the evil eye on you, and it turned out to be the master himself!"

When Khadijeh had left, Khosrow and Hormoz came in. Khosrow threw an arm round his mother, saying, "Hello, mother dear! Would you like me to fan you a little?" Then, "What can I do to make you better?" Hormoz was smiling, and asked after Zari's health as he stood politely by the bed. Khosrow put his face next to his mother's and said, "Mother, please can Hormoz and I have our dinner in my room?"

"Why, dear?"

"We've decided never to speak to English officers again from now on. We're not even going to have anything more to do with their Indian soldiers."

"But McMahon isn't English, he's Irish."

"What's the difference?" asked Hormoz.

"He's not even an officer, he's a reporter," said Zari.

"Well he's probably a spy," said Hormoz, "otherwise why shouldn't a young man like him be wearing an officer's uniform in wartime? He's younger than Singer, isn't he? I'm sure Singer sends him here to find things out from my uncle."

"You shouldn't judge people like that when you don't know anything about them," Zari reprimanded gently. She was about to go on and tell them that McMahon even dreamed of independence for his country and wrote revolutionary poetry, but she decided against it and just gave them permission to have dinner in Khosrow's room. She wasn't in the mood for explaining or defending.

205

As the boys were leaving, Zari said, "Khosrow, tell Khadijeh to give the twins their dinner and put them to bed."

When Yusef came in, he switched on the light, even though the bedside lamp was still on. The bright light bothered Zari's eyes, but she didn't complain. When McMahon came in, he reached out and put on the dressing-table light, and sat on the stool in front of it. Zari had not noticed until then that the middle finger on his left hand was missing. He had gained weight, and seemed to have more wrinkles on his forehead.

"I hear your story has been published," said Zari. "I'm glad."

McMahon smiled. "I'll read it to you, even though I'm afraid your headache might get worse!" He said. Turning to Yusef, he added, "Are you rationed for drink?" He was speaking English distinctly that night. Maybe he was trying to modify his thick Irish accent or perhaps even to hide it.

He took a sip and began. His voice was like a lullaby and Zari closed her eyes. Yusef sat next to her on the bed.

19

The old Charioteer gathered up his flowing white beard, a souvenir of millions and millions of years, and used it to dust the Golden Chariot of the Sun. Then he reached for the gold key which was dangling from his belt and headed for the East. Yes, it was time now. The Sun would be arriving wearily on his way. The old man opened the gate to the East with his key. The Sun was late today. But finally he showed up, yawning and dusty from his travels. The Charioteer brushed off the dust from the Sun with his thick white beard, and polished his beams. The Sun climbed into the Chariot, ready to begin his journey across the sky. But he didn't start right away, and the Charioteer waited.

"The Master sent you a message," said the Sun, "that's why I was delayed."

"His wish is my command," replied the old Charioteer.

"He sent His regards and said He wants you to clean out the Celestial Attic right away, throwing out or burning all the odds and ends. But His most important instruction is for you to take out the stars belonging to His subjects from the attic and send them down to Earth. He wants everyone to take possession of their stars from now on."

"Do you think cleaning out the Celestial Attic is such an easy thing to do?" grumbled the old Charioteer. "We've stored things in there for over five hundred thousand years; you can hardly find anything for all the rubbish."

"You know the Master," said the Sun. "When He gives an order, He means it."

With that, the Sun took off, and the old Charioteer was left to clear out the Celestial Attic, mumbling under his breath as he went, "Why doesn't He just wipe out the whole species from the face of the Earth and be done with it! They'll never be up to any good, these humans! What a waste to have blessed them with a spark of His own spirit! After all, they go back to that unruly creature, the ape. When He was watching over them Himself, they never stopped bringing disasters upon each other; now He wants to give them a free rein over their own lives! How he spoils these earthlings! How He lets them get away with things. Ever since they managed to stand on two legs, He has become very excited and talks of nothing but the 'noble human race'! I know all about that noble race. From what I hear, they have few talents besides slaughtering and oppressing one another . . ."

Grumbling, he walked on until he reached the Celestial Attic. There, he first reached for the Tablets of Destiny, stone and clay tablets which had the fortunes of people predicted and written out in an outlandish script. He broke up all the tablets and threw them away into space. He also disposed of the remaining odds and ends like old wings belonging to angels and cherubs, burnt-out stars and meteors which had never reached their destinations . . . Then he started on the files belonging to ancient gods. What a huge pile! He collected them all in a corner of the attic and went to the adjacent hall where replicas of the ancient gods were stored. There were all kinds of gods . . . tree gods, serpent gods, star-, fish-, and sun-gods, and finally, both winged and wingless human gods. In a corner of the hall he spied a battle-axe, which he used to chop down Ashur and Shiva.

He had had his fill of these gods. Suddenly he caught sight of Gilgamesh, the legendary hero. "How dare you!" He exclaimed in surprise. "Posing as one of the gods . . . !"

In a twinkling, the old Charioteer turned him into dust and blew him away.

When he got to the beautiful, shapely goddesses, the old man stood gazing for a while and reminisced. He thought of those days when Ishtar and Isis and Nahid and Aphrodite used to tease him with playful remarks. Every so often they would wink at him or perhaps Nahid would let him have a drink from her pitcher of water to refresh him. He had to push back the tears as he broke the replicas of the goddesses, but he couldn't bring himself to break Nahid's pitcher. Actually, he felt a pang as he destroyed Merduk, Mithra, Quetzalcoatl and Apollo too. In their heyday, these gods had never been too hard on their subjects. They even showed them

208

some compassion from time to time. But the god Benu seemed to have somehow disappeared at the very moment the Charioteer was breaking up the Tablets of Destiny which Benu himself had inscribed.

Before long, the old man began to feel hot. He came out of the hall to look at the sky. The Sun, in his Golden Chariot, had reached the mid-point of the heavens. The Charioteer returned to the attic and pulled out the papers concerning the holy cities and mountains ... records of the cities of Ur, Nineveh (later named Karbala), Benares, Chichen Itza, Jerusalem and other holy places, as well as records of the Himalayas, the Zagros mountains, Mount Olympus, the Andes, Mount Sinai, the Calcutta Hill, Mount Hera and any other mountain frequented by the ancient gods or used by them for their rendezvous with a favoured mortal. All these records he put on top of the files of the ancient gods.

There was almost nothing left now in the Celestial Attic except for one file containing several pages on the sacred trees ... the Tree of Knowledge, the Lotus Tree, and others. On the rest of the pages were lists of talismans, prayers and other palliatives which the Master had created over the past five hundred thousand years for his noble human race. The old Charioteer picked up all the papers and records and existing files from the Celestial Attic and piled them in one corner of the sky. Then he rubbed his hands together and made a spark which he held out to the pile, setting everything on fire.

The old man didn't wait to watch them burn. Instead, he went to the cupboard where he stored and locked away all the stars which he had swept up with his celestial broom from the sky every dawn. After all, if he didn't stow away the stars somewhere for safe-keeping, they would be scattered all over the sky and anyone passing through might choose to play marbles with them. Anyone, even the Sun, or the idle angels and cherubs. He removed the gold key to the cupboard which hung around his neck, opened the cupboard and called out, "Children! Come along and give me a hand!" His voice echoed round the heavens, and from every corner of the sky, millions of cherubs rushed to his aid. In a twinkling, they had prepared all sorts of sacks and bags sized according to every city, town and village of every earthly country, and they also made a variety of ladders with sun-beam rungs to go down to Earth.

The cherubs were having a field day. One of them would read out the list of people in order, another would hold the sack open, and the third would throw in the stars as the name of each owner was announced. When the sacks had been filled up, the old Charioteer tied and sealed them one by one, and then handed them to the cherubs. Each cherub was given one sack with a list of people whose stars it contained, and in return they gave a receipt. The Charioteer appointed one supervisor and five assistants for them, and ordered the ladders to be lowered to Earth.

It was a sight worth seeing. Imagine! Millions of sun-beam ladders, with millions of cherubs carrying sacks full of stars, rushing down those ladders. The old man had seen many interesting sights in his lifetime, but never anything like this. He had witnessed the day Lucifer stood up to the Master, quarrelled with him and left; he had seen Gabriel's wings burn away, and had been there the day the Master commanded the lotuses in every earthly lake to open while He sent the Light of Wisdom to that man sitting cross-legged beneath the tree . . .

The young cherubs were to knock at every door on Earth, and give each person his or her own star. "From now on," they were to say, "it's up to you!" Actually, they were free to phrase that message any way they chose.

Now the old Charioteer went to the West to see the Sun off on his course. Climbing out of his Golden Chariot which he left to the Charioteer, the Sun said, "Well done!"

"I'll have to think of a solution for the Master's cloak," said the old man. "From now on there will be no more stars on it at night until He has time to create some new ones."

"Why should that be up to you?" replied the Sun, before bidding the old man a chilly goodbye.

The Charioteer was glad his task was over. He ran a hand over his thick, woolly beard and thought, "Well now that I've got the chance, I might as well clean up too!"

It seemed a shame, but he decided to chop off that impressive beard which reached all the way down to his toes. As he did so, bit by bit, he covered the whole sky with the shavings. Then he broke Nahid's pitcher and poured the water over his head and body, washing himself thoroughly in the process. He looked quite a bit younger in the end. With all this water, the heavenly river of the galaxy swelled. Meanwhile, the sky over Earth was looking very cloudy. There was even some thunder and lightning and much rain,

210

but the cherubs were not in the least frightened. They knew the old Charioteer had broken Nahid's pitcher of water.

Thrice the Sun came and went, and there was no news of the young cherubs, their supervisors or their assistants. Every day the Charioteer would sit in a corner of the heavens, gazing on the planet Earth as it spun like a top around the Sun in space. Little by little, he began to worry. "What if they've lost the way," he thought. "What if their sun-beam ladders have got soaked in the water from Nahid's pitcher and then burned to cinders in the lightning?" The heavens were empty; empty of stars, empty of cherubs ... and still there was no message from the Master.

On the morning of the fourth day, he heard some noises in the distance. It sounded like the beating of wings, and the rustle of a breeze. Then the noises became more distinct. It was like a cosmic ringing, a melody which arises from the orbiting of planets and galaxies. Ladders were hoisted skywards, and soon enough the cherubs appeared. The Charioteer smiled. How the little cherubs had grown in this short time! How tall they had become!

He came forward to welcome them, all the while looking out for the supervisor and his assistants. Most of the cherubs didn't recognize him at first, but those who did said at once, "Why do you look like that? We came back because we missed playing with your beard."

They all began talking at the same time about their experiences on Earth, and there was such a din no-one could be heard above the others. The Charioteer suddenly thundered out in a voice which penetrated the noise, "I've had enough!" Then, when everyone had quietened down, he asked, "Where is the supervisor I sent with you?"

A cherub who was taller than all the rest stepped forward and said, "He didn't come. He stayed behind, and asked me to replace him."

"What happened to the assistants?" asked the Charioteer.

"They stayed too," said the new supervisor; "you know, one hundred and eighty thousand, three hundred and twenty-five cherubs stayed on Earth. With the supervisor and assistants, that makes one hundred and eighty thousand, three hundred and thirty-one."

"Why?" interrupted the Charioteer. "What was happening on Earth?"

All the little cherubs shouted together, "The Earth is so interesting, everything is alive there!"

The Charioteer clapped his hands to his ears. "You're deafening me!" he said. "One person at a time! You, supervisor, you tell me."

"You see," said the new supervisor, "the Earth is genuine. It's real. It's not imaginary or illusory. It's not nebulous, fleeting, or chimeric. It is solid. Your feet are on firm ground, and everyone and everything isn't floating."

"What do humans look like?"

"They come in all shapes and sizes. None of them look alike, but they are all real, made of flesh and blood. You know, down there everything grows, everything is in a state of flux. Everything is subject to the laws of creation, evolution and decay. There, nobody and nothing is eternal."

"I gathered that when I saw you. Now tell me about your mission."

"We really enjoyed ourselves. We celebrated their festivities. They had wars too, as well as poverty and disease. We wept for them."

"What did you do with their stars?"

"We gave each star to its owner, from the young to the old. The assistants gave me a report of their work on every continent. I've summarized all the reports for you here." And the new supervisor took out a folded piece of paper from underneath his right wing, and read out loud, "As you had instructed, the cherubs were to hand each person his star, with the words, 'We now entrust you with your own star so you know you are henceforth free. You must be your own support and refuge.' The reaction of the earthlings was the following: the children's eyes sparkled upon seeing their stars, and they quickly took them and started to play with them. When we left, they were still playing. The old people merely said, 'It's too late now' As for the youth and the middle-aged—and they are the ones who run most of the affairs of Earth—their reactions were mixed. All the people in this group received their stars, but most of them, no matter how much we explained, could not grasp what the Master meant. Some of them almost immediately lost their stars. Others hid their stars in their pockets, smug with the knowledge that they had a star tucked away. Only a few amongst these people understood very well. Some of them said, 'This is the way we have always been. We had no expectations from any celestial or earthly

212

stars, as we neither believe in destiny nor in complaining about being born under a good or bad star.' This group of people used complicated words, and the cherubs didn't always understand. Even their fellow earthlings had difficulty understanding them. Then again, one or two others from this group said, 'What a good thing it is that each person has found his own star.' These were an odd group, and in every country we came across a few of them. Some had beards, but not quite as long as yours used to be. These people immediately went to work on their dictionaries, striking out a lot of words from the vocabulary; words such as destiny, fortune, chance, fate, pre-determined and pre-ordained and all the other synonyms or equivalents. They were trying to replace these words with new ones rooted in 'freedom' and 'liberty' as we were leaving."

The Charioteer smiled. "One of these days I shall have to visit Earth," he said. "From what you tell me, it sounds very interesting."

McMahon fell silent. Zari opened her eyes. It felt as though she had just woken from a pleasant dream.

"What a story!" she said.

"Did you understand all of it?" asked Yusef.

"Whatever I didn't understand I pieced together with my imagination." Then turning to McMahon, Zari said, "Actually, at first I was expecting to hear a children's story."

"You see," he explained, "your daughters planted the germ of this story in my mind ... the first images I had were those of someone sweeping the sky and a sackful of stars inside a dark cupboard. But to tell you the truth, no matter how hard I tried I wasn't able to write a story for the children themselves, to pay back my debt to them. It turned out as you heard it."

Yusef laughed; he got up to pour some wine for McMahon and handed him the glass. McMahon took a sip and said, "It's good wine, where can one buy it?"

"You know," Yusef said, "now that I've heard your story again, it occurs to me your favourite theme is that same one you keep repeating in your poems." McMahon didn't say anything, so Yusef continued, "You're trying to atone for the sins of others."

Zari no longer understood what her husband meant. She was

213

about to ask him, when she heard Abol-Ghassem Khan's voice from the parlour.

"Where's everybody hiding?" he called out. Then he appeared in person. He blinked and said, "I heard there was a feast in this house tonight, so I got myself here on the double!"

20

A s Kolu began to regain his strength, he made himself a slingshot with which he pestered the sparrows in the garden until they could have no peace on any branch. There was still room to be grateful, however, since of all the window panes in the main building, only the pantry's had been broken. That day Zari had given Kolu a hard slap on the back of his hand, saying, "I've had more than enough of you!"

And Kolu had sat underneath the orange-blossom tree, crying and sobbing loudly to be taken back to his mother and brother.

Every Sunday before dawn, Kolu would get up, undress, and jump into the pool with the copper crucifix around his neck, waking Zari up with the noise. Then he would get out of the pool and, according to Gholam, dress in his new clothes, gulp down a little breakfast and rush off to see the black-robed man at the Missionary Hospital. Just before noon, he would return home and instead of his usual hello, announce, "I am a Christian." By lunchtime, though, he had clean forgotten it, and reverted to swearing by Hazrate Abbas again.

That last Sunday, Kolu had come home later than usual. Zari was in the kitchen, preparing provisions for Yusef's trip, so they could have some dinner ready when they reached Zarqan that night. Kolu came into the kitchen and eagerly preached to Zari and Khadijeh about Jesus Christ. He also mentioned Judas and asked Zari whether that ungrateful scoundrel was to be found in the Jewish quarter. Then he said with a sigh, "I am a lost lamb of Jesus." He clasped his hands in prayer before his lips and continued, "O Jesus who art in heaven. Let's see if you can find me and take me home to my mother!"

Khadijeh scolded him. "You stupid boy, repent before Allah!

215

Go wash out your mouth!"

"Leave him alone," said Zari quietly.

"Every night from now on I'll talk to Mr Jesus and pester him until he comes to me. After all, what kind of shepherd is he to abandon all his lambs and go and sit up in the sky? If he's true to his word, let him come down and take me . . . if he takes me with him then I'll give him my father's flute which I've hidden under the bedclothes. But if he doesn't, may Hazrate Abbas strike me down if I don't hit him one in the middle of the forehead with my slingshot when I come across him!"

He dug a hand into his coat pocket and brought out three copper crucifixes which he showed to Zari. "The fang-toothed woman gave me these charms," he said. "One is for my mother, one for my uncle, and the other for my uncle's wife—I'm taking these for them as souvenirs." He held one of the crucifixes in front of Khadijeh and said, "Kiss it!"

Khadijeh shoved his hand away. "You idiot!" she snapped. "Go back to your mother!"

Zari thought, "None of them have ever accepted him as a son in this family. Not even myself or Ameh Khanom."

"The fang-toothed woman told me Jesus is everywhere—in our village too," Kolu went on. "She said any child who calls out, 'Mr Jesus!' He immediately says, 'Yes, my child.' But I'm too old now so I can't hear him."

That evening Yusef decided to take Kolu with him to the village. Zari couldn't help thinking, "What does the poor boy imagine now? That Jesus found him?"

Kolu couldn't keep still for joy, so much so that he left his slingshot behind, even though he knew he wouldn't be going straight to his family. First he was going with Yusef to Zarqan until someone could be found to take him to the lowlands. Clearly the poor lad felt that every step away from Yusef's homestead was a step closer to his own village . . .

They departed, and Zari found herself alone during the long, turbulent nights, filled with nightmares. Nights so long, it seemed they would never be followed by morning. As time drew on, her thoughts became more distressed and her dreams more agitated.

Ameh was an expert at interpreting dreams. Everyone—even strangers—acknowledged this. Sometimes total strangers would telephone her and recount their dreams. She would greet them politely, and then proceed to give her interpretation, in the hope of doing a good deed. She also had a handwritten manual of dream interpretation which she would refer to in case of difficulty. But even Ameh was unable to unravel two of Zari's dreams. She leafed through her book carefully, but she still couldn't find the key to those two dreams. And it was for this reason, according to Ameh, that of all Zari's dreams, those two were constantly repeated.

Zari would dream that she stood stark naked in the middle of an unfamiliar square, surrounded by thousands of staring men and women. She also dreamt that it was exam-time at school, and a dark-skinned, scowling examiner was standing before her. Yet no matter how hard she tried, she didn't know any of the answers. She racked her brains and sweated and her pulse raced, but still she was unable to answer the questions. In the morning, she could no longer remember what the questions were.

Ameh instructed her to beg a piece of bread from a beggar and then eat it so she would remember the questions.

One night Zari dreamt that a two-headed dragon swallowed her husband whole, as he was galloping along on his mare. When she looked closely, she realized that the two-headed dragon looked like Captain Singer, dressed in a Scottish tartan kilt with embroidery all around the edge. This particular dream Ameh interpreted easily. She said it meant that Singer would become a public laughing-stock, but Yusef, like Jonah, would learn patience and endurance in the whale's stomach. The darkness inside the whale would enlighten him so that he could understand the secrets of the universe.

A few nights later Zari dreamt that the Governor had tossed Yusef into the furnace with his own hands. Yusef had burnt to a cinder, but nevertheless managed to grope his way out. Ameh interpreted the fire as the biblical one which had descended upon Abraham and then turned into a flower-garden. Yusef's coming out of the fire meant that he had passed his ordeal. And although Ameh's words reminded Zari of Siavush's story, she kept quiet. Because that night, in the tent of the tribal chief . . . that night when Malek Sohrab took a bet with her over a Brno gun, and she had lost but never paid up . . . that night they had talked of Siavush the whole time, and teased Zari because she knew about John the Baptist and not about Siavush, and they had explained to her that Siavush had passed through the fire and come out vindicated . . .

217

Ameh went on with her interpretation. "The furnace is clearly the same one in which the wicked Khuli woman hid Muslim-ibn-Aqil's children. Burning to a cinder signifies being purified and vindicated because, as you know, the meaning of a woman's dream is always the reverse of the dream itself."

Another night just before dawn, Zari dreamt that Kolu had struck Yusef right in the middle of the forehead with his slingshot. Ameh didn't bother to interpret this one saying that dreaming just before dawn has no significance.

Ten days after Yusef's departure, it was rumoured that Malek Sohrab had become an outlaw. Everyone who came to the house had something to say about it. Gholam told Zari that Malek Sohrab had taken to the mountains with a thousand gunmen and was hiding in an inaccessible spot.

One day Khosrow told her excitedly, "He's close to Yasuj now, with two thousand fighting men. And he still hasn't come down the mountain—what a man!"

A few days later, Hormoz showed up and commented, "Auntie, you know how much I admire bravery, but I think brave men should also have a sense of timing."

Abol-Ghassem Khan often came along in a hurry to pick up Hormoz and take him off to his highness the Governor, but each time Zari would coax him into staying awhile, plying him with some of Tavuus Khanom's oldest and best wines, and pressing delicacies on him until she managed to draw out some news.

"I hear Bibi Hamdam, Malek Sohrab's mother, went to Army Headquarters," Abol-Ghassem Khan told her. "She barged into the captain's room without permission and threw herself, in those wide breeches of hers, at the major-general's feet. She begged immunity for her son, and promised to bring him to the authorities herself. The major-general advised her to do that as soon as possible, at which point Bibi Hamdam pulled out a Quran from her bosom and tried to make him swear not to harm her son. But the major-general only kicked the old woman's hand away."

Then Sakineh, the woman who came to bake their bread, told them, "Bibi Hamdam has hired forty people to read the Quran and chant the An'am verse every day. It's hair-raising! Oh Lord, I beg you by the purity of the saints, to spare the life of Bibi Hamdam's

218

son, and meanwhile to spare this poor, sinful servant's son from the military draft too!"

In despair, Zari took up her old addiction of reading newspapers. But she couldn't find even the slightest mention of Malek Sohrab's name in any newspaper. Her habit did, however, lead her to a certain news item in one of the leading local papers. She had been alone in the garden that evening when the newspaper arrived and she had taken it from the delivery-boy herself. It was two weeks since Yusef had left. The item read like this:

"In Gratitude"

"The gracious Khanom Ezzat-ud-Dowleh, one of the charitable and kind-hearted ladies of this town, has been appointed by the Women's Society to visit and inspect the houses of the Mordestan District, as well as the women's prison. All the houses of the above-mentioned district have been cleaned and disinfected under her supervision, and this charitable lady, out of boundless generosity, has bailed out and set free one inmate of the prison who, out of ignorance, had engaged in earning an illegal livelihood. The Governorship of Fars extends its gratitude to this humanitarian and benevolent lady for her services."

Although Zari was not surprised to read this piece of news, it still depressed her. She crumpled up the newspaper and threw it away. She took refuge in the orangery, pacing about under the orange-blossom trees, feeling unequal to any task that might require concentration. She decided to go to the stables to find Gholam and ask him whether he had any more news of Malek Sohrab. But she changed her mind, knowing that the poor man might be half-undressed or even naked in the heat, or perhaps having a quiet smoke. For a moment, she thought of going to visit Bibi Hamdam, but decided against that too. She wasn't in the mood for the loud chanting of Quran reciters, and she knew that the instant Bibi Hamdam set eyes on her she would begin to wail and press her for a solution to her problem. And of course, if Zari had any idea what to do, she would not be feeling so distraught. Everyone knew that Bibi Hamdam's existence was tied to that of her son, and everyone knew too that Malek Sohrab, despite his size and stature, was nothing more than a child before his mother.

She thought of following Ameh Khanom and the children to Mehri's house, but she realized she didn't feel like putting on a long-sleeved dress and a head-scarf in that heat. Mehri's second husband, Mohsen Khan, was a very strict man.

Zari knew her restlessness and depression had much to do with sheer fatigue. Every summer she would spend at least two or three weeks at their village where a change of air, long walks and horse riding prepared her for the autumn and winter ahead. But this summer, with its disease, famine and war, and her own unexpected pregnancy, had made a prisoner of her, confining her to the house, the prison, and the asylum. She decided to arrange a weekly reunion with her former classmates ... an afternoon reunion, perhaps ... first at her house, then at Mehri's. Of course Mehri herself would be willing, if only Mohsen Khan would allow it. Their husbands didn't get along, otherwise she and Mehri, regardless of how often they saw each other, were still the same steadfast friends.

She went to the bedroom and searched in her drawers for knitting needles and wool in order to knit away her anxiety and depression. But neither knitting needles nor wool could be found. Her glance fell on a box full of glass beads. She picked it up, along with her sewing kit and went out on the verandah to string the glass beads. She looked out towards the garden which seemed to have lost its bloom. Dust had settled on all the trees, smothering the yellow, burnt-out leaves. For an instant she thought the trees were staring back at her. Then she saw them shiver and nod and then quieten down again. "They're getting ready for their sleep," she mused, "but the sparrows are awake on the branches, complaining to each other like a bunch of mother hens at the public baths!"

The sun had completely left the garden when, suddenly, she heard the neighing of a horse. It was the mare, not Sahar. Thank God! Yusef was back from the village. It was true what they said about hearts that talk to each other. Whenever she began to miss him desperately, Yusef would somehow turn up all of a sudden. She decided not to complain about how long he had been away this time, how anxious and wretched he had made her, how endlessly he had abandoned her to imaginings and nightmares and frightening rumours and unjust expressions of gratitude!

Gholam came out of the stables. Seyyid Mohammad, Yusef's steward, entered riding the mare, with the roan horse in tow. Zari felt a pang. She stood up. The box of glass beads in her lap fell to the ground and broke open, scattering the beads all over the rug. Well, perhaps Yusef had got off along the way, gone somewhere on an

220

errand. Seyyid Mohammad dismounted and gave the horses' bridles to Gholam, whispering something in his ear. Gholam threw his hat on the ground, and Seyyid whispered something more to him. Slowly, Gholam led the horses away to the stables. Zari ran toward Seyyid Mohammad, out of breath.

"Where's the master?" she asked.

"He's coming in Malek Rostam's car. Don't panic, nothing's happened," he answered.

Gholam and Seyyid started to behave mysteriously. Gholam ran out of the garden hatless, while Seyyid came to the pool to wash. He took out a comb from his pocket and combed his thick moustache. Then, taking a stone from the driveway, he washed it and placed it on the ground as he stood to pray. But Seyyid wasn't one for praying. Besides, what kind of prayer was this? Without a proper ablution and, although the sun had set, without the evening call to prayers?

Then Ameh arrived. It was very odd. Wordlessly, she stood to pray on the verandah still dressed in her outdoor veil. Without her prayer-mat. And without bringing the children. It was a long time before the car carrying Abol-Ghassem Khan drove in. Zari was certain something had happened but she didn't want to ask. She didn't have the courage. They began themselves, brother and sister, to tell her.

By the time Malek Rostam's green car drew up to the poolside and stopped, she knew what had happened, but she refused to believe it until she saw for herself. Malek Rostam and Majid got out and she knew her husband would not be stepping out. She knew he would never again climb in or get out of a car ... where had she read that so-and-so was riding on a wooden horse? Yusef was sitting stiffly on the rear seat, covered with a cloak and his hat pulled over his eyes. She heard Ameh's voice saying, "Welcome, brother. So you've come home ... " and Ameh began to sob. Abol-Ghassem Khan was wailing at such a pitch that he must have been heard in every corner of the house. Zari placed a hand over Yusef's ice-cold one, with those long stiffened and separated fingers. She looked at his ashen face, his chin which had been bandaged with a blood-smeared handkerchief, the blood which had already congealed. She took it all in, but could not believe it.

"Without saying goodbye?" she asked in bewilderment. Gholam let out a wail. Zari asked again, "All alone?" And now everyone

221

wailed. She wondered where from within their throats they managed to bring out those sounds? And why couldn't she? She could see that Ameh had torn open her collar and was sitting on the stone ledge of the pool. Zari kept asking, "But why?" And then the car, and the trees and the people and the pool all swam around and around and went away from her.

When she opened her eyes, she found herself stretched out on the rug on the verandah. All the garden lights were on. Did they have guests? There was an odour of mud-plaster in the air. Ameh Khanom was massaging her shoulders, and her body, neck and face felt moist. There was commotion all around. They had propped Yusef up on a wooden bed by the pool. A hatless Gholam was sitting behind him, rocking gently back and forth and repeating, "My master!" Haj Mohammad Reza the dyer, with his arms dyed purple to the elbow, was unsuccessfully trying to remove Yusef's boots. Abol-Ghassem Khan was standing over them.

"Haji, cut the boot open," he said. And he shouted for a knife.

Yusef didn't have his cloak on. He wasn't wearing his hat either, and Zari thought she must be dreaming. Lately she had had nothing but nightmares—perhaps this was yet another bad dream. She thought she was dreaming of a man they had forced to sit on the wooden bed, and they were cutting open his boots with a knife, but she couldn't see his face. She dreamt that Malek Rostam was holding the torn boot in his hand and shouting, "O woe is me, woe is me!"

She thought, "What do they call this kind of shouting from the guts? Bawling? Bellowing? Hollering? No, there's a good word for it, but I can't remember it now." Then she imagined she was dreaming that Majid had put his head on Yusef's cloak by the bed, and was sobbing out loud. But maybe she wasn't dreaming, since her eyes were wide open.

Abol-Ghassem Khan came to the verandah. He took out a white handkerchief from his pocket and blew his nose as though he had a cold. His eyes and his long nose were bright red. He blinked and said, "Sister, how quickly you've been widowed! And not even thirty yet! Oh my! Oh my!"

"Control yourself, man! Don't frighten a pregnant woman more than she is," Ameh said.

"Pregnant?" Zari knew she was pregnant, but her mind simply refused to acknowledge what had happened.

"How did you know?" she asked Ameh.

"From your eyes."

Again Zari had the feeling she was dreaming. A man seemed to be sleeping, sprawled over a bed, and despite the heat they had covered him with Yusef's cloak. But she didn't recognize the man. She dreamt that three men were sitting on the children's bed, talking about the man who was laid out on the other bed.

She managed to distinguish the voices: "My sister is right," Abol-Ghassem Khan was saying, "it wasn't time for his ideas. Brother, if your spirit is present, forgive me. I envied your intelligence and understanding and education, but as I didn't have those things, I'd make fun of you. Brother, you had the freedom of a cypress, reaching out—"

Then Majid's voice, "Yes, but don't be upset now. He knew himself that it wasn't time for his ideas. But he used to say—many times he told me himself—that our duty is to hasten the time for those ideas."

And Malek Rostam's voice, "I know that any day now they'll get my poor brother Sohrab, as well. They'll set up a gallows in the Mashq Square and everyone will go to watch."

The voices mingled with the sound of crying.

"Don't you think one wants to say and do the right things? But when you've started on a downhill course, the only way to go is down and then you're sunk . . . " Whose voice was that?

Footsteps could be heard on the gravel of the driveway. But they stopped when they reached the verandah and then resumed again. Zari closed her eyes, feeling as if all her life-forces had been drained and spent, like a squeezed fruit. It was as though a snake had slithered down her throat and coiled itself around her heart, with its head erect, ready to strike, and she knew that for the rest of her life this snake would stay coiled right there around her heart, so whenever she remembered her husband it could sink its fangs into her bosom.

At Ameh's insistence, she got up and let herself be led by the arm to the parlour. Women were sitting all around on chairs or on the carpet, most of them fanning themselves and whispering together. The men were in the other rooms. She could hear their voices. It was as if they had all been waiting outside the garden gates for her husband's corpse to arrive, with its fair locks bloodied beneath the hat, all the way down to the fair moustache where the blood had

223

clotted, and then they could all come in ... the women stood up at the sight of her, but Zari couldn't see anyone clearly enough to recognize them. Ezzat-ud-Dowleh was the only exception. Zari's gaze locked for an instant into her cobra-like face, framed by the gaudy hair, and then some sparkling yellow, red, blue and black glass beads took form and danced before her eyes. Most of the women peered at her carefully, shaking their heads and crying. From the other rooms, the men's voices could be heard, topped by Abol-Ghassem Khan's loud weeping.

"If anyone knows, please tell me too ... I'm at a loss ... " he was saying.

But Zari's eyes and tongue were dry. Not a tear, not a word. She went out to the verandah and sat on the rug. Khosrow, riding Sahar, came through the garden gates and cantered straight to the verandah. He let Sahar go and rushed to his mother.

"Is it true?"

Zari bent her head and busied herself collecting the glass beads from the rug.

"Did you pass your exam?" she asked. All the lights were on. How could he not have seen his father's sprawling corpse beneath that cloak? Why did he keep asking if it was true?

"Why are you so late?" Zari asked.

"Those of us who'd passed treated the others to paludeh ice-cream. But then the janitor came and told me uncle had called to say father was shot but he was just wounded, and he'd come straight home on horseback. Is it true? Where is he now? At the hospital?"

She suddenly hugged her son and kissed him, and then the tears began to flow.

Before long, a lot of people were embracing her and weeping aloud over her and her fate—to have been widowed so soon, to have to raise four orphaned children. Already everyone knew about the fourth. Ezzat-ud-Dowleh came forward too, but she neither embraced her, nor did she cry. She just said, "I hope this will be the last of your sorrows. At least he's left you enough to raise your children in comfort." Hardly saying goodbye, she went away, hobbling down the stairs with a hand to her back. She headed towards Malek Rostam who was sitting on a cane chair by the pool. Malek Rostam stood up and gave her his seat. You could tell Ezzat-ud-Dowleh was talking and Malek Rostam listening. She

224

seemed to shed a few tears too, since she kept dabbing at her eyes with a handkerchief. A voice announced: "The droshke is here." Ezzat-ud-Dowleh rose and, on Malek Rostam's arm, walked down to the end of the garden.

A few hours later Zari found herself lying on the bed in the cool basement with Khanom Hakim standing over her head. The fountain was on, and she could feel a cold, wet handkerchief on her forehead. She felt the sting of a hypodermic needle. Once, twice, three times ... she could see Khanom Hakim placing the cold wooden ear-trumpet on her belly and listening.

"The baby be all right," she said. "Tonight be best for the burial."

Zari heard Ameh Khanom reply, "Why don't you keep to your doctoring! Do you think my brother was a criminal to be buried at night?"

And again Khanom Hakim's voice asking, "Why be so unpleasant? All three children be delivered by me. So will be fourth."

Zari realized she was being questioned. "Why you be not coming sooner to me?"

Zari gave no answer, and Ameh replied rather harshly, "It's all your 'be this' and 'be that' which has driven everyone mad! If only ... "

"If only you would get lost." Someone had said that in Zari's mind, because Ameh Khanom didn't finish her sentence. Nevertheless, Khanom Hakim seemed to have heard the voice in Zari's mind.

"Be this the reward for service and self-sacrifice?" she complained indignantly in a trembling voice. "We be in strange town with dry air, away from brother and sister and friends ... medicines be free, treatment free."

This time the voice in Zari's mind shouted, "Get lost! Everyone get lost!"

Khanom Hakim had gone, and Zari could see Khosrow with a fan in his hand. She felt a cool, gentle breeze on her face ...

"Khosrow," she murmured.

Khosrow brought his head closer.

"Do something for your mother ... go to Dr Abdullah Khan early tomorrow morning ... tell him what a disaster—tell him to come by and visit me for a moment."

"I'll go right now," Khosrow said, getting up.

225

"No, my love, go tomorrow morning."

Ameh came in and Zari heard her say, "Get up, son, go and eat your dinner. Then to bed. For your late father's sake, be a good boy and go right away." How quickly they beseech you by your late father, thought Zari ... and sometime after that Khadijeh's voice announced, "There's a man at the door. He says he's come to give us a hand as an act of charity. He says he dreamt last night that one of Imam Ali's devout servants had just entered the kingdom of God ... "

Zari knew they had set up a tent around the pool, and were about to wash her husband's corpse in the pool-water. She knew the pool would be emptied and the water drained that very night, channelled quietly into the garden. The water that had cleansed her husband's body and washed away the dried blood would irrigate the trees. And Hossein Kazerouni would work the treadwheel from midnight to refill the empty pool by morning.

Her ears perked up at the sound of Seyyid Mohammad saying, "What can I say? Better left unsaid." Whose question was he answering? Zari opened her eyes. Seyyid was squatting by the door of the basement, rolling a cigarette. Ameh was sitting on the bed at her feet. Abol-Ghassem Khan and Khosrow were there too. Seyyid licked the thin cigarette-paper and striking a match, said, "What can I say, really? No-one knew how it happened. The peasants were ready to die for their master. I don't know. Maybe it was the work of the gendarmes, or some others ... this business about Kolu's uncle rushing all the way from Kavar to shoot the master and then racing back home is a load of nonsense. It's trivializing the matter; it's even an insult. Whoever had a hand in it, started this rumour themselves. When I got on my horse to come down to the plain, Kolu stopped me and said, 'I shot the master.' I said, 'What did you shoot him with?' He said, 'With my slingshot.' Later I heard he'd said a gun. Then he'd said his uncle had done it. I know they've told him what to say. They think they can fool us. We couldn't find a single trace of Kolu's uncle having been at the village, no matter how carefully we investigated. How could he possibly have gone there without being seen? Yes, he does have a rifle. The master bought if for him himself after Kolu's father died."

Seyyid broke off to take a puff. Then he continued. "Early that morning we'd gone to the store-rooms. The master broke the seals on the doors with his own hand and distributed pulses and dates

226

and flour among the peasants. He teased them and joked with them. He told the women that if they sold their share to buy gold bracelets or go on a pilgrimage, he would disown them. He told the men that if they dared convert their provisions into money to buy new bedclothes and new wives, he would know what to do. Everyone was happy. The master was the happiest of all.

"Before lunch we went up to the upstairs room in the old fortress. The master sat on his cushion. We'd rolled away the mosquito-net. Elias brought the hookah and set it down next to the master. I asked, 'Shall I remove your boots?' He said, 'No, I'll smoke a pipe and we'll go down to the plain.' Then he asked, 'Has the camel-driver come?' 'Yes,' I answered. Elias said, 'Sir, this agent of Singer's is back again.' "

Abol-Ghassem Khan's voice interrupted Seyyid's narrative. "Everyone who came here tonight told me to hush up the matter completely, that the situation is very dangerous. The whole thing comes from the very top—" And Zari wondered how a man who had been howling with grief only a moment ago could possibly speak like that now.

Ameh's irate voice didn't let Abol-Ghassem Khan finish his sentence. "Bless my soul!" she exclaimed, "Now they want to blot out the blood that's been shed! Brother, listen to me. Hire a lawyer. If you don't, I'll do it myself."

"Sister, I thought you were about to leave for Karbala?" said Abol-Ghassem Khan sarcastically.

"Now my Karbala is right here," said Ameh with a cry in her voice. "Happy is the martyr whose blood is one night old. For us, it hasn't even been one night yet."

"Sister, you women are not aware of the things that are going on here," Abol-Ghassem Khan said gently. "Let's say I engaged a lawyer. Who do you think they'll charge with the murder? I'll tell you: Kolu and his uncle ... or some other miserable peasant, or perhaps even this very Seyyid here. They'll manipulate things so that eventually we forgive the scapegoat ourselves, or else Kolu will turn out to be the murderer, and he's a minor. Isn't that so, Seyyid?"

"If any court decides to act so unjustly," replied Seyyid, "I'm willing to go out there and rouse all the peasants, single-handed. In the whole village, the master was—"

"But what's the use? The little money my brother's orphans have left to them will be wasted. Besides, what if they arrest you first? Do you think they can't?"

"Uncle," Khosrow said, "in that case Hormoz and I will go and round up the peasants for action. Mr Fotouhi will help us too. And if our money is wasted, it doesn't matter. I'll earn my own bread. Of course I can't do that now. For the time being our mother might have to sew for a living until I grow up"—and suddenly he broke into tears.

Zari wanted to come down from her bed and embrace her son so that they could cry together, but she couldn't. She wasn't even able to open her mouth to say, "Don't cry, my love." What had Khanom Hakim's shots done to her?

Ameh cursed away. "O Lord," she said, "why did you create me a wretched, veiled female? If I were a man, I'd show them the meaning of manhood."

Zari expected Abol-Ghassem Khan to lose his temper, but he merely complained quietly, "All right. Go ahead and insult me by saying I'm not a man. But what else can one do besides surrender and consent?" After a pause he added, "Well, all right. These are problems for later, anyway. Give me some time to see what I can do."

Khosrow turned to Seyyid Mohammad and asked, "Isn't Singer's agent that fat man with the pock-marked face?"

"Yes, that's him," Seyyid answered. "After Elias announced him, he came up to the top room of the fortress. First he conveyed Captain Singer's greetings, then he said, 'I've been told to ask you to be sensible. What's the use of distributing wheat among the peasants? Peasants don't think of tomorrow. They go and sell it for several times the price on the black market.' The master laughed— that was the last time he laughed—and answered, 'Go and tell Singer that instead of him and his sort getting fatter by the day, let our peasants get a little richer.' The agent said, 'Captain Singer thinks your best interest lies in not touching the rest of your provisions.' The master answered, 'Since when do I ask Singer about my interests?' I remember every word of that conversation. The agent then said, 'Captain Singer says they can break the locks on the storerooms and take the wheat. Not only the wheat, but also the barley, the pulses and dates that they need. They have a written mandate from the Governor too. After all, they'll be paying you cash. Is that such a bad deal?' The agent went on, 'At a stretch

228

they'll buy the provisions second-hand from the peasants, and they won't be losing on it either. The government has doubled the exchange rate of the pound.' Then the agent bent over and whispered some things in the master's ear which we couldn't hear. But the master lost his temper and shouted, 'To hell with all of them! Don't threaten me with gendarmes either, I'm not afraid of them. If you dare, go and break the storeroom locks with your gendarmes. You have the mandate.' Then he calmed down and said, 'At this point in time provisions have nothing more to do with their war. It's fallen in the hands of their trading company, and the trading company deals in food supplies.' The agent wiped the sweat from his forehead and said, 'Sir, I beg of you, don't be stubborn. Don't fall out with these people, they'll harm you.' Then he asked, 'Aren't we from the same town?' The master replied, 'Yes, unfortunately we are.' The agent said, 'These people aren't really in need of your provisions, but they're afraid of the example you'll be setting.' The master said, 'Actually, that's precisely my intention. In Hamadan people closed their shops and didn't allow a grain of wheat to leave the city gates. Here they've wrecked the Darvazeh Quran gate . . . ' Again the agent whispered in the master's ear for two or three minutes. When he'd finished, the master went deep into thought. He seemed upset, but stayed resolute. He just said, 'Tell Singer I give Sohrab provisions, not weapons.' I was about to go. I had barely crossed the threshold when I heard a gun fire. I turned around, saw the pipe fall over and the master tip to one side. Blood started to gush. Mohammad Mehdi and Elias ran inside . . . they gave a hand, but the agent didn't budge. I yelled at him and told him to get lost."

"Maybe it was Singer's agent who shot him," said Khosrow.

"No, that man is such a coward, he would fall over if you said 'boo' to him!" Seyyid said. "We moved the master off the cushion. I lifted it. They had dug a hole under it the size of my hand. The master was still conscious. He opened his mouth to talk, but he couldn't. I brought my head close to his. He said, 'Kolu . . . Kolu . . . take him . . . to his relatives . . . Zari . . . Zari . . . my children.'" Seyyid paused, then continued, "I sent a messenger to Kavar to tell Malek Rostam, and I sent Kolu along with the messenger before any fools got their hands on him to tear him limb from limb. I took the camel-driver and Mirza Agha Hennasab with me down to the plain and I waited until they loaded the camel with provisions. I got a receipt from the Mirza Agha and came here. Here's the receipt. I don't know if I did the right thing. But I know if the master were alive, that's what he would have done."

"What was Mirza Agha Hennasab doing there?" It was Ameh's voice.

"He'd come with the camel-driver from Malek Sohrab," answered Seyyid.

With an effort, Zari managed to sit up. "I wanted to raise my children on love and non-violence," she said. "Now I'll raise them on revenge. I'll give Khosrow a gun."

"I don't blame you," said Abol-Ghassem Khan. "What they've done is unforgivable. But you can't wash away blood with more blood. We have to wait and see what happens."

Zari lay down again and fell asleep. She began to dream that a strange tree had grown in their garden and Gholam was watering it with blood from a small watering-can.

21

Zari was awake. In her mind, someone seemed to be talking. Saying nonsensical things. Things that Zari knew she had heard or read somewhere. Sentences followed each other, but she was not expecting them. Where had they been suspended in her memory to be appearing now?

"My, but all our wise men have abandoned this town . . ."

"O Dark, dark, dark, amid the blaze of noon . . . it's me Eilan-ud-Dowleh, it's me Veilan-ud-Dowleh . . . I'm burning, burning, burning. There's enough fire within me . . . but because you're younger, you can't take it . . . how this painted dome, the world, reeks of mischief . . ."

She squeezed her eyes together to block out the flood of sentences plaguing her, but that only made it worse. Now the painting that one of the mental patients had done in the asylum kept appearing before her eyes. The painting depicted a butcher's shop. An icon of the Imam Ali and the image of the young butcher with his hand cut off could be perceived against the shop wall. The shop itself was filled with giant hooks as far as the eye could see, but instead of mutton, there were people hanging by their feet from those hooks, and blood was dripping from their throats.

She opened her eyes. It must have been well after midnight because there was no electricity and they had lit candles. She saw Abol-Ghassem Khan sitting on the carpet, hugging his knees. Ameh was sitting across from him. Khosrow was there too, as well as Malek Rostam. Seyyid Mohammad was standing in the doorway of the basement. The smell of opium, cigarette smoke, alcohol and charcoal mingled in the air. She could hear the steward's voice in her state of semi-consciousness. He was talking about the funeral and his voice seemed to have gone hoarse as if he had just come

231

down the Mortaz-Ali mountain carrying a jug of wine to go to the grave of the Seven Sufi Saints. Now he opens the tap of the jug and starts to drink. Red drops spill from his thick moustache on to the nameless graves. He puts the jug under the cypress tree and sleeps on a cold slab of stone. When will the jug of wine turn into holy wine? By dawn? By the time the sun rises? "Gone are the days when people could find a purified drink to use for attaining a mystical state of mind like Hafez," Zari thought in her reverie. "Now they have to swallow gunpowder instead. Gone are the days when they sat humming by a stream and reflected quietly on the passage of time, content just to be with a rosy-cheeked young lover. Now they have to stand next to the dam of life, with its flood charging straight at them, slapping them so hard in the face, they're left reeling for good. By the way, what was the word for shouting from the guts? There was a good word to describe it ... but it had to somehow convey piercing or boring. You see, if a person can't let out a certain kind of scream when they're hit with the flood, the thunderbolt, or the thrashing of life, their heart is punctured instead, and then all those people with riddled hearts go for each other's throats trying to destroy one another until they're sent off to prison. Or else it goes to their heads, and they lose their minds. Meanwhile, a spoilt, silly, pampered young woman is taking bread and dates to prisoners and lunatics every Thursday. She has a vow to fulfil. But that woman herself is perhaps struggling on the verge of lunacy at this very moment, which is why her mind is ticking so. So fast, she can't stop herself ..." And suddenly Zari was seized with fear. "Am I going mad?" She tried to sit up, but it was as if she had been nailed to the mattress.

When she lost consciousness, she would dream. Awake, either someone would be talking randomly inside her head, or she would intensely relive bygone incidents drawn out from the recesses of her mind. She no longer distinguished past from present. Sometimes random events materialized before her which she didn't recollect ever having seen or heard. She strained to keep her eyes and ears open, to assure herself that Ameh and Khosrow and the others really did exist, and she could recognize them and hear them. But her eyes and ears would only stay at her service for a short while, and then sooner or later they would drift away from the present reality again.

She could hear Ameh's voice, "How did Ezzat-ud-Dowleh

manage to get here with those leg-pains of hers? I suppose she came to satisfy her curiosity and see what's going on. Her eyes really lit up whenever she looked at Zari. I told myself how happy poor Zari had made her enemy." And she broke off, crying.

Then Malek Rostam was saying, "Ezzat-ud-Dowleh asked after my brother Sohrab. At first she said she'd heard he was under siege. 'Where did you hear that?' I asked her. She seemed taken aback. 'Well they'll get him anyway,' she said, 'and then Lord have mercy on poor Bibi Hamdam. Whatever you suffer, it's at the hand of your children!' And she burst into tears. Because of her connections with the Governor's family, I thought she might know something, and I tried to prise out of her where she'd heard that Sohrab was surrounded. But she eluded me and said, 'When did I say such a thing? I just said his friends gave him away ...' Anyway, she changed her story a hundred times ... she said Malek Sohrab was tired, that he had no food or water, that he's turned himself in. When I was helping her into the cab, she said, 'I've heard Bibi Hamdam has begged the Governor for mercy for her son, and now she's gone to bring Sohrab on his own feet to be executed!' I nearly tore off her wig, I was so angry, and wanted to beat her up as much as she could take. But all I said was, 'Khanom Ezzat-ud-Dowleh, if you have any specific information, please tell me.' I even made her swear by her darling son Hamid, but she denied knowing anything and pretended it was all rumours. I got into the droshke with her and afterwards rushed to Bibi's house. No-one would answer the door. What if the major-general's promise of a pardon was only words and he'll go back on it ... what if—"

"Forgive me for saying this," interrupted Abol-Ghassem Khan, 'but considering the hell Malek Sohrab raised in the battle of Semirom, I doubt if they would give him a pardon. It's like the story of the husband who said to his wife, 'I told you to dance, but I didn't mean you to overdo it!'"

Yet all Zari could see, clear as day in her half-awake state, was a vision of people coming at dawn to the Baq Takht square, carrying rolled-up rugs on their shoulders. The women were wearing ordinary chadors with face veils, or the large, wide chador with a thin face-cover. The men were crawling on all fours. O Lord, have the townspeople gone stark raving mad? Wasn't this Shiraz, the town where angels bent down to kiss its very soil? I must remember who it was who wrote a eulogy of Shiraz ... Sounded like ...

Mohammad-ibn-Yusef Saqafi. I memorized the title. Yes, this is the land which will nurture many thousand men of bounty. It's the seat of the Sufis, the wellspring of our country, the essence of our Imams' spirituality . . . oh my, oh my! So where have they gone? Where are these people that are not coming forth now? I've heard a hundred times myself that all our wise men have abandoned this land . . . they asked a sparrow why he didn't come in winter; he replied, "What good did you do me in summer that I should come again?"

And now here's Nana Ferdows. There's a small rolled-up rug inside the bath bowl she's carrying on her head. And here's Ezzat-ud-Dowleh leaning on Ferdows, limping along. Oh dear, look! Ezzat-ud-Dowleh sits down on the rug in front of all those people without her veil, and her gaudy hair is showing. No. It seems as though she's wearing a wig like a turban. Here's Hamid Khan, her son. The bastard reaches out and pulls at Ferdows's breast. He's pulling very hard. Ferdows gets up to go about her business. Her legs are tapered and shapely in those transparent stockings. Everyone is staring open-mouthed at Ezzat-ud-Dowleh and her son and Ferdows. Then they burst out laughing.

Where has Ezzat-ud-Dowleh's husband been all this time and why is he arriving only now? Maybe he's escaped from the grave. He's been dead for a long time, you know. Oh look, he's wearing a cashmere brocade cloak and a brimless hat in this heat. His hat is very, very tight and it's squeezing his forehead. There's a perforated hole in the corner of the hat too . . . Oh I know! He's back to kill Massoud Khan all over again. He reaches under his brocade cloak and brandishes a long pistol which he aims at Massoud Khan and bang . . . bang . . . bang . . . he drags the corpse on the ground and abandons it on the green by Seyyid Abol-Vafa's shrine. But it seems as if Massoud Khan isn't dead. He rolls in the grass among the cucumbers and the pumpkins and eggplants. He opens his eyes and stares at all the people who've come to watch him. "Water!" he moans. Soon there's pandemonium in town. Massoud Khan is dead. He died in Haj Agha's arms in the droshke. There's no-one to calm down the crowd. They're about to raid the Jewish quarter. They're charging into the houses. People are running to the roof-tops and hoisting a British flag to proclaim that they're under the protection of His Majesty's British government. What chaos! The men who are on the roof-tops jump down quickly to the ground.

234

Each man is carrying a basin on his head. They put the basins down on the ground. In each basin is a severed head dripping with blood. What a lot of noise they're making!

They've tied Malek Sohrab's hands behind his back, but he's laughing so hard he could fall over. He staggers to the left and right. Children follow him, clapping and chanting, "Bring him here! Bring him here! Give him to the bride!"

Now they're erecting a gallows in the middle of the Baq Takht. What a loud hammering! Why didn't they do all this earlier so Malek Sohrab wouldn't have to wait? The men's eyebrows have grown so bushy, they cover their eyes. The men push back their eyebrows so they can see better. The women, sitting on the rugs, are straining to see what's going on. There's room for everyone. But they all have a problem with their eyes. How the eyeballs spin around! Maybe their eyes have rolled to the back of their heads! No. The men had their eyes under their eyebrows, didn't they? But the women are so wrapped up in their veils, you can't tell where their eyes are.

They bring Malek Sohrab to the gallows, but instead of putting the noose around his neck, a soldier with a gun on his shoulder comes and ties him to the stake. Malek Sohrab gives the soldier a surprised look and says, "Gently! Not so tight—you're hurting my foot." And then he says, "That's better now." And he laughs. He laughs so heartily, it echoes all around the Baq Takht. The same soldier tries to blindfold Malek Sohrab with a black handkerchief but Malek Sohrab says, "There's no need for that! Pull the trigger as quickly as you can. On the temple, between the eyes, in the heart, aim wherever you please. It doesn't make any difference if you do it sooner or later. I'll be standing right here. I've been waiting here for you for a long time. You can even chop me up with an axe."

Oh no, the ropes have turned into such snakes! Thank goodness Haj Mohammad Reza the dyer has arrived. He's wrapped some felt around his hand, takes the snakes' heads one by one, and thrashes them to the ground.

And here comes Bibi Hamdam in her wide breeches. She shouldn't have come. Why should anyone come to the hanging of her own son? Maybe Malek Sohrab's first wife is being avenged this way. Weren't Sohrab and his wife madly in love? Yes, they were. But Bibi Hamdam wouldn't stop talking about infertility and childlessness. Wait! The Quran reciters are here too. There's no

235

need to count them. They'll arrange their voices in unison and chant the Al-Rahman verse ... Malek Sohrab's poor wife used to say, "Bibi Hamdam, if you wouldn't plague us about having children every minute, we wouldn't worry about it ourselves and ruin our happy life together." And she'd told the story of another barren woman. What a night that had been! They were in the village and Zari was pregnant with the twins. Her pregnancy had reminded Bibi Hamdam of her desire for grandchildren. None of them could sleep a wink. It was so hot. Zari's hands and feet felt as if they were on fire. If she tried going outside the mosquito net, mosquitoes would attack her ... She was parched with thirst. Further away, Malek Sohrab and his first wife were sleeping under their mosquito net. Bibi Hamdam had stayed indoors. There was a lot of noise; first the chanting of religious mourners, then the barking of dogs, next the tinkling of sheep-bells as the sheep stirred in their sleep, even the sound of crows quarrelling about whether the sun was coming up or not ... and all Zari could think of was the story Malek Sohrab's wife had told:

"A woman who desperately wanted children went to a dervish. He told her to fast for forty days and on the fortieth day to go up on the mountain and wash her body under a waterfall. But there was one condition. She was not to think of monkeys. She was allowed to think of all sorts of things, but not monkeys. Five times the woman went up the mountain and stood under the waterfall, each time after forty days of fasting. Yet she could not rid herself of the thought of monkeys. Each time the one thing that crossed her mind was the image of a huge, hairy monkey. Finally she went back to the dervish and said, 'Your remedy didn't work. If you hadn't mentioned monkeys, I would never have thought of them in a hundred years. But now that you have ...'"

And here's Captain Singer with his short, pleated tartan kilt which he has embroidered all along the edge himself! He sits behind the Singer sewing-machine and sews away ... But this is no time for sewing! How fast he treadles the machine! His eyes run from one end of the fabric to the other. He does a zig-zag stitch. No, it's lattice-work. The material is as full of holes as a sieve. Now he's standing up to make a speech.

"Ladies and gentlemen," he says, "Give alms! We have brought you civilization as a gift." His eyes fall on Zari, and he says with a smile, "When madam gives you hand, you kiss madam's hand."

People are clapping, but not for Singer. They're clapping for the little cherubs who are coming down sun-beam ladders with sacks full of stars. The cherubs come amongst the people and give each person his own star. Zari receives hers too. The cherub tells her, "Now it's up to you. Our heavenly Master is weary. Very, very weary." But Zari loses her star. Now she's searching everywhere, rummaging in every cupboard, and throwing out all the rubbish from the attic. She hunts in every trunk in the store-room, but nowhere can she find her star. She is wandering in the garden. She looks on top of the brick walls and under the trees. She asks Khadijeh, "Have you seen my star?"

A tearful voice says, "Now that you haven't found any saffron, make some halva from chalk instead." It's Ameh.

A doleful voice sighs, "You can make halva with chalk, but you can't eat it." This time it's Malek Rostam.

And again Ameh's voice which sounds stronger, "Khadijeh, make some yellow-rose halva for my young flower who died ... alas! alas! The tears dry up, but the sorrows remain."

The door slammed and someone entered. Zari opened her eyes. Seyyid Mohammad said, "They answered the telephone. His Holiness the head of the Sufi dervishes said we could have the memorial service in the House of Ali. The Imam's house is open to everyone."

"Fancy being parliamentary deputy of this town and not being able to hold your own brother's funeral in the Vakil Mosque! Ah! well, write it down, Khosrow ... what date is the day after to-morrow?" Abol-Ghassem Khan had been speaking.

"The thirty-first of Mordad." It was Khosrow's voice.

"Write down, 'On the occasion of the tragic passing away of our dearly beloved young ...'"

"Passing away?" interrupted Ameh's voice. "Put down, 'martyrdom'!"

"Sister, I'd be grateful if you'd let us do what we have to do. I persuaded him with a great deal of difficulty to print the announcement, but the man set down a thousand conditions ... one of his conditions ..."

"I think you should write martyrdom too," said Malek Rostam.

What a foul odour there was in the air! If only a passer-by would throw out the charcoal brazier. If only he would ask, "What's wrong with your patient here; why is he lying like a corpse, like a dead body, on the bed? Let me take him to the garden underneath that grafted fruit-tree. Outside, the sky is full of stars."

Zari's heart would race away and palpitate, then race away again. She would close her eyes and see a truck on fire, burning away. An officer comes and stretches out on top of a dead soldier in a trench.

And again Ameh's voice, "It's cat-shit. They've left the top of the coal-bin open and the cat's dirtied inside it. Khadijeh, come and take away the brazier. I don't want it, after all." Then she went on, "Have all the rooms been cleaned? Did they drain the pool? Did Gholam sweep the garden?"

And now Zari sees a little girl with braided hair tied up in ribbons, standing by the herbalist's store on top of the Moshir Hill. She needs seven ingredients to make black shoe-polish, by order of her physics teacher. Actually, that shoe-polish will never turn out properly; she'll make a gel like black frog-spawn and no-one knows whose fault it is—the girl's, the physics teacher's, or the herbalist's? The herbalist has gone to the back of the shop to look for the seven ingredients. It's late afternoon and the girl is in a hurry to get back to school to make shoe-polish during the fourth lesson. Suddenly a man on horse-back approaches her. The rider is Prince Charming himself; he looks so handsome and erect on his horse. He has green eyes . . . they shine like emeralds in the sun. And now as he stands in the shade, they look moss-green.

"Do you know how to get to the Sang-e Siah, my dear?" he asks. The girl panics. There is no-one around that afternoon. Still she ventures, "Do you want to go to the Sibavayh grave?"

"No, my dear. I want to go to the house of Sufis, the Khan-i Qah."

"Are you a dervish, then? You want to go to the House of Ali?"

The rider laughs and his white teeth glisten. "No, I'm not a dervish," he replies. "My steward is a dervish. He's ill and he's staying at the Khan-i Qah. I'm going to visit him."

"Well then, go straight ahead. Then turn right. After that, turn left, and another left . . . But you can't go on horseback. The little back-alleys are full of bumps and stones."

Now that she's given him directions, why isn't the rider going away? Why is he looking her up and down? Yes, I understand. He's wondering why she, of all women, should be without a veil.

"I must explain," she thinks to herself, "or he'll think I'm Armenian."

"My father was Mirza Ali Akbar Khan Kafar," she says out loud; "he stated in his will that I should never wear a veil."

The rider takes off his hat. It's a strange-looking one with a brim, but it's not the new pahlavi hat. He bows to the girl and says, "I never asked why you're not wearing a veil."

And he leaves.

But what will? As if there had been anything to bequeath! That very afternoon, with the shoe-polish gel still on her hands, there is news of unrest in town. The English headmistress lines up all the girls and tells them to put their face-veils in their satchels and that heavier veils would be brought for them from home. But unlike other times she doesn't nag and say, "This country doesn't deserve to be civilized." Her glance falls on the girl with braided hair and ribbons, and she asks, "Zari, do you know how to wear a chador?"

Whether or not she knows how to wear a veil is irrelevant, because there's no-one at home to bring one to her. Khanom Hakim has been cutting up her mother's breast at the Missionary Hospital, and that's where they're keeping her for the time being. Who knows how long it will take for her to get better? Her brother's away doing his military service and he won't be back for a long time. Their old maid-servant is too feeble-minded to find out what is going on in town and to bring her a veil. Well, everybody is leaving the school now. Nazar Ali Beg the Indian janitor agrees to fetch a chador and face-veil for her after all the other pupils have left. But it would take so long for everyone to leave.

Servants arrive to take the girls home, bringing them the veils which they put on before leaving. But there she is still, all by herself. Now she is alone with Nazar Ali Beg and it's getting dark. She's afraid. Nazar Ali Beg has a long moustache which droops lower on one side. His face, too, is slightly crooked. He explains that ruffians have poured into the streets and alleys, tearing away at women's face-coverings or men's brimmed hats, and that eventually they'll get to the school too, and break all the windows. She's afraid of Nazar Ali Beg because he keeps saying in his funny Persian, "Khanom, good Khanom!" But at the same time, she doesn't want him to go fetch her a chador, leaving her all alone in that vast school-building.

Suddenly she has an idea. She decides to call the house of the head dervish and ask Mehri to send her a chador. She's glad she's had such a good idea. She prays the rider she saw that afternoon is

239

still at the dervishes' house. She telephones and then sits by the pool and daydreams. She dreams that she's riding with Prince Charming on his horse; they're galloping towards Baba Kouhi, the mountain dervish, and she's singing for him:

"The lips of the Turkoman maiden should not have been created so perfectly ... "

They're knocking at the school-door. Yes, it's him. The girl smiles when she sees him. But this time he's on foot and hatless, and is carrying a parcel wrapped in newspaper. He holds out the parcel and says, "Here, put it on. I'll take you home."

"Sahib, good Sahib!" says Nazar Ali Beg.

The girl doesn't know how to keep the veil on properly, and it keeps slipping off.

"Do you have a safety-pin?" the man asks Nazar Ali Beg. Nazar Ali reaches behind his coat collar and produces an ordinary pin.

The girl walks off with the man, though she can't really see where she's going and nearly trips.

"Why did they bother you ... ?" she manages to ask.

"There wasn't anyone else. The dervishes had disappeared into their little cubicles. Mehri Khanom, the niece of the head of the dervishes, asked me to deliver this chador to you on my way. She said your name is Khanom Zahra. My name is Yusef."

The headmistress of the English School had taught them, on being introduced, to extend a hand, smile and say, "How do you do!" But how could she? Both her hands were taken up—one with her chador, the other with her books. The man continues, "I knew your father. I used to study English with him, until I went abroad. He was a great man, in his own right. He inspired noble ambitions in his students."

The girl remains silent. "Mehri Khanom has been telling me that your mother enjoys going under the surgeon's knife," the man says. "She enjoys having part of her flesh cut off and thrown away. Apparently every day she finds an excuse to go to the Missionary Hospital—one day it's a bruise on her big toe, another day it's a lump in her breast ... "

"You mean to say Mehri doesn't think my mother has cancer and she's wasting her time with all this surgery? I hope to God that's true."

The girl is looking at the man's shoes. She stops abruptly and says, "Your right shoe-lace is undone."

The man bends over and ties his shoe-lace. How quickly she's become familiar with the stranger! It's as if she's known him for years. And what does the man think now? That she's the kind of girl who comes away with him easily and even confides in him! Thank God she's wearing a veil and face-cover, and no-one will recognize her. Thank goodness there isn't a soul in the Jewish quarter. What if the man thinks she planned all this to catch him? Well, in fact she had. Mehri had realized this too and tried to help her.

"Mehri's face is as lovely as a flower, isn't it?" she asks. The man smiles and says, "I didn't see her face. She was wearing a veil."

"We were classmates up until the sixth grade. Every day we'd gather round the stove and she would teach us the Quran and religious law. Then she would tell us the stories she'd read in the Thousand and One Nights. She has a good voice too. She sang us Masnavi poems . . . the one that goes, 'I sight the King in any guise . . .' I've forgotten the first part."

"I want an eye to sight a King
To sight the King in any guise."

The girl has to make an effort to control herself. She's about to say, "I sight you!"

That was really why she quoted the verse in the first place.

"Has anyone ever told you your voice is as soft as velvet?"

The girl doesn't make a sound.

"You were talking about Mehri Khanom . . . " says the man.

"Anyway, she left school to get married . . . I don't know why her husband divorced her after a year. The husband died soon after. They say her uncle, the head of the Sufi dervishes, had cursed him . . .'

"Do they stuff your head with these superstitions at the English School?"

The girl is hurt and stays silent.

"What class are you in?" asks the man again.

"Eighth grade in Persian and ninth in English," answers the girl, still hurt.

There is no-one in the back-alleys. No-one has lit the street-lamps. The girl wants to lift her face-cover but she doesn't dare. It's a good thing she knows her way home by heart and is familiar with all the bumps and ditches. She could walk home with her eyes shut.

"Mehri Khanom talked about you all the time," says the man. "She said you once dealt your headmistress a severe blow by reciting the poem about Samson's blindness in front of the Oriental Missionary Council . . ."

"The poem just happened to come to my mind. I didn't mean to be cheeky or anything."

"You're modest, too!"

Now they've reached the bazaar and they're both quiet. In the bazaar they have lit a few oil lamps which they've placed on stools in front of the shops. But all the shops are closed. There are seven or eight policemen roaming around. There's quite a din but it's coming from the sword-makers' section. In the main bazaar itself, a few people are going on their way.

"They've blamed it on them again!" mutters the man. The girl doesn't understand what he means. Or maybe she didn't hear correctly.

They reach the vaulted passageway which is darker than anywhere else. The man takes the girl's arm, and the girl flushes. Her whole body seems to be flushed, in a way she has never experienced before . . . Now they reach the girl's house. She politely invites him to come in and have a drink, but she's praying he won't accept. He doesn't come in.

"I remember you had a winter-sweet bush in your house in those days," says the man.

"We still do."

"They're hard to grow, but when they take well, they flower every year . . . and what long-lasting, fragrant flowers!"

She both wants him to go and yet she doesn't. She asks him out of the blue, "Have you done your military service?"

"I'm going this autumn."

"It takes two years, doesn't it?"

"Try to grow up as soon as you can."

And again Zari doesn't understand his meaning. Later when she tells her mother the story, her mother agrees that God had sent the stranger to save her girl . . . and then . . . three years later, when that same man comes to ask for her hand . . .

What pandemonium in the garden! She had been having good dreams. Obviously she must be getting better if her nightmares and delirium have left her in peace. Someone was roaring in the garden: "Ya Hu, Ya Haq, Ya Ali." It was Seyyid Mohammad's voice.

242

"Khadijeh, what happened to the lemon juice?" Gholam asked.

Zari thought he must be drunk. "Take him to the Seven Saints," she said out loud.

Ameh came towards her. "Did he wake you up?"

Zari opened her eyes. Only Ameh was left in the basement with her. "They'll wake the children with their noise. They'll frighten them," Zari said.

"Don't worry. Mehri is keeping the children tonight; she'll keep them tomorrow too. I sent Khosrow up to bed on the roof after a thousand pleas."

The noise in the garden abated for an instant. From somewhere, the monotonous chanting of the Quran could be heard like a hum. Someone was retching. Retching. Someone else was cursing out loud and saying, "You're sitting up there watching, are you? Why don't you step down here for a second, taste your own broth which you've been giving our folks ... I spit on the bloody—"

Someone started to sing:

"A houseful of drunks already
More drunks have now arrived!"

Ameh put a hand to Zari's forehead and said, "They've been sitting around together drinking so much spirits, they're all drunk now." And she added with concern, "You try to sleep."

"What if Khosrow wakes up and falls off the roof? I wish you'd sent him off to Mehri's too."

"Hormoz is sleeping on one side of him, Majid Khan on the other."

"Ya Hu, Ya Haq, Ya Ali!" It was Seyyid Mohammad's voice in the distance. Close by, a man's incessant weeping broke the thread of her fantasies, and Zari felt as though that sound would never end. She opened her eyes. She saw Malek Rostam sitting with his head in his hands, sobbing out loud. Abol-Ghassem Khan was sitting there too, pale as a corpse, as if he were the one who had died.

"Malek Rostam Khan, please stop crying for this poor woman's sake. She'll wake up," said Ameh.

"I told Khanom Hakim to give her a shot that would put her to sleep," said Abol-Ghassem Khan. "I said if she stayed awake she wouldn't last till the morning. This blow will shatter her by dawn. I wish she'd given me a shot too."

243

The weeping hasn't ceased but Zari's mind has fled all the misery and sorrow . . . and sees herself hand in hand with Yusef crossing a field of wheat. The golden wheat is ripe and bends its head to the twilight breeze. Zari and Yusef come to a stream of water and sit down until it gets dark . . . they're sitting in the dark and holding hands, and Zari feels as though there's no-one else in the world besides herself and Yusef. She puts her head on Yusef's shoulder and listens to his heartbeat. How long did they sit in the darkness without talking?

That night they sat by the window in the darkness and stared out at the garden . . . that night Baba Kouhi told their fortunes, reading from Hafez, "The harvest of our work in this world is not so important!" And he recited the ode to the end. Then he predicted, "It will pass in the twinkling of an eye. It's as close as the mouth to the lip."

Baba Kouhi went to his own room while Zari and Yusef sat in the darkness and stared at the town-lights. They came down the mountain holding hands in the blackness of the night. That night, in the twins' bedroom, Yusef took the keychain from Marjan's pillow and put the lights off. He held Zari's hand while they stood still in the darkness, listening to the children's breathing. Then they slept together stark naked under the mosquito net, waking Khosrow up with their noise, and he called out to his father. Yusef hurriedly pulled on his night-clothes and went to him, saying, "Go to sleep, son, it's nothing." He came back and they both sat up in the mosquito net, their hearts pounding so loudly they could hear it, and they waited for Khosrow's breathing to become even again. And all those days and nights which came and went . . .

Again Ameh's voice, but Zari didn't want to hear it. She was having pleasant dreams, yet the voice imposed itself, "I have a black scarf and dress myself, but Zari doesn't. My poor brother disliked black. When Zari's mother died, he didn't let her wear black for more than forty days. I had to give a scarf and dress of hers tonight to Haj Mohammad to be dyed black. I gave all the bed sheets to be dyed black also. He said he would stay up the whole night to do the clothes and sheets. The weather is warm; they'll be dry by morning."

"The sheets?" asked Abol-Ghassem Khan.

"I want to cover all the rooms in black. I'll throw black sheets over all the seat-cushions around the room."

244

But Zari is in the village now, not in the basement of their house. She is in the village, and she knows that they are reaping the last field. She knows Yusef is waiting for her by the mill. She is supposed to reach him before the sun leaves the fields, and it's a long way there. She comes out of the landlord's house. The village women in their chadors are squatting, washing their tea-things in the stream of water which issues from the landlord's house. They greet Zari when they see her, and she stops to chat with them. She points to Kolu's mother's rounded belly and says, "You've filled your pot again!"

She looks at Goldusti, Kolu's aunt who has just got married and is wearing heavy make-up. Zari says, "You're having a good time of it, aren't you?"

Kolu is there too, idling about. Zari pats him on his wavy hair and says, "Run to Seyyid Mohammad. Tell him to saddle the horse and bring it here."

Kolu giggles and runs off.

Zari mounts the horse and rides through the harvested fields. The wheat has been piled around like so many heaps of gold. The men are stacking the hay, tying it in bundles with black rope and loading it on the mules. The men greet her as she passes by every field. She returns their greeting kindly and rides away. When she reaches the upper village, she is surprised. Just above the lowlands they have covered up the doors of all the houses with mud. It looks as if the village is deserted. Yes, actually there are a few people—several tribal women going on their way. But the tribe has already migrated to its summer quarters. She saw them going away herself. They pitched tent for a few days in the upper village and then left.

She leaves the fields and the men and women behind. And she reaches the last field moments before the sun disappears. The men are still reaping. The women gleaners, wearing black scarves on their heads, sit in a row to one side of the field. She knows Yusef always tells the men to reap carelessly so the gleaners can pick up something for themselves afterwards. It's for this reason that the gleaners always bring two large woollen sacks with them. She spies Yusef sitting on a rug in front of the mill, smoking the hookah, a thin cloak thrown over his shoulders. Yusef sees her too, and comes forward to greet her still wearing his cloak. He sweeps her off the horse and puts her down on the ground. "Come share my cloak," he says. "You're sweating; I'm afraid you'll catch cold."

245

Then he says, "The sun was on your hair and made it look the colour of musk-willow in the distance."

Zari sits on the rug, wrapped under Yusef's cloak. The miller has planted three Marvel of Peru bushes in front of the mill, and now, at sunset, he is watering them from a tin watering-can. He is covered with white flour from head to toe. Even his eyebrows, eyelashes and hair are powdered white.

The miller brings a tin tray which he places on the rug before them. There are two loaves of round bread which he has baked himself, a bowl of home-made yogurt, and a bunch of fresh spring onions. He has also put salt and pepper for them on two bits of paper. Zari prepares a large mouthful of bread and yogurt which she offers to Yusef. Yusef laughs and says, "I know you're hungry, coming all this way. Eat it yourself." And how hungry she is . . .

Behind the mill is the landlord's summer-crop, watered by the stream which turns the mill. Yusef gets up and goes. When he returns, Zari sees that he has filled his cloak with something. The miller brings a brazier full of coal-fire. A blackened old kettle is sitting in the corner of the brazier. He places the brazier on one side of the rug. Yusef has picked a lot of corn-cobs. He puts them on the fire and fans them with the top of a cardboard box which the miller has given him.

Zari and Yusef go over to the gleaners. Their sacks are brimming, and they've tied them together with a piece of rope. The men help the women heave the sacks on to their shoulders before they start off. Zari falls in step with a middle-aged woman who is one of the last to leave.

"Mother, why are you wearing a black scarf?" she asks.

The woman doesn't seem to hear. Instead of answering the question, she blesses Zari. "May you live long, my dear. May Allah bring you health and prosperity."

"Why are you all wearing black scarves?" Zari asks again.

The woman hears her this time. "Bless you, my dear," she says, "tonight is the eve of Savushun. Tomorrow is the day of mourning. If the Khan's guide has arrived, we'll be there by the cock's crowing . . . as soon as we arrive they'll start beating on the drums and the kettle drums."

"Where is this Savushun?"

Again the woman hasn't heard. "No, my dear," she answers, "we'll be going on mules. Your servant Mohammad Taghi has brought the mules, and he's waiting for us under the Gissu tree. He'll be getting a whole sackful for the fare."

The woman stops. She's becoming talkative. She continues, "When we arrive, we all sit around the arena in a wide circle. They bring hot tea, bread and gingerbread ... as well as rose-water drink, sweet grapes ... they hand out lunch and dinner on the eve of Savushun. In the middle of the arena they've put firewood which they set alight. All of a sudden you look up and you see the night has faded. But it's well before dawn when, God bless him, he appears high up on the mountain riding his steed. You'd think he was praying right there on horseback. He lifts a Quran to his brow and prays for all Moslems in the world. God Almighty. He is wearing black from head to toe. Even his horse is black. He comes down and jumps over the fire on horse-back. We women clamour and scream. The men cheer, the boys whistle, they play drums and kettle drums, and suddenly you see the sunrise, and the whole arena is now bright."

Zari enjoys listening to the woman's talk. "Well, what happens next?" she asks.

The woman has fallen behind her fellow-gleaners; she's following them with her eyes. Zari notices and says, "No, you go ahead and catch up with them. You'll be late."

"By the time they pack their things and gather the children, I'll soon catch them up." And the woman adds, "Bless you, my dear, you're our mistress and benefactor. Now you want me to tell you this story."

"All right, let's go together," says Zari. "You can tell me on the way."

Again, they walk in step. The middle-aged woman continues, "God bless him, he comes all alone towards the arena. He circles slowly. He's thinking. How can he fight so many of the accursed enemy single-handed? From one side of the arena the Princes of Earth come to the middle to see if he'll allow them to help him."

"Princes of what?"

"One group are holding some soil in their hands and wear flowery brown headgear. They are the Princes of Earth. Another group have fans in their hands, and are fanning themselves; these are the Princes of Air. Others wearing black and holding torches are the Princes of Fire. They come to his aid from the three corners of the arena. Finally, from the fourth corner, a wandering dervish

247

appears, chanting the name of Ali ... " The woman sighs. "Ali, my saviour ... don't abandon your humble believers ... in justice," she says. "The dervish's begging-cup is full of rose-water drink. He takes the horse's bridle and says, 'Drink a sip of this in the memory of Imam Hussein's thirsty lips.' But he throws the drink to the ground and dismisses the princes. All alone, waiting for the accursed enemy, the rider stays there on his horse. He has no sword, no bow and arrow. The sun has now spread from one end of the arena to the other ... Suddenly the accursed enemy, riding their horses, charge from all four corners. Thirty or forty of them attack his holy person. They fight ... the drums roll ... they beat harder and harder on them ... and now so loud and fast, your heart is about to explode.

"Finally they pursue his horse and drag him down from it. They tie the bridle around his blessed neck. They put the saddle on his shoulders. They tie his hands behind him, but he doesn't utter a sound. His bare black horse stands there neighing so loudly it echoes all around. One of those villains is dressed as the executioner. He comes forward and takes the horse's bridle which they've tied around his highness's neck. This man is mounted, but that poor, lonely captive is on foot. They drag him all around the arena, and he keeps stumbling and getting up again. He's bloodied, his black clothes are torn and covered with dirt. But he doesn't moan or show his pain."

The middle-aged woman is crying and she wipes her eyes with the corner of her black scarf. She blows her nose before continuing between tears, "Then that villain dismounts and puts a sword to his noble throat. He covers his face like a sheep and places his head at the edge of a basin ... He sharpens his knife before our eyes ... Sharpens it like a razor. But by the will of God, the blade will not cut. Then he lays him face down and puts the knife to the back of his neck. The oboe plays so mournfully ... oh so mournfully. Suddenly you see his horse covered with blood, just like that! His mane is dripping with blood. Our elders say that once, in Solat's time, his highness's black horse hadn't been able to bear it and had died of grief right there. I've seen the poor animal's tears several times with my own two eyes." She pauses and wipes her eyes again.

"We women put hay over our heads in mourning. Our men take two mud-tiles each which they beat together to shake dust and hay

248

over their feet, and then they do the same over their heads . . . "

Zari feels her eyelids burning. She nearly puts an arm around the woman and cries along with her. But they've reached the Gissu tree now. The woman says goodbye, blessing her again, and a man who is probably Mohammad Taghi comes forward to help the woman remove the sacks from her back and get up on the mule . . .

Zari and Yusef are riding their horses side by side.

"Do you know what Savushun is?" Zari asks Yusef.

"It's a mourning ritual. All the people of the upper village observe it tonight."

"Is that why they've covered up the doors of their houses with mud?"

"Yes, their trip will take a few days."

"A village where houses have no doors, and where the inhabitants meet under the Gissu tree to go to the Savushun together!" Zari says sadly.

"In other words, the mourning of Siavush's death. The people of the upper village leave every year after the harvest and return in time for the corn-threshing."

They both fall silent. It's getting dark on the lowlands. They ride their horses and stare ahead. Zari's eyelids are burning as tears roll quietly down her cheeks. So quietly Yusef wouldn't know. But she is already sobbing. She cries with all her heart.

A hand wiped away her tears. It was Ameh's hand.

"I beg you by Yusef's departed spirit not to cry," said Ameh.

"I was crying for Siavush," said Zari, sitting up. "At first I didn't know about him, and I disliked him. But now I know him well and I feel sorry for him . . . I was standing under the Gissu tree, crying for Siavush. Pity I don't have long hair, otherwise I would have cut it off and hung it on the tree like all the others."

What had she said to hush them up? Why were they staring at her? A silence and a stare you couldn't endure. Zari felt as though something fell and shattered inside her. Who had told her once, "A storm raged within the folds of my body"?

Abol-Ghassem Khan put a hand to his waist, stood up and came towards her. "How many times did I tell that poor soul not to let this weak, fragile woman go so often to the asylum? But he wouldn't listen . . . " he said.

"For heaven's sake, man, don't go jumping to conclusions," said Ameh.

249

"Someone was telling me the story of Savushun," said Zari. "How he'd been all alone and the enemy numbered a thousand . . . of course, he couldn't overcome them single-handed . . . "

Malek Rostam spoke up from where he was sitting, "Abol-Ghassem Khan, sir, please sit down." And he whispered something quietly.

But Zari managed to catch what he was saying. "Don't worry," she heard him say, "she hasn't gone mad. Why can't someone cry for Siavush?"

Abol-Ghassem Khan beat himself on the head and said, "Who's Siavush? What's the Gissu tree? The world is spinning and crumbling all around me . . . under the rubble . . . a pity, a thousand times a pity."

"I've attended Savushun many times myself," Malek Rostam said. "When the Ta'zieh passion play was banned, that was stopped too. And the Gissu tree is famous all over the lowlands."

"The first time I saw the Gissu tree, from a distance I thought it was a wishing tree with all those bits of yellow, brown and black ribbons hanging from it," explained Zari. "But when I went closer, I realized those ribbons were in fact braided locks of hair. Hair that belonged to young women who had lost their husbands . . . or sons, or brothers . . . "

Why was Abol-Ghassem Khan frightened and listened to, but still didn't believe, whatever they were telling him? Why did Ameh too start to doubt and didn't say anything anymore, but Malek Rostam kept reassuring them it was all right to cry for Siavush? Zari put her head on the pillow again and thought, "If only they would just let me be happy in my own thoughts, riding horses in my dreams, walking over reaped fields, sitting hand in hand with Yusef by the piles of wheat . . . I'd put my head in Yusef's lap and he would rub my temples with his fingers and say, 'I'm willing to bet you're going to be just fine.'"

22

Finally that bloated night of nightmares and terrors released its grip on Zari. At dawn, she got up. Her knees were shaky and her mouth had an acrid taste. She went out to the garden and listened to the sound of water pouring from the stone head into the pool. She washed her hands and face. The coolness of the air, the freshness of the garden, the smell of the moist earth, the chirping of the early sparrows, the clean water which had reached half-way up the pool—all of these revived her somewhat.

They had left the wooden beds in the shade of the building next to the pool, and covered them with carpets. Khadijeh came out, carrying a tray which she placed on one of the beds.

"I knew you would feel better in the morning," she said, greeting Zari. "Thank God! I broke an egg for you, I burnt some wild rue to ward off the evil eye. I tried all kinds of vows and prayers."

She spread a tablecloth on one of the wooden beds, and put some knives and plates on it. She went away to fetch the samovar and came back with it minutes later, boiling and ready for the tea. Zari sat down cross-legged by the tablecloth. Her stomach growled with hunger.

"We couldn't find your keychain last night even though we searched everywhere for it," said Khadijeh. "There's probably some sugar, tea and saffron in the store-room. I know we have a bottle of sugar syrup . . . by the way, Khanom, we're short of fans, too."

"Where are they reciting the Quran?" Zari asked. "The voices seem to be coming from around the well."

Khadijeh stood and stared at her. "They've put the body in the cistern, between big sacks of snow. It was coolest there," she said, and looking Zari over carefully, began to say, "You've changed so much overnight . . ." but she finished her sentence, "My poor

251

mistress, what have you done to yourself! You've lost so much weight. Do you remember my uncle's wife who swallowed opium once? I was the one who saved her. She looked just like you do this morning."

Just then Gholam came in through the garden gates followed by Haj Mohammad Reza the dyer. Gholam was carrying an iron in one hand, and Zari's black dress and scarf in the other. Haj Mohammad Reza, wearing a long-sleeved black shirt, was balancing a large bundle on his head with hands which matched the colour of his shirt. Zari took her things from Gholam and went to the bedroom. She put the dress on with difficulty; it had become too tight. Digging a hand into the pockets of her dress, she found a crumpled and blackened two-toman bill in the right one. She glanced involuntarily in the mirror. She didn't recognize herself. She switched the light on and took a closer look. Several strands of hair had turned white, and her parched lips had lines around the corners. Her darkly-circled eyes seemed to have sunk in their sockets. She thought, "It's not true when they say all of someone's hair turned white overnight."

She went to the parlour which had been stripped of all its decorations, even the radio. Gholam and Haj Mohammad Reza were spreading black sheets on the cushions arranged around the room. Haj Mohammad Reza stood up when he saw her. He averted his eyes awkwardly and asked after her health. Zari thought, "Poor soul, he's been up the whole night dyeing all this material." It seemed as if he had read her mind because he surveyed the black cushion-covers with satisfaction.

When Zari came out to the garden, Ameh had just finished her morning prayers, and Abol-Ghassem Khan and Khosrow were having breakfast. Khosrow was wearing a black shirt which hung over his grey trousers. Zari sat at one end of the table-cloth, next to the samovar. She poured herself and Ameh some tea, but her hands were shaking and her head swam. Ameh broke two eggs, carefully disposing of the whites in the bowl underneath the samovar tap. She dropped the yolks in a cup, added some sugar, and started to beat it. Zari followed Khosrow with her eyes as he got up and went through the garden gates. Involuntarily she spoke her thoughts, "The poor man has been up the whole night dyeing all of us black!"

Ameh raised her head as she was beating the eggs and changed the subject. "Sister, did you find your keychain?" she asked.

252

"Keychain?" asked Zari distractedly. Then she smiled and said, "Khadijeh was shocked to see me a few minutes ago. She said I looked like one of those people who've eaten opium and been rescued in the nick of time. She said I'd aged a thousand years overnight. No, she didn't say that. I don't remember what she said . . . I didn't recognize myself in the mirror."

"Khadijeh had no business saying things like that to you!" Ameh replied.

Abol-Ghassem Khan looked at Zari. He stared and shook his head. "Didn't I say so, sister?" he said. "Last night you said I was making things up about her because I was interested in her money."

Again Zari spoke her thoughts out loud. "I think Khosrow's gone to fetch Dr Abdullah Khan."

Ameh bit her lip and said, "When time heals her wounds, she'll be all right."

Hurriedly she poured some milk over the egg yolks, stirred it and handed it to Zari. But suddenly Zari wondered what Abol-Ghassem Khan had meant? Blood rushed to her face. Her heart pounded in her chest and again she felt as though something had shattered inside her.

She felt she had to explain. "In the asylum," she said, "the first thing every patient says is that he's not mad and he shouldn't have been brought there. But Abol-Ghassem Khan, you can be sure I haven't gone mad . . . you see . . . well, it was all so sudden . . . " She left her sentence unfinished. She was not entirely convinced herself. What if she really had gone mad and didn't know it? A fear more insidious than the terrors of her recent nightmares gripped her, larger than anything she had ever experienced. She felt chilled to the bone but the palms of her hands were sweating. She had to show Abol-Ghassem Khan, and, more importantly, prove to herself that she hadn't gone mad. She ate her breakfast delicately, even though her appetite had gone, remembering to thank Ameh for the milk and eggs which she had hardly been able to swallow. Then she got up and called Khadijeh and Gholam. She sent Khadijeh to borrow fans from the neighbours, and then to fetch her keychain from the children at Mehri's. Then she sent Gholam to find tea and sugar at any cost.

Khadijeh returned with an armful of fans and said, "Khanom Mehri and Mohsen Khan were quarrelling, so I didn't dare go inside for the keys."

Gholam came back and said, "I went all the way down the street, but no-one has opened their shop yet!"

All the time Zari's eyes were glued to the garden gate in expectation of Dr Abdullah Khan. At first Hossein Agha the grocer and his brother Hassan Agha the local corn-chandler came in, clad entirely in black. Then the two distillers from next door arrived, sweating from the loads on their back. They had each tied a black armband around their bare arms, otherwise they were dressed as usual in a pair of drawers and an undershirt. They put their loads down next to the pool, opened the burlap sacks at the top and rolled them down carefully. Holding their hands in turn underneath the mouth of the stone head, they caught some water with which to sprinkle the roses and the eglantine inside the sacks. Soon the fragrance of the flowers filled the area in front of the house. Zari looked at the flowers and thought, "How far they went to get these ... they've spent the whole night picking those flowers, and in the darkness too ... how many thorns did they get in their hands? Why didn't the youngest son go with them? I hope he hasn't come down with typhus as well!"

Gholam, still hatless, approached Hossein Agha and said,
"Brother, I came to you earlier, but your shop was closed. See if you can get us some sugar, tea and saffron, will you?"

Hassan Agha, Hossein Agha and the distillers left. In the driveway, they came across the old distiller himself who had put on Gholam's worn-out suit and thrown a black shawl around his neck. They stood and talked to the old man who followed them back on the way he had just come.

A droshke drew up at the garden gate and Zari wanted to rush forward and greet the long-awaited Dr Abdullah Khan.

She was longing to make him tell everyone, "Khanom Zahra hasn't gone mad. She's had a shock, that's why she seems distracted. Don't watch her so closely, because then you really will drive her mad!" But it was Ferdows who came out of the droshke, taking Ezzat-ud-Dowleh's hand as she stepped out. The old lady descended with a lot of difficulty, and giving her arm to Ferdows, limped slowly up the driveway until she reached Zari who was standing in front of the house in a state of disbelief. The sun had just risen, and before Zari could collect herself from the surprise of this early morning visit, the woman had thrown an arm around Zari

254

and was saying, "The news came so suddenly last night, I wasn't myself at all and I left without saying goodbye or realizing what I was doing. All night while everyone was fast asleep, I couldn't close my eyes. You're like a daughter to me, and your late mother was my twin soul. God forbid, she'd always say, 'Ezzat-ud-Dowleh, I'm a dying woman. I leave my child in your hands.' Alas! Alas!"

She sat on the wooden bed—the same one that Yusef's broken body had occupied the night before, but which was now covered with a carpet. Rubbing her leg, she asked, "Where's my sister?"

She was swathed in black, including the gloves, scarf, socks . . . when had she had time to dye her hair black? Come to think of it, why should she dye her hair black at all?

"I said to Ferdows, 'Get up, child, let's go there first thing in the morning'," continued Ezzat-ud-Dowleh. "'Maybe we can give them a hand or something.' After all, what good is our so-called sisterhood if not for times of need?" It was lucky for Zari that she managed to hold her tongue. If this woman accused her of madness too then she would be done for. It would give Ezzat-ud-Dowleh a week's worth of gossip with the Governor's family!

"My dear child," said Ezzat-ud-Dowleh again, "what kind of dress is this you're wearing? A dyed thing, and ironed to a shine, too. It's not nice in front of people, and it's too tight for you."

Zari, who had her eyes on the garden gate, didn't reply. But Ezzat-ud-Dowleh wouldn't let up.

"My dear girl, why aren't you paying attention? Now go along like the nice lady that you are and allow Ferdows to let out your dress for you. There's probably some room left—she'll open it at the seams."

Zari noted silently that those beady eyes didn't miss a thing. But she made no effort to move.

"By the way," said Ezzat-ud-Dowleh, "I nearly forgot. I've brought you something which I know will really make you happy. A keepsake from your late husband—no, you're not paying attention to me at all . . . look!"

Reluctantly Zari shifted her gaze from the garden gate. Ezzat-ud-Dowleh took out a small box wrapped in white paper from her handbag and gave it to Zari. Zari held it in her hand, not knowing what to do with it. Again she stared at the garden gate. Ezzat-ud-Dowleh gave a little laugh and said, "Go on, open it!"

Zari mechanically undid the wrapping. Inside was a black velvet

255

box. She opened it, and saw her emerald earrings shining at her from their small velvet case. She felt depressed. The earrings which Yusef had put in her ears on their wedding night with his own hands. Yusef's eyes had shone like those very emeralds in the light.

Ezzat-ud-Dowleh smiled. "I knew it would make you happy," she said. "Last night I went straight from here to the Governor's house. I decided that since I'd been responsible for having my dear child's earrings taken away, I had to get them back myself."

"Do you think I can be fooled like a child?" said Zari. And she closed her eyes. She felt dizzy.

Ezzat-ud-Dowleh neither scolded her nor complained. She merely said, "Ferdows, my child is not feeling quite herself because of her grief. Poor thing! Take her to her room. Tight clothing is bad for a pregnant woman." She put a hand to her brow and cried a little. Then calming down, she advised Zari in a motherly tone, "Zari dear, put the earrings in a safe place. It will get very crowded here today."

Zari walked off, feeling like a robot with rusty springs and loosened hinges. Ferdows took her hand to keep her from falling. They went to the bedroom together. Zari took off her dress, put the velvet box on her dressing table and stretched out on the bed.

"Where's the sewing kit?" asked Ferdows.

"I don't know," replied Zari. She felt dizzy and nauseous. This must be the way madness begins, she thought.

She wished Ferdows wouldn't talk, but Ferdows kept on chatting.

"Khanom Zahra," she said, "it's a good thing you and I managed to be alone. These people can get up to anything!"

If only she'd shut up, thought Zari.

"Are you listening to me?" asked Ferdows.

"No."

"I want to put you on your guard. Last night mother and son were up the whole time, scheming behind your back. I stayed awake on the roof and listened. God Almighty! In the middle of the night she dyed her hair and put henna on it ... actually it's a wonder she doesn't think she's the Almighty!"

Zari didn't respond, though her interest had been kindled. Ferdows had found the sewing kit and was opening the seams of the dress.

How efficient she is, Zari thought silently.

256

Still undoing seams and re-stitching them, Ferdows continued, "When Khanom got home, Hamid Khan threw himself at her feet again, flattered her and played up to her and finally he said, 'Mother, I must have this woman at any cost' ... God forbid, he said that every night he'd slept with his wife he'd thought of you. All three of his children had been conceived thinking of you ... bless my soul! A grown man like that making up all kinds of verses and poems for you! If you only knew the kinds of things he said ... "

Zari didn't want to know, but Ferdows went on, "Well, to cut a long story short ... Khanom was not easily persuaded. She kept saying that you bring bad luck, that your brother-in-law wouldn't let anyone lay a finger on your money, that you're pregnant and no-one can wed a pregnant woman. Hamid Khan said he'd wait. Khanom ... "

If Gholam hadn't knocked on the bedroom door just then to announce Dr Abdullah Khan, Zari would have vomited.

"Ask the doctor to wait a minute while I get dressed," she said. And to Ferdows, "Khanom Ferdows, please hurry."

"Right away."

But Ferdows kept on talking, and Zari didn't stop her because now Dr Abdullah Khan had arrived and would relieve her mind one way or the other.

"He pleaded with her until she gave in," Ferdows went on, "so he asked her to get to work on you from the very next morning. What lies she strung together in front of me! Actually Khanom was a born liar. How she pretended to care about you! Don't be fooled, she's after your blood ... there, I'm all done." And she handed over the dress which Zari put on with a sigh of relief. Maybe she had felt dizzy because of the tightness of the dress.

As she looked Zari over, Ferdows added, "And she didn't go straight to the Governor's either. Hamid Khan made her telephone the Governor's daughter. Khanom sent a piece of her own jewellery in exchange for yours. My worthless husband Kal Abbas went and fetched it."

"Thank you," said Zari. "Now go and tell the doctor I'm ready."

Dr Abdullah Khan came in, leaning on his stick. He seemed older than on the day Zari had seen him in Khanom Massihadem's room. Or perhaps she hadn't looked at him closely enough then. The doctor sat on Zari's bed, took her hand in his and said, "What's the

257

use of reaching a grand old age like mine? When a precious young man like your husband dies, I begin to hate myself. Here I am clinging to life with both hands while our young men are taken . . . "

"My husband didn't just die, he was killed," said Zari sadly.

"I know. Your son told me everything on the way. I congratulate you. A clever boy like him could take his father's place for you. May the Lord bring both of you prosperity." He paused and said, "An old man like me shouldn't step into a house which has lost a young man of his kind. I'm old and useless now. His mourners must surely look at me, shake their heads and think, 'Old man, you're alive, and our young one has been martyred!'"

"No-one thinks of you like that. You're the salt of the earth to all of us."

Dr Abdullah Khan raised Zari's hand to his lips and kissed it. Zari tried to withdraw it out of modesty. The old man sighed and said in a pensive voice, "I don't know where I read that the world is like a dark room which we enter blindfolded. One of us may have his eyes open or others may try hard to open theirs; perhaps it's even destined that one person should be touched with a ray of light from above so he may see and understand all for an instant. Your husband was one of those rare people who'd never shut his eyes from the beginning. His eyes and ears were alert. More is the pity he had such a short time . . . "

He spoke like one who had taken in everything there was to know. If there was a God, He had shown Himself for once to this man in the course of his long life . . .

The old man continued, "I've told Khanom Qods-ol-Saltaneh many a time that that brother of hers was a genuine human being. He was an enlightened man."

"But you're enlightened as well, you're . . . "

"Now tell me what's ailing you?" interrupted the doctor. "Your son begged me to come and visit you. I said to him, 'Dear boy, for the wife of such a one as he was, I'm ready to go to the ends of the world. Besides, I'm very fond of your mother herself . . . she is a queen among women.'"

Zari had no fear or embarrassment in telling Dr Abdullah Khan the truth. "I've been so distraught since last night," she confessed, "I can't control my mind. I'm afraid I might be going mad . . . I feel tempted to imitate the lunatics I've seen." And she added in tears, "All last night I was caught up in nightmares. Khanom Hakim gave

258

me three injections but they didn't seem to do any good and I couldn't fall asleep. I kept seeing horrific scenes. I said nonsensical things. And I've been feeling dizzy all morning."

The old man stood up and went to the window, looking out on the garden. "Don't let me hear you say things like that," he told her with his back to her. "If you were distressed or even delirious, it was perfectly natural. Khanom Hakim couldn't have given you tranquillizers, either. She gave you a camphor injection to stimulate your heart and the other two shots were distilled water."

Again he came and sat down next to Zari.

"So you're saying I haven't gone mad?" Zari asked innocently.

"Absolutely not."

"And I won't go mad either?"

"I assure you you won't."

He stared into Zari's eyes and continued in a soothing voice, "But you have a malignant disease that cannot be cured by my hand. You must get rid of it before it becomes chronic. Sometimes it's hereditary."

"Cancer?" asked Zari.

"No, my dear; don't you understand? It's the disease of fear. Many people have it—I told you it's contagious."

Again he took Zari's hand and said prophetically, "I have one foot in the grave, so listen to the words of this old man, my dear. In this world, everything is in one's own hands. Madness, fear, even love. A human being can if he so desires, move mountains, dry up the waters, create havoc everywhere. A human life is a chronicle. It can be any kind of chronicle—a sweet one, a bitter one, an ugly one ... or a heroic one. The human body is fragile, but no force in this world can equal man's spiritual power. As long as he has a strong will and some awareness."

He paused and took out a green bottle with a white top from his pocket. He gave it to Zari. "There's a special kind of salt in this bottle," he said. "Keep it in your pocket and every time you feel unwell, open it and smell it. Drink a glass of sweetened willow-water too." He got up and said, "I know you're a lady. A real lady. I know you're strong and brave enough not to run away from the bitter reality. I want you to prove that you are worthy of such a man as your husband was."

He picked up his stick which he had hung on the edge of the bed and said, "Here is some news that will make you happy. Take heart.

259

The day before yesterday, Khanom Massihadem was discharged from the asylum. She's much better and by the time you're ready to give birth, she'll be completely recovered."

Zari felt as if she'd been freed from a cage. A man of wisdom had given her hope and encouragement. Not one but a thousand stars were lit in her mind. She knew now that she feared no-one and nothing in the world.

They went out into the garden together. Abol-Ghassem Khan was sitting on the children's bed with Malek Rostam and Majid Khan. When he saw them, he got up and went towards them.

"Well, doctor," he blinked, "what did you think? What did you find?"

"If you ask me," replied the doctor, "your sister-in-law must be very strong indeed just to be standing on her two feet. Her distress and anxiety are natural. It's no joking matter. But all of you around her must leave her in peace."

Zari saw the doctor all the way to the gate. She kept searching in her mind for a suitable word to express her gratitude but she couldn't find it. Maybe he felt her helplessness, or perhaps he just wanted to bid her to be patient, or maybe it was for his own heart—at any rate he murmured the following verse:

"Be patient, o heart, that the Just One,
Will not let such a gem fall to Evil."

Zari knew that Dr Abdullah Khan was a member of the Hafeziun group who held sessions in memory of the mystical poet Hafez at his gravesite. They recited his poetry, drank wine which they threw on the mystic's grave, and even played the tambourine and the lute.

She said quietly, "Please recite some more. Verses which will give me strength to go on."

The old man smiled, and said:

"Let us do good deeds, lest we take our soul,
In shame to the other world."

He stood under the elm tree to catch his breath. "I didn't recite that verse for you," he said. "I said it for myself."

"You've done your work in this world," said Zari. "Your life-story is a heroic one. But my poor husband's tale was tragic and unfinished." And without intending to, she leaned against the tree and wept quietly behind her hand.

23

They had arrived for the funeral procession. First came all the relatives and close friends. The women were shown to the howzkhaneh and the men to the parlour. Ezzat-ud-Dowleh took the seat of honour amongst the women. Ferdows had donned a tight black dress and a sorrowful expression as she lent a hand with the serving. Anyone who didn't know would have thought Ezzat-ud-Dowleh was next of kin, the way she was ordering everyone around. The minute she set eyes on a newcomer, she would talk effusively about Yusef's youth and tragic end, of his good looks and knowledge, of his faultless English, of the poor innocent widow and children he'd left behind . . . she would go on and on, sobbing loudly. Occasionally she would even beat her chest, but not too hard. Every so often Zari would take a whiff of the salts Dr Abdullah Khan had given her to prevent herself from crying at her words. Ameh was nowhere to be seen. Eventually, when Ezzat-ud-Dowleh started a lament, and talked of "a tree which had been cut at the roots and felled to the ground", Zari left too.

It was after eight-thirty in the morning when Abol-Ghassem Khan's friends arrived. But there was no more room in the parlour so they had to sit on the children's bed in the garden. Zari sat across from them near the sacks of eglantine and red roses which had been left at the edge of the pool. The pool itself was brimming with crystal-clear water.

Hossein Agha and Hassan Agha, each with a full sack on his back, passed by Abol-Ghassem Khan's friends as they made their way to the pantry. The distillers from next door, again without the youngest son, followed them, balancing pitchers on their shoulders. Then three other men arrived, carrying large empty vessels. Zari's eyes filled with tears on seeing them.

261

Abol-Ghassem Khan came out of the parlour and joined his friends. A fat, dark man was saying something quietly while the others listened with worried expressions. The town's newspaper manager was shaking his head and the former parliamentary deputy was racing through his rosary.

Ferdows approached Zari with the tray of drinks. "You help yourself first," she said. "This one is willow-water sweetened with rock-sugar . . . Did you see the way she was play-acting? Now she's pretending to faint."

Zari took the glass from her and asked, "How did you know I should drink sweetened willow-water?"

"Khanom sent me to eavesdrop. Let her keep hoping you'll miscarry—you're not unprotected and alone like me. She wanted to know what you and the doctor were saying to each other all that time. I told her I didn't understand a thing of what you were talking about because you were whispering. I just heard the doctor say that the world is like a dark-room with upside down pictures and we're all lost and wandering about in it . . . Khanom called me an imbecile and told me what a waste of time it had been for a distinguished lady like her to try and train me. Khanom Zahra, if I have just one day left to live, I'll take my revenge. When my mother was in prison it was a good chance to . . . "

Zari cut her short saying, "Take the drinks over to the gentlemen, the ice is melting."

Ferdows went to Abol-Ghassem Khan's friends. The notary, who was Chinese-looking, said something to Ferdows and she giggled. Gholam went to greet some men dressed in black whom Zari didn't recognize. They made way for two porters, one of whom was carrying an upright candelabrum on his head, the other a lustre. Covered with sweat, the porters went as far as the pool where others helped them place their loads on one of the wooden beds. Another man stripped to the waist, holding the emblem of the Ta'zieh passion play, garnished with flowers, tulips and lengths of brocade, and topped with a feather which swayed to the movement of his step, carefully lowered the emblem past the garden gate. The men indoors looked out from the parlour windows and the women had come out of the basement to watch. Ezzat-ud-Dowleh, however, was not among them.

By nine or nine-thirty in the morning, the garden was filled with men dressed in black. But they were still arriving in droves, and the

262

last group had flagellating chains with them. Finally, they brought in the mock wedding chamber, the Hejleh Ghassem, which nearly made Zari break down and sob, but she managed to control herself by taking out the smelling salts and busying herself with opening the top.

Abol-Ghassem Khan's friends approached her. The former deputy had crewcut white hair, and no longer carried his rosary. The notary really did look Chinese. The newspaper manager took Zari's hand in his, and said that all of them had to attend a meeting at the governor general's office about bread supplies, so he regretted that they could not be present for the funeral procession. But on everyone's behalf he offered his sympathies and condolences to Zari and "Abol" and Khanom Qods-ul-Saltaneh, and he prayed that, God willing, they would all live to old age and never suffer loss in the family again. The others listened, and when he had finished they left. But the newspaper manager would not let go of Zari's hand. He said quietly, "I hope you understand my position if I don't print news of the event. Even the funeral announcement was placed purely for your sake and that of my friendship with Abol."

Zari withdrew her hand and said bitterly, "Funeral announcements have always been permitted."

A few minutes later, Abol-Ghassem Khan came and sat next to her. He was very pale and his nostrils were trembling. "Sister," he said, blinking rapidly, "I know you're more sensible than the rest of them. For heaven's sake, say something to these fools. My own stupid sister doesn't seem to understand. She keeps saying she wants them to turn this dog-infested town into a holy Karbala. And our ruffians keep praising her and egging her on." When Zari didn't budge, he pleaded with her, "Sister, I beg of you, for the sake of that tragically-departed soul, get up and say something."

So they went to Khosrow's room together where, according to Abol-Ghassem Khan, the town ruffians had gathered. Malek Rostam and Majid, wearing black ties, were standing by the doorway. Zari's glance travelled from Haj Mohammad Reza the dyer, who was squatting by the doorway, to the others. Seyyid Mohammad, Hossein Agha and Hassan Agha had their backs to the window. Seated on Khosrow's bed were three men. One she recognized as the tall, broad-shouldered Mashallah Qari; another was Fotouhi, who wasn't wearing a tie; and the third was Mr Mortezai who had put on his religious robe. The rest of Yusef's sworn companions, along with a few others also in mourning dress but whom Zari didn't recognize, were seated on chairs brought from the parlour. Ameh Khanom, wearing an Islamic black scarf, was standing tall and upright behind Khosrow's desk. None of the men had shaved.

"Here is my late brother's wife," Abol-Ghassem Khan announced. "Do whatever she says. You've shut down the bazaar, so be it. But to circumambulate the Shah Cheraq shrine with the body, and have the crowd flagellating in the courtyard; to have Mr Mortezai saying the last prayers with full sermon from the shrine balcony ... upon my word, don't even think of it! What with the foreign army in town, there will be rioting ... You've dragged all these people here for nothing."

Turning to Zari, Majid said, "Khanom Zahra, you know yourself we had sworn allegiance to Yusef. Now that they've killed him, they want us to sit here and not even give him a proper burial. Our simple objection ... "

Zari didn't let him finish his sentence. "They have killed my husband unjustly," she said. "The least we can do is to mourn his death. Mourning hasn't been outlawed. In his lifetime we were always frightened and we tried to frighten him off too. Now that he is dead, what else can we fear? I, for one, have nothing more to lose.... " Her voice was trembling. She brought the bottle of salts to her nostrils and inhaled its freshness deeply.

"Well, bless my soul, sister!" Abol-Ghassem Khan exploded. "Now you've really put me to shame! Why don't you understand, woman? When this many people take to the streets, if someone leads them on to rioting, who could possibly stop the tide then?"

"Abol-Ghassem," Ameh said, "your brother's corpse is at your mercy now. Don't sit by idly and watch his blood being trampled on."

Zari, looking at her, was reminded of Hazrate Zeynab, defending her martyrs.

"I have reliable information that you'll be stopped," Abol-Ghassem Khan told them, "then there'll be bloodshed. I won't allow it. My poor brother wouldn't have wanted to hurt a fly. He treated his peasants like an older brother ... Don't torment the departed soul."

"I lived with him for fourteen years," Zari said with a sigh. "I know that he always spoke of courage ... of justice ... "

264

The serpent which had coiled around her heart the night before reared its head to strike, and her throat constricted. She left her sentence unfinished, but now her mind shone like a torch, and she knew that no-one in the world could ever dim it again. She swallowed and went on, "Do whatever you have to do today ... if you don't do it now, there will never be another opportunity." Then, after a pause, she said to Abol-Ghassem Khan, "Today I came to the conclusion that one has to be brave in life for the sake of those who are living ... but it's a pity I realized it so late. To atone for that ignorance, let's mourn our courageous dead the way we should."

"A blessing on this noble mother of our race," murmured Seyyid Mohammad.

"Bravo!" came from some strangers in mourning clothes.

Mortezai recited in Arabic from the Quran: "There is Life to you, O ye men of understanding."

"This way we shall prove that we've not been annihilated yet, and we value the blood that's been shed," Fotouhi added.

"Sooner or later it'll be my brother's turn," Malek Rostam reminded them. "They'll catch up with him in the heat of these cruel mountains, and drag him into town to the sound of horns and drums. They'll hang him on charges of insurrection, and everyone will come out to watch."

Abol-Ghassem Khan, venting his ill-feelings on Malek Rostam, said, "You talk as if your brother is the Prophet's son! Of course they'll hang him. No-one's forgotten the bloodshed in Semirom. How much government property was raided! How many innocent people were killed! If there's such a thing as penance in this life, then he must pay for all that killing..." Blinking rapidly, he continued, "How ambitious can you get! He changes colour every day like a chameleon. One day he's a slave to the Germans, the next he's serving the British, and before you know it, he's turned against them too! Just like the treacherous Shemr..."

Malek Rostam interrupted him.

"If a person knowingly makes a mistake, he can try to make up for it. But now's not the time for putting Malek Sohrab on trial, and you're not a judge either."

"Actually, you yourself have been parading a little too freely in public these days," Abol-Ghassem Khan retorted. "If I were you I'd put on a chador and make a getaway to the mountains through the back door of this garden."

At that, Malek Rostam's tribal blood began to boil. He answered sharply, "Some people hide under black chadors to slip away to the Consul at the British Consulate. My brother and I use them to hide from the Consul and his men."

"Gentlemen!" Fotouhi intervened. "This is no time for quarrelling. We were supposed to come to a decision about the funeral procession. Khanom Zahra agrees . . ."

"But I'm against it!" Abol-Ghassem Khan interrupted again. "And by rights I'm the legal guardian of my brother's children. Sister, be sensible, listen to my advice."

Zari couldn't stand on her feet any longer. She sat on the bed next to Fotouhi and said, "His body's not buried yet. I don't want to argue with you. But while he was alive, you each had a tight grip around his throat and he had to keep raising his voice to be heard until he was finally killed for it. And now . . . let people show at his death that he was in the right. Besides, justice and truth haven't died with him, there are others to consider."

Abol-Ghassem Khan, blinking nervously, raised his voice in anger. "It's women like you, who follow their husbands like so many sheep, that bring about these tragic events!"

"Don't make me say this," Zari answered calmly, "but more than one person was responsible for the blood that was shed, including yourself. Maybe I'm to blame, too."

"You've got something to say for yourself, have you? Well, well! I'll say it in front of everyone, then. Now that you've come into a bit of easy money, you've forgotten that a woman is, after all, only a woman. A woman is like the lining of a garment, she exists to uphold and support a man. But you just blindly endorsed whatever mistakes that poor man made . . ."

Zari felt that the snake sitting alert inside her was speaking out now. "You're only worried about your post as a deputy, about all the plans you've made for when you become one. An eye operation, a good set of teeth from the famous Dr Stump . . . Haven't you said as much yourself? Maybe you even want to get remarried . . ."

Abol-Ghassem Khan looked at her in total astonishment. "Fie, for shame!" he spat. Then he composed himself and added, "You don't know me well enough. I'm the kind of man who spent sixteen solitary years, night after night, when my wife died . . ."

Zari was going to say, "What about the various temporary wives . . . What about the shoemaker's daughter who rubs herself all over with ox's gall-bladder stone to fatten herself up ..." She felt completely reckless, and in such a state that, if someone had handed her a gun which she knew how to use, she would have been prepared to shoot. She stood up and said, "Just a few minutes ago your notary ..."

Majid Khan, trying to mediate, stepped in. "Please, I beg of you ..." he said. "Mr Abol-Ghassem Khan, Khanom Zahra. It's hardly the time for this sort of thing."

Fotouhi motioned everyone to be silent. "Let's not waste our time with discussions about each other's private lives," he said. "Let's approach the matter in another light. The killing of Yusef Khan is, from your point of view, a personal matter, whereas from ours, it's a social issue ..."

Again, Abol-Ghassem Khan interrupted Fotouhi, saying, "I know the rest by heart. You want to make the most of this killing. Create riots in town and cause innocent people to be killed. There are several truck-loads of soldiers blocking the town's main roads. What with the foreign army in town ... I suppose you know what you're doing."

The coffin, swathed in eglantine and red roses, was to be taken from the driveway of the house by Hossein Agha, Hassan Agha, Majid Khan and Fotouhi as pall-bearers. Malek Rostam insisted on carrying the coffin too, but Zari dissuaded him, saying that Abol-Ghassem Khan had been right about one thing: the tribesman had shown himself too carelessly in public. She made him promise to put on Khadijeh's chador after they had all left and escape to a safe hide-out through the back door of the garden.

Malek Rostam merely responded by saying, "It doesn't really matter any more. Whatever's going to happen will happen."

Abol-Ghassem Khan begged the ladies to stay at home for lunch. A bite to eat could be arranged at his humble abode, and it wasn't wise for them to attend the burial. Khanom Ezzat-ud-Dowleh would remain at the house too.

The emblem and the candelabrum went before the coffin while the Hejleh Ghassem followed it. Abol-Ghassem Khan gave his arm to one of Yusef's sworn companions, and extracted a black handkerchief from his pocket which he used for dabbing at his eyes every so often. Zari and Ameh walked alongside him.

The door of the stable was open. The roan horse was feeding, but the mare and Sahar were standing quietly on the side-path, with Khosrow and Hormoz holding their bridles. Zari felt sick with grief at the sight of the horses and the boys. The mare's saddle was completely covered with black fabric, with Yusef's hat on top and his gun strapped to the mare's neck. They had covered Sahar with a white sheet stained randomly with red ink like a bloodied shroud. When the mare saw the body, she picked up her ears and drummed her hoofs on the ground. Zari felt as if her own heart were being trampled on. Then the mare neighed twice. Zari thought she saw tears rolling down the horse's flared nostrils. She remembered what the middle-aged woman had told her about Savushun, all those years ago.

Khosrow and Hormoz led the horses behind the Hejleh Ghassem. Abol-Ghassem Khan rushed at them and pulled the blood-stained shroud off Sahar. He bunched it up and threw it under one of the elm trees. Then he gave Hormoz a hard slap on the face, knocking his glasses to the ground. "What kind of nonsense is this?" he shouted. "Everything is being run by women and children all of a sudden! Take the horses back to the stables, you fools! My God, they make you livid with anger!"

The emblem of the Ta'zieh had by now been carried as far as the garden gate. Its porter, the man stripped to the waist, bent over to lower it, his bare back glistening with sweat. Everyone stopped. Hormoz picked up his glasses from the ground, shook out the broken bits of glass from the right lens and put them back on. Just then a car, sounding its horn, pulled up at the garden gate. An Indian soldier got out, bringing with him a white flower arrangement adorned with black ribbons in the shape of a cross. Entering the garden, he headed towards the coffin and tried to put the flowers on it. But the pall-bearers, standing on tip-toe, lifted the coffin out of his reach. Khosrow dropped Sahar's bridle, went to the Indian soldier and took the flower arrangement from him. One by one he plucked the flowers from the cross and threw them in front of the horses. The horses sniffed at the flowers but didn't eat them. The Indian soldier stared with bulging eyes at the black-clad mourners, as if he couldn't believe what he saw. The crowd was so silent you could have heard a pin drop. Abol-Ghassem Khan put a hand on the soldier's back and led him to the car, whispering something to him which the man seemed not to understand since he answered aloud

268

in a language no-one recognized. Then the car sounded its horn again and drove away.

Now the youngest son of their neighbour, the distiller, came running up to them, panting and sweating, with an armful of wild flowers. Khosrow took the flowers and smelled them before placing them on the coffin which the pall-bearers now lowered.

By this time the sun had penetrated every nook and cranny. Coming out of the garden, Zari noticed that all the shops in the side-street were closed. Haj Mohammad Reza, using pairs of wooden poles, had draped lengths of black material all along both sides of the street. Usually he tied colourful fabrics in red, blue, green and orange on them, or else dyed silks and wool to dry off in the sunlight.

They had barely gone half-way up the street when they saw a bare-headed Gholam approaching with the twins. Reaching Zari, Gholam spat and said, "Mohsen Khan telephoned, so I went and fetched them . . ."

Zari and Ameh stood aside to let the procession go ahead, but the crowd waited. Zari bent down and kissed the children. Mina was holding the keychain which she gave to her mother.

"Now take us so we can watch too!" she said. "Oh look at the lights! Look at all the stars!"

Abol-Ghassem Khan, who had gone ahead a few steps, came back to warn Zari, "They'll be trampled on. Sister, please take them to Khanom Ezzat-ud-Dowleh."

"No, Ameh Khanom," Zari replied. "Leave them with Ferdows."

At that, the twins started to cry. None of Ameh's pleading and cajoling had any effect. Finally Gholam picked Mina up and Ameh took Marjan as the crowd made way for them to leave.

Along the main road, policemen were either scattered randomly or walking around in pairs. In the side-street opposite, a truck full of soldiers was waiting. When the policemen first sighted the funeral procession they simply stood and watched, but when the procession turned towards the main road, the policeman in command blew his whistle, bringing his men into a line to block the crowd's path. But the Ta'zieh emblem had already been carried into the main road and its front feather seemed to nod in greeting to the crowds spread out on the roof-tops and pavements. What loudspeaker could have drawn the people to the street in such numbers?

269

The police officer came towards the crowd and shouted, "Gentlemen, except for the relatives of the deceased, everyone else must disperse." He waited. Abol-Ghassem Khan remained standing with his back to the crowd. Zari turned round to look. Men dressed in black were still flocking out through the garden gates. Then a voice proclaimed in Arabic, "There is but one God!" In unison, the crowd repeated the sacred phrase.

The policeman shouted again, this time on behalf of Abol-Ghassem Khan. "Do you hear me or not? The honourable Abol-Ghassem Khan cannot speak out because of his grief . . . to thank all of you. The weather is hot. He bids you gentlemen farewell."

A voice from the crowd replied calmly, "We are all related to the deceased."

Hossein Agha, who was one of the pall-bearers, signalled to Seyyid Mohammad to replace him as he walked up to the policeman and addressed him. "Sir, a young man has been killed unjustly. We're mourning his death. That is all."

"I'm asking the crowd, very politely, to disperse," the policeman declared in a loud voice. "Go back and open your shops. If you don't, your trading licences will be revoked. That's an order. Do you understand? If you don't obey, I'll have to resort to force . . ."

This time, Mashallah Qari came forward. He said, "Sir, you know what kind of a fellow I am, don't you? When I say something, I stand by my word. We don't mean to stir things up. We're just mourning one of our fellow-townsmen. Imagine it's Karbala here and today is the massacre of Ashura; you don't want to be Shemr, do you?"

Someone cried out, "O Hussein!" And the crowd enthusiastically echoed, "O Hussein!"

Zari thought bitterly, "Or imagine it's Savushun and we're mourning Siavush."

"I told you to disperse!" The police commander shouted even more angrily, "I'm going to smash that candelabrum to pieces!" And he made for the upright candelabrum which was being carried on a tray over a porter's head. The man with the candelabrum had come right up against the line of gendarmes blocking the main road. His companion nudged him in the side and whispered something in his ear. The man turned to the right and went off to stand by the dried-up gutter along the street, the candelabrum pendants jingling to his movement.

The policeman turned around and motioned to the truck full of soldiers in the side-street opposite. The truck's engine revved, and the vehicle swerved noisily, coming to a halt a little beyond the Ta'zieh emblem on the main road. The crowd watched the truck. An officer stepped out. He was stout, with a perspiring face, and he had three stars on his epaulette. He came over and stood by the policeman.

"As God is my witness," he said, "I don't want any of you to come to any harm. We have families too. Go back to your work and livelihood."

The crowd seemed to take heart at the captain's gentleness. Mashallah Qari stepped forward again and said, "Sir, you know what sort of a fellow I am, don't you? As long as I'm around, I'll make sure our brothers and sisters here are safe and sound. We'll take the body to the Shah Cheraq Shrine, go round it, mourn and flagellate for a while . . ."

"What! The Shah Cheraq?" shouted the captain, quickly losing his temper. "Right in the centre of town? Whoever gave you permission to do that? Can't you be spoken to in a civilized way? Now, go straight back to where you belong!"

He took a few steps towards the main road and motioned again to the soldiers in the truck. One by one the soldiers got out, rifle in hand, and lined up behind the police. The captain turned to the crowd and, wiping the sweat off his forehead with his hand, said, "That man's always been trouble, dead or alive."

Zari thought she was the only one who had heard the insult to her husband, but Hossein Agha turned to Abol-Ghassem Khan and said, "The poor man hasn't been buried yet, and you let them insult him like that?"

The captain slapped Hossein Agha sharply across the face, making his nose bleed. "You shut up!" he barked.

Abol-Ghassem Khan took out a silver cigarette-case from his pocket which he opened and held in front of the captain.

"Captain, please have one," he said, blinking. "I seem to recognize you. Aren't you the son of Agha Mirza Mehdi, the porter at the oil-maker's caravanserai? Your father respected the dead . . ."

"Is this the time to be pulling out my pedigree?" the captain shouted angrily. "Why do you lead these people on?" Turning to the crowd, he yelled, "I told you to get lost!"

Hossein Agha had cupped his hand under his nose. "How can we

271

do that?" he asked. "You're blocking our way."

The captain dealt Hossein Agha several more blows on the back of the head. "Why are you jabbering again?" he bellowed. "Didn't I tell you to shut up?"

They began to grapple with each other. Just as Mashallah Qari had pinned the captain's arms behind him, the police commander blew his whistle and the policemen and soldiers charged the crowd, hitting out left and right with their batons or rifle-butts. But the crowd managed to make its way down the main road. First Fotouhi and Hassan Agha, then Majid and Seyyid Mohammad, out of necessity, left the coffin on the ground by the side-street and followed the crowd into the main road.

The road itself became blocked. Cars were backed up in both lanes; several carriage-horses shied. The noise of drivers cursing and lashing at their horses, car drivers honking and vainly attempting to reverse, mingled with that of the mourners who had taken out their chains and begun to flagellate amidst the general hubbub and confusion of the crowd.

The man carrying the candelabrum tried to cross the dried-up gutter to reach the sidewalk, but he was pushed by the crowd and the candelabrum crashed to the ground, breaking into bits. The man, with the empty tray still on his head, squatted down to pick up the bits of crystal. The others, however, managed to escape to the sidewalk with the Ta'zieh emblem which they leaned against a wall. A group of people helped make way for the Hejleh Ghassem to be taken back to the garden.

Now all the crowd had poured into the main road and the coffin, decked with flowers, was lying abandoned by a wall along the side-street. Only Zari and Abol-Ghassem Khan remained. Wordlessly, they tried to pick up the coffin. It was heavy. The eglantine and red roses had withered, but the wild flowers were still fresh. Zari looked down the main road for help. Suddenly she heard gun shots. The people who had been watching from the shop roof-tops retreated a little.

Zari spotted Khosrow who was struggling and shouting, "Let me go!"

A policeman was holding both his arms with one hand, and Hormoz, wearing his one-eyed glasses, was punching the policeman on the chest.

Those who were injured or unconscious were being carried off by others, many of them with torn clothing revealing naked flesh underneath. What a cloud of dust there was in the air! Meanwhile, no-one could be found to help them pick up the coffin from the ground, and Zari was against dragging it on the dirt all the way back home as Abol-Ghassem Khan suggested. Feeling sick to the stomach, she had to resort to her smelling salts again.

Eventually four buses, honking non-stop, managed to scatter the crowd and open up a way for themselves. They narrowly passed the truck, now empty of soldiers, hitting the deserted sidewalk with a thump. The odd remaining spectator dodged the vehicles as they pulled up and parked, one after the other, beyond the Ta'zieh emblem. Indian soldiers peered out from the bus windows and the crowd, which had momentarily retreated, converged again, shouting and clamouring.

The captain approached Zari and Abol-Ghassem Khan. "I think you ought to go and bury the body right away," he told Abol-Ghassem Khan. "I'll find you a car. When you get a crowd roused up . . . " He pulled out a handkerchief and wiped the sweat off his face.

"I have a car myself," Abol-Ghassem Khan answered.

An Indian officer got out of the first bus and pushed his way through to the captain. He saluted and said in broken Persian, "We on holiday. Soldiers been visiting Shah Cheraq. Only two days' holiday."

"You can see for yourself that the road is blocked," the captain informed him loudly.

"All right, all right," said the Indian soldier.

But Zari knew, and was quite certain the captain knew too, that the route the soldiers had taken could never have led to the shrine.

At this point Zari noticed Majid and Haj Mohammad Reza the dyer holding Khosrow and Hormoz by the hand, leading them towards the side-street. They helped Abol-Ghassem Khan lift the coffin, but they didn't let go of the boys' hands. This small group, followed by Zari, returned to the house and took the body to the cistern. Abol-Ghassem Khan sent Haj Mohammad Reza for more ice, praying that he wouldn't return empty-handed. By now the garden was filled with wounded people. Several half-conscious, bloodied men with their shirts ripped open had collapsed on to the wooden beds. Two men were washing their faces at the pool, and drinking from it even though the water was no longer clear.

273

Zari went to the basement, hoping to find the twins there. But instead she found Ezzat-ud-Dowleh, lying on the bed with Ferdows at her feet, fanning her. The pool-fountain had been turned on, and no-one else was there.

Zari found Ameh and the twins in the bedroom. The curtains had been drawn and the room was half-dark, but Mina still spotted Zari, and she got up from Ameh's side on the bed to throw herself with open arms into her mother's embrace. Zari kissed her on the eyes which were moist from crying. Marjan was sitting on Ameh's lap and didn't get up. She just stared at her mother with round eyes.

"Mother," said Mina, "the old man didn't say Nargessi, Narengi. He kept saying 'Ouch! Ouch!' His head was hurt! It was bleeding . . ."

"But you were supposed to stay at Aunt Mehri's," said Zari.

Mina kept staring at the curtains of the window which opened on to the verandah. "Why did you let them into the house?" she asked. "Now they'll take dadash's horse and father's horse away . . . that boy was hurt there . . . " and she pointed to her arm.

"I asked you why you didn't stay at Aunt Mehri's," Zari repeated.

Mina pointed at Marjan, who was still in Ameh's lap, and said, "This cry-baby was scared and cried. She kept saying, 'I want my mama' . . . Ameh didn't let us look . . . he kept his head under the tree like this, it was bleeding . . . " She paused and threw an arm around her mother's neck. "Aunt Mehri and Uncle Mohsen were fighting. Aunt Mehri cried. Uncle Mohsen said, 'I'm scared!' Then he hit Aunt Mehri. And this cry-baby started to cry . . . "

"I didn't want it to be like this, and I didn't think it would turn out like this," Ameh said.

"But I don't regret it," Zari said. "As Yusef used to say, a town mustn't be completely empty of real men."

"I wanted them to mourn the poor martyr's death, but I didn't want it to end up in fighting and violence. As my late father always said, in any war, both sides are losers."

Mina, still holding on to Zari, said, "Father will come and scold us. My brother will say, 'Where's my horse, then?' I'll say, 'Brother, Sahar was hurt and died.' All right?"

Now that Zari had her keychain she could fetch the first-aid box from the cupboard to treat the injured. The noise still continued, as did the gun-fire. In the midst of all this, the telephone kept ringing stubbornly. Abol-Ghassem Khan went to pick it up. It was obvi-

274

ously for him because he was a long time answering, and when he left by the garden gate, he seemed in a great hurry. Soon afterwards, Hormoz left too. But Majid remained, holding Khosrow's hand in his own, sitting next to Zari on the bed while Zari rubbed some ointment on to Khosrow's other wrist which was puffed and bruised from the gendarme's grip.

"Does it hurt a lot?" Zari asked. "I think it's dislocated."

"No, mother. And anyway, I'm not more precious than father, after all. When he was shot ..." He didn't finish his sentence. Instead, he smiled at his mother and said, "Even if it hurts, it'll get better."

"That's my man!" Zari said with a smile.

That night, they moved the body from the cistern and its bags of ice to the boot of Abol-Ghassem Khan's car. Ameh, Zari, Khosrow, Hormoz and Abol-Ghassem Khan sat in the car and drove around Seyyid Haj Gharib's grave as a ritual gesture. Ameh Khanom cried all the time, sobbing, "O my poor lonely one!"

But Zari had no tears. She wondered whether Ameh was referring to the solitary saint, or Yusef's loneliness. She could only wish for her own tears to flow, and a safe place to sit and weep for all the lonely and estranged people in the world; for all those who had been killed unjustly and buried secretly by night.

When they reached the Javan Abad cemetery, the grave had been prepared and they lowered the body into it by the light of a lantern Gholam held. Seyyid Mohammad wanted to say the last prayers but he couldn't remember them properly. At Gholam's signal, Khosrow pulled back the shroud, crying behind his hands. Gholam and Seyyid threw a handful of earth over Yusef, while Ameh wailed, "My martyr is lying right here. My brother is right here. Why should I go to Karbala?"

But Zari felt nauseated with everything, even with death. A death which had had no last rites, no departing prayer, no proper burial. She decided not to have anything engraved on the gravestone either.

When they got home, several letters of condolence had already arrived. Among these, only McMahon's really touched her, and she translated it for Khosrow and Ameh:

"Do not weep, my sister. A tree will take root in your home and

275

many trees in your town and even more in your land. And the wind will bring the message of each tree to the other, and the trees will ask the wind, 'did you see the dawn as you were coming on your way?'"

Glossary

Agha—or Aqa. Roughly meaning "Mr." or "Sir".

Ashura—the tenth day of Moharram, the day of the martyrdom of Imam Hossein at Karbala.

Babi—a member of the Babi sect, founded by Seyyid Ali Moham-mad of Shiraz, and considered heretical by Shiites.

Bibi—mother.

chador—full-length veil. Women of higher class would use indoor and outdoor veils, often made in a variety of luxurious fabrics.

droshke—an open, horse-drawn carriage similar to its Russian counterpart.

Ezhdehakosh—a clan of the Qashqai tribe of southern Iran.

Farsi-Madan—a clan of the Qashqai tribe.

Fassayakafikohomo'allah—a phrase in Arabic meaning "Then God shall be sufficient for you".

Ghassem wedding chamber—a miniature structure carried at the head of Shiite funeral processions to remind mourners of the untimely martyrdom of Qassem, son of Hassan, who died just before his marriage-day.

giveh—woven canvas summer shoes or slippers.

halva—a type of pastry commonly served at funerals.

Hazrat—meaning "saint" or "holiness"; thus Hazrate Abbas, Hazrate Massoumeh, Hazrate Fatemeh, Hazrate Zeynab, all refer to holy persons, in this case the immediate family of the Prophet Mohammad.

howzkhaneh—roughly equivalent to a basement, where people retire in the heat of the day, and which generally has a small pool with a fountain.

277

Imam—Islamic religious title which refers both to the family of the Prophet Mohammad, and to clergymen of the highest authority, e.g. Imam Juma. Thus, also, Imam Reza, eighth Shiite Imam, or Imam Hossein, grandson of the Prophet Mohammad, or Imam Ali, son-in-law of the Prophet, on whom the Sufi sect of dervishes in Iran is focused, as well as being the legitimate Caliph and heir after Mohammad's death, according to Shiites.

Kahn/Khanom—titles meaning "Mr." or "Mrs." Khanom Hakim literally means "lady doctor". Khan can also refer to tribal chiefs or feudal landlords, as in Yusef's case.

Khuli—in Shiite lore, a man who had hidden Imam Hossein's severed head in the furnace in his house.

Masnavi—a form of verse popularized by Jalal-ud-Din Rumi, the great Persian mystic poet.

Nakir and Monkir—two angels believed to interrogate the dead on their first night in the grave.

Ramadan/Ramazan—Islamic month of fasting.

Rowzeh—a ritual gathering in popular religious practice, to lament the martyrdom of the Shiite Imams. Special food is prepared for the occasion and distributed amongst the poor.

Seyyid—honorific title used for men to denote descent from the Prophet Mohammad.

Shahnameh—epic book of poetry written by the Iranian poet Ferdowsi, dating to the eleventh century. The mythology created by Ferdowsi figures largely in all aspects of traditional Iranian culture. Thus, Rostam and Sohrab – the legendary son killed at the hand of Rostam, his own father. Esfandiar the invincible, Ashkabus the warrior, Akvan the demon—are all characters from this epic.

Sheikh San'an—from Farrid-ud-Din Attar's "Mantiq-ut-Teyr" or "Conference of the Birds". The story of a prominent clergyman who fell in love with a Christian girl, renouncing his high position and followers to prove his love for her.

Siavush—legendary Iranian prince, whose stepmother conspired against him and who was forced to undergo a trial by fire.

Sobhi—a popular radio story-teller for children.

takht—large, multi-purpose wooden bed or platform. Can be used as seating over a small pool for coolness in the afternoon, or as bed under mosquito netting.

tar—a stringed instrument, played by plucking.

Ta'zieh—an Islamic Shiite passion play re-enacting the martyrdom of the Imams at Karbala. It often serves as inspiration for various mourning rituals, and was banned by Mohammad Reza Shah Pahlavi for the religious fervour it was liable to create. Marhab, Shemr (who beheaded Imam Hossein), Yazid (the Omayyid Caliph), the farangi (or European), the unwanted Zeynab, Hend, who rapaciously tore out the liver of the Prophet's uncle, and Fezza, are all villains of the play.

toman—ten rials, i.e. unit of Iranian currency.

Tuba tree—a tree in Paradise which has all manner of heavenly fruit.

Walazalin—the last phrase of the opening Surah of the Quran.

Ya Hu, Ya Haq, Ya Ali—a chant used by Sufi dervishes.

zither—a stringed instrument with flat sounding-board played on table.

Zurkhaneh—Persian "gymnasium" where the national sport—a type of rhythmic exercise with weights—is practised to chanted music.

Chp 4 Ameshgui

Chp 6 : Story of Bibi
o Kerbala

Chp 10 mental asylum